Rachel's Pudding Pantry

Caroline Roberts lives in the wonderful Northumberland countryside with her husband and credits the sandy beaches, castles and rolling hills around her as inspiration for her writing. Caroline is the Kindle bestselling author of the 'Cosy Teashop' series. She enjoys writing about relationships; stories of love, loss and family, which explore how beautiful and sometimes complex love can be. A slice of cake, glass of bubbly and a cup of tea would make her day – preferably served with friends!

If you'd like to find out more about Caroline, visit her on Facebook, Twitter and her blog – she'd love to hear from you.

f/CarolineRobertsAuthor
@_caroroberts
carolinerobertswriter.blogspot.co.uk

Also by Caroline Roberts

The Desperate Wife
The Cosy Teashop in the Castle
The Cosy Christmas Teashop
My Summer of Magic Moments
The Cosy Christmas Chocolate Shop
The Cosy Seaside Chocolate Shop

Caroline Roberts

Rachel's PUDDING PANTRY

HarperCollins*Publishers*

Harper*Impulse* an imprint of
HarperCollins*Publishers*
1 London Bridge Street
London SE1 9GF

www.harpercollins.co.uk

First published by HarperCollins*Publishers* 2019
2

A catalogue record for this book
is available from the British Library

ISBN: 978-0-00-832765-1

This novel is entirely a work of fiction.
The names, characters and incidents portrayed in it are
the work of the author's imagination. Any resemblance to
actual persons, living or dead, events or localities is
entirely coincidental.

Set in Minion Pro 12/15.25pt by Palimpsest Book Production Limited, Falkirk, Stirlingshire

Printed and bound in the UK by CPI Group (UK) Ltd, Croydon CR0 4YY

MIX
Paper from
responsible sources
FSC
www.fsc.org **FSC™ C007454**

This book is produced from independently certified FSC™ paper
to ensure responsible forest management.

For more information visit: www.harpercollins.co.uk/green

*For Alfie – my first
grandchild*

The proof of the pudding is in the eating

Old English Proverb

She is the perfect
example of grace
because she is a
butterfly
with bullet holes
in her wings
that never regretted
learning to fly

J.M. Storm

Chapter 1

COMING HOME TO CHOCOLATE PUDDING

Heading back down the grassy slope, Rachel caught a glimpse of golden light ablaze over the vista of the Cheviot Hills, the sky above filled with cloudy trails of mauve, grey and orange – the sun set early here in Northumberland in March. Though she'd lived here in this valley all her life, every now and again this landscape with its vast, dramatic beauty simply took her breath away.

Rachel was on the farm's quad bike, with Moss her faithful border collie on the back, having checked the fields were secure and ready for the new lambs and ewes. Earlier that afternoon, and working with the tractor, she'd put out some hay and bales of straw in large rectangular stacks to provide some shelter for the animals.

She paused for a few seconds looking towards those high hills that rose steadily from the valley where Primrose Farm nestled. Down here at the lower levels, there was grassy pastureland that led to brooks and streams, which ran cold and fresh from the moorland peaks above.

Despite this stunning panorama, there was a biting

chill to the wind this evening, especially when you were on the back of the quad. Rachel's fingerless gloves were no match for the nippy spring weather, and as the sun dipped the temperature cooled even further. It was six o'clock and time to head home to the farm.

She could see the farm's outbuildings down in the valley; the lights were on in the lambing shed where Simon, their farmhand, would be settling down to work for the night. Beyond that, there was the old barn, which they used mostly for storage nowadays, and a warm welcoming glow came from the honeyed-stone traditional farmhouse where she knew her mum, Jill, and young daughter, Maisy, would be waiting for her.

Rachel couldn't wait to arrive back and get cosy. She drove down the grassy bank, pausing to close the gate to the farmyard, parked the quad securely for the night, and walked towards the farmhouse porch where, even before opening the door, the sweet, warming smells of home cooking greeted her. Ah, bliss, Mum must have been baking. Rachel wondered what delights awaited her. Jill was a fabulous baker, mostly of the old-school-pudding-and-cake style, and boy were they good. They certainly cheered both stomach and soul, and were just what Rachel needed after a cold day out on the farm.

She took off her green wellington boots in the porch, and then opened the door to the kitchen where the rich chocolatey aromas were truly mouth-watering.

'Mumm-ee.' Little Maisy flew across to give Rachel a big hug, her blonde wavy hair bouncing as she ran.

'Hello love, everything right?' Jill turned from where she was washing up at the old stone sink to greet her daughter with a warm smile. Jill's dark brown hair, which she wore in a loose bob, was peppered with grey nowadays.

'Fine, thanks. So, you've been baking again, then?'

'Yes, felt like getting the old mixer back out.'

'That's great,' Rachel smiled. It had been a while since Mum had made any of her puddings and cakes, despite her having loved her baking so much. The kitchen had been the hub of so many sweet and scrumptious creations during the whole of Rachel's childhood. Coming in from school, Rachel would often wonder what pudding delight might be waiting for her. She used to try and guess by the scents that greeted her at the door. Today's smelt undeniably of cocoa.

'Ooh yes, it's the chocolate one,' Maisy said, as if reading Rachel's thoughts. 'I've been helping, haven't I, Grandma?'

Yes, that was the smell she'd recognised, that rich chocolate sponge and sauce. It was one of Rachel's favourites.

'You certainly have,' Jill answered. 'You've been a great little helper . . . been sifting the flour for me and all sorts.'

It was lovely to see the friendship and love so apparent between grandmother and granddaughter. And, it was wonderful that Jill was baking again too, returning step by step to the things she once loved to do.

'Oh my, I don't think I can wait. It smells divine, Mum. I'm famished.'

'Well, supper's not ready for another half hour yet, I'm cooking a stew,' said Jill.

'That sounds great . . . but a *whole* half hour . . . I couldn't have a little taste of that pud just now, could I?' teased Rachel.

It was sitting there, still warm on the kitchen side by the Aga, tempting her. Moss had sniffed it out too, standing tall with his nose to the air, before he settled down, resigned to snooze beneath it.

'Why don't we have pudding *before* dinner, Grandma?' Maisy asked cheekily, with a big grin.

'Well, I don't know about that,' Jill answered.

Rachel was nodding in time enthusiastically with her daughter now.

'Pretty please?' Maisy's grin widened.

'You'd have to be sure to eat all your dinner, mind . . .' Jill's resolve was weakening, 'But well, maybe just this once, why not.'

'Yay! Yesss!' they cried out. The three generations of Swinton girls started giggling together. And, it was lovely to hear laughter back in the farmhouse once more.

'Come on, then.' Jill organised some dessert bowls and spoons, and dished out three portions for them, pouring over some of the spare dark and glossy chocolate sauce she'd made, with a swirl of double cream to finish. They sat together at the old pine table that had been the focus of many a family meal and celebration over the years – Christmases, birthdays, anniversaries – where they'd shared stories of their days and lives, and of late where they had shared their tears. It was the very same table where Rachel had sat as a little girl herself, and it was very much at the heart of their farmhouse home. Now, watching her young daughter sat next to Mum, digging into the delicious homemade pudding, was the most comforting sight and made Rachel feel all warm inside.

There were soon plenty of 'Umms' and 'Ahhs' coming from Rachel and Maisy as they tucked in with delight. The pudding melted in the mouth, with rich cocoa-sweet flavours.

'Thank you, this is wonderful, Mum,' Rachel said.

It felt like a big move in the right direction for Jill, and for their newly shaped family. For a while now, the laughter had stopped, and her mum had stopped her baking too, saying that it hardly seemed worth it. There had been, still was, this huge, gaping hole in their lives . . . yet, slowly but surely, they were trying, and beginning, to knit it back together.

Chapter 2

TROUBLED TIMES AND MIDNIGHT PUDDING

The farmhouse kitchen was lit by the glow of a single lamp at the desk where Rachel sat staring at her laptop. Jill had gone up to bed an hour before and little Maisy was tucked up fast asleep, no doubt hugging her favourite soft-toy lamb, in her lilac-painted room that had been so carefully and lovingly decorated by her grandad. The tug at Rachel's heart was strong right then, for her father to whom she could no longer go for advice, and for the three of them who were here trying their best to hold the farm together.

The clock ticked away on the kitchen wall. It was already past midnight. However long she looked at those figures, they weren't going to get any better. Rachel sighed, rested her elbows on the wooden desk and held her forehead in her hands for a few seconds, her dark wavy fringe tumbling down over her fingertips. *She wasn't going to let this beat them, no way.* Primrose Farm had been in their family for generations. She *had to* keep it going for the three of them, for their future, and also for their animals – the sheep and cattle they'd reared and cared for over so many years. What they had all been through, two years ago now, could *not* be in vain.

But every month, when she drew up the farm accounts, it was plain as day that any profits had been squeezed further and their income was down. They lived a frugal enough life as it was. Luckily, they didn't need fancy clothes or holidays. The only one getting new shoes or clothes was Maisy, as she was growing so fast. Rachel felt the tension knot across her brow. She got up to make herself a cup of tea and, fetching the milk from the fridge, spotted that there was some of Mum's gorgeous chocolate pudding left. She helped herself to a slice and warmed it in the microwave – a little cocoa magic might help lift her spirits.

Rachel knew the time had come to talk about the farm's struggling finances with her mother. She'd tried to protect her from this until now – her mum had had enough to cope with – but it was only right that Jill knew what they were facing, and they needed to approach this as a team. If it meant selling a couple of fields for the sake of the farm, Rachel mused, then so be it, *except* she wasn't quite sure how Jill would take that news. And, any income from that might only be a drop in the ocean.

There might be other avenues they could explore. Farming friends in the area had started doing bed and breakfast ventures. In fact, traditional farmhouse B&Bs were becoming quite the thing. After all, they lived in the most beautiful Northumbrian valley in the foothills of the Cheviot Hills, but with Maisy so young, Rachel was wary of opening up their home to strangers. There must be other ways to diversify.

For tonight, however, her head was tired and fuzzy, and she was feeling cranky. It was hard to think clearly any more. Time for bed. Tomorrow was for taking things forward. Yet, having to tell her mum the truth about their dire financial situation filled her with a gnawing anxiety. It was one conversation she *really* wasn't looking forward to, but it would have to happen soon.

'Hey, Moss.' She smoothed the head of the black-and-white sheepdog who was lying down beside her. 'Come on then, boy.'

It was time for him to go back out to his kennel in the yard. He was meant to live outside, but often sneaked in for the warmth of the Aga and some affection. Rachel liked him there with her, to be honest; he was great company as well as being excellent when working with the sheep, her dad having trained him well. How much they both missed him.

Chapter 3

STICKY TOFFEE PUDDING AT DAWN

A week later, and lambing at Primrose Farm was in full flow.

'Come on then, petal. Let's get you to bed,' Rachel said.

'But Mu-um.'

'No buts, Maisy. It's already past your bedtime, and it's school again tomorrow.'

It was Sunday evening, the weekend was coming to a close, and her *almost* five-year-old daughter needed her sleep. Oh yes, her little girl's birthday was fast approaching at the end of the month – yet another thing to think about, party planning – but Rachel was too tired to get her head around the thought of entertaining a host of excitable children just now. With late nights, early starts and a couple of all-nighters completed, the lambing brain-fog had well and truly descended.

'But who will look after Pete? And how will I know he's all right?' Maisy sounded genuinely concerned, a frown forming beneath her pale-blonde fringe. She had been helping Rachel to bottle-feed the pet lamb over the weekend since his mother had rejected him (being a triplet, and the weakest of the trio).

'Well, that's easy Maisy, because it's my turn on night shift tonight, so I'll be there with him.'

'Oh.'

'Yep, I'll be keeping a very close eye on him,' she reassured. 'And all the other sheep and lambs too, of course. So, I'll let you know how Pete is first thing in the morning when you wake up.'

That seemed to appease Maisy. 'O-kay.'

'Come on, then. I'll come up and read you a bedtime story.'

The little girl got up from the large farmhouse kitchen table at the same time as her mum.

'Night, Maisy,' called Jill from across the kitchen. Rachel was both surprised and delighted to see that her mum was baking again this evening.

Maisy dashed over to give her a goodnight kiss. 'Night, night Grandma . . . Ooh, are they for me?' As she was lifted up in her grandma's arms she caught sight of a batch of vanilla cupcakes that were cooling on the side.

'They might be. You can have one in your packed lunch for school tomorrow. But now, it's time to brush your teeth and get to bed.'

'Aw, not fair!' The little girl gave a cheeky, hopeful smile.

'Tomorrow,' Jill said kindly but firmly, smiling back, as she ruffled her granddaughter's soft wavy blonde hair.

Maisy slid down and scampered back to Rachel. 'Can we have the Floss story please, Mummy?'

'I should think so.'

Her daughter loved the countryside tale with its lovely illustrations of the sheepdog and his new family.

They were soon settled upstairs in Maisy's small but prettily painted room. Maisy was tucked up in her bed under her unicorn print duvet with her cuddly lamb toy that she'd had from being a baby. Rachel began reading, her voice rhythmic, soothing. Both mother and daughter enjoyed the farmyard tales. The books they had read over and over were familiar and reassuring, with a sense that everything would be all right in the end. After all they had been through in the last two years, they really needed to believe in that.

Maisy's eyelids were getting heavy by the last page. Unfortunately, so were Rachel's – she could *so* climb under that duvet with her daughter and curl up, but there'd be no sleep for her tonight. Nature and the farm wouldn't wait. The ewes and lambs needed her care.

Simon, their trusted farmhand, had already worked all last night and most of this afternoon, snatching only a few hours' kip in between. This was her shout. She didn't mind really. The lambing night shift was often peaceful, out in the barn with just the sounds of the sheep baaing and the hoots and calls of nature at night-time from outside. She had done this for many years now, each springtime, learning alongside her father. She wanted to make him proud and show him she could do well, that she would carry on and do her best by Primrose Farm and the livestock there. After all, it wasn't just the animals that were relying on her now, her mum and her daughter needed her to make sure the farm kept going too. It was their home as well as their livelihood.

She shifted carefully off the bed and leaned over to give her little girl a gentle kiss on the forehead, trying not to disturb her. 'Night, petal.'

'Night, Mummy,' came a whisper, Maisy's eyelids already closing.

'Time for a quick cuppa before you head out?' Jill asked, as Rachel came back downstairs to the farmhouse kitchen.

Rachel glanced at her wristwatch. 'Nah, I think I'd better get across to the shed. I told Simon I'd let him go at seven.'

'Well, give me a minute and I'll make up a flask for you. You can't go out without some food for the night. There are some ham sandwiches ready in the fridge wrapped in foil. Oh, and I've also made some sticky toffee pudding . . . there's an individual portion I've put aside just for you.'

'Oh, great, thanks Mum. I love that stuff.' It was wonderful to see her mum with a little of her old spark back, slowly coming back round to the things she used to love.

'I know. Got to keep the troops fed, and your energy levels up.'

'Definitely. I'll not argue with sticky toffee pudding. And, it's great to see you baking again, Mum.'

'And you've got your phone?' Jill neatly bypassed the comment.

'Yes, of course. And . . .' Rachel went to the coat peg in the porch and checked everything else she needed was in her old Barbour waxed-jacket pocket: a pen-knife which had been her dad's, string, her lambing cord which was sometimes necessary with a difficult birth. 'Yep, got all my kit.'

'Well, have a good night out there. Hope it stays nice and calm for you.'

'Me too.'

Jill packed her off with her bundle of food, a large flask of tea and a tin mug in a well-worn rucksack.

'Come on, Moss. You can come too.' Rachel whistled at the sheepdog who was settled by the Aga, having snuck in with her earlier. He leapt up, eager to help.

Rachel walked across the yard, headed round the corner of the old stone barn and down a short track to the lambing shed. Dusk was moving in with its long shadows and cooler air. The light was fading softly from its grey-peach glow, diffusing into the indigo of night. She heard the peeping call of an oystercatcher, spotting a pair of them – a dart of bold black and white – overhead, with their distinctive long orange bills.

She soon reached the lambing shed – a large, steel-framed structure. It was more modern than the other buildings on the farm. The lights were bright in there and the smell as she entered was earthy, of straw and sheep.

'Hey, Simon. All been okay?'

Their middle-aged farmhand looked up. He had dark hair that was greying at the temples and a rugged but friendly face, lined from years of working outdoors. 'Aye, grand. Just keep an eye on number 98 over there. She's got twins but one of her teats isn't working, so she's struggling to feed them both for now. You might have to supplement them a bit when you're feeding the pet lambs.'

'Okay, thanks for the heads up, and how's Pete? That's the pet lamb from Friday. Maisy's named him.'

'Aye, he's grand. A little fighter, that one.'

'Phew, that's good, Maisy'll be distraught if anything happens to him.'

Life and death were normal processes at the farm, but it was hard at times not to get attached to individual creatures, especially when they were cute little lambs and you were only going on five years old. In fact, it was still pretty hard at twenty-four, Rachel mused. Her dad used to say she was far too soft back when she was a little girl herself, and that she shouldn't name the animals, but Rachel couldn't help her caring nature. She'd try her utmost to keep her animals alive and well, even in the most forlorn of cases. Her dad had reminded her that sometimes you had to be cruel to be kind.

'Aye, well, we'll do our best by him,' said Simon, bringing her back to the here and now.

'Naturally.'

'Everything else has been pretty steady. A few of the

ewes and their lambs have gone back out into the fields from yesterday. They all seem fine.'

'Right, well, I'll let you get away.'

'Thanks, lass. I must say I'm ready for some kip.'

'Oh, hang on, Mum's sent over a couple of cupcakes for you.' Rachel dug a small package from her bag.

'They'll be grand with a cup of coffee when I get in. Thank Jill, won't you?'

'Will do and you're welcome.'

Simon set off leaving Rachel alone with Moss and the sheep. She switched off the radio that Simon had left playing. In the daytime she liked the chat and the music, but at nightfall it was nice to appreciate the peace, interrupted now and again with the sounds of the baaing of the new lambs and the ewes.

Rachel toured the shed, making a check of the livestock. The ewes waiting to lamb were penned together in a large section and the majority seemed fine just now. There were mostly Cheviot Sheep on the farm – a hardy breed ideal for the hilly landscape. One Cheviot was showing signs of being close to giving birth. Also, one of the Texels – a larger, stocky breed of sheep that they only had a few of – was circling in a separate pen and seemed restless. Rachel would keep a close eye on those two.

The new mums and lambs in their individual pens seemed happy as Rachel made her way around the shed. She checked the teats of number 98 – there was still no milk coming on the one side. She'd make up the evening feed soon and help these two new lambs out, as well as bottle-feed the three smaller pet lambs – including the famous Pete – then she'd need to fill the teat trough for the four others that were bigger.

After doing the feeds and a further check of the sheep, Rachel settled down on a straw bale with a warming mug of tea from her flask. There was a sense of calm in the lambing shed, especially as night began to fall, when you were the only person there. Moss settled himself at her feet. She could mull over her day, think of her plans for the coming weeks, her sketchy ideas for the farm still prominent in her mind, or try to grab a few precious moments of stillness. It had been a lovely sunny day and the evening felt mild. Spring had definitely sprung in Northumberland, which was good news for the lambing – the ewes and lambs suffered in the wet and cold, especially if the bad weather was prolonged. Memories of a recent winter that had lasted far too long came bleakly to mind, and she gave an involuntary shiver. Sometimes, in Rachel's heart, it felt as cold as ice looking back to that time. Spring, though uplifting, could also be a bitter-sweet time for Rachel.

She swiftly shifted her thoughts back to the here and now and pulled out a paperback from her pocket. She settled to read for a while, losing herself in a world of tearooms and tangled love affairs. It was a pleasant escape in a world of troubles.

In the early hours of the morning, the Cheviot ewe she'd spotted earlier began to give birth; the sac was showing and the lamb presenting. Rachel watched closely. It was straightforward and the mother sheep managed well on her own – the second lamb appearing a short while after the first, and the ewe licking them clean. Both lambs were up on their legs within minutes, and soon began suckling. Nature was an amazing thing. It was still a mini miracle to Rachel every single time – watching new life blossom.

Rachel was well aware that farmers could sometimes be viewed as hard, but it was more a case of having to be practical. She cared for every single animal at the farm and its livelihood. Yes, the farm was a business, of course, and financially at times a very tough one – the animals were reared to be sold on at the end of the day – but farming was so much more than that. These sheep, their predecessors, and the small herd of cows they kept, had been here with them for many years. She was guardian of the land too. From being a little girl, this farm and its valley had a huge piece of her heart.

Rachel felt her tummy rumble as she did another tour of the animals. One Texel was still up and down and circling a bit, but nothing seemed imminent, so Rachel decided to have her sandwiches and some more hot tea. It was beginning to get chillier now, she could see her breath misting, but with her thermal layers, double socks, woollen jumper and coat, she stayed warm. She unwrapped the foil package her mum had made for her. The ham was thick and tasty and the fresh wholemeal bread was spread with a touch of honey-grain mustard.

Delicious. She gave Moss a crust and sipped her tea. An owl hooted outside, then all was quiet again. The brightness of the shed a beacon in the still of the night.

An hour or so later, the Texel was beginning to show properly. She seemed agitated, not wanting to lie down for long. Rachel perched on some bales nearer to the Texel's pen – there were just twelve of them on the farm. Two had already lambed successfully a couple of days ago and were already out in the field. Within another half hour, all the signs were pointing to an imminent birth, but she seemed to be struggling, and a panicked sheep running around with a lamb about to be born was not a good thing. Rachel put her sheep-wrestling technique into action and dived onto the back of the ewe – the Texels were a large, muscular sheep and needed some force to tackle them down to the ground. The ewe could then be turned on her side. It would make it easier for both ewe and lamb.

Damn it, Rachel was on the sheep's back but the ewe was still fighting it, thrashing her legs about, so Rachel used an old shepherd's tip handed down from her dad and grandad and pulled off her coat, placing it over the ewe's head. The creature did settle somewhat, thank heavens, enough that Rachel could check her rear and see the lamb's nose and feet there. It could well be a large lamb. The birth might just take a while, but Rachel also knew that you couldn't afford to leave it too long without intervention.

Twenty minutes later, and nothing had changed, so

Rachel attached her lambing cord and began trying to help the little creature out, heaving back against the prop of a straw bale. This was like the bloody enormous turnip of Maisy's bedtime stories; nothing was giving, and the ewe was trying to get up again, panting and bleating. Rachel knew that the situation would soon be life-threatening for both sheep and lamb. She needed to call someone right now, someone experienced and stronger than herself. *Think, think.* Simon lived over fifteen minutes' drive away. Next door was Tom's farm – he'd no doubt be busy with his own sheep, but as he had a bigger farm she knew he had two farmhands, so one of them might well be on duty with him. With no time to waste, she pulled her mobile phone from her pocket, still trying to keep the ewe wedged to the ground as she made the call.

The dialling tone rang four or five times, then – finally – he picked up.

'Tom.'

'Rachel, is that you . . . is everything okay?' He sounded rather bleary, he must have been sleeping.

'Not really, I've a Texel in trouble. The lamb seems to be stuck.'

'Right.' Instantly, he sounded alert. 'I'll come straight over.' They both knew the seriousness of the situation.

Rachel put her phone back in her pocket and stayed with the ewe, trying her best to keep the creature calm and grounded.

*

The welcome sounds of a quad rolling up outside came a short while after. Tom arrived with a brief 'Hi' and then went straight into action. Rachel stayed at the ewe's head, whilst Tom got to work below, having to use the cords himself. He was tall and strong, but even then, he had to heave with his back set against the straw bales. At last, after much effort, the lamb came free. It was large, with a mass of mucus around it . . . and it didn't move. Tom carefully wiped the mucus away from its mouth and gave its body a firm rub. Still no movement – the poor thing seemed lifeless. He blew into its mouth, once, twice.

'Come on lad, you can do it.'

And there was a flicker of life, a twitch of a leg initially, then it lifted its damp woolly head, raised itself to a tentative stand and shook itself down – shocked at its arrival into the world. The mother sheep shifted across instinctively to lick it.

'Thank you, Tom.' Rachel found herself feeling a little emotional. Fatigue and the stress of the situation suddenly crashed in.

'Hey, you're welcome. Good call getting me out.' Tom smiled.

'I know. I was struggling. I need some stronger muscles.' It was frustrating at times not having the physical strength that was required for the more challenging jobs on the farm.

'Hah, now we don't want you looking like the Hulk or anything,' Tom joked, his dark brown eyes shining.

'Hi, little chap.' Rachel moved across to see the new-born lamb, who thankfully seemed fine after his ordeal coming into the world. She'd let him and his mum settle for a few minutes together and then she'd do her checks on the lamb. But just now, they all needed a breather.

'Would you like a tea, Tom? And . . . I've got some of Mum's sticky toffee pudding here.'

'Now you're talking. Well, that's certainly worth getting up at 3 a.m. for.' He grinned.

Rachel poured out his drink from the flask, passing over the now communal tin mug. Tom took it, his forearm smeared with muck and blood, but neither were worried about dirt and grime; it was par for the course in the lambing shed.

They sat together side by side on a straw bale.

'God, I really appreciate you coming over.' The relief began flooding through Rachel.

'No worries. You know I'm here to help . . . any time. I've always said that.' He gave her an earnest look.

'Thanks. You've been so good to us.' He was such a great family friend – had helped see them through the toughest of times. In fact, sometimes she worried he'd think they were a bit of a pain – the women from the farm next door. They tried not to pester too much, doing their best to remain self-sufficient at Primrose Farm, but tonight really had been an emergency situation.

Tom was a little older in his mid-thirties. They had known each other since childhood, though Tom had been a teenager, whizzing up and down the lane on his quad bike, when Rachel was just a small girl. He'd lived on the family farm next door virtually all his life, except when he'd got married and moved away. Then, when his father's arthritis hit hard several years ago, his parents had moved out to a bungalow in Kirkton, allowing Tom to take over the main farmhouse and the running of the farm with his then-wife, Caitlin. They'd divorced three years ago – pretty acrimoniously, so Rachel heard – and he'd been living there as a single man ever since. They saw a lot of each other on the road and out and about, being neighbours.

'So, how long are you on till?' Tom asked.

'Ah, Simon's back at seven. A twelve-hour shift for me. I'll see Maisy for breakfast time and then I'll get my head down for a few hours' sleep once she's gone off to school.'

'Ah, a few hours of blessed kip.'

'Then, I'm back on again tonight.'

'Relentless, isn't it – lambing time. Feels never-ending. It's only around three weeks overall and it seems like a bloody year.'

'We'll get there. Same every year. Like a horrid hangover, you come out of it threatening never to rear any more sheep, and then by market time you've forgotten how bloody awful it is and you're tricked back into it again.'

'Hah, yeah.'

Rachel began rummaging in the rucksack for Jill's pudding and poured herself another mug of tea.

'To the hardy Cheviot Hill farmers,' she said. She raised her tin cup. 'Cheers.'

She passed Tom a portion of the rich, treacly pudding and a plastic spoon – Mum always thought of everything.

'And to sticky toffee pudding.' He smiled, digging a spoon into the sponge. 'God, this is delicious. Fuel of the hill farmers.'

'Hah. Absolutely!'

After chatting for a while, Tom headed back to snatch a few more hours' sleep. As she'd suspected, he had been in bed when she'd called, trying to make the most of a rare night off from the lambing shed. Rachel felt a little guilty for disturbing his night, as he'd have plenty of his own work to do on his farm today.

It wasn't long until dawn began to break with golden morning light filtering in through the gaps in the shed door. On her own once more, Rachel dealt with another birth – a single healthy lamb who came into the world without a fuss – and soon enough, it was time to head back over to the farmhouse and her family.

Thank goodness it had all worked out in the end for that little Texel. And, looking at the clear sky above her as she walked back across the yard, thank goodness for another warm dry day. The weather this spring was being kind to them. It hadn't always been so. She walked past the old stone stable building that was no longer used. Remembering that fateful spring morning two years ago, she felt a shudder run through her.

Chapter 4

PET LAMB PATROL

Maisy was already up when Rachel got back to the farmhouse. She and Jill were busy setting out the breakfast things at the large pine kitchen table. Maisy was struggling, carrying two bulky cereal boxes, and dropped them down quickly on the table as her mum appeared.

'Mumm-eee! How's Pete?'

'He's good, Maisy. He had a great night and is feeding well.'

'Ooh, can I go feed him?'

'After school, yes. You've got to get ready and have your own breakfast now.'

'Oh, not fair.'

'He's already had his breakfast today, anyhow,' Rachel added.

'Cup of tea, love?' Jill asked, switching the kettle back on, already knowing the answer.

'Yes, please, I'm desperate for another brew.'

'Has everything been all right? I thought I heard a

vehicle in the early hours?' Her mum had a frown of concern across her brow.

'Yeah, I had to call out Tom. One of the Texels was in difficulty.'

'Oh, did you manage okay?' As a farmer's wife, Jill was well aware of the problems you could experience with lambing. She had often helped out herself in the past, but lately shared her time between the lighter farming duties and helping to look after Maisy.

'The lamb was stuck. It had been going for too long and I was getting a bit worried, so I called Tom in. He did a great job. The ewe and lamb were both fine in the end. It was just a really big lamb.'

'Ah, well I'm glad everything was okay with the little chap. All's well that ends well.'

'Yes, and thank heavens for Tom,' added Rachel. 'The poor guy, I think I woke him up. Been trying to catch a few hours' sleep himself.'

'Oh, he's a lovely lad. I'm not sure what we'd do without him next door. He's been a godsend.'

Lad. It made Rachel smile – he was well into his thirties. Her mum made him sound like he was thirteen. But yes, he had been a great friend to the family and a brilliant support, especially since they'd lost Dad.

'Can I see Tom, Mummy?' Maisy piped up, now sat at the table and digging a spoon into a bowl of Rice Krispies.

'Well, not right now.' Rachel sat down next to her daughter, cradling her mug of tea. 'He's probably either back in bed, or in his own lambing shed. He's a bit busy just now, Maisy. We'll give it a week or so, then you can go across and say hello when lambing is over.'

'Ah, lambing is *sooo* boring.'

'What do you mean? You love Pete and the other lambs?'

'Yeah, but all of the grown-ups are *too* busy.'

'Yes, that's 'cos it's so important. You'll just have to be patient, petal. It's our job.' *And, it's what pays the bills*, Rachel added mentally.

'Maybe we can ask him across for Sunday dinner this weekend as a thank you?' chipped in Jill. 'I'm sure he'd be glad of that. Even if it's just for an hour or so if he's got a lot on.'

'That's a nice idea. I'll mention it if we cross paths in the next couple of days,' said Rachel.

Maisy was nodding animatedly, happy with that idea.

Time was slipping on and the school minibus would be arriving at the end of the farm track at 8:20 a.m. sharp. 'Right Maisy, time to finish your cereal and go up and brush your teeth. Then it's shoes on, rucksack at the ready, and I'll walk you to the bus.'

'I'll go if you like, Rachel,' Jill offered. 'You might want to get off to bed.'

'No, it's fine, Mum. I'd like to go.' However tired she felt, even at lambing time, she liked to spend some time with Maisy before and after school.

'Well, are you peckish, pet? You haven't eaten any breakfast yet. Shall I make you some scrambled eggs for when you get back?'

'That sounds perfect. Thank you.'

They kept a dozen or so of their own hens, who wandered around the farm, pecking away and fluffing their feathers. They were happily free range by day and settled in their coops at night, which kept them safe from any foxes or other prey. Their eggs were delicious with orange-gold yolks – just perfect served scrambled or poached on thick farmhouse toast.

Ten minutes later, Rachel and Maisy had left the house and were out in the yard.

'Can I see Petie before I go?' Maisy gave her mum the cutest of smiles.

'Maisy, you're in your smart school clothes and best shoes. You'll get filthy in the shed.' Rachel did have her wellies on though. Looking at her daughter's cheeky grin, she caved. 'Ah okay, a quick one-minute hello. But just look, no touching, as we haven't got time to go and wash hands again. Come on, I'll carry you across.' She hoisted her up onto her hip and headed across to the lambing shed.

The pet lambs were sectioned off in a pen near the front, so Rachel lifted Maisy to look in at them.

'Hello, Petie boy! See you later!' Maisy shouted, waving at the little fella.

He looked up and gave a baa in return, then skipped towards them, hopeful of another feed. The other pet lambs were snuggled together beside a large bale of straw. They all seemed to be doing fine, although one – number

34 – was still a lot smaller than the rest. Rachel would have to keep an extra eye on him, but he seemed lively enough just now, getting up to his feet.

They spotted Simon across in the shed and gave him a wave.

'Have a good day at school, Maisy,' he called across.

'Hello, Simon. I will.'

'Morning, Simon. Everything been okay since I left?'

'Just grand, lass.'

'Right, we'd better go, Maisy. Don't want you missing the bus.'

The two of them made their way down the farm track, hand in hand. Thankfully, Maisy enjoyed school. She'd only started six months ago but had settled in well at Kirkton's First School, in the small market town that was just three miles from the farm. Maisy was such a sociable girl, she enjoyed seeing her friends as much as the learning.

The lane down to the road was bordered by grassy banks and spring had arrived with a mass of pale-yellow primroses, that nestled beneath the hawthorn hedges each side. At the roadside verge there were clusters of bold yellow daffodils swaying in the breeze, ready to welcome any visitors to the farm. Rachel made sure she kept the grass each side of the farm gate short and well-tended. Her dad had always insisted the entrance was neat and tidy. 'First impressions, Rachel. First impressions,' he'd say in his deep, resonant voice. She took a deep breath, feeling that familiar pang of sorrow.

She spotted her good friend Eve, heading down the lane towards them with her little girl, Amelia – Maisy's bestie. They had walked down from their nearby cottage. It saved the minibus an awkward turnaround in the narrow lane.

'Hi Eve. Hello, Amelia.' Rachel gave a cheery wave.

'Hiya, Rachel. You okay? Surviving lambing?' Eve asked, pulling a grimace. It was well known in country circles that lambing was *the* most exhausting time of the farming year.

'Yes, we're getting there. Bit of a tense time last night though . . .'

The bus then arrived, pulling up beside them, and the girls got on with their school bags and packed-lunch-filled rucksacks swinging. The adults hopped on too, saying a quick hello to Ted, the driver, and checking that the girls had everything with them and that their seatbelts were done up. After a kiss and a 'Have a good day' each, they got off again, waving as the bus set away.

'*So*, you were saying? An eventful night?' Eve asked.

'Oh yes . . . life in the lambing shed. A Texel was in trouble, the lamb stuck. But thank heavens it was all fine in the end . . . with a bit of early-morning help from Tom.'

'Ah, the delectable Tom. Your dishy next-door farmer.' There was no hiding that Eve, despite being happily married to Ben, had had a bit of a crush on Tom for several years now, which always amused Rachel. Eve hadn't batted an eyelid when their childhood friend Tom had moved away to the city – largely under influence, or so Rachel heard, from his new wife Caitlin – but ever since he'd arrived back at the farm, newly single, Eve had seen him with new eyes. 'I still haven't worked out how he hasn't been snapped up,' she continued dreamily. 'His divorce was ages ago.'

'Hmm, maybe once bitten twice shy.' Rachel knew that feeling well. 'Anyway, I don't know why you're gushing on – you're already taken. *And*, he's at least ten years older than us pair.' The two girlfriends had been a year apart at school, Eve being the older, but they had always lived nearby and been good friends, sharing the ups and downs of their teenage years. They were now the grand old age of twenty-four and twenty-five respectively – though after ten days of lambing and hardly any sleep Rachel felt about sixty-four.

'Eight years older than me, actually. He's thirty-three.'

'Is he now, and how do you know that?'

'It was his birthday a few weeks ago. He happened to mention it to Ben down in the pub.'

Tom was a nice-looking chap, Rachel supposed, but he'd always been a family friend. She'd known him as a neighbour from being a little girl. However much Eve had a crush on him, Rachel found she couldn't even begin to contemplate him in that way.

'So, what are you up to today?' Rachel asked, happy to change the subject.

'Well, I have a new project actually. I'm quite excited about it. You know how I love making things . . .'

Eve was the most talented craftsperson Rachel knew,

making the most gorgeous felt soft-toy animals, and her knits were fabulous – her cute tractor design jumpers were a triumph – as well as bootees, children's cardigans, hats and scarfs. At Christmas and birthdays, she usually turned up with a lovely handmade present. She also turned her hand to making gift cards, doing woodwork, needlecraft, you name it. Rachel had named her the bunting queen of the valley after she'd made a gorgeous strand for Maisy's birthday party last year. It was *so* pretty, with flags of pastel spots and stripes and vintage roses.

'Yes . . . come on, tell me all about it then.'

'I'm looking into starting a little craft business and joining Etsy,' Eve continued. 'So I can start selling some of my stuff online. As always, we could do with a bit more cash in the household, but it's hard finding a job that fits around school hours and isn't too far away. But the best thing is, I can do all this from home, other than nipping to the post office for organising the postage. *So*, what do you think?'

'That sounds a brilliant idea. I imagine you've done your research and looked into everything, and yeah why not. It looks a great platform. I've bought the odd thing from there myself. Hey, good for you.' Rachel then had to stifle a yawn. 'Sorry, that's nothing to do with your project. I haven't slept since yesterday afternoon, and even then, it was only for a couple of hours.'

'Oh crikey, hun. Well you'd better get yourself off to bed. Is it night shift *again* tonight for you?'

'Yep, no rest for the wicked.'

'Or farmers.'

'Too true. And, hey, good luck with the crafting, Eve. Once the lambing's over I will resurface and join the real world again, I promise. We'll have to have a coffee and a proper catch-up.'

'We will, indeed. Or maybe a drink in the pub. I'm missing my mate. Bye, Rach.'

'See you, Eve.'

'Sweet dreams, hun.'

'Thanks.'

Walking back up the road, Rachel thought how great it was that Eve was starting her own business. Little seeds had also been sown in Rachel's mind. They really needed to think of something else they could do at the farm. A new direction. Diversification. Something that fitted in with their farming lives, and with Maisy of course, that had the potential to improve their income. But *what*, was the million-dollar question.

Oh yesss, the bliss as her head hit the pillows. Rachel snuggled down under a soft duvet with the bedroom curtains closed against the brightness of the early spring day. The sounds of the birds tweeting away outside soon began to fade as Rachel drifted into much-needed sleep.

When she came to, a tractor was droning in the distance and the birds were still singing. A glance at her wristwatch told Rachel it was almost 2 p.m. Goodness, she'd been asleep for nearly five hours. It felt like five minutes! She yawned and stretched. She'd better get up, give her mum a hand, and then go and see how Simon was getting on. Crikey, it was only another hour until the school minibus would be making its way back up the lane and Maisy would be home.

Rachel pulled on some tracksuit bottoms and a T-shirt, popping an old fleece over the top. The farmhouse was never that warm, except in the kitchen by the Aga, as the thick stone walls kept it cool. Her father had been born within these walls. And, being brought up here as a little girl, Rachel remembered seeking out the kitchen and its warmth, standing on a little stool and watching Jill press out a batch of scones that would bake with the most enticing aroma, ready to dollop with jam and cream later, or helping to stir a batter mix for lemon and sugar sprinkled pancakes which would sizzle in the pan.

'Hello love, welcome back to the land of the living,' Jill greeted her as she came through into the kitchen. 'There's some soup on the stove, and some crusty bread I've been baking.'

'Oh, thanks Mum, excellent.' Rachel lifted the lid on the pan – leek and potato – yum, her favourite. It was steaming away, hot and ready. Her mum must have kept it simmering for her. Jill was a star, like the cogs in the wheel, keeping the family fed and watered, as well as taking an active role in the farm. Rachel counted her blessings for having such a supportive parent. She admired how Jill had kept going so stoically, especially considering the circumstances; the three of them often struggling to find their way in this new uncharted landscape. Maybe keeping busy was the only way to keep afloat.

'Oh, I popped out to the shops for a few essentials while you were sleeping, happened to see Tom on my way back, so I've asked him across for Sunday lunch. He seemed delighted. Goodness knows what he cooks for himself, a man there on his own all the time.'

'Hah, I'm sure he can cook, Mum. It's not the dark ages. And I bet he pops across to Jim and Barbara's often too.' His parents only lived a few miles away, after all.

'Yes, but still, I'm sure he'll enjoy being looked after. It's a busy enough time on the farm. And, you don't tend to cook a roast dinner for one, do you now.'

'No, I suppose not. Thanks for asking him.' It would be a lovely way of thanking him for his help and support last night, not to mention the past months.

'Be nice to have some company here, too,' Jill added.

It was true that farm life could be quite isolating at times, especially out in rural North Northumberland. Yes, it was beautiful and quiet and such a special place, but that also meant you were quite some way from towns, cities, cinemas, airports. Mostly you didn't think about it, just got on with it. But often it was just the three of them there: Rachel, Jill and Maisy. Sometimes, Granny Ruth, her dad's mother and Rachel's last surviving grandparent, would visit as she lived not far away on the far side of Kirkton, but other than her, Simon, Eve and the

34

bus driver, it could be days before she saw anyone else
– in fact weeks at lambing time.

School bus time soon came around again. Rachel strolled
back down the lane to meet Maisy, scanning the fields
on the way, checking that the sheep and lambs that had
recently been turned out from the lambing shed seemed
okay. The minibus was already pulling up at the lane end
as she got there, with Maisy skipping down the steps
within seconds to give her a big hug. Rachel had a quick
chat with Eve and Amelia, and then they were on their
way back to the farm.

As they walked together, Rachel asked about her
daughter's day and what she'd been doing. Painting,
reading, *really hard* spellings and skipping with ropes at
playtime was the answer. As they neared the top of the
track Maisy went unusually quiet, then she stopped
walking suddenly and looked up at Rachel with a serious
expression on her face.

'Mummy . . . why haven't I got a daddy?' she blurted
out.

'Oh,' the question floored Rachel momentarily.

'Well?' Maisy chanted. 'Amelia's got one and Nell's got
one, and even Harry says he has one but he only sees
him on Saturdays.'

'Oh Maisy, of course you have a daddy. Everyone does.
It's just that . . .' Rachel knew she had to frame the words
carefully, not wanting Maisy to feel unwanted. 'Well, he's
not here much. He lives a long way away.'

'Why doesn't he live here . . . with us . . . like Amelia's daddy? Doesn't he like me?'

Rachel's heart went out to her daughter. *Because he's an irresponsible, immature, selfish little git* came to mind.

'Oh petal, of course he does, he loves you. It's just a bit more complicated for us. Your daddy and mummy aren't together – a bit like Harry's, but because your daddy is so far away it's hard for him to come and see you, even on Saturdays.' She was trying her best to explain the mess that adults make of their lives and their relationships in simple terms for a young child. 'He did come and see you a year ago, don't you remember?' It was actually a bit more than that, but a year sounded better.

Maisy stood shaking her head, whilst screwing up her little face as though she was trying so hard to remember. Blimey, Rachel realised, thinking about it, it was more like sixteen months ago, just before Christmas. Maisy would only have been three-and-a-half. He'd turned up out of the blue with a Christmas gift for his daughter, and a twenty-pound note to help Rachel out. (Hah – that had gone a long way, *not*! Did he even realise what a pair of children's shoes cost?) He'd never managed to pay any formal child support, being mostly unemployed, or so he'd told the authorities. But in a way, for Rachel, it was easier not having him around. They could manage just fine themselves, on a budget of course. They didn't need his kind of inconsistent and unreliable support. Oh yes, a kiss and a hug for Maisy, empty promises to visit more often, then – poof – he'd be gone again.

'Remember the monkey toy?' Rachel asked, trying to help Maisy out.

The little girl nodded.

'Well, that was your Christmas gift from your daddy.' It was now sitting on the shelf in Maisy's bedroom – after being hugged for several months, and with no further appearance from her dad, Monkey had got moved aside in favour of the soft-toy lamb she'd had as a baby from Grandma Jill.

'Oh,' was all Maisy said. She went quiet again for a few moments. 'Well, it *is* my birthday soon,' she piped up, her face brightening. 'He could come to my party.'

Rachel didn't want to give her daughter any false hope, but yes, she'd send a text to his last known number. She thought she had an email address she could try too. But she wasn't holding out a lot of hope. 'Well, I'll try. We'll invite him, shall we?' Maisy was nodding vigorously. 'But I still think he might have to be at work, a long way away.'

Who knew whether he even had a bloody job?! Or money for a train fare, or a car he could use. Argh, why the hell had she chosen her first love so poorly? She was seventeen when it all happened and so bloody naïve. He'd dipped in and out of her life for the next two years, never able to commit to anything even then. By the time she'd seen past the boyband-style good looks and charm and realised how useless he was, it was too late, she was pregnant with Maisy. But in all honesty, she couldn't wish it hadn't happened either, Maisy was far too precious to wish away.

Chapter 5

BREAD AND BUTTER PUDDING AND
SUNDAY DINNER

Sunday rolled around in a blur of lambing late nights and early starts.

When Rachel got up from a few hours' sleep on the Sunday lunchtime, having done the previous night shift in the lambing shed, the smells that greeted her as she opened the kitchen door were delicious! Jill was preparing a roast beef dinner with all the trimmings. The meat must have been cooking away in the Aga, along with roast potatoes.

'Wow, that smells divine,' Rachel commented.

Maisy turned around, perched on her little wooden stool beside her grandma. 'Mummy, I'm Grandma's special helper today. We've made bread and butter pudding for Tom,' she said, grinning.

'That sounds very scrummy.'

'Hello love,' Jill added. 'It'll be ready in a half hour, so if you want to take a shower first.'

'I'll just grab a cup of tea.' Rachel stifled a yawn. There

was never enough sleep nowadays. She ran her fingers through her bed-head hair, finding a strand of straw stuck in it. No wonder her mother was suggesting a shower, she probably looked like that scarecrow character, Worzel Gummidge, right now. She switched on the kettle, asking Maisy about her morning, and listened to her chitter-chatter whilst she sat at the big pine table, cradling her mug. The tea started to work its magic, and Rachel began to feel a little more human. 'Right, I'll just whizz upstairs and get ready then.'

'See you soon, Mummy. Don't forget Tom is coming so you need to brush your teeth and your hair too,' said Maisy seriously.

My, she really must have been letting standards slip these past few weeks. Rachel looked down at her grubby jogging bottoms and T-shirt. She certainly hadn't brushed her hair as yet either. As she moved, she realised there might also be a slight whiff of sweat mixed with odour of sheep about her – nice. Hmm, Maisy might in fact have a point. Rachel shook her head smiling. Nearly-five going on fifteen, that girl!

Tom arrived at one o'clock prompt with a warm smile, a bottle of red wine and a unicorn-themed colouring book for Maisy. He had also 'made the effort', and was out of his usual dirty-denim farm gear, dressed smartly in a pale-blue shirt and a pair of beige chinos.

'Hello, Tom,' Jill greeted him, whilst stirring the gravy. 'How's the lambing going?'

'Fine. About three-quarters through now. There's a light at the end of the lambing-shed tunnel.'

'Yes, we're getting there too,' added Rachel. 'Thanks again for your help the other night.'

'Ah, you're welcome. These things happen. It's all part of the job.'

'Well, it was really appreciated,' Rachel confirmed.

Tom then lifted Maisy up in his arms and ruffled her blonde hair. 'Hi, Maisy. How's tricks?'

'Good . . . Is that for me?' She'd spotted the colouring book he'd brought in with him and scampered down as he nodded, saying, 'Aha, it is.' Delighted with her gift, and after adding a quick 'Thank you,' she went off to find her crayon set.

'Take a seat, Tom,' Jill said. 'Make yourself at home. Dinner won't be long.'

Sat at the table next to Tom a short while after-wards, Maisy piped up, 'Tom, have you seen Pete, my lamb?'

'No, not yet.'

'Can we go and see him now, Mummy?'

Rachel was about to carve the joint of beef, as the final stages of the meal were coming together. 'I'm sure Tom's seen enough lambs of his own this week . . .'

'It's okay, I don't mind,' he said, smiling.

'Well, maybe after dinner, Maisy. In fact, it's nearly ready now, so go and wash your hands, and then you can help put some water glasses out on the table and three wine glasses for the grown-ups.'

'O-kay.' Maisy headed reluctantly off to the downstairs bathroom.

'Tom, maybe you'd open the bottle of red you brought?' Rachel asked, hunting down the corkscrew in the cutlery drawer. They didn't generally have wine with their meals. It was considered a bit of a luxury in their squeezed budget of late.

They were soon all sitting down to eat around the farmhouse table. Rachel had served out the plates of roast beef and crispy Yorkshire puddings with a selection of fresh vegetables, golden roast potatoes and Jill's gorgeous gravy. At Jill's request, Tom had taken up the seat at the head of the table. Rachel felt herself stiffen seeing him sit there. For a second, she could picture her dad, Robert, in that very place settling down for his Sunday roast. When she was big enough, she'd carefully carry his dinner plate across to him, piled with meat and vegetables and one of Mum's delicious Yorkshire puds. Dad would give her a wink and a big smile. There were so many memories just waiting to creep up on Rachel. Tom was most welcome, of course, but it was still difficult seeing someone else sat in her father's place.

The dinner-table conversation flowed as they chatted about their respective farms and Maisy told Tom all about her swimming lessons and the animal paintings she'd done. They ate and talked, and drank the wine. It was a lovely way to spend a Sunday afternoon and a real treat after cold nights and long days lambing.

'This is truly delicious, ladies, thank you. I hardly

bother cooking a roast dinner for myself. It just takes too long. I come in starving usually and need something straight away.'

Jill gave Rachel a knowing glance. 'Don't beat yourself up Tom, you've got your hands full,' she replied.

'I do cook, but simpler stuff. Steak, gammon, pasta, pop a pizza in the oven, that kind of thing.'

'Grandma's made pudding too!' Maisy added, gleefully.

'That sounds good.' Tom grinned.

'There's bread and butter pudding or brownies. I don't like the nasty currant things in the pudding, so you can have mine,' the little girl offered Tom.

'Well, remember you need to finish your dinner first, Maisy,' her grandma reminded her. 'Including the broccoli trees.'

'A-huh. I know.'

'I can certainly recommend the bread and butter pudding, despite the *nasty* sultanas,' added Rachel with a wry smile. 'It's divine – the custard's all light and fluffy and nutmeg-flavoured.'

'It's my grandmother's recipe,' Jill beamed proudly. The recipe was handwritten in the family's baking cookbook, which Rachel had nicknamed 'The Baking Bible', and though Jill knew the instructions off by heart, she still liked to have the page open at Grandma Alice's swirly handwriting as she prepared the ingredients. It almost felt like she was there beside her.

It was lovely to see her mother smiling, Rachel thought. Jill had been weighted with grief for far too long.

They were soon tucking into bowls of bread and butter pudding, with its golden crispy top, soft fluffy custard and sultana middle, with a blob of thick cream melting down over it. Maisy was already happily sporting sticky fingers and smudged lips from her chocolate brownie.

'This is amazing, Jill,' Tom enthused. 'Takes me back to visiting my granny in her cottage kitchen years ago. The Aga was always on and there was always something smelling wonderful, ready to come out of the oven just for you. She used to make this pudding too, I remember it well.'

'The old recipes are often the best, I think. I have a whole book handed down from my mother and her mother before her, with extra recipes I've discovered over the years popped in there too. Along with my stalwart Mrs Beeton's of course, and a few tweaks from Mary and Delia.'

'Berry and Smith – they're Mum's best friends, you know,' Rachel added with a grin.

'You know, you could make a business out of selling these, Jill, and that glorious sticky toffee pudding I had the other night. Bet you have more pudding delights up your sleeve too, by the sounds of it. I'd certainly be queuing up to buy some.'

'Oh, yes, proper old-fashioned puddings,' Rachel agreed. 'You might just be on to something there, Tom.' The seed of an idea that had started in her mind the other evening was finding its first shoot. 'What do you think, Mum?'

'Well, I don't know about that. I'm just a home baker, that's all.' Jill batted away the suggestion. 'Any seconds for anyone?' she added, spotting that Tom's dish had been swiftly cleared.

'Blimey, I'm full as a tick . . . but you know what, that's an offer I can't refuse, so maybe just a spoonful. I have a feeling I'm being fattened up.' Tom laughed.

'Definitely.' Jill grinned.

Rachel looked across at Tom. He was of medium build, but well-muscled, and was around six foot tall. His physical lifestyle meant he was fit and well, and he could no doubt pretty much eat what he liked without putting weight on. He caught her glance and smiled warmly across the table. His eyes were a deep liquid brown – she'd never really noticed quite how dark they were before.

'I don't think I'll be able to move after all this, but I really should be getting back soon to check on my ewes.'

'You still haven't seen Pete,' chanted Maisy.

'Of course, you can show him to me on my way back,' said Tom.

'You've surely time for a cup of tea first?' suggested Jill. 'Let your meal settle for few minutes at least.'

'That'd be great, Jill. Just a quick one. And thanks again to you and Rachel. This has been a real treat.'

'It's been lovely to have you here,' Jill added.

Rachel nodded in agreement. 'Yes, thanks for coming. It's been really nice.'

*

Fifteen minutes later, and Rachel, Maisy and Tom were on their way to visit Pete the lamb.

'Now then, you have to be gentle with Pete as he's only little.' Maisy was in full bossy mode, as though Tom had never had anything to do with a sheep in his life.

He and Rachel shared a look of amusement.

'Of course, Maisy,' he answered in a serious tone. 'So, which little guy is he then?'

'This one.' She pointed, peering over the metal railing. 'Come on, Petie boy.' The little lamb perked up, seeming to know his name, and trotted towards them, followed by the others. 'Mum, can we feed him?'

'Yes, I don't see why not. I'll make sure Simon knows he's had his tea, when he comes in.' She was having a night off tonight herself – oh yes, that would be bliss. A hot bath and cosy bed were calling her name already.

Rachel scooped out the lamb. His short wool was soft and curly-ridged under her hands. 'I'd better go and mix up some milk feed for him and the others.' She passed him to Tom, who knelt down so Maisy could stroke Petie. 'Won't be a sec.'

When she came back a few minutes later, Maisy and Tom were deep in conversation about the lambs that had been born the night before. He then told her about the Texel he'd had to help out with a few days back, and she was fascinated.

'You had to use *a rope*, Mummy?' Her little girl's eyes were like saucers now.

'Hah, suddenly lambing's not so boring then, Maisy.'

It was lovely seeing them chatting away though. Tom able to bring the drama and the magic of the lambing shed alive for her little girl. It reminded her of times with her own father for a moment, whisking her back to being a little girl on this very farm . . .

'Quick, Rachel lass. This one's about to give birth.' Her dad grasped her arm firmly but kindly with his strong farmer hands, guiding her towards the pen. 'We'll leave her be and just watch from here, quietly now. She's doing a grand job by herself by the looks of it.'

And they sat together on a straw bale, overlooking the pen. The ewe was panting heavily, as she lay on her side. There was a show of some whitish sticky stuff, and . . . oh . . . wow . . . two little black-and-white hooves pushing through. Then, all of a sudden, out it all came in some weird balloon-looking thing. The mum was soon up and licking her baby . . . a whole new lamb . . . a whole new life.

Nearly twenty years ago and Rachel had been allowed to stay up late for a few precious hours with her dad in the lambing shed.

She was just five years old. But she'd never forget that special day – some memories lasted a lifetime.

Rachel was jerked back to the present as Pete the lamb kicked out hungrily, spotting the bottle in her grasp.

She realised with embarrassment that her eyes had misted with tears, and she turned away for a second to compose herself. *Breathe.*

'Better get this little one fed then, Maisy. You take the bottle now,' Tom said.

'I've done it before. You do it like this.' She tilted the angle just right, as the lamb made jerking sucks on the teat.

'Great, you've got it down to a fine art, I see,' said Tom.

Once the milk was emptied, which didn't take Pete long at all, Tom stood up to put him back in the pen. 'Sorry folks, but I'd better go.'

'Aw.' Maisy pulled a face.

'Come on Maisy, Tom's already stayed later to see Pete.' Rachel looked across at Tom. 'I bet you've got loads to do too.'

'Certainly have. A farmer's work is never done.'

'You can say that again.'

'Bye, Tom,' Maisy said reluctantly, hugging his leg.

'Bye, Maisy. Be a good girl for your mum now.'

'O-kay.'

Rachel watched him as he walked to his pick-up truck and set off along the drive with a wave and a toot especially for Maisy. She had a warm feeling she couldn't quite explain as she watched Tom go. He was great to have as a neighbour. It felt like they had someone on their side.

Chapter 6

PUDDINGS AND PLANS

Later that evening, with Maisy in bed and Mum up in the bath, Rachel sat at the kitchen table with her laptop out and a mug of hot chocolate, chewing the end of her Biro. She had loads of the farm's paperwork to catch up on. There seemed to be a never-ending stream of documents and reports to complete and return. She was tired but thank heavens she wasn't needed in the lambing shed tonight.

It was quiet and cosy in the kitchen with the warmth of the Aga, and Moss there lying beside her too. They did have a small office, but Rachel preferred working here, in the hub of the farmhouse. She got some admin work done and then she found herself mulling over the conversation at dinner and – more crucially – Tom's suggestion whilst they'd been spooning in their bread and butter pudding. Might there be something in this pudding-making idea?

It might just give Jill a new focus, a sense of purpose, Rachel mused. She'd been lost since her husband's death two years ago; it was almost like a part of her had died with him and it was so sad to see. Baking was something she'd always loved doing, and Rachel could see that little spark reignited within her when she was back with her recipe books and ingredients in the kitchen these past few weeks. *And*, any income it might produce certainly wouldn't go amiss in helping out the farm's finances. They needed every penny they could get at the moment. The first lambs wouldn't be ready to go to market for sixteen weeks yet, and the end-of-year subsidies were being stretched thin as it was. Oh crikey, she still needed to have *that* conversation with her mother – about just how big a financial hole they were in – but the lambing season had stalled that particular conversation. And Rachel realised she'd been ducking out of it too. She really didn't want to give her mother anything else to be concerned about, not when she was finally showing the first signs of recovery.

Rachel did enjoy baking too, when she found the time. Her raspberry and white chocolate cheesecake, sugary-crisp yet soft-in-the-middle meringues and carrot cake had always been hits with her family and friends. Once lambing was over, and with Maisy now at school, she'd have a bit more time to experiment in the kitchen once the daily farm chores were done. She might even get The Baking Bible out herself and have a go at some of the old favourites too.

She googled 'starting up a catering business', jotting down some notes. She and her mum could easily sign up for the hygiene qualifications they'd need – that's if her mum warmed to the idea. Then Rachel found herself googling 'puddings'. A feast of delights hit the screen – taking her back to her childhood with Mum there in her pinafore, Dad sat at the farmhouse table and something sweet and comforting about to come out of the Aga – golden syrup sponge, sticky toffee pudding, treacle tart, and jam roly-poly . . .

Smiling to herself, Rachel remembered the time when Dad couldn't decide which pudding he wanted. It was a toss-up between three, she seemed to remember, so Mum just went ahead and made a whole feast. He said that that was real love right there on a plate, as he helped himself to a generous portion of each two hours later, laughing that he was only having so much to please his lovely wife.

Rachel scrolled over the images with an ache of loss in her heart as she looked across at Dad's empty chair. Why did he have to go and leave them? How the hell had that happened? So many whys and unanswered questions. She felt a tear crowd her eye.

But it was no good getting nostalgic. She had to hold it together to keep the farm going for the three of them now, look at ways of making it more profitable, to keep them afloat. She couldn't be the one to let them all down, to see it sold off. Primrose Farm was their legacy – and their beloved home.

So, if the pudding idea could help the farm, and as it was something Jill really enjoyed, it was worth at least looking into. There were plenty of people who stayed locally in holiday cottages who might like a treat, there were busy mums and wives with little time to bake, people on their own like Tom, the elderly – a whole host of potential customers who might like to buy a lovely homemade pudding.

There was a pudding on the screen now, the packaging wrapped in muslin. Hmm, Rachel's mind turned to Eve, her crafting friend. She'd know how to make something similar. Ooh, maybe they could have a selection of puddings, wrapped in something pretty with a bow around and a 'Primrose Farm' tag.

The ideas were rolling now. For the first time in a long while, Rachel felt a spark of excitement.

This was definitely food for thought!

A little while later, Jill came down from her bath.

'Hey, Mum. Feeling more relaxed now?'

'Yes, love. That was just what I needed – a hot soak in some bubbles.'

Rachel wondered whether to share her newly hatched pudding idea. She'd seen how her mum was starting to enjoy her baking again, but would suggesting that she turn her flair into something more business-like take away all the joy from it? Would Jill feel pressured to help out if she knew how tight their finances really were? And could letting her in on the farm's dire financial state undo all the progress she was making?

No, Rachel decided to hold back and keep these

thoughts to herself. She was afraid to broach this just yet, uncertain as to how it would be taken. She'd have to find some other way to stop the farm's overdraft deepening for now. Her mum's positive progress through that painful journey of grief was far more important than any business venture idea. She was just glad that the old Jill was slowly but surely finding her way back home.

Chapter 7

UNICORNS AND CUPCAKES

Life on the farm was far too busy for Rachel to mope about dwelling on their problems, however big they were. There was lambing to get on with, the small herd of cattle to be fed and mucked out, plus there was the persistent mountain of paperwork to trawl through.

Maisy's recent question about her missing father was also playing on Rachel's mind – now she was growing up, how was this affecting her? And thinking of her growing up, there was also a birthday to plan for. Maisy's special day was approaching fast. Rachel was determined to give her daughter a wonderful birthday, but how did you make a little girl's party special on a shoestring budget? Rachel sighed. *Oh well*, she rallied, if anyone could do it, she and Jill could.

It was Saturday of the following week, and the day of Maisy's birthday.

'Mumm-ee! Come on, come on. It's today!'

'Ah . . . hi, Maisy . . .' Rachel was trying to come to

from a foggy haze, with a very excited five-year-old bouncing up and down on her bed.

'Grandma's making pancakes too!'

Five-year-old . . . that was it! 'Oh fabulous . . . happy birthday sweetheart.'

Rachel stretched and rubbed her bleary eyes. Last night had seen her up until past midnight as she tried to get the surprise party venue ready after Maisy had gone to bed. So, just as her knees were buckling and her eyelids drooping, the grand finale was that eighteen young children were due to arrive today at 2 p.m. Rachel was getting palpitations just thinking about it.

Down in the farmhouse kitchen, Jill was busy making a breakfast of pancakes for them all as a treat, along with thickly buttered toast and mugs of warming hot chocolate.

'Good morning, birthday girl,' she called to Maisy. 'You'll need some pancakes to help you grow big and strong, I bet?'

There was a choice of scrumptious pancake fillings all lined up on the side: lemon and sugar, banana and home-made toffee sauce, or chocolate spread. Maisy plumped for the chocolate ones, Rachel for a lemon-sugar closely followed by a toffee-banana. She figured she'd need her energy levels up for the day ahead, after all. Jill sat with them soon afterwards with her own lemon stack, and a well-earned mug of tea.

There were some birthday gifts for Maisy to open – one from Grandma Ruth and a couple of small ones from Rachel and Jill, including a new party frock for today. Their main present was outside ready for Maisy to discover later – they'd been saving hard over the past few weeks, the household expenses being on an extra-tight budget to do so. Jake's parents, who now lived further south, near to Leeds, had sent something on in the post too, which was kind of them. Typically, there was nothing from Maisy's dad himself, and no word on his whereabouts or even whether he'd got Rachel's message about the party today. Rachel tried to push that particular worry to the back of her mind.

Jill had set to work baking and by mid-morning twenty-four cupcakes were neatly lined up on the cooling rack in the kitchen, ready to be iced and decorated with sugar-paper unicorns and hundreds-and-thousands sprinkles. There were also two large Victoria sponge bases she had made, ready for Rachel to sandwich together with jam and buttercream and cover with royal icing. Rachel was then to create the birthday cake bonanza with an arch of rainbow-coloured icing, some edible flowers she was yet to craft and a sprinkling of coloured stars. She had bought the cutest sugar-paste unicorn and a number '5' to then pop on the top.

Rachel's mind spun as she listed all the things left to do: icing the cake, finishing the decoration of the barn party venue, setting up the bouncy castle and slide . . . Along with Granny Ruth, she and Jill had been saving for ages to get the new play equipment for the party as

Maisy's main birthday present. They hoped it would be a wise purchase and help entertain the rabble of children at the party, as well as provide hours of fun for Maisy and her friends for the summer months to come.

Rachel began colouring strips of icing with food dyes to make the rainbow arch. She had ready-made stars to sprinkle over and was going to cut out and delicately mould some flower shapes from the left-over coloured icing.

Fifteen minutes later, Jill walked past the kitchen bench where she was working just as she was putting on the finishing touches with the unicorn topper. 'Wow, that looks great. I'm impressed.'

Rachel had thought the rainbow was a bit skew-whiff, but as she stood back and looked at the finished cake, she could see it wasn't bad at all – yes, a pretty good effort.

'Maisy will love it,' Jill confirmed.

Rachel hoped so; her little girl had already been disappointed this morning, after *once again* asking if her daddy was going to come to the party. She'd been asking every day this last week, but despite Rachel sending numerous texts, phoning and leaving answerphone messages as well as trying a couple of emails to his last known contact address, Jake hadn't bothered to respond. Rachel had tried to let Maisy down gently, but she knew that her daughter was still clinging onto the belief that he'd turn up.

Jake hadn't made it for the last three birthdays, so

Rachel didn't expect to see him at this one. She didn't actually even know where he was in the country, or if he still *was* in this country. His parents lived over a hundred miles away too, so they wouldn't be visiting, though they had sent a gift and always kept in touch with Maisy at birthdays and Christmas and the like. Rachel didn't think even they knew where their son was most of the time. In some ways, it was easier for Rachel that he did keep his distance so she could get on with raising Maisy her own way. But it was Maisy who was starting to need him now, or at least to need to know who he was. *Who he was*, was in fact an unreliable, commitment-phobic, selfish tosser. In reality, he might well be a disruptive influence and a disappointment to Maisy, Rachel mused, but maybe that was unfair. Perhaps, by some miracle, he might have grown up a bit himself by now, and of course her daughter did need her dad. She certainly wanted to be like the other kids who had dads around, her little girl having become more aware of his absence since starting school. Well, if he did turn up it would be a bit of a shock and a minor miracle, but only time would tell.

With the birthday cake completed, Rachel needed to crack on with getting the barn ready. She passed Moss in the kitchen, giving him a pat on the head, and headed through to the porch to pull on her wellies.

'Come on Moss, boy, let's go and get this party started.'

Rachel headed across the yard and yanked open the

two heavy wooden barn doors that shaped into an arch. A sparrow darted out – it must be nesting in there. The morning light filled the space and the honeyed-stone walls glowed. It really was pretty in there. For years it had been hidden in dust and straw, with heaps of old sacks, discarded tools, and a few bags of sheep feed. Yesterday, they'd had a damned good clear-out, moving what was useful to one end of the lambing shed, discarding the rest. The flagstone floor was brushed clean, and the cobwebs and dust dispersed – it had taken some time!

Rachel did a quick count of all the chairs they'd ferried in there. They had nineteen bottoms to seat plus parents – hmm. She took out her mobile phone. She needed a friendly neighbour.

'Tom?'

'Hi, Rachel. All okay?'

'Yes, thanks. I just need a bit of a favour.'

'Okay, ask away.'

'It's Maisy's birthday today and we're having a bit of a party for her friends. I'm here getting the barn ready, but I've realised we haven't enough chairs for everyone.'

'Hah, it'll be bedlam. And yes, I thought her birthday was sometime soon. She'll be excited.'

'She sure is. She's across with Eve and Amelia just now, whilst we get everything ready. There're eighteen children coming . . . I can't wait,' Rachel groaned. 'Anyway, do you have any spare chairs that we could borrow for this afternoon? Just some old ones will do, we don't need anything fancy.'

'Hah, there's not much fancy in my house. I can bring across my patio ones and my kitchen set.'

'Yes, please, that'd be brilliant. Cheers, Tom.'

'No worries. I'll be across in a while. I'm just up at The Ridge checking the ewes and lambs.'

'Okay, well there's no mad rush, just whenever you can make it before the two o'clock kick-off, if at all possible.'

'Yeah, that's fine. See you soon.'

'You're a star. Thank you.' Rachel put away her phone.

Tom really was turning into a bit of a knight in shining armour these days, though she hoped she wasn't leaning on him too much and becoming a pain.

Time rushed by in a whirl of bunting-fixing and paper-chain-hanging. Tom had arrived with the chairs and didn't bat an eyelid when Rachel asked him to blow up thirty fuchsia-coloured balloons and to help lay the tables with paper plates and unicorn napkins.

She glanced at her watch – it was gone one-thirty already.

'Crikey, we've only got half an hour to go. Maisy'll be back any minute too, to change into her party dress.'

'Well, I'll let you get on. I have bought a little some-thing for the birthday girl, so I'll pop back across with it in a while,' Tom said.

'That's very brave. Are you sure you're up to handling nineteen four and five-year-olds?'

'Well . . . I can try, but I'll leave it at least an hour or so, let them all settle in. When are they expected to go?' He gave a wry smile.

'Hah – good thinking. It finishes around five-ish.'

'Best of luck then, and I'll see you all later. Wish Maisy a lovely time from me.'

'Will do.'

'It looks great in here by the way,' he added, scanning the barn as he turned to leave.

'Yeah, I'm really pleased with it. And, it'll be far better than them all going crazy in the house.'

'Hah, yes – well, have a good time!'

Jill arrived with a tray of clingfilmed sandwiches and freshly baked sausage rolls, just as Tom was about to leave.

'Don't tempt me.' He grinned, eyeing the platter hungrily.

'Go on, help yourself. A sausage roll won't hurt, I've made a double batch. There's a load more in the kitchen.'

'Well, it'd be rude not to, I suppose.' He took a bite of the crispy, melt in-the-mouth, sage, onion and sausage goodness. 'Delicious!' And with that he set off in his truck, giving a farewell toot.

Five minutes later, Eve turned up with a very excited little girl in tow – in fact two!

Maisy dashed out of the car. 'Mumm-ee, we've been making finger puppets for the party. Animal ones – look, they're so cute. There's one for every party ba . . .' She stopped in her tracks and stared, open-mouthed at the inside of the barn. 'Wow-wee!' she shouted, running in and doing a lap of the trestle tables. 'A-maz-ing!'

Phew, she liked it! Rachel and Jill were beaming, their efforts having evidently been worthwhile.

'Right petal, well you need to go upstairs and get changed into your new party dress right now, before all your friends get here.'

'Ooh, yes.' And Maisy skipped off towards the house, Amelia by her side, with Moss on their heels scooting across the yard, picking up on the buoyant mood.

'Shall I stay and help?' offered Eve. 'Amelia's already in her party gear, and I've got time on my hands. No point heading back home just to turn around again in twenty minutes.'

'Aw, you are a star. That'd be great. Could you help Mum bring across the rest of the food whilst I'll check Maisy's getting dressed and ready okay?'

'Yeah, no worries. Looks really great in there by the way,' Eve nodded at the barn. 'Think we'll need to borrow the barn for all our kids' parties. Save the wreckage to our own homes.'

'Hah, we'll see how it goes first! You might not be saying that by the end. It could be kiddie carnage.'

'Well, at least you can just close the doors on the barn afterwards and retreat to the farmhouse for a glass of wine.'

'True.'

'Do you think we could close those doors for a while during the party too?' Rachel added cheekily. 'Adults outside and the kids in.'

The two friends chuckled.

'It'll be fine,' rallied Jill. 'What's the worst a bunch of five-year-olds can do?'

Eve and Rachel both looked at each other, pulling a grimace. *Anything could happen!*

Chapter 8

BIRTHDAY TREATS, TEARS AND
CHOCOLATE PUDDING

With Musical Chairs, Pass-the-Parcel, and the fabulously peaceful-for-the-parents Sleeping Lions game completed, it was time for the birthday tea.

The party food looked amazing, and Jill, Rachel and Maisy beamed proudly as the adults 'Oohed' and 'Aahhed', saying how delicious it all appeared, and the children tucked in. There were homemade sausage rolls, mini sausages, neatly cut triangle sandwiches, crisps and two 'hedgehogs' made of pineapple and cheese on sticks that Granny Ruth had brought with her – basically silver-foil-covered grapefruits with spiky snacks and some wiggly stick-on eyes. And, that was before you even got to the dessert selection of unicorn cupcakes, mini jam tarts, jellies and rocky road squares!

'Granny Ruth, you need to come and sit here next to me.' Maisy patted the chair next to her, with Amelia already settled on her other side.

Rachel caught Granny Ruth's eye and had to suppress

a giggle as she sat down with all the children. But, she soon looked like she was having a ball, smiling broadly and passing around the plates of treats.

'I love your hedgehogs, Granny. They're *sooo* cute,' said Maisy.

'Ah, thank you pet. I'm glad you like them. I used to make them just like that for your grandad when he was a little boy.'

'Really? That must be ages ago.'

'Yes, it was.' And there was a tell-tale glisten in Granny Ruth's eyes as she spoke.

Rachel found herself with a lump in her throat and Jill said she'd better head back across to the farmhouse to warm her individual sticky chocolate puds, which she was to serve with a blob of thick cream or local vanilla ice cream for the adults.

Amongst the attendees were Eve, Charlotte – another close friend of Rachel's who lived nearby and worked as a teacher at a primary school – several of the school mums and a couple of the dads, and Jill's closest friend, Jan, who was also a farmer's wife. They could relax for a few precious minutes whilst the children were busy tucking into the party food – lulling their minders and parents into a false sense of security ahead of their imminent sugar rush!

With just one hour of the party to go, Rachel rushed up to get ready for the big 'Birthday Cake Lighting Ceremony'. As she headed across the garden, Maisy came up and grabbed her hand.

'Hey petal, you all right? Enjoying your party?' Rachel asked.

'Yes, it's good, but is Daddy coming?'

Oh my, she was still hoping, bless her.

'Nicholas says he's not real,' Maisy then blurted out. That figured . . . he was the brat-kid who Rachel had seen fighting over the last cupcake. 'That I don't really have a daddy, but I do, don't I?'

'Of course you do, Maisy, but like I said, Daddy's a long way away right now and I really don't know when he'll come back.' She could only be honest (though economical with the full detail) with her little girl. Lies would just lead to more disappointment. Maisy brushed away a fat tear with the back of her hand, breaking Rachel's heart. She lifted her daughter up into a hug. Sometimes, as much as you tried to protect them, they still got hurt.

'Hey sweetheart, you go and have some fun with your friends. Show them your brilliant new slide and bouncy castle. I bet Nicholas hasn't got one of those in his garden.'

'O-kay, yes. I will.'

Rachel popped her down next to the garden gate.

'Come on, Amelia,' Maisy called her best friend to her side. 'Come see. I've got a new slide!' The others heard and were soon dashing forwards too.

Tom's truck then appeared on the driveway. He parked up and made his way over, avoiding an incoming tide of excitable children. 'Hi Rachel, Jill.'

Several sets of ladies' eyes seemed to light up as he

approached the gathering, Eve's, in fact, turning into saucers.

'So, where's the birthday girl?' He seemed unaware of the effect he was having. He was holding a gift, wrapped up in Peppa Pig paper.

Maisy heard him, turned in her tracks, and ran to him gleefully. 'Tom!'

'Hey, I heard it was someone's birthday today.'

Her eyes lit up as Tom handed her the present. She couldn't wait to open it and promptly sat down on the driveway to tear the paper off. It was a bracelet-making set along with a storybook, some acrylic paints and coloured card with lots of glitter and sticky shapes to decorate it with.

'Thank you, Tom, thank you!' she squealed.

Rachel was proud her daughter had remembered her manners. The little girl gave him a quick hug and then ran off to be with her friends who were enjoying the bouncy castle and slide.

'Survived?' Tom asked Rachel, with an understanding smile.

'Just,' she replied. 'Do you fancy a tea or anything? There's birthday cake coming shortly too.'

'Well, now you've got me.' He gave a grin.

'Hi, Tom.' Eve came across rather coyly, and Rachel left the two of them chatting whilst she went to fetch Tom a mug of tea and organise the candle-lighting for the birthday cake.

*

'Happy birthday to you! Happy birthday to you!' they all chorused.

The unicorn cake was met with delight, and Maisy's face was a picture – she actually couldn't speak. Rachel felt a happy tear crowd her eye.

It was time to blow out the candles. Maisy scrunched up her face and made a silent wish. Rachel had a feeling she might well be wishing for a daddy – one that came to birthday parties. She felt a lump form in her throat for her little girl, and for the little girl inside herself too, still yearning for her own daddy to come back home, even though the adult in her knew that that was never going to happen.

Jill sliced the cake up into rectangles of moist sponge, jam and icing. They ate it from napkins out in the sunshine, then the adults watched the children play once more. The early April day was warm and pleasant. The sky ultramarine with wisps of puffy white cloud. The fields, hills and countryside where their sheep and cattle grazed, were spring-green and bursting into life all around them.

After eating a slice of cake and a sausage roll, Tom stood to say his goodbyes to the group. He then came across to Rachel. 'I'd better be heading back.'

'Well, thanks so much for taking the time to come across. I know Maisy loved seeing you.'

'It's no problem. She's a great kid. And hey, you've done a brilliant job here, Rachel. The barn, everything. She'll have had a real special day.' His hand rested on her shoulder for a brief second. It felt reassuring, warm.

'Thanks.'

Tom then set off back to work at the farm next door. It was so nice that he'd made the effort to call. And, Rachel smiled to herself, it had certainly cheered up Eve's day by the soppy look on her face.

The party was wrapping up for another year, and after a flurry of farewells, a few tired tears, happy hugs and party bags distributed, it was finally time for home. Quiet – phew.

Back at the house, Maisy crashed out on the old armchair by the Aga – Granny Ruth's favourite seat. It had most likely been there when she and her husband, Grandad Ken, had lived in the farmhouse themselves with Rachel's dad growing up as a little boy. There were so many memories over the generations in this farm, and there was a sense of history and comfort from that. Rachel placed a cosy blanket over Maisy, giving her tired daughter a kiss on her forehead, and set about doing the last of the washing-up in the kitchen.

Jill arrived back from dropping off Granny Ruth, and Rachel poured out two glasses of left-over fizz as they collapsed at the kitchen table, with Maisy now sound asleep in the chair. A wave of fatigue hit Rachel.

'Well, I'd say that was a success,' pronounced Jill.

'Yes.' Rachel stifled a yawn. 'Thanks Mum, for all your help. I couldn't have pulled that off without you. All the food was just brilliant, and the second round of Sleeping

Lions out in the garden was a triumph.' In fact, two of the children had actually gone off to sleep.

'The old games are the best.' Jill winked.

Rachel glanced over to check that Maisy was still sleeping, before lowering her voice. 'Mum, I'm a bit worried about Maisy, lately.'

'Oh . . . why's that, pet?'

'She's been asking about her dad, and why he's not around. I think the other kids at school have been asking questions and teasing her.'

'Oh dear . . . bless her.' Jill sighed. 'It's a tricky one, isn't it. I don't suppose you heard a thing back from him about her birthday, either?'

'Now then . . . what do you think?' Rachel asked, ironically.

'Well, we can only be honest with her, Rachel. Be there to field her questions. She's growing up, she's bound to be curious.'

'Yes . . . I think she's missing him. Well, missing a father figure anyway. Especially with Dad . . .' Rachel couldn't bring herself to say the words.

'Yes, I know, I know, love. We've just got to be strong for her. Be her mum, dad, grandparents . . . everything. Families come in all shapes and sizes, especially these days.'

'You're right. Thanks, Mum. We can only do our best, can't we.'

'Indeed. And, today was a pretty good shot at a super birthday party for her.'

'It was. Well then, I don't think *I'll* need any help getting off to sleep tonight.' Rachel gave in to another yawn.

'Nor me.'

They spent a few quiet moments sat in the kitchen, Rachel looking out of the window at the view; the fields with their white woolly sheep dotted about and the valley below – all green and lush, and rather beautiful. The gentle foothills of the Cheviots which cradled their lovely farmhouse. Rachel gave a tired, yet contented sigh. It was lovely to stop for a second and take in the scene – sometimes you were so busy you forgot to look.

Later that evening, Rachel carried Maisy upstairs and, after a nice warm bath, they started reading Tom's birthday book, all about magical adventures at a fairy glen – a good choice.

Maisy's head was heavy on the pillow.

'Night, night, Maisy. Happy birthday, my love.'

'Night, Mummy.' Maisy went quiet for a second and looked thoughtful. 'Mummy . . . do you think . . . maybe Tom could be my daddy?' she said sleepily.

'Oh, Maisy. It doesn't quite work like that, sweetheart.' Rachel kissed her little girl gently on the forehead. 'Night, night, petal. Sweet dreams.'

If only life was that simple.

Chapter 9

COFFEE, CHAT AND CHOCOLATE
BROWNIES

A few days after the party, reality was hitting home all too hard for Rachel. With lambing over and birthday dreams delivered, the cold hard facts of the farm's ever deepening financial woes were impossible to avoid. Rachel could no longer shield Jill from the truth, as leaving their heads in the sand any longer would lead to far bigger issues – and the chance that they might lose the farm altogether. That was one thing Rachel could not risk.

The time had come to face the music. Maisy was at school, Rachel had done the morning's farm checks and she and Jill were pottering around in the farmhouse kitchen.

Rachel took a deep breath. 'Mum, we need to talk.'

'Okay, right. What about . . . you sound awfully serious?'

'Well, it is.'

'Does it warrant a cup of tea?'

'Yes, I think maybe a gin actually.'

71

'Ah . . .'

Jill quickly put the kettle on and set about making a pot of tea, placing a small milk jug and two cups in the centre of the pine table.

'It's the farm. We're struggling, Mum.' Rachel found herself all choked up just saying the words aloud. Yes, she'd known it herself for some time, but telling her mum made it all much more real. She was incredibly worried about how it would affect her.

'Oh . . . Well, it's always been a bit of a juggling act, love. Even years back.' Mum's tone was light.

Rachel realised that she'd not quite grasped the seriousness of the situation. How very wrong it had all gone since Dad's death.

'It's getting harder and harder to earn a living, Mum. I didn't want to have to involve you, I hoped we might see a turnaround, but the prices for sheep aren't looking too good for when we come to market, and our costs are forever rising. We are already struggling with an overdraft now and if things carry on the way they are, in a few months' time we'll hit rock bottom – the farm's subsidy payment for this year is already nearly used up.' Most of it had disappeared into the black hole of the farm's overdraft straight away.

'It's gone *already*?' Jill looked shocked.

'Yes, I'm sorry, Mum.'

In fact, at any point the bank might pull the plug on them and that would be it. Rachel held back from voicing that last hammer blow.

'Oh dear . . .' Jill grasped the edge of the table. 'Well, it's not your fault, pet. It's the way things are, have been, for a long time. Your dad . . .' Jill couldn't finish that sentence. Instead, she stirred the teapot and poured out the tea on autopilot.

There were a few seconds of heartfelt silence between them.

Jill took a deep breath. '*So*, what do we do?'

Rachel had already been thinking so much about this. 'Okay, one, I think we have to sell some land. Just one or two fields for now, to get some extra income in to keep us afloat.' It wasn't ideal and was very much a last resort. Losing land was heart-breaking and there was always a sense of shame within the farming community somehow, in letting it get to that. But sod it, they had already been through enough, who gave a stuff about rural tittle-tattle? If it meant keeping the rest of the farm together, giving them time to find some way out of this, then so be it.

Jill couldn't help the sigh that escaped her lips. There were a few seconds before she said pragmatically, 'All right, if needs must. But that still won't solve the long-term income problems, will it?'

'No . . . but . . .' Maybe it was time for Rachel to share her pudding business ideas. Sow the thought that they might be able to do things differently. She didn't have much else up her sleeve. 'Look, Mum, I've been doing some research. We need to do something new, to diversify.'

Jill was nodding, listening.

'So hear me out. I'm thinking . . . puddings,' Rachel continued. 'A pudding business. Something we can do from here. I think it might have legs.'

'Oh, blimey. So, how do you see it working?'

'Well, you're great at baking. And you really enjoy it, don't you?' Rachel felt nervous broaching the idea.

'Well yes, but . . . a *business* . . . I'm sure there's a darn sight more to it than just enjoying baking, love.'

'Of course. I know that. But what if we made the farm kitchen our base? We can do the qualifications like health and hygiene we might need, both of us, and just start small, give it a try. Make some puddings to sell. Just have a think about it, yeah . . . And in the meanwhile, I'll look into it some more.' Rachel was trying to gauge her mum's reaction, but Jill's face was hard to read. 'So, what do you think?'

'It's a lot to take on board, pet. I'll need a little time.'

Rachel didn't like to say that *time* was one thing they didn't have on their side. But she knew her mum needed a bit of space to get her head around all this. And that was fair enough. After all, Rachel herself had been mulling it over for several weeks now.

'Okay, I understand. Promise you'll at least consider it, yeah?'

'I will, pet.'

'And tomorrow, I'd better make that call to the land agent,' Rachel stated, facing up to the worst of it.

Jill placed her hand gently over her daughter's on the table top, then nodded her acquiescence sadly.

*

A week later, there was a large wooden sign mounted on a post by the farm gate. It read 'Land for Sale' and it tugged at Rachel's heartstrings every time she saw it.

One evening soon after the sign went up, Jill went along to the local WI meeting for a talk on jewellery making. She'd come home deflated, telling of the hassle she'd had from a certain Vanessa Palmer-Pilkington there. 'Honestly, that woman was probing so much. Wheedling for information. Was it the whole farm up for sale? She was so sorry to hear it, blah, blah, bloody blah. She wasn't sorry at all, just wanted some juicy gossip to tell her neighbours and the village.'

'Oh dear, doesn't sound like it was the best of nights for you, Mum.' That was such a shame too, as Jill had still been a bit reclusive of late. Rachel had hoped that getting out and about more would do her good.

'Bloody woman was like a vulture at the end of the talk circling me, looking for every juicy scrap of information. Pretending to be concerned, when all she wanted was some tittle-tattle.'

'Well, don't worry about her, Mum.' Rachel knew the woman was a bit of a nightmare. 'Some people have nothing better to do with their lives. I bet the others there were supportive.'

'Oh yes, I do have some nice friends there, of course. And all the farming folk know the tough issues we face every day in this business. Anyway, I was getting fed up with Vanessa's constant wheedling, so I told her we were using the money from the sale of the fields to build a new indoor swimming pool. Well, you should have seen her face. It was a picture.'

'Hah, I love it. Go, Mum.'

'Well, that shut her up. She moved off swiftly then. And Jan, who was there beside me, nearly choked on her tea and biscuits. We couldn't stop chuckling.'

'Good for you, Mum.'

It was never easy in such a small community where everybody knew everybody's business – or at least they *thought* they did.

'So, what was the jewellery talk like?'

'Good, actually. Very informative. She'd brought some really pretty examples too. It was just the end with old V.P.P. that spoilt the night a bit, that was all.'

'Well, I think you handled it brilliantly. We stand tall and we fight back, Mum. We can hold our heads high. I, for one, am proud that we're trying to keep things going here, whatever that takes. We can only do our best.'

'I know, I know that, love. I just wish certain people would mind their own bloody business.'

'Yes. I know. So, why don't we rename her? V.P.P.: Visible Panty-line Palmer – has a nice ring to it, don't you think? Then every time we see her, it'll make us smile.'

Jill spluttered on her tea. 'Hah, that's genius!'

For all her fighting talk, Rachel had to admit that she was desperately worried too. What if the land didn't sell soon? Or what if it did but the money they received didn't make enough of a difference in the long term?

She swallowed down her fears and managed to smile across at her mum. 'We'll be okay, Mum. Together, we'll find a way.'

The next day, after the heart-to-heart with Mum, puddings were very much on Rachel's mind. Not just that she could eat a very generous portion of some left-over lemon pudding that she knew was still in the fridge right now, but also, and *more-so*, that there might actually be something in this pudding-making business idea. Thinking back to Maisy's party last week, the parents had raved about Jill's sticky chocolate pudding – and Charlotte wouldn't go home without the recipe. Rachel was desperate to dig a little deeper, and find out what her mum was really thinking, but knew she'd asked for some time – and it was only fair to give her that space.

Of course, Jill would have to be fully behind the idea to make it work, as they'd be relying heavily on her commitment as well as her baking skills. But they could start small, Rachel mused, test the waters. Sign up for their health and hygiene course together and trial a few sales locally. There were bound to be some nearby shops who'd be interested in stocking local farmhouse-made puddings, or perhaps they could even try a stall at the local farmers' market.

Rachel had given herself a headache looking at their accounts again this morning and yes, whilst they were still just about okay, their heads above water for now, they'd need money to keep the farm going until the first lambs were ready for market and beyond. There were wormers and medicines to buy, machinery to keep going, their farmhand to pay, the household bills to cover too. The list could go on . . . and on.

It was when the land agent had come around to value the fields that reality had really hit home. He'd pushed them to make a larger acreage available, suggesting that three or four fields might be more saleable, but Jill and Rachel hadn't been ready to give up too much land. They'd compromised at two, understanding that something had to be done, but he'd warned them that unless it was a local farmer or someone wanting a field or two for a pony to graze, it might not be snapped up that quickly. They'd have to see, but neither of them had felt ready to allow too much of the farm to go just yet. There must be some other way . . . if they could just think creatively.

Yes, she'd have to do lots more research on this pudding business idea, find out if there were any grants available for such things to help them get set up, and she *really* needed to talk over this idea properly with her mum. Without the Queen of Primrose Farm Puddings by her side, it was a non-starter.

Chapter 10

COFFEE, BROWNIES AND CHAT

The next morning Rachel had been checking the boundary fences and was trying to repair a bolt-hole that the lambs were escaping from.

'Want a coffee?'

Rachel jumped. Eve's head popped over the hedgerow.

'Jeez, Eve, you frightened the life out of me!'

'Sorry, hun. I spotted the quad, knew you'd be about somewhere. I was on my way back from Kirkton, been getting a few groceries.'

'Let me just finish securing this fence here – the lambs have been making a bid for freedom.' She was weaving a mesh of chicken wire through the existing fencing to stop the gap.

'Okay, call up at the cottage when you're ready. Be nice to have a catch-up.'

'Yes, I'll do that. Thanks.'

When she got to Eve's ten minutes later, there was a cafetière of coffee ready on the kitchen side along with a plate of chocolate brownies – the room was smelling of cocoa-coffee gorgeousness.

'Shall we take it outside?' Eve suggested. 'It's nice and sunny.'

'Sounds divine, coffee and a view.'

Eve picked up a tray and loaded the goodies onto it, along with a couple of mugs. 'To be honest, the dining room and lounge are covered in my craft stuff just now. There's not a lot of space left in the cottage. It's driving Ben crazy, but I need to keep it all somewhere handy, especially when I'm mid project.'

They settled at a slightly rickety table-for-two, on a flagstone patio to the rear of Eve's cottage. Their stone two-bedroomed cottage was rented from grumpy Mr Macintosh, whose farm bordered Primrose Farm on the opposite side from Tom. The farmer didn't keep the cottage in the best state of repair for them but the young family did their best with it and always kept the garden tidy. The cottage itself, though pretty, was tired-looking, with its white wooden window sills in need of a re-paint, but it was still full of character and Eve was happy there.

'So, what are you making just now?' Rachel took a sip of rich, delicious coffee.

'Children's toys . . . knitted and felt mice, rabbits, a fox, sheep, teddy bears. Hang on, I'll fetch one to show you.' Eve stood up to go back into the house.

'The kids at the party loved those finger puppets by the way. Thanks again for doing that,' said Rachel, whilst she was still in earshot.

'You're welcome, glad I could help you out with the entertainment.'

Eve went on into the cottage and came back a couple of minutes later with some extremely cute knits.

'Aw, these are so sweet,' Rachel exclaimed.

'I'm selling them as a set of three online. Like a friendship group.'

'They're brilliant. You are so clever.'

Knitting and delicate craft work had never been Rachel's thing. She just about knew how to sew a button back on, but it wouldn't be too neat a job. She was far better handling real animals or driving the tractor. She had always been a bit of a tomboy and relished getting stuck in around the farm. It was her dad who had taught her how to drive the tractor, just slowly around the yard to start, at the age of fourteen. She'd been watching and learning for years up until that point though – right beside him in the warmth of the cab. Oh yes, she could still remember his voice from that first lesson. 'This is one powerful and heavy machine, mind, lass. You treat her with respect,' he'd said in his warm but cautionary tone. She'd felt so proud sat there at the wheel, with a beaming smile. She'd be happier with a spanner and screwdriver than a needle and thread any day. But, hey, each to their own.

'So, it's going well so far, the Etsy thing?' Rachel asked with interest.

'Yes, I've got a few orders already. I'm so glad I made that leap.'

'That's great . . . Actually, we're thinking of setting up something of our own from the farm, me and Mum.' Rachel felt it was time to share her idea. It would be good to get some honest feedback.

'Ooh, I'm all ears. So, what's the plan?'

Eve was her closest friend, and the truth spilled out. 'Between you and me, we're struggling a bit. Finances are really tight and we need to think of other ways to make a living and support the farm.' It was actually a relief to speak to someone about this, other than her mum. She knew she could trust Eve to be discreet.

'Well, if there's anything at all that me and Ben can do to help . . .'

Aw, bless her. They didn't have a lot to spare for themselves. And, putting money into Primrose Farm at the moment would be like donating to a black hole, Rachel feared.

'Thanks Eve, I really appreciate the offer but we'll be fine. We just need to think creatively and out of the box on this. Then we can shore things up a bit, that's all.'

'So, what's your idea then, hun?'

'Okay, so what's the one thing *guaranteed* to put a smile on your face when you come into Primrose Farm?'

'That's easy, Jill's amazing cooking. I always leave about two stone heavier whenever she's been baking away in the kitchen.'

'Exactly! So, that's the nub of it, I keep coming back to the idea of Mum's puddings.'

'Ooh, interesting. Well, you know that I'm a big fan.

They are just divine. I still remember that strawberry and passionfruit pavlova she made for the barbecue we had here last summer. And her sticky toffee pud on a cold winter's night . . . mmmnn.'

'Ah yes, that's always been one of my favourites.'

'So, you're thinking of selling puddings then? That's such a great idea. Where and when can I buy some?' Eve clapped her hands together enthusiastically.

'Well, we're still thinking about outlets. I wondered if maybe the Kirkton Deli would be good to try, what do you think? It's on our doorstep and Mum knows Brenda there pretty well.'

'Yeah, that sounds a great place to start. No harm in asking anyway.'

'Yes, I'm feeling really positive about it, but I just get the feeling that Mum's a little reluctant just now, despite her being a brilliant cook. I'm looking into everything in detail and doing my homework. I've said I'll help Mum as much as I can with the business side, as well as with the cooking too.'

'Hmm, I see.'

'I don't want to push her too hard, but I can see this really working. We *need* to do something, Eve, I don't want the farm to get into deeper trouble. We've chatted all about the pudding idea, she obviously loves her baking, but then . . . well, I think she's really lost her confidence lately.'

'Oh, Rachel. You've all been through so much . . . it's no wonder.'

'I know,' Rachel's tone softened.

'Whatever you decide, we'll support you. Whatever you need to make this venture work, say the word if we can help. And tell your mum she needn't worry about whether or not they'll sell, she makes the best puddings around. They'll be queuing down Kirkton High Street like it's the Harrods' sale.' Eve grinned.

Rachel felt wrapped in a warm glow of friendship. 'Thank you.'

They ate some of the gorgeously-gooey chocolate brownies Eve had made and sipped rich strong coffee, chatting about country life, their girls' latest antics, a smattering of rural gossip. Apparently Melanie Bates had got engaged, and there'd been sightings of escapee pet rabbits appearing amongst the rural burrows – there'd be a medley of black, white and brown ones soon enough – and there was the drama of a couple on their hiking holiday who'd had a fall on some loose shale further up the valley, resulting in a broken leg and the air ambulance having to be called out.

'Right, best stop this gossiping, I should get myself away,' Rachel announced ten minutes later. 'Mum'll be wondering where I've got to, and I've a list of chores still to finish on the farm before school's out and the whirl-wind that is Maisy arrives home.'

'Yes, I'd better make a few more of these animals to fulfil my orders. It's been great to catch up. See you soon then.'

Rachel glanced at her watch. 'Yeah, at the bus stop in

about three hours. How does it roll around so quickly? And thanks for the coffee. It's been really good to chat.'

'You're welcome. It's nice to get you back out from the lambing shed.'

'Hah, absolutely.'

'Well, you all take care. Oh, and best of luck with your pudding plans.'

'Thanks, hun. I'll keep you posted.'

When Rachel arrived back at the farm, Jill handed her a parcel that the postman had just delivered. Her mum couldn't disguise the frown that had formed across her brow. Rachel was curious and, as she looked closer, she recognised the scrawled handwriting of Jake, her ex. It was addressed to Maisy. Most likely a late birthday gift, Rachel mused. She turned the parcel over in her hands. He was there loitering on the edges of their lives, unpredictable, unreliable. She wondered how Maisy would feel about this reminder of her dad's long-distance relationship – if it could in fact be described as a relationship, him being far more absent than present.

Rachel couldn't help the twist of anger in her gut that he hadn't even bothered to get a gift to his own daughter *on time*. It always seemed like Maisy was an afterthought to him. Maisy should *never* be an afterthought.

Chapter 11

FULL STEAM AHEAD

A couple of days later, Rachel made her way back into the warmth of the farmhouse for some lunch after being out in the tractor spreading fertiliser on the Low Pasture, preparing it for growing grass to make hay. She was quite happy driving the tractor, with her country music on her iPod to keep her company, her favourite at the moment being Colbie Caillat's 'Try'. And at least she'd had a dry and comfy seat for the morning.

As Rachel slid off her wellies at the porch, the sweet, warming smells of home baking once again greeted her. She opened the kitchen door to find Jill humming away to the radio, with Moss lying down quietly by her side, and an array of ingredients, bowls and baking trays around her.

Rachel smiled to herself. Her mum looked so content there in her baking haven; it was a scene that warmed Rachel's heart like nothing else, she could stand there and watch her forever. The family Baking Bible was open beside her, and Jill was concentrating on the page, her reading glasses propped on the end of her nose. She then weighed out some glacé cherries before taking a can of pineapple rings to hand.

'Hi, Mum.'

'Oh Rachel, hello love.'

'You look busy.'

'Oh, I was making some cherry scones just before, and then I thought about my mother's old recipe for pineapple upside-down pudding. I thought we might have a can of pineapple rings in the cupboard to go with the spare cherries and, hey presto, here we go. I found the recipe written out here, in her lovely loopy handwriting. Yes,' Jill smiled to herself, remembering, 'Granny Isabel always used to make this as a bit of a treat. Pineapple was rather decadent back in the day. So, I thought it might be an idea to treat ourselves today, too. It's high time there was a bit more light in our lives.'

'Absolutely.' It was wonderful to see Mum happier, with glimpses of her old self shining through, and she was evidently enjoying her baking. Could Rachel chance mentioning the pudding business idea again? It seemed the ideal time to broach it, and time was beginning to run short on their nose-diving finances – as yet, there had been no interest in the two fields they'd put up for sale.

'Mum, look, I don't want to pile the pressure on or anything, but did you get a chance to think about the pudding idea? Of trying to sell some? You're so talented, and I know everyone's been raving about your chocolate puddings since Maisy's party.' There had indeed been some thank-you texts from parents gushing about how delicious they were.

Rachel spotted the tell-tale frown straight away. Damn, she'd broken the lovely spell that her mum's baking had cast over the kitchen.

'Well, selling them to paying customers is a bit different than offering some puds around at a party.' Jill sounded unsure of herself, nervous in fact.

'I'm sure people would buy them! I've heard so many "yum", "scrumptious", and "divine" compliments being thrown around whilst collecting Maisy after school, and if that's anything to go by, well, they'll be queuing up.' Rachel grinned at her mum.

'Oh, I really don't know, love,' Jill answered honestly. 'I do like my baking, but it's more for pleasure, for us as a family. It was . . . well, it was always about Dad coming home to a hearty meal and a lovely pudding to look forward to, about you and Maisy tucking in. About Grandma Isabel and Granny Ruth, and all those recipes handed down from the generations before. I don't know if making it into a business would spoil all that. Like it might lose its heart somehow . . .' She gave a small sigh.

'But, maybe, you could share all that with lots more people. Give them a taste of a hearty farmhouse pudding, one made with love, instead of some packet mix or one off the supermarket shelf loaded with preservatives and such like.' She paused, her tone then becoming serious. 'We need to try something new to help farm, Mum.' Rachel stopped talking, feeling that she had pushed far enough.

Jill was nodding, but her look was of concern, of wariness. 'Oh, Rachel, love, I'm just not sure.'

Jill was notably quieter than usual for the rest of that afternoon and evening, and Rachel felt saddened that she had spoilt her mum's magical baking moment. So, late the next morning, after coming in from her farm chores and with it all still mulling over in her mind, Rachel felt an apology was called for. She caught up with Jill collecting eggs at the hen house.

'I'm sorry, Mum. I shouldn't have pushed you yesterday about the baking business. I'd just got excited about the idea. But if it's not for you . . .'

Jill looked up, wicker basket in hand, with several chickens clucking happily around her feet. 'No, you were right, I need a little shaking up. I've had my head stuck in the sand about the farm's finances for too long now, hoping it would all somehow magically improve. I don't think I felt I could cope with any more bad news . . . So, I *have* been thinking, in fact, more than that . . . I've called in and spoken with Brenda when I went into town this morning . . . at the Deli in Kirkton. She *really* liked the idea of selling some of our puddings, especially as they'd be locally made. With the busier summer season coming up, she said she'd be happy to try a few there should we decide to go ahead.'

'Oh wow! That's great news, Mum.' And so *wonderful* that Jill had come on board with the idea.

'So,' added Jill animatedly, having evidently been

thinking more on the project herself, 'which flavours do you think we should try first?'

'Oooh, now then, your sticky toffee is the bee's knees and my all-time favourite, so that's a must, and the sticky chocolate from the party was really popular. What about just keeping it simple while we start out and do those two to begin with?'

'Hmm, we can always add more pudding varieties later, I suppose.' Jill stood, framed by the stone outbuildings of the farmyard with the rolling hills behind, the warm April sunlight giving her a golden glow.

'Exactly, this is great, Mum. I love the new enthusiasm. You seem excited about the idea. What's changed?'

'I've just been thinking about it, that's all. And, I did bump into Jan on the high street this morning too and we got chatting.' Jan was also a farmer's wife, and understood their lifestyle and situation all too well. She had been Jill's close friend over many years. 'We ended up going for coffee and she was telling me all about how the Glen-Robertsons have set up their jam and chutney business at their farm. It seems to be going really well. So, I thought, you know, *why not*. We can at least give it a try. So, I thought right, let's do this thing, and I popped right on into the Deli.'

'Oh, that's brilliant, Mum. I'm so pleased you're excited about all this. Life's too short to not give it a go, hey.' *And didn't they know that.* 'In fact, I think we need to book on to our hygiene courses as quickly as poss. I've found out that we can do them online, so we can study together over the next few evenings when Maisy's in bed. It'll be like old times . . . do you remember when you kept me going through my exam revision, up until midnight with a constant supply of cocoa and flapjacks?'

'I'd better get baking some supplies then.' Jill smiled warmly.

Oh yes, there was no time like the present. Rachel felt a buzz of hope fizzing through her.

She phoned Eve that same afternoon to continue their chat about the pudding idea, and also to ask if she'd think about designing some packaging for them. She was imagining something pretty with an old-fashioned, country feel.

'So, you're going to give it a try. How fabulous,' Eve said cheerily. 'Oh yes, Primrose Farm Puddings. Sounds great, doesn't it.'

Rachel hadn't got as far as a name yet, but yes, that was simple and ideal. 'Brilliant! Yes! I like it.'

'Hmm . . .' Eve started, 'I suppose the puds will have to be made in something like a metal foil tray with a lid, so I'm thinking traditional muslin or maybe a pretty cotton print tied with a ribbon bow as packaging, and a card label.'

'Love it already. Yes, the two puds we are starting with are both baked, so that sounds about right. I knew you'd come up with something great. Your mind is a well of craft genius.'

'Hah, not sure about that . . . So, sticky toffee and chocolate flavours, you say.'

'Yep, that's it. To start with, anyhow.'

'Ooh, so there could be a whole range of puddings soon? Scrummy, I can't wait to try them.'

'There might well be, in time, but we'll just take it slowly to begin with. One step at a time, Eve. I don't want to put too much pressure on Mum, either. She was nervous about it all initially, though she does seem really on board with the idea now, which is great. But I do hope she's not just going along with it for my sake. So, back to the packaging, if you can come up with a few ideas and samples for us to have a look at – we'd pay you for the designs of course – then that'd be brilliant.'

'Sounds great. I'll do some trial ones to start, see what you and Jill think of them first. Ooh, I love a new challenge and this is right up my street,' Eve enthused. 'I'll let you know as soon as I've got some ready. It'll probs take me a day or two, as I've got a couple of Etsy orders to make up.'

'Oh, that'll be fine, Eve. We've got to pass our hygiene certificates and there's a check to be made on the kitchen facilities by the council before we can actually make anything to sell, so a few days is no problem at all. And, it's great that you're all up and running with your Etsy now too. Well done you. Well, aren't we the entrepreneurs,' said Rachel, smiling, feeling the frisson of excitement between them. 'How's it been going?'

'Well, just a few orders so far. Some of the knitted toys

and a couple of jumpers – the tractor one seems popular. But it's a good start.'

'I'm delighted for you.'

'Thanks, and like I say, give me a day or so, and I'll get some packaging designs made up for the puddings. Then you and your mum can come over and see what you think.'

'Perfect, thank you.' Rachel found herself with a big grin on her face.

Team Primrose Farm Puddings was coming together.

Rachel had gone straight online after the call and booked the two courses for health and hygiene. She didn't want to waste time getting started on this, and to be honest they couldn't afford to financially either. In the back of her mind, she also wanted to make sure her mum didn't have second thoughts and waver.

Whilst on the computer she took a look at her emails. There were a few pieces of farming admin to address, and then she spotted an email that must be from Jake, at some new email address. The subject line was simply 'Hi'. Rachel felt a bit queasy. It was always unnerving hearing from him; it left her wondering what his real agenda was.

Hmm, first that late birthday present for Maisy. What now? Maisy had been so excited that day when Rachel passed the gift on to her, her little sunny face so full of hope as she ripped open the parcel. *Her daddy had remembered her.* It had turned out to be a dress a size too big; he hadn't even bloody well remembered her age. Maisy had put it on regardless, sporting the baggy floral item around the house and doing little twirls, bless her.

And now a message. Was he trying to come back into their lives? She should be pleased for Maisy's sake, but it always seemed to spell trouble when Jake reappeared, stirring things up, only for him to just drift off and disappear again soon after.

She took a deep breath and braced herself to read the email:

> *Hi Rach,*
>
> *How's tricks? Hope Maisy got her gift ok and likes it. Say a big hi to her from her dad.*

Oh yes, say hello from the dad who's never here just to get her all wound up again.

> *How're you and your mum doing? Still on the farm?*

Of course, working hard to keep it all together and support your daughter.

> *I'm down in Bedford on a job at the moment.*

Oh, so he *is* working, so where's the child support? All Maisy gets is a toy monkey one Christmas and a dress a year too big!

Thinking of coming up North this summer, so I'll deffo call in and see Maisy then.

Great, *not* – can't wait for that to happen then.

How is she? At school now? She must be. All grown up I bet. Send a photo.

A photo – he needs a frigging photo to recognise his own child!

Send her my love and a big hug.
Cheers,
Jake x

Rachel felt all churned up. Her fingers were trembling on the laptop's keyboard. Hah – so he thought he could flit in and out of Maisy's life, just like that? But, if she mentioned to her daughter that he was planning a visit, he *still* might not even turn up – given his past track record. Rachel had heard it all before. There was no way she'd be telling Maisy that her dad might be coming up this summer – she couldn't raise her little girl's hopes just for them to be dashed. No, Rachel would hold strong and wait and see.

She didn't even know how to answer the message. Hearing from Jake always sent her into a bit of a spin. The implications for Maisy were complicated, and there was always the fear that maybe one day he'd want to come back up this way for good, perhaps even look for custody of Maisy – just the thought of that made Rachel feel sick. Maisy hardly knew her dad. And the one thing Rachel was sure of was that he was in no way reliable. *Argh*, she'd reply later. A polite response, but nothing overly friendly.

It was many a year ago now since she'd fallen head over heels for that lad, taken in by a handsome face, a cheeky smile and a host of false promises, when she'd been a naïve teenager herself. The first time she'd met Jake was at sixth form, when he'd turned up in the autumn term as the good-looking new lad who'd grown up near London. His life before his arrival in Kirkton sounded so exciting, with trips to the big city, party nights, and a host of cool friends. All the girls in her year were totally into him, with his blond hair, that flash of a smile and easy chat. She knew he was a bit of a charmer, but that was just him. He was so much more confident than the other lads at school who suddenly seemed so much younger, naïve. Jake was fresh, interesting and very different from the local farming lads. And the crazy thing was that he seemed to like Rachel too, and would single her out to chat with at break-time; about music, life here in Kirkton, and his plans for travelling. And then, when he asked her to go along with him to the local nightclub over in Berwick, just after he'd passed his driving test, well, she almost hyperventilated.

Dad hadn't been so sure about this, of course. When he heard of the planned night out he said that they were too young to go out drinking and clubbing. But Rachel argued that anybody who was anybody went, even if they weren't quite eighteen. And Dad didn't know, but she'd already sourced a fake ID to get into the club. Dad insisted he needed to meet this lad who was showing an interest in his daughter, and Jake was promptly invited to Sunday dinner. Sat around the farmhouse kitchen table, it was the first time Rachel had seen Jake looking distinctly uncomfortable, as he was being quizzed on his plans for the future, which he seemed rather vague about. Well, who the hell knew what they wanted to do with their lives at seventeen years of age, anyhow? That's what Rachel had thought back then, that her dad was being old-fashioned, had forgotten what it was like to be young and carefree. The world was their oyster, they didn't need to have it all mapped out. But hey, hindsight was a wonderful thing.

Weeks of schoolyard kisses, parties, dancing, drinking and fun, falling in love and first sex. And then there was Maisy, just a bud of life within her.

The thing was, Rachel had had to grow up and fast. And Jake hadn't.

Rachel was thrown back to the present by the phone ringing. She was the only one in the farmhouse as Jill had popped to Kirkton to do some food shopping.

'Hello, Primrose Farm.'

'Hi, is that Rachel? It's Nick from the land agents.'

'Oh, hi. Yes, it's Rachel speaking.' Had something happened with the two fields they had put up for sale? Perhaps there was some interest at last.

'So, do you want the good news or the bad news?'

'Umm . . .' Rachel faltered.

'Well, the good news is we've had an offer in.'

'Wow, great.'

'The bad news is . . . it's substantially below your asking price and the valuation.'

'Oh, so how much exactly?'

'It's an offer of five hundred pounds an acre.'

'Blimey, that's just taking the mickey. That land is worth at least fifteen hundred pounds an acre. Can I ask who the bidder is?'

'Yes, it's a Mr Macintosh, a neighbouring farmer of yours, I believe.'

Ah . . . typical. The tight-fisted miserable old bugger. That was akin to stealing at that price. Oh yes, he'd know they were in financial straits. Could see the gain for himself by buying the land at *way* below the commercial value. He'd be rubbing his hands with glee, no doubt. Well, she wouldn't give him the pleasure. They'd rather keep the land at Primrose Farm and struggle on somehow than sell it for that.

Rachel's hackles were up, thinking of how their neighbour was ready to prey on their misfortune. 'Well then, you can go back and tell good old Mr Macintosh that it's an insult of an offer. There's no way I'd consider selling at that price.'

'Yes, I did think that your answer might be along those lines.'

'No other interest so far?' Rachel asked, trying to remain hopeful.

'I'm afraid not.'

'Oh well, we'll just have to wait and see.'

'Yes, of course, you'll have to give it time. Unless, you're thinking of adding more land to the sale? That might create more interest.'

'Not just yet, but I understand what you're saying.' Rachel really wasn't ready to give up more of the farm, everything her father had worked for and her heritage – not just yet, not until she had exhausted every other avenue. Unfortunately, time really wasn't on their side . . .

Chapter 12

IT'S A WRAP

It was a beautiful spring day. The sky was a hazy blue, punctuated with fluffy, cotton-wool clouds, and the daffodils were out in full bloom. Rachel was walking down Primrose Farm's lane, Moss padding along obediently at her side. She reached the end of the track and found Eve waiting at the school bus collection point with a big grin on her face.

'They're ready!' her friend announced.

'What? Ooh, do you mean the pudding packaging? Have you made some designs already?'

'Yep, I'm so pleased with them, but . . . I'll let you make up your own minds. Why don't you and Jill come up to the cottage, in say fifteen minutes, and have a look? I'll put the kettle on. Maisy can come and play with Amelia.'

'That sounds a great idea. I'll walk Maisy home, then catch up with Mum and let her know. I'm sure she'll be happy to come across. Ooh, I'm excited to see them now. Spill . . . are they patterned, checked, floral, plain?'

'You need to wait and see.'

'Spoilsport.'

'No, I just think it's best you see how they work. First impressions and all that. Just like your customers will.'

'Yeah, you're right. Well then, this is a special occasion which I believe deserves cake. Do you have anything in?'

'No, sorry. Been too busy doing all my crafting these past few days.'

'Well, I'm sure Mum was baking earlier today. I'll see what she was rustling up. There's always something tasty in our kitchen these days. If we're lucky, she may even have been testing out some new puds. We'll bring something along, don't you worry.'

'Now that sounds a plan.'

Rachel, Jill and Maisy were soon jumping into the farm's battered old Land Rover and heading across to Eve's place to see the pudding packaging samples. They parked by the old stone cottage and walked up the pathway that was bordered by sunny daffodils and soft-pink tulips.

Eve came to the door with a cheerful grin. 'Hello, hello. Come on in, my lovelies. Welcome to the mad house. Sorry, it's a bit chaotic here just now, but I'm so excited to show you what I've made so far. Would you like a cup of tea or anything?'

She led them through to her dining room, which looked like an arts and crafts Aladdin's cave – where the table and dresser were piled with bundles of colourful material, balls of wool, scraps of felt, buttons, threads and ribbons in all shades, and more.

'Oh yes, tea would be lovely,' Rachel answered. 'But can we see the packaging ideas first?' She didn't think she could wait.

'Of course. Right . . .' Eve had some material samples placed at the centre of the pine table top, next to a box of coloured satin ribbons. 'Well then, eek . . .' she sounded rather nervous. She opened a cardboard box and from it set out four options which she'd wrapped earlier, using the correct size of metal foil containers that Jill had chosen to bake her puddings in. 'Here are your pudding packaging ideas.'

Each had a different floral print that had a gorgeous vintage-farmhouse look. Any of the patterns would work brilliantly, and Eve had tied thin satin bows around them, which looked beautiful.

'Of course, the material wrap will come off before baking, but they just look so pretty. And I can change any of the patterns or the colours of the bows to whatever you prefer. I've got some other samples of materials here.' Eve sounded slightly anxious as she pointed to the other colour options.

Jill just stared at the package designs with a huge smile on her face.

'Oh wow,' said Rachel, 'I love them. They look old-fashioned in a lovely vintage kind of way.'

Jill had a glisten to her eye as she spoke. 'Aw, they look like something Grandma Isabel would have made.' She gave a little sniff. 'This pattern is just adorable.' She was pointing to a small floral print in red and green, with tiny red roses.

'Oh, and I *love* this one,' Rachel added, pointing to another floral pattern but with browns, yellows and orange shades that had a seventies feel. It had been tied with a deep-brown satin bow. 'This has chocolate pudding written all over it. Don't you think, Mum?'

'Yes love, and the red roses one could be for the sticky toffee. Do you like the green ribbon or the red on that?'

'Hmm.' Rachel rubbed her chin, as she considered.

'I think I'd go green,' Eve commented. 'I'm thinking countryside, farming colours.'

'Yes, I'd agree,' said Jill buoyantly.

'Just to warn you though, I may not always be able to get exactly the same material prints,' added Eve. 'To keep the costs down initially for you, I've bought remnants and samples, but they are all new material. I know you made it clear you can't have anything pre-used to wrap food. But, I'll get online as soon as poss now that you've chosen, and see if I can order some more of these two patterns at least. I've enough to last for a while anyhow.'

'No worries,' said Rachel. 'There are so many lovely options here Eve, I'm sure we can find other styles we love too. And maybe as we expand our range with other puddings,' she gave Jill a wink, 'we can go for some of these other lovely designs.'

'Oh, I'm so happy you like them.' Eve looked more relaxed now.

'I knew you'd come up with something special, Eve. Never doubted you for a minute,' said Rachel, with a smile.

'Right then, I'll get the kettle on now. Phew.' Eve went off to the kitchen, leaving Jill and Rachel grinning at each other.

They were soon chatting over tea and homemade ginger shortbreads – delish. Jill had come up trumps on the baking front as per usual. Amelia and Maisy came running in from Amelia's bedroom where they'd been playing, to take a biscuit each and zoom off again.

'Having fun girls?' Rachel asked.

'Yes, we're playing shops,' answered Maisy, already on her way back out of the room. 'Amelia is selling her toys. We have them all lined up and I'm the buyer.'

'Sounds good.'

They scampered off, happy in each other's company.

'So, how's the Etsy stuff going?' Jill asked Eve when she'd brought in the tea, interested to find out more. 'Rachel's been telling me all about it.'

'Yes, it's not just us starting a new venture,' added Rachel.

'Well, it's early days, but I've got off to a good start, yeah. There've been a few orders in already. I've sold some felt animals, a few knits and some of my new wooden hearts and stars. I'm personalising the hearts with messages and names on, whatever people want really. In fact, I've just got an order for a wedding gift, for a hanging wooden heart, to put the couple's names on and the wedding date.'

'Oh, that's wonderful, Eve. Well done you,' said Jill.

'We're flying the flag for small businesses from home. I love it,' said Rachel. 'Cheers ladies.'

They picked up their teacups and gave them a happy and hopeful sounding clink together.

'Cheers everyone,' said Jill.

'To crafts and puddings!' proclaimed Eve.

'And lots of sales,' added Rachel.

These were exciting times, but they all desperately needed these businesses to work out. Maybe with a little luck – and a good dollop of teamwork – they had a chance of pulling off something special.

Chapter 13

A VERY GORGEOUS APPLE CRUMBLE

They were brainstorming over beer. Well, cider in Rachel's case.

The promised post-lambing-shed night out had finally materialised, so Eve, Rachel and their close friend Charlotte were having an evening out at . . . wait for it . . . The Black Bull Inn in Kirkton. Okay, so it wasn't anything plush – the hour's travelling to either Newcastle or Edinburgh and a certain lack of finances had put them off going further afield. And, so it was that the three of them had ended up in their local pub; the best of the two in the village. It was cosy and friendly, with dark wood furniture, a well-worn deep-red tartan carpet, some quirky examples of farming memorabilia and some scary-looking tools – Rachel daren't think what they did with those in the olden days. There was a hearty choice of lagers and ciders, and the usual round-up of locals at the bar.

The girls were sitting chatting away at a table near one of the pub's front windows.

'Ah, it's so nice to get out. Just for an evening, child-free,' Eve said, then couldn't help but yawn.

'Hah, well, you're looking lively. We want you up dancing on the tables in an hour or so.' Rachel laughed, giving Eve a friendly nudge.

'I might be sleeping *under* the table at this rate. Sorry girls, life's just so busy at the mo. What with all my crafting and keeping up with Amelia and stuff at home.'

'Well, I don't have a child of my own, but put your-selves in front of a class of twenty-five seven-year-olds daily and see how that feels.' Charlotte was a primary school teacher in the local town of Alnwick.

'Hmm, think I'd actually prefer life in the lambing shed than a class full of children to cope with.' Rachel grinned. 'It never stops though, does it. There's always so much going on. It's the same at the farm. Full on with the sheep, it'll be calving any time, and now we're trying to set up the pudding business.'

'Ooh yes, so come on Rach, tell me all about this scrummy-sounding pudding business you're planning,' Charlotte enthused. 'And *please*, tell me your mum is making that divine chocolate stuff that we had at Maisy's party.'

'Well, progress is being made. We've now set aside an official area in the farmhouse kitchen as Mum's special baking zone. Poor old Moss is allowed nowhere near it, bless him. He's very put out. We've passed our health and hygiene certs, ta-dah.' Yes, she and Jill had sat and studied together over the past few evenings and passed with flying colours, much to their relief. So, another step in the right direction. 'We've bought in all the ingredients to make a start and I have a fab packaging design, care of my trusty assistant here . . .' Rachel smiled, gesturing at Eve, who gave a mock bow. 'And, we have our first retailer all ready to go, the lovely Brenda at the Kirkton Deli.'

Yes, it was all coming together. And with Jill about to make her first official batch of puddings tomorrow, it would be a reality very soon.

'Wow, that all sounds great. I hope it goes well for you and your mum, Rach,' said Charlotte. 'You so deserve this.'

'Thanks Charlotte, that means a lot.'

'It's such a brilliant idea, isn't it,' agreed Eve. 'Now then,' she added with a cheeky glint in her eye, 'if your delectable neighbour Tom was a pudding, which one would he be?'

'Ooh . . . now you're talking,' Charlotte answered. 'Hmm, I reckon ginger. Yes, a bit spicy and strong, but all soft and gooey on the inside.'

'I think he'd have to be *the* most delicious and moist chocolate brownie – all that dark hair, tanned skin and intense eyes.' Eve added her opinion with a doe-eyed smile. 'What do you think, Rachel?'

Did she really have to play this game? Two sets of eyes were looking at her, waiting. 'Okay, well he's really sweet . . . so maybe . . .'

'Sweet? *Sweet?* That man is hot, with more sauce than I can possibly imagine,' declared Charlotte.

Eve hooted with laughter at that point. 'Oh, I might change my mind,' Eve said. 'Maybe sticky toffee then, all over his body.' The white wine was definitely getting to her now; she didn't drink much generally. But Rachel knew she was all bark and no bite, just fantasising a little. She really was happily married to hubbie Ben, just letting off a little night-out-with-the-girls steam.

'Well then?' Charlotte was waiting for Rachel's answer.

'Oh, I don't know.' Rachel felt herself blushing and came out with the first pudding that came to mind. 'A nice crumble. Comforting.'

With that, the pub door opened and in strolled the man himself. There was Tom, dressed casually in a red-checked shirt and jeans, looking clean and fresh (not always a given in the farming community), and, by the look of his still-damp hair, he'd just made it out of the shower. Eve's eyes lit up instantly. Rachel cringed – what if he'd heard them as he came in?

Eve and Charlotte were suddenly giggling like a pair of teenagers beside her. Tom spotted their little huddle, smiling quizzically at all the hilarity. Rachel was not about to enlighten him on the subject of their conversation and merely said a brief 'Hello' with an awkward wave as he passed their table. He made his way to the bar where he started chatting with some of the other local lads.

'Ooh, your sexy crumble of a neighbour appears,' said Charlotte, not that discreetly.

'Behave.' Rachel shook her head, exasperated. 'I thought Eve was bad enough.'

'Just window shopping,' commented Eve coyly. 'Shame we can't handle the goods though.'

'Eve, shush.' But Rachel couldn't help but giggle, especially when Tom looked over at them, no doubt wondering what they were so amused about.

Charlotte got another round of drinks in, and the evening flowed nicely with chat and more laughter, the girls talking about what was going on in their lives now as well as reminiscing over stories from their youth. It was great for Rachel to let her hair down a little – sometimes she forgot how young she still was, only in her mid-twenties. With a child and a farm and her mum to look after, at times she felt more like forty-four than twenty-four. Just a few years ago, when her friends had been out nightclubbing, being carefree and chatting up the lads, Rachel had had a young baby in tow, and was leading a life of nappy changes and feeds. She never wished she hadn't had Maisy, that wasn't it. But life for a young, rural-based single mum was often isolating, even though her mum and dad had always been a great support. At nineteen, she'd had responsibilities at a time when her friends were living totally different, carefree lives.

A short while later, Tom made his way across to their table.

'Hey, I enjoyed the party the other day.'

'I assume you mean Maisy's,' Rachel answered, smiling.

'Seeing as we've both been holed up in the lambing shed for the past month.'

'Hmm, I wouldn't mind being holed up in the lambing shed with someone . . .' murmured Charlotte beside Rachel, who received a swift dig in the ribs to stop her saying any more.

'I do indeed,' Tom continued. 'How is she doing?'

'Oh, she's fine. Full of energy. Buzzing around the farm like a little bee. She loved that book that you got her, by the way.'

'Great. Bit of a gamble in WHSmith's on which to choose actually. Not quite au fait with the reading tastes of five-year-olds.'

Rachel was suddenly taken back to that conversation with her little girl the night of her birthday, Maisy declaring that she wanted Tom to be her daddy, seeing as her own bloody father had never turned up to her party. Rachel looked up at Tom for a second. And *really* looked him. She'd known him for years. He'd been the older kid next door when she was little; a teenager racing around on his quad; a married man who went away for a while; the single farmer next door . . . She remembered him taking her to see his terrier pups when she was just a small girl. He must have been, what, sixteen? He was so gentle with them all, and proud as he told her all about saving the one she was holding – the frail runt of the litter – explaining that his dad had said she wouldn't make it, as she lay so still, but he had persevered with rubbing her, clearing her tiny mouth, puffing gently between her new-born lips, and that little pup turned out to be the mum of Mabel – his latest dog.

To Rachel he was just Tom. But she had to admit, perhaps there *was* something nice about him. He was tall, his dark hair short and slightly scruffy, he had kind eyes, a kind heart too, she was sure of that.

Whoa, where had these rogue thoughts come from? Hah, it was being around Eve and Charlotte, their crushes must be rubbing off on her. She shook the crazy thoughts away but had the feeling that she might just be blushing.

'So, what's the crack then?' Tom turned his attention to the other ladies, as he pulled up a stool at their table.

'Oh, normal stuff. Life, children, work, never enough hours in a day,' said Eve.

'Never enough wine in a glass,' added Charlotte cheekily, shaking her near empty glass of rosé. 'Come on Eve, it's your round. Can we get you a drink in, Tom?'

'Thanks, but I'm fine. I've just had the one pint, now I'm sticking to the Coca-Cola. I've just nipped out for a quick break while Adam's there. Got a feeling I might be needed to help with the calving tonight.'

'Oh right, hope it all goes well.'

'Oh, have you heard the news? Rachel's setting up a pudding business with her mum,' announced Eve.

'Now that *is* good news. So, you're really making it happen then?' He turned to Rachel with a warm smile. 'Good for you. So, when and where can I buy something?

You know I have been waiting for Jill's takeaway puddings all my life.'

Rachel had to grin. 'Well, we'll be starting by selling some in the Kirkton Deli this coming week. We're just trialling it, it's early days yet.'

'Brilliant. There's a sticky toffee with my name on it there then.'

'You might even get to be the first customer,' Eve joined in.

'*No*, that's me. I'm in for a chocolate pudding as soon as they open on Monday,' Charlotte announced, coming back with their drinks.

It felt good making plans, having hopes for a new beginning, however small to start.

By ten-thirty the girls felt pretty shattered. It was a school night, so Charlotte said she'd better be getting off soon. Eve was back to yawning again and whilst she wasn't quite asleep under the table as yet, there were no signs of any of the three of them partying till dawn or dancing on the tables tonight.

'Right, well we might as well make tracks.' Rachel finished off the last of her cider. Charlotte's boyfriend, Sam, was coming to pick her up. He had also offered to take the other two girls home, as both Jill and Eve's husband couldn't leave the little ones, who'd hopefully be tucked up fast asleep in bed by now.

Tom was also putting on his jacket at the bar. He walked across, spotting them getting up to go. 'I'm heading off too. Can I give anyone a lift?' he offered.

'Ah, well, Sam had said he'd take us as he's picking Charlotte up. But, I suppose if you're already heading in our direction . . .' Rachel responded. Charlotte and Sam lived in a hamlet across the other side of Kirkton.

Eve was nodding. 'Yep, makes sense. Thanks, Tom.'

Outside the pub, they said their goodbyes to Charlotte, as Sam was already there parked up, the three of them promising to catch up again soon.

Tom drove them home through the dark country lanes, which felt extra twisty-turny now they'd had a drink or two (well, maybe five!). Eve and Rachel sat chatting in the two passenger seats in the front cab of the pick-up.

'Been a good night, hasn't it?' said Eve.

'Great – a bit of time out and good fun. Just what we needed.'

'Well, I'm looking forward to a nice chocolate brownie when I get back,' Eve began, ending up in a fit of the giggles once more.

'What is *up* with you lot tonight?' asked Tom, glancing across at the pair of them.

'*Nothing*. Just Eve's idea of a joke, that's all.' Rachel then dug her friend in the ribs in the hope of silencing her.

'Or a nice comforting crumble.' Eve's sniggering continued.

Rachel couldn't help but grin. 'Sorry, Tom. Not quite sure what's got into her.'

'A bottle of wine,' piped up Eve.

'Hah, yes.'

Tom just smiled to himself.

It wasn't long before they arrived outside Eve's cottage.

'Here we go, Eve. That's you home,' Tom stated as he pulled up.

'Thanks so much, Tom. You're a star.'

'You're welcome,' he replied. He watched her get safely through the front door before he turned his vehicle around and headed back along the lane to Primrose Farm.

As Tom pulled onto their farm track, the 'For Sale' sign was there as clear as day – illuminated in his head-lights. 'So, I see you've put some land up for sale.'

'Yeah . . . it wasn't an easy decision but we needed to do something.' Rachel went quiet for a few seconds.

'Ah, I see.' Tom's tone was gentle, understanding.

No-one else knew the difficult situation they were in other than Jill and Eve, though with the board now up outside the farm, people might be drawing their own conclusions soon enough. But, she felt she could trust Tom not to gossip.

'We didn't have much choice in the end, the farm desperately needs to release some cash.'

'I'm sorry to hear that, Rachel.'

'Oh Tom, it's been so bloody hard.' The cider was helping to pull down Rachel's guard, plus the kind, thoughtful look on Tom's face told her that she could trust him with the truth. 'I feel like I'm letting Dad down somehow, selling off a piece of his farm . . . But, I can't let it go under. I can't let it all go.'

'Of course not. You're being practical, doing what you have to. I understand that. I think your dad would have, too.'

'Thank you.' Rachel let out a slow sigh under her breath. 'Well, I had a crazy offer in today from guess who?' Now that she had started talking it felt good to share her burden. 'Bloody Mr Mac. And do you know what he offered?'

'Go on.'

'Five hundred pounds an acre.'

'No, no way. That's a joke.'

'I know, nothing like trying to kick you while you're down.'

'Well, I hope you bloody well said no.'

'Of course, I did. We're not *that* desperate.'

'Well, have you thought about renting the land instead? That way you get to hold onto it whilst earning some income and keeping your options open.'

'Oh . . . hmm, well, maybe we could, but who'd want to rent just one or two fields?'

'*I* would.'

'You would?'

'Yeah, I could do with some extra fields for hay this year. And, it's on the doorstep. It could work for us both. You get some rent in and I get more land to use. I'm more than happy to pay the going rate.'

'Well, yes, that could work.' Rachel was surprised, a

little stunned in fact. Could it be that easy? Was Tom actually handing her this offer on a plate?

'Look, just think about it. You've got a lot on your mind and you'll want to talk it over with your mum, of course.'

It almost sounded almost too good to be true. 'Tom, why are you so good to us?' The cider really was loosening her tongue now.

'Hey, I'm just looking out for you and the family, Rachel . . . any neighbour would in the circumstances.' A jolt of a memory passed between them then, with a shared look that spoke a thousand words.

'Hah, not Mr Mac though.' Rachel broke his gaze and swiftly moved the conversation on. 'But thanks Tom . . . you're a really special friend, you know that.' Her hand reached to brush his shoulder.

His tone softened. 'I know what you've all been through,' he said meaningfully. 'I just want to see you're okay.'

In the half-light of the pick-up's cab, Rachel could see his warm smile reach right through to his dark brown eyes. Before she knew it, she'd leaned across, and was now only centimetres from his face. He smelt all fresh, his aftershave cool sea-notes and citrus.

Oh my goodness, what was she doing? Surely, she wasn't thinking of kissing him? What was up with her? Cider, that was it – she must have drunk far too much of the potent stuff, and all that lusty talk from Eve and Charlotte must be rubbing off on her. Tom was just a friend, a neighbour. Damn, she'd better get out of the pick-up *right away* before she embarrassed herself any further.

'Right then.' She opened the door and made a dash for it, calling out, 'Thanks for the lift,' over her shoulder.

'You're welcome,' came Tom's amused-sounding voice from the open truck window. 'Night, Rachel.'

'Night.' She kept looking forward, making a beeline – well, a slightly wonky beeline – for the farmhouse. Luckily, Mum had left the outside light on for her.

All was quiet and dark as she stepped inside. Maisy and Mum must be in bed asleep. Rachel stood at the kitchen window and saw the headlights swing around in the drive and then the red tail lights as Tom's truck moved away.

What had just happened there? Or was she making something out of nothing? It was just the excitement of the evening out that had got her, and something about being that close. But it suddenly all felt different . . . Like something was beginning to shift beneath her feet. Was it empathy, attraction? Hah, she'd never felt like that with Tom . . . *ever*. It was bloody disconcerting, whatever it was. Mind you, she reminded herself, she did have a bloodstream full of cider. Alcohol, that was it, warping things all out of proportion. It would seem irrelevant in the morning. Just a neighbour giving her and Eve a lift home. Just Tom.

Chapter 14

A PUDDING PRODUCTION LINE

Oh boy, was Rachel struggling the next morning. Her brain felt bruised, like a herd of cattle had trampled over it through the night. It was past nine-thirty, and Rachel still had the headache from hell hanging around. She wasn't used to drinking alcohol these days – she should have known better, as it always kicked back at her with a vengeance the next day.

After a swift cup of coffee she forced herself out to check on the livestock. On inspecting the sheep in the Low Pasture, she spotted an abscess lump on the neck of one of the ewes. It was an infection and she knew she'd have to act quickly to help the animal. She got her first-aid kit from the Land Rover. It'd need lancing and then some Dettol wash. Oh, jeez, this was no job to undertake with a hangover, but needs must. She held her breath as the needle went in. Yuck!

Rachel was gagging as the pus came out. The stench was horrendous and her stomach heaved. She cleaned the wound and then set the sheep on her way. It was all Rachel could do to stop herself from vomiting. She steadied herself before walking back to her vehicle, where she sat for a few moments, feeling a bit giddy. God, she was never setting foot in a watering hole ever again.

As she was heading back across the yard to the farmhouse, for a much-needed cup of tea and some paracetamol, her phone pinged with a text. She took it out to see it was from Eve.

How's the head, hun?! Mine's not too great. X
Not good x, she replied.
Did you get any crumble last night after I'd left? X

Hah! Rachel couldn't help but laugh out loud reading that comment, which unfortunately made her head pound even more. Oh yes, it was all coming back now: their giggly conversation on puddings and men, well one man in particular.

Then, she remembered nearly kissing that particular man on the cheek and her fleeing the scene. Bloody hell, how embarrassing.

No, of course not, she answered herself. The near-kiss was one scenario she was going to keep to herself.

She was at the front step taking off her muddy wellingtons when Eve's reply pinged back.

Shame – you could have told me all about it and I could have lived every moment through you!! X

Rachel was smiling and shaking her head at the same time.

As she entered the farmhouse kitchen, Jill rushed towards her, excitedly waving a letter in the air.

'It's from the council, we've passed the inspection! What a relief, eh? The kitchen area has been given the all-clear. Now that we've passed the exams too, we're good to go.' Jill beamed across at Rachel.

'Oh, that's wonderful!' It was all coming together, and it was brilliant to see Mum so enthusiastic about it all.

'So, let the pudding making begin,' announced Jill. 'Hah, my kitchen can now become a pudding pantry.' She was grinning as she stood beside the kitchen surface where she'd just laid all her ingredients out ready – flour, butter, brown sugar, dates and their own fresh farm eggs. 'Blimey, I'm feeling the pressure now. I've got to make the best puds of my life, haven't I?'

'Don't worry, just do what you always do, Mum, you're a natural. Just pretend you're baking for me and Maisy. Your puddings are always delicious.'

'Right, okay. Well, I've got several hours before Maisy's home from school. I think I'll get cracking straight away. No time like the present.'

Though she was evidently nervous, it was lovely to see Jill so animated. Maybe this new project was just what she, in fact what *they all*, needed.

*

When Rachel came back into the farmhouse kitchen two hours later, after having put down some more straw and checked on the cattle, the smell of baking was divine. They only had a small herd, and it was coming towards the end of calving now with just one cow left to calf out of their fourteen ladies, so Rachel was keeping a close eye on her. Simon had been with her through the night, but there was still no sign as yet. Thankfully the calving this year had been pretty straightforward, and most of the cattle were already out in the fields as the spring grass had started growing.

The source of the gorgeous aroma was a dozen freshly baked sticky toffee puddings, all lined up on the kitchen side in their foil containers, oozing with delicious toffee sauce. They were standing on racks to cool, ready to have their lids popped on and be wrapped in Eve's beautiful vintage-style floral cotton material with a ribbon bow.

'Oh, hello, love.' Jill looked slightly anxious. She also looked uncharacteristically ruffled – her apron was askew and there was a thick dusting of flour in her hair and on her jumper. 'Well, what do you think?'

'If the smell's anything to go by, I think I'm in pudding heaven.'

'Aw, thanks. Can't help but feel a little nervous though. I hope Brenda manages to sell some of them.'

'Just look at them Mum, of course they'll sell. I have very high hopes.'

'Well, I think we should take these ones to the Kirkton

Deli as soon as they've cooled and are all packaged up,' said Jill.

'I'll take you down there,' offered Rachel. 'Yes, I think we should go together to deliver our first ever order, and then we can mark the occasion with a celebratory cup of tea and a slice of cake at The Cheviot Café.' She glanced at her watch. 'If we go soon, we'll just have time before the school bus comes. What do you think?'

'I think that sounds a lovely idea.'

'You might just want to get that flour out of your hair first,' Rachel added cheekily.

'Oi you, I've been slaving away here!' Jill teased back.

They made a little production line of the pretty cotton wraps, which had already been cut to size by Eve, and they carefully secured them with the green satin ribbon bows. Eve had also designed and created pretty tags for them, with a list of the ingredients on the back and a best before date for them to fill in.

'There is one here I made as a spare,' added Jill. 'Before we let these loose on the public, do you think we ought to do a taste test? In case I've gone daft and confused the salt with sugar or something.'

'Well, I'm up for taste testing. Absolutely!' Rachel's hangover had finally subsided, and a big spoonful of sticky toffee sounded just what she needed right now.

'After all, the proof of the pudding . . .' Jill started.

'Is in the eating,' Rachel finished for her, with a huge smile. 'Fetch us a couple of spoons then.'

Jill dished a generous portion out into two separate

bowls. Rachel grabbed her spoon and dived on in. *Oh my*. The sponge of the pudding was so moist and delicious, the sauce treacly-butterscotch warm, and when Jill added a blob of thick cream that melted over it, it was elevated to an even more heavenly zone.

'Well . . . ?' her mum's tone was anxious.

For a second or two, Rachel couldn't speak. The explosion of deliciousness in her mouth taking over.

She finally found the words. 'Oh my goodness. Honestly Mum, there's no doubt that these will sell. And once people have taken them home and tasted them, I'm sure they'll be coming back for more.'

'Crikey, thanks love. And if I can help put a few more coffers in the farm pot, then I'll feel very proud. You seem to have been pulling more than your weight out on the farm lately.'

'Hah, I'm younger and stronger for the more physical farm work. I really appreciate all your help with Maisy here on the home front, and that frees me up to get on working with the animals.' Rachel enjoyed the farm work even though it was demanding sometimes. The farm felt a part of her soul. It didn't feel like a job as such, it was more a way of life. She couldn't imagine working in an office or a shop, being cooped up inside all day.

'Well, the pudding making is ideal for me. I mean, if it goes well.' Jill still had a natural edge of caution about the new venture. 'I can be here in the farmhouse baking and still be with Maisy when she's not in school.'

'I know, it'll work out great.'

'Well, let's not run before we can walk, hey. We'll see how this lot go down with the general public first.' Ever the voice of reason her mum, but Rachel noted a lovely hint of excitement there in her tone too.

As they sat in the old Land Rover twenty minutes later, about to set off to their first ever retailer with the puddings safely stowed in a box on Jill's lap, she looked across at Rachel and seemed to steady herself. 'I think your dad would be proud of us.'

Rachel nodded, and bit her lip. Oh my, that had got the water works going. She couldn't help herself and had to wipe away a fat tear that had plopped almost instantly down her cheek.

'Yes,' she replied turning to her mum with a brave smile, 'I think he would.'

Sometimes her heart still felt so raw, even though she tried to hide that from her mum. This was one small step to getting the farm back on track – there was still a long road ahead. But yes, she acknowledged, they should be proud of themselves.

'Oh Mum, if only he was still here. If only we could have . . .' Rachel stopped herself. They couldn't turn back time or wave some kind of a magic wand. What was done, was done.

'I know, I know, love.' Jill placed a hand gently on Rachel's shoulder. 'We have to just keep going forward.'

'One step at a time,' Rachel took up, trying to smile at her mum, still with tears glistening in her eyes. She gathered herself, took a slow breath, then added, 'And today's one big step, yeah?'

'Yes, absolutely, so let's go.' Mum sniffed and wiped away a tear or two of her own, then patted the box as though it were treasure.

'Come on then, let's hit the road.' Rachel put the truck into gear. 'These puddings need new homes.'

Fifteen minutes later, it was wonderful to see their puddings sat proudly on the shelf in the Kirkton Deli. Brenda had put them straight out into the refrigerated counter. It was real! The Primrose Farm pudding business was up and running.

'These look fabulous,' said Brenda. 'And the packaging is so pretty.'

'We have Eve to thank for that,' said Rachel.

'Oh, well, they're lovely. I don't think we'll have any trouble selling them. In fact, I might have to take one home for myself tonight.'

'Well, when I bring the next batch of chocolate puddings in tomorrow, I'll bring an extra one for you – complimentary of course,' offered Jill.

'That sounds grand. Thank you.'

'No, thank *you* for giving us this brilliant opportunity and a retail outlet,' Rachel replied.

'So, we'll be back tomorrow with the second lot of twelve if that's okay, and then we can see how it goes. Fingers crossed.' Jill gave a hopeful smile.

Just then, the door chimed as a woman came in and

started browsing the shelves. She stopped and scanned the counter where Brenda had set out the Primrose Farm Puddings.

Rachel found she was holding her breath. 'Right then, we'd better be off and let you get on, Brenda. See you tomorrow.'

'Yes, thanks ladies.'

At the door, Rachel couldn't help but look over her shoulder to see if the lady might be interested in their puddings. She heard Brenda saying, 'Hello there, can I help you with anything?'

She and Jill couldn't really hang around watching and listening though, so left discreetly, but by the looks on their faces, they'd both have loved to be flies on the wall just then.

Who might their first customer be?

They celebrated with tea (Jill), hot chocolate (Rachel), and a slice of Victoria sponge each in the tearooms on the high street.

'Wow, we really did it, Mum.' Rachel beamed.

Jill smiled back. 'Yes, we did. Fingers crossed they'll go down well, and that Brenda's not left with a stockroom full of old puddings.'

'I think word's out already. I know Eve's telling everyone she knows, and Tom's already said he'll be popping in to buy one. I saw him in the lane earlier today. He asked me to text him once they were in.' Oh, yes, he'd pulled up beside Rachel as she was out on the quad and she'd felt a rash of a blush warm her neck and face. Thankfully, he hadn't mentioned anything about dropping her off the other night.

'Aw, that's nice of him.'

'You'll be the Queen of Puddings soon, I'm sure.' Rachel raised her hot chocolate mug. 'To Primrose Farm Puddings. Cheers!'

'Yes, cheers! Ooh, blimey, can you believe it; we're officially baking entrepreneurs! Not bad for a pair of farmers!'

There was a frisson of positivity and a jangle of nerves between them. And yes, things were starting to look up at last.

Chapter 15

THIRTY-NINE PUDDINGS AND A PANTRY

Though they were making some headway with the puddings for sale at the Kirkton Deli, there was something nagging Rachel. It was two weeks after they'd started the business and they had sold a grand total of thirty-nine puddings – which was brilliant – with a further order to supply more on a weekly basis. The support from Brenda had been wonderful and the feedback from her customers so positive – even Tom had popped into the farmhouse to say congratulations, and tell them that he'd already tried out both flavours and was smitten.

However, this evening, Rachel was sitting before her laptop looking at the farm's monthly accounts for April. The income so far from the pudding business after costs was less than fifty pounds for the two weeks, and though it might yet improve, with the Deli naturally taking their own cut was it ever going to be enough to make a real difference? And on the farm side of things, the bills kept going up and profits coming down.

No wonder her dad had felt the weight of the world on his shoulders.

She and Jill kept a tight rein on their finances as it was. They hadn't treated themselves to anything new clothes-wise for a couple of years, not that it really mattered. The sheep and cattle weren't bothered what they turned up in, and most of Rachel's clothes ended up in a permanent state of grubbiness. It wasn't as though she went out anywhere dressy.

So, Rachel mulled, the business had started fine in theory, but they needed to up the ante with production and also find a new outlet. Being so rural, the next town where they might get some trade would be Alnwick, and that was twenty miles away. After taking out the extra costs involved with delivering the goods – and Rachel hadn't even factored in an hourly rate for Jill – in reality it would hardly be worth it. Rachel sighed; she'd had such hopes for this enterprise, but had she been unrealistic?

They would continue to supply the Kirkton Deli, of course, but there had to be some other way too. If only they could somehow get the customers to them . . . But how?

Rachel made herself another cup of coffee, the caffeine-boost probably not ideal at this time of night, but she needed to stay awake a while longer to try to fathom things out. She knew she'd need to speak with her mum about it all too. She suddenly felt guilty for getting her into all this pudding malarkey, getting her hopes up, yet not having worked everything out enough herself first. The slim profits they'd make would hardly dig them out of the farm's financial pit.

Rachel let out a frustrated groan.

It was twenty past four in the morning, with the grey light of dawn creeping in at her bedroom window, when Rachel drowsily came to with the seed of a thought forming in her mind. They didn't need to be trailing around Northumberland using up fuel and time chasing business, what they needed was something here on the farm.

Puddings, the farm ... what were they good at? Making people feel cosy and welcome, that was for sure. Just a few years before, they'd had friends and neighbours gathered here for summer barbecues, there'd be coffee mornings in the farmhouse kitchen for charity, Christmases with family and friends all welcome, even the postman would be calling in for a mince pie and a chat. The kettle was always on, and any caller would know there'd be something delicious ready to come out of the Aga. Mum really was a brilliant baker. The puddings were definitely the way forward ... but how?

Maisy's party in the barn had gone down well, and whilst Rachel didn't fancy having a tribe of kids turning up daily, the barn itself would soon tidy up. There were already electrics and water to the building, and it had gorgeous old stone walls and was brimming with countryside character – as well, admittedly, with cobwebs, dust and strands of hay. But, with a bit of work, some TLC and hopefully a rural grant to help fund it, it might even make a nice café, or tearooms, or . . . a *Pudding Pantry*. She woke right up at that lightbulb moment of a thought and sat up in bed.

Yes, they could serve tea and coffee . . . cake . . . and puddings galore . . . *here* on the farm. They could sell their range of puddings to take away too, as well as keeping their lovely supporter the Kirkton Deli supplied. Jill would be the main cook naturally, and Rachel would help with some of the cooking and serving at the tearooms around her farm work and maybe if it started to get busy – it was worth dreaming big – they could in time employ a waitress to help out.

That was it. That was bloody well it! Rachel felt a rush of emotion.

Welcome to the Pudding Pantry at Primrose Farm!

Chapter 16

GRANDMAS AND GINGER PUDDINGS

Rachel felt like dashing across the landing right away to wake Jill up and see what she thought of the idea, but she couldn't disturb the house, not at this hour, and risk waking Maisy before school. So, she sat up in bed for a while planning, then tiptoed across to the dressing table where she grabbed her laptop, took it back to her duvet zone, and started researching grants for farms and rural projects, saving any important links and information.

There must be other people who had converted barns into tearooms, so she tap-tapped away and a new search followed on diversification in farming. What were the pitfalls, the problems, the gains? By five-thirty she felt shattered, yet buzzing too, with a headful of dreams, and plans for their barn, to consider further. Finally, she laid down her laptop, curled herself under the covers and slept until her alarm went off at seven, dreaming of puddings and sunny days on the farm and happy-ever-afters.

*

After Maisy was away to school, and with the cattle and sheep checked for the morning, Rachel came back to the house to find Jill humming away in the kitchen measuring out flour, with a line-up of ingredients beside her.

'Are there any more fresh eggs, Rachel love? Would you mind checking for me? With all this baking I'm doing we're getting through our supplies fast. The hens won't be able to keep up soon.'

'Yes, of course, I'll nip back out. Ooh, what are you making this time?' Rachel peered over her mum's shoulder into the mixing bowl.

'I'm trying out a ginger pudding. The rhubarb's nearly ready in the garden too, so I thought I might serve it with some stewed rhubarb and a blob of cream.'

'Sounds delicious. Right, I'll get cracking then and fetch some eggs.' Rachel smiled at her own pun and took up the wicker basket used for egg collecting which sat by the porch door.

They had a dozen or so hens and one cockerel; they were mostly the bronze-feathered Rhode Island Red type – known to be good layers. They lived free range around the farm during the day, and were put back into their hen house at night (to keep them safe from any foxes), and produced the most golden-orange-yolked eggs, with a gorgeous flavour. Rachel walked across the yard and checked inside the hen house first, gathering nine eggs from the soft straw beds, but invariably there were several more eggs to be found in the nearby hedgerow and in the verge to the side of the old barn – the hens had their favourite laying places.

Back inside soon after, Mum broke the eggs into the mixture and set her trusted Magimix away. The smell of ginger and soft brown sugar was soon fragrant in the air, even more so twenty minutes later when the mixture had started to steam in a large pan on the hob.

'This one's a bit different. You steam it the old-fashioned way in a pudding basin.'

'I think it's going to be a hit already,' Rachel said with a smile.

'My own mother used to make this years ago. I haven't made it in ages. Hmmn, just the smell brings back memories.'

Granny Isabel, Jill's mother, had lived in a village in the Scottish Borders about a half hour drive away. She was warm and friendly, with a wicked sense of humour, white curls, and striking green eyes that Jill always said Rachel had inherited. They used to visit often when Rachel was a child, happy memories of walks and play in the country hills near the house, and she always put on a wonderful Sunday afternoon tea with some kind of gorgeous pudding or two, right up until the old lady died nine years ago.

Puddings had been a part of their shared past.

'Yes, it's funny how food can do that,' Rachel commented. 'Even down to the smells here in the kitchen. They can take you back to another time.' Right now, she had a feeling of comfort and warmth, memories of traybakes and cakes, soups and puddings, of coming in from helping her dad on the farm, wet through and cold, to something hot and delicious to eat.

Memories of her other granny flooded in now too; Granny Ruth, her dad's mother, now eighty-one, and Rachel's last surviving grandparent. She used to be here in this very kitchen baking when Rachel was a little girl, back when the farmhouse was still Granny and Granda's. Granda had sadly passed away a few years ago, and Ruth still lived in their cottage on the edge of Kirkton village, where they had been since passing on the farmhouse to the next generation.

Ruth particularly loved to spend time with Maisy and hear all about her activities and about life on the farm. It was evident she found it harder to visit since Dad's death, but it didn't stop her coming. She was a good baker too, despite the arthritis in her fingers, and there was often a crumble or a slice of homemade cake to be found in the larder at her cottage.

Rachel popped the kettle on as Jill cleared the surfaces and began to wash up. 'Tea?'

'Sounds good, thanks, love.'

Rachel knew this was the ideal time to mention last night's big idea. She poured hot water into the teapot and placed it along with two mugs on the mat at the centre of the pine table, giving it time to brew.

'Right, I'd better keep an eye on the clock. It'll take around two hours to steam.' Jill took up a seat. 'You never know, if it's a good one we could introduce some of these to the Deli too.'

'Well, yes, let's definitely look to do that . . . Look Mum.' Rachel had to steel herself. 'I've been thinking. The baking you're doing is brilliant and I'm so happy you're on board with it all and trying out new recipes. Really, it's great.'

'Well, I have to admit, after my initial concerns, I'm enjoying it. Ooh, and Brenda said she had a lady in yesterday who took two of each flavour to take home with her to Edinburgh, after trying a sticky toffee on her holidays here.'

'Well, that's just fabulous. But . . .'

'Why do I get the feeling you're about to burst my bubble?'

'I'm not, honestly. It's just I kind of think we need to blow the balloon up a whole lot bigger.'

'What on earth do you mean?'

'Well yes, the puddings for sale at the Deli are doing well and that's great. But even if we sell, say, twenty a week, hopefully thirty, and then get a new outlet thereafter, by the time they take their cut, and with all our costs, we're still not making much of a profit to really help the farm out.'

'Oh,' Jill looked deflated.

'It's good that we're on the right lines, don't get me wrong. But what we need to do is think bigger, think differently. In fact,' Rachel paused, aware she was about to launch a whole new idea in the mix, 'think about having an outlet right here.'

'Like a shop or a stall, do you mean?'

'Not quite. We need more than that. I feel we're a little out of the way for just a shop. We need to draw the customers in . . . with somewhere to sit and relax. A tearoom . . . or, a Pudding Pantry.'

'Crikey, you *have* been thinking. So how on earth do we suddenly do that?'

'I was thinking of the barn. Maisy's party worked so well there. We'd have to do some work to it of course. We could hopefully get some grants in place, and I can save some of the monthly rental we're now getting from Tom on the fields. It'd all have to be done on a careful budget, of course.'

'Oh Rachel, that'd be a hell of a lot of work. The barn's in a bit of a state. We'd need a working area for a kitchen to start, and that won't come cheap.'

'Yes, I know there's a lot to consider. But I'd like to look into the idea more, Mum. I'm thinking of getting some companies in for quotes, actually.'

'Blimey, it all seems rather sudden. You always were one to jump in feet first.'

'Don't worry, I'll do my homework first. And, only if you're in agreement, of course. It will need both of us on board to make this work.'

'Look, I don't want us to rush in and get this wrong, Rachel. It's a big thing.' Jill's tone was calm but serious. 'You still have the farm to work, that'll take several hours a day, and there's Maisy to think of too. And . . . if it didn't work out, we might well be even worse off and lose the lot, the farm too. I don't want to dash your plans by any means, but this needs careful consideration.'

'I know, I know. I'll do some more research and we'll keep up the pudding making to supply the Kirkton Deli just now. That will hopefully continue to get our name out there, as well as helping prop up our income a bit. It'll all take time.' Rachel took a slow breath, remembering the most recent farm accounts.

Jill spotted her concern. 'But I don't suppose we have a lot of time, do we?'

'With the farm finances the way they are just now, Mum, realistically . . . not a lot. And if it's something we feel we should do, then we need to make it happen sooner rather than later before the main summer season starts – to take advantage of the holiday tourist trade. Don't you think?'

They were already in early May. Could a facelift to the barn really happen by the summer holidays? Or was it all just pie in the sky?

'Okay then, I'll do some research too.' Jill suddenly sounded upbeat. 'I'm sure I'll have friends of friends who've done something similar. There're often new ventures within the farming community in the area. I'll ask around. But we can't afford to get this wrong, Rachel. I'll not take any unnecessary risks.'

They shared a look, as they thought of Dad, the farm, their precious legacy.

'I know that, Mum,' Rachel replied earnestly.

But doing nothing at this point wasn't a great option either.

It was a wet afternoon, so Rachel made the most of being stuck indoors by researching further into local building companies and electrical firms as well as grant opportunities. During a break in the rain showers, she wandered across to the barn, opening its creaking wooden doors and turning on the single electric lightbulb that hung from a wooden rafter above. She walked in and stood, looking around her. The two trestle tables were still left from Maisy's party, but otherwise it had all been cleared. The barn's honeyed-stone walls and smoothed-over-time flagstone floor were just waiting to be transformed. With a little building work, some imagination and hard graft, they really could bring this place to life.

A shaft of warm spring sunlight beamed in through the open doors and, for a few seconds, Rachel half closed her eyes and dared to dream. Yes, there could be a small kitchen area and a wooden counter over there at the far end, with a selection of quaint tables and chairs, maybe a pine dresser with a jug of sweet peas and blue-and-white patterned vintage plates and teacups on it, resting against the back wall.

Oh, and of course, a display of delicious homemade pudding and cakes and scones . . . in fact all kinds of foodie delights. Cheesecakes, pavlovas, crumbles, brownies . . .

'Rachel?' Jill's voice came from the yard.

'In here,' she replied.

'Oh . . . I wondered where you'd got to.' Jill came on in.

'I was just imagining how it might be . . . our Pudding Pantry. All set out with tables and chairs and cosy lampstands.'

'Daydreaming, were you, love?'

'No . . . not daydreaming. I want this to be real, Mum. I've got a good feeling about this. Can you picture it . . . a kitchen and a counter over there, piled with your amazing puddings and bakes, people gathered happily chatting over tea and scones, or sticky toffee pud and coffee?'

'It is a lovely thought. But,' Jill seemed to hesitate, wary of breaking her daughter's reverie, 'we do need to be careful, love. So many businesses fail.'

'I know.' But, were some dreams worth the risk? Or was she being foolish? Rachel needed to find out more at least.

Back in the farmhouse, she made a couple of calls and had two building companies lined up to visit within the week to give a quote for the basic renovation work.

The good news was that grants and rural schemes were available for this kind of diversification, but on reading the small print, what was worrying was that most grants needed a good solid investment from the farmer themselves *and* could take several months to come through should they even be agreed. Hmm, quite where that kind of financial investment would come from was beyond her at this stage. But that wasn't going to stop

Rachel's plans and dreams just yet – she'd get some quotes to start and cross that bridge when she came to it.

She lost herself in research and all too soon it was time to go and collect Maisy from the school bus. As it was drizzling, she nipped to the lane end in the Land Rover – Moss leaping in the back to join in. She just had time for a quick hello and catch-up with Eve, when the school bus came into view and pulled up. The first off was Maisy, bouncing down the steps in her royal-blue school uniform, rucksack swinging off one shoulder, one sock up and one down, and a beam of a smile on her face. She ran over to give Rachel a big hug.

Maisy was full of chat about Eleanor's mum bringing in her two gerbils Bubble and Squeak for show and tell.

She started giggling as she said, 'Aw, they were so cute and naughty. Do you know what Bubble did?'

'No?'

Maisy and Amelia then collapsed with infectious, sunny laughter. 'He pooed . . . all over Mrs Watson's hand.'

'Oops.' Rachel couldn't help but smile, imagining the classroom scenario.

'Oops, poops,' said Maisy cheekily, giggling again.

'Come on then, let's head home. Bye, Eve, bye, Amelia.' Rachel gave them a wave as she got back in the Land Rover.

Maisy rubbed Moss's shaggy coat affectionately as he came to greet her with a lick as she took up her seat beside Rachel. 'Hey, Mossy boy.'

'Let's go then.'

'Can we have hot chocolate when we get in?'

'Well that depends, have you been a good girl at school?'

'Of course, I was the best!'

'The best? Well, I suppose that's deserving of a nice cup of cocoa.'

'By-ee!' Maisy called to Amelia and her mum, as they moved off.

Back at the farmhouse soon afterwards, they had their hot chocolates – Grandma-Jill-style with whipped cream and mini marshmallows on the top – and then later they tucked into a supper of cheese and ham omelettes with salad.

'Right Maisy, I'm going out to check on the sheep. Do you want to come and see how Pete's getting on out in the field? He's a big boy with all the others now.'

'Oh, wow. Does he like it? I bet he's made some new friends.'

'He probably has, and by the way he was gambolling around like a loony this morning, I think he was very happy, and enjoying the fresh grass to eat.'

Rachel and Maisy popped their coats on. Though the rains had passed and it was a pleasant evening it would soon cool, and it was often nippy when riding on the open-air quad which was easier to use in the fields. Rachel gave a quick whistle to Moss who was up like a shot from his prone position in the porch. He was sadly banished from the kitchen for health and safety reasons just now with the pudding business underway, but he sneaked as close as he could, bless him. Rachel made sure she still gave him lots of attention though, and he was her companion on the farm for most of the day, sat happily in the back of the quad.

The sheep and lambs were spread over two large fields, with the latest arrivals and the newly turned out pet lambs being in the one nearest the farmyard. Pete came running up to the quad, seemingly excited, and Maisy got down to give him a pat and a cob of sheep nut which made him very happy.

'Hi there, Petie, do you like your new field?' Maisy was chatting away with her four-legged friend and he baaed his response. They both then gave him a good rub on the back – Rachel had to admit she was fond of him too – before moving on to see the others. Rachel spotted a ewe that was limping and needed her foot trimming. She dealt with it and finished with a douse of antiseptic. Then they drove up to the top of the hill and sat side by side on the grass, sharing one of Jill's melt-in-the-mouth chocolate brownies and looking out at the view before them: rolling green fields, rising moorland near to Doddington Hill and away on the horizon the dark blue glimpse of the sea. It was so calm up here, quiet, other than the odd baa of a sheep and tweet of a bird. A place to chat in comfort about their day, a place to catch up and just breathe.

'All fine at school today, Maisy?'

'Yeah, good. I played with a new girl today, Bethany.

She was nice . . . but not as nice as Amelia. But Mrs Watson said we had to let her join in our game.'

'Well, that's a kind thing to do. And I expect she was a bit shy. It's hard when you're the new one.'

'A bit like Pete in the field, I suppose.'

'Yes, a bit like Pete.'

'He's making friends. I saw him playing with those other lambs.'

'Yes, and I'm sure Bethany will too, as long as you are all friendly to her.'

It was a lovely mum and daughter moment, sat chatting as the sun began to fade in the sky, their sheep and cattle content in the fields below. The farmhouse light was a welcoming glow in the valley, where Grandma Jill would be getting some milk warmed on the Aga soon, ready for Maisy's bedtime. Their valley was peaceful and, despite its problems, the farm, their home, was such a comfort.

Chapter 17

THE CATTLE ARE LOWING

The next morning, after checking on the hens, Rachel was striding across the yard towards the trill of the house phone. She daren't run with a basketful of eggs. She heard it stop and then start all over again. She wasn't sure where Mum was, maybe out hanging the washing in the garden. Rachel placed the eggs down at the front door and ran in, in case it was Maisy's school or something.

'Rach-el?' The voice was male and sounded gruff.

'Ye-es.'

'There's a bull and a dozen or so of your cows and calves trampling all over my barley crop. I suggest you get yourself over here right away.' She recognised the deep, angry tones of old Mr Macintosh, their neighbouring farmer, whose land was on the opposite side from Tom.

Oh shit. Cows could do some serious damage if left to their own devices. They must have broken through the adjoining hedge somehow. And yes, Mr Mac would be extremely grumpy if his crop was ruined. *Shite. Shite.*

She was already grabbing the Land Rover keys as she replied, 'I'm right on my way, Mr Macintosh. Which field are they in?'

'Ah, you'll see them soon enough, lassie. They're in the one right by the road when you come along the lane.'

She suddenly thought better of going on her own. Cattle were often a nightmare to herd, especially if they got themselves into a panic.

'I'll be there as soon as I can.' She put the phone down and ran to the garden where, as she'd guessed, her mum was hanging out the clothes to dry.

'Mum, can you give me a hand? The bloody cows have got out.'

'Oh blimey, is Macduff leading his ladies astray again?' Macduff was their Aberdeen Angus bull, a huge and rather handsome, but wayward, black beast. Jill raised her eyebrows exasperatedly as she quickly pegged out the shirt that was in her hands, leaving the rest in the basket. 'Right then, where are they?'

'Sounds like they're trampling all over Farmer Mac's barley crop. He's not a happy man.'

'Damn. No, I don't suppose he will be. And that's one neighbour we don't want to get on the wrong side of.'

Rachel started relaying the phone call as they leapt into the truck.

'Oh blimey, this is a nightmare.' Jill went a bit pale.

The two of them knew all too well the havoc that even a few escapee cows could cause. The Land Rover engine rumbled into life and they set off, leaving a trail of dust on the farm track. They stayed quiet, feeling anxious, as they zipped the half mile along the lane.

It was so hard keeping the perimeter fencing in check. Rachel would go out on the quad regularly to take a look, but all it took was one weak link and a tasty-looking crop in the next-door field, and the weight of a bull would bring it down in no time, leaving a nice pathway for the rest of the herd to follow. Oh my, she hoped they hadn't done too much damage already. Mr Mac had sounded furious.

Soon enough, they had passed Eve's cottage and were further along the lane, approaching the neighbouring farm gate. The field next to it was sporting a crop of barley shoots. And, yes, there they were, a dozen or so of their errant cattle plus their new calves with a frazzled-looking Mr Macintosh with a large stick in his hand, desperately attempting to herd them to the set-aside verge of the field, trying his best to keep them off his precious crop. But as Rachel got out of the Land Rover, she could see the tell-tale hoof marks and a trail of trampling from the adjoining field. Aargh!

She leapt out of the vehicle. 'I'm so sorry, Mr Macintosh.'

'Aye, well there's no time to mess about. Let's get them rounded up and off my land. I'll be wanting some kind of compensation for the damage, mind!'

'Of course, of course,' Jill reassured him from her stance beside Rachel.

From the magic pot of money they didn't have, Rachel mused with a heavy heart.

'Let's herd them this way to the gate,' Rachel suggested. 'And I'll take them down the road way and home. Okay?'

'Aye, that'll stop them crushing my crop further.'

'Mum, will you go ahead and stop any traffic on the road?'

'Yes, love.'

'Come on,' Rachel started calling as firmly yet calmly as she could, as she raised her arms in a sweeping action. Mr Mac had stirred them up enough already with his hollering; what they needed was calm assertion. 'Come on Macduff. Come on cows.'

Mr Mac got behind them; they were quite happily chewing his set-aside grass now. They looked up nonchalantly, then started slowly shifting. Once Macduff got himself moving, the others started to follow, thank heavens.

Mr Mac jumped on his quad and that rallied them along further, with Rachel walking with arms spread widely and encouraging shouts, keeping the herd together. With Jill ahead, they went on down the lane, back up their own farm track, and Jill opened the gate on the first grass field they got to. The cattle could go in with the sheep for now, she'd herd them on later, back into their original field, once she'd had a chance to look at that damaged fence line.

'Sorry again, Mr Mac.' Rachel was extremely apologetic as she closed the field gate. The frazzled farmer was by her side on his quad with the engine running – the noise seemingly grumbling away at her.

'What a palaver.' Mr Mac was shaking his head. 'Mark my words, I'll be in touch about the damage, mind.'

Oh yes, she was sure he would. He'd probably be miffed that she'd rejected his measly offer on the land too. She sighed to herself; yet more money to come out of the dwindling pot. Argh, there was always something.

As the old farmer turned his quad to go, she heard him mutter, 'Tsk, bloody women playing at farming.'

Rachel felt her face flame, and the heat rise up her neck. The damned cheek of it. Things went wrong at times with all farmers, *men or women*. In fact, she was sure there was a time when she was little when *his* cows had made their way into Primrose Farm. Her dad had been furious as there'd been some risk of disease. Some people sure did have short memories and quick tongues.

Chapter 18

PROSECCO, PLANS AND MINI MERINGUES

The next morning, once Maisy was at school, Rachel and Jill were out fixing the damaged fence from where the cattle had escaped. It was a gorgeous morning, warm and dry, the birds singing happily in the green-leafed hedgerows around them. From here, they could see all the way across their grassy fields down to the valley where Primrose Farm nestled.

Jill stood up tall, stretching out her stiff back from all the physical work, and took in the view. 'It's beautiful here, isn't it?' The words came out almost as a sigh. 'It's far too precious to lose.'

Rachel stopped tugging at the rotten fence post, and pulled herself up tall, drinking in the gorgeous vista next to her mum. 'Yes,' she whispered, wondering where Jill's words might be leading.

'I've been thinking over everything these past few days, love. And you're right, life does need to change here. We've been stuck in a rut these past few years. Well, we've just been trying to get through one day at a time, I suppose.'

'That's all we could do, Mum. It was the only way to make it through,' Rachel answered, knowing just how hard life had been. In the early days after Dad's death, it was hard just to get up, get on, to even bother to make supper. But having a farm-load of animals all waiting for you, and a young child who needed you, made you rally, drag your body out of that bed, and get on with it.

'Well, it's high time we started looking forward, Rachel. Primrose Farm needs a future, and your idea of having something based here seems the right way to go. I've been mulling it all over and . . . yes, why not, I think we should go for the Pudding Pantry plan. At least, let's give it a try, anyhow.'

'Wow, that's great, Mum.' Despite the words, and her joy that Jill had made a huge leap forward, Rachel couldn't help but sigh herself; last night's research into funding and grants had kept throwing up stones at her, in fact massive bloody boulders. 'But . . . the problem is, I've been looking further into applying for grants, and for the works we need, we'd have to find sixty per cent of the set-up costs. Even with the rent we're getting from the fields, and even if we saved for six months, we still couldn't possibly put by enough. The Pudding Pantry couldn't happen until next year at least, maybe not even then. I'm sorry Mum, I know I got all carried away with the idea, but we don't have the funds we need to start up with. I've been looking at all angles and I just don't know how we can do it.'

Mum was quiet for a few seconds, looking out across

the green rolling landscape of their farm with the hedge-rows of hawthorn now studded with confetti-style May blossom and their fields dotted with sheep.

'I've been doing some research too, and yes, I've seen you need to contribute a capital sum for the rural grants scheme. But there's something I haven't told you.'

Rachel turned to face her mum, Jill having her full attention now.

'You see, I have some savings. Nothing major. I was keeping it as a stand-by, as a little last-resort pot for Maisy's future. It was from a small life insurance your dad had set up many years ago. It's only a couple of thousand but it might just be enough to make a start on those quotes you've had for the work in the barn.'

'Oh, but Mum, no, if you've kept the money back with that in mind, then we must keep it for Maisy.'

'I kept it for Maisy's future, yes. And the more I think about it, *this*, this Pudding Pantry idea, it *is* Maisy's future *and ours*. If the farm can't survive as it is, then we all go under and there'll be no farm or future for us here anyway.'

'Oh . . . I'm not sure what to think. It had all seemed so far out of reach, but now . . .' Rachel was stunned, having told herself it could never happen. Yes, it was a risk. Mum's last savings at stake, along with the future of the farm, but they were at risk of losing that already. 'What if it doesn't work out though, Mum? Just as you'd feared?'

'Is anything guaranteed in life, Rachel? Look at what happened to us all before . . .'

Rachel took in the words as she gazed across the green

fields of their valley, pausing to look at the farmhouse itself. She saw the barn there opposite it, like a beacon of promise, its stone walls lit honey-gold in the morning sunshine.

'Well?' Jill was waiting for her response.

Rachel turned towards her mum. She looked at her face and couldn't help but notice the fresh twinkle in her eyes – a sparkle of promise, and hope.

'Wow, okay then, yes! I think we should do it. For the three of us.' Rachel's mouth stretched into a broad grin.

'For the three of us,' Jill echoed, taking her daughter's hand in hers.

There was a palpable sense of excitement at Primrose Farm with Pudding Pantry plans afoot. They'd chosen a local building company to work with (who'd given a reasonable quote *and* had a sound reputation) who could start in four weeks' time. That would take them towards mid-June. The work itself, they'd been advised, should take around one month, so the Pudding Pantry might be open by mid-July – how amazing – and hopefully just in time for the school summer holidays.

In the meanwhile, Jill was still baking the popular sticky toffee and chocolate puddings for the Kirkton Deli. The farm kept Rachel busy, but with the cows now calved and all the animals out in the fields, farm life was far simpler and she had more time to help Jill.

They needed to get an order made up quickly, as Brenda had phoned them to say she'd had a flurry of sales, so later that day Rachel, Jill and Maisy set up an afterschool pudding packaging production line. The radio was on, and they were singing away to one of Mum's old favourites, the happy beat of The La's 'There She Goes'. Jill was pouring rich toffee sauce over the sponges that she'd already baked in their foil containers, Rachel was in charge of lidding, and Maisy set out the material squares, ready for Rachel to wrap and tie with a bow. Maisy then had to stack the finished puddings very carefully, checking they stayed flat to avoid spillage, in the cardboard box ready for delivery.

'You're doing a great job, Maisy,' Rachel praised. She could see how serious her little girl was, with a furrow of concentration on her brow, making sure she didn't tilt the cartons as she carried them.

'Were there any pudding spares, Grandma?' Maisy asked hopefully, as she put the last one into the box. 'I do think we should try them to make sure they're okay.'

'Yes, quality control is essential,' Rachel agreed with a grin.

'Oh yes, I know what you two are like. There's a chocolate one already in the fridge that I kept back.'

'That's what we like to hear.' Rachel gave a big thumbs up to Maisy, who started giggling away.

'Got to keep the workers happy,' Jill commented with a smile.

'Yes,' agreed Maisy.

'Absolutely, or we'll go on strike, won't we, Maisy?' Rachel jested.

The farmhouse kitchen was a happy buzzy place to be just now. The pudding production line had brought it back to life.

That evening, Rachel was browsing on Instagram and Google for interior design inspiration – *on a budget*. She wanted the barn to look pretty with a country feel, and be welcoming and cosy. She'd printed off some pictures of white-painted wooden furniture, and for lighting she'd spotted the most gorgeous glass chandeliers that could hang from the wooden rafters. They would add a touch of sparkle and warmth, though in reality, she mused, they probably couldn't afford something like that. Then, there was the counter area to create, but she struggled to visualise how it might all work together.

What she needed was an artistic friend in tow. So, she caught up with Eve at the school pick-up the next day, telling of her design thoughts.

'Ooh, this all sounds great, Rach. You know what, me and you need to brainstorm all this properly. Come up with all sorts of ideas for your Pudding Pantry and choose the best ones to move forward with, then of course you can chat them over with Jill. What do you think? You could call around one evening this week?'

It sounded a fab idea, and better to thrash out her thoughts with a creative friend before launching them half-formed on Jill just yet.

'Yes, that sounds great, and I'm sure Mum'll be happy to be keep an eye on Maisy for an evening.'

'Perfect, just let me know which day. Bring your pics along and any of your ideas so far. And,' she added with a cheeky wink, 'we need to plan over prosecco. Nothing breeds creativity like a bit of gorgeous fizz.'

'Now you're talking! Sounds good to me, thanks Eve.'

Thursday was the agreed prosecco planning night.

Rachel had settled Maisy in bed, and Jill was going to use the time to make another batch of chocolate puds to build up supplies. Then she was planning on making the most of a quiet night to have a lovely bubble bath and read her latest crime book.

'Off you trot,' she'd said to Rachel. 'Don't you be worrying about time, you go off and enjoy yourself.'

Rachel headed over to Eve's on the quad. She could always walk back and fetch it in the morning if the prosecco proved plentiful. It was a mild night, a little cloudy but warm. The evenings were drawing out now that they'd reached mid-May, so it was still light, with an early smattering of stars starting to appear. Eve greeted her with a hug and a kiss at her cottage front door, suggesting they sit outside in her back garden.

'There isn't actually much space inside at the moment anyhow, what with all my latest crafting mid-flow – the place is bursting at the seams with felt and woollen balls and sequins – it's like a haberdashery on a high!' Eve laughed.

'Oh, can I see what you're making?' Rachel loved all the things that her clever, artistic friend created. Eve was so talented. Rachel also wanted to see if there might be some crafts that would be ideal to sell in their Pudding Pantry shop. Oh yes, she had decided a little shop area could work well within the tearooms and had already mooted this with Jill who was more than happy with that – she couldn't wait to share the idea with Eve. They would have puddings for sale to take away, as well as a counter full of goodies to eat in, but Rachel could also imagine a dresser filled with Eve's gorgeous craft creations – children's toys and gifts, wooden wall plaques, pretty candle-holders and more. It was a chance to showcase her friend's talent, and return the favour for all the help she'd offered on the packaging designs – as yet, she'd insisted on not taking a penny from them.

'Come on then, come and have a look in the dining room, also known as my craft zone. I'll warn you though, it really has taken over.'

Amongst the scraps of material, needle sets, coloured card, scissors, balls of wool, and reels of ribbons, were some finished toys made of felt and fabric. They were the cutest things – all animal designs: a red squirrel, hare, hedgehog, mice, sheep, cows, dogs, and cats, dressed in tweed waistcoats or mini floral pinafores, and some with just bow ties (the hedgehog must have been hard to clothe!). They were similar to the finger puppets that Eve had made for Maisy's party, but were much bigger and easier for a child to hug.

'Aw, these are adorable, Eve.'

Then, Rachel spotted some of the woodwork items stacked up on Eve's dresser – hearts and stars and hanging plaques bearing little messages like 'Home Sweet Home' or 'Life Is Beautiful'. She particularly like the distressed-wood drinks coasters with 'Gin Time!' and 'Prosecco Moments!' There was also a box of handmade cards. Rachel sifted through them, an array of 3D and cut-out designs all crafted beautifully – 'Happy Birthday', 'Thank You', 'New Baby' and more. These were all things that would surely sell well in a countryside shop and café.

'You're amazing, really.' Rachel smiled broadly at her friend. She then spotted some delightful bunting flags strung on white satin ribbon just perfect for a new baby's nursery. 'Ooh, this is gorgeous Eve, do you think you could make me some bunting for the Pudding Pantry? Something vintage looking . . . I'm not sure what colour schemes to go for yet, though I have seen some pretty white wooden furniture designs. We'll have to have a think on what might work best.'

'Of course. And yes, we'll brainstorm all things puddings and tearooms and barns. Let's go and get a glass of prosecco poured,' Eve announced with a smile.

They were soon sitting outside in the twilight hush at a little wrought-iron table for two with a glass of prosecco to hand, crispy-sweet mini meringues that Eve had made and a bowl of strawberries between them.

'I'm so excited for you and this project.' Eve grinned. 'You've all been through so much, and I'm so proud of you taking this new step forward. It's brave and it's wonderful, and I really do think it can work.'

'I bloody well hope so.' Rachel took a sip of prosecco.

'Do you remember all our dreams and big ideas back in the day? When we were playing dress-up, I wanted to be a fashion designer, draping you in all sorts of colourful scarves and knits . . .'

'Hah, well you really are making them now, with your gorgeous children's jumpers and the knitted toys.'

'Not quite London fashion week though.'

'No, but . . . hey, don't run yourself down. They're great and you're using your skills, your passion, your creativity.'

Eve nodded in acknowledgement, softly smiling. 'And then there you were, ever practical, happier in wellies than high heels, even though I could make you totter around in your mum's special pair of stilettos that were way too big for you, whilst you were making plans for the farm. And, when you were a teenager you had your dream of going off to agricultural college to learn all the latest farming developments. You already wanted to make a difference back then.'

'And then there was Maisy to think of, of course,' Rachel commented. Reality had taken over.

'Yes, well, you just had to hold fire on those big ideas for a while, and you've done a brilliant job of being a mum. That's a huge achievement in itself, hun.'

'And . . . there was Amelia following soon after,' added Rachel.

'Well, yes, but then I was all settled with Ben, and couldn't wait. I think you'd made me all broody. Life just turns on a sixpence sometimes . . .'

There was a moment of quiet when they must have both

been thinking of the much harder times that had followed at Primrose Farm, then Eve gave a sigh and a smile. 'And now this, you and Jill being brave enough to go ahead and change things at the farm. It's maybe not quite panned out quite how you'd imagined way back then, I know it's been so tough, but here you are; strong and determined, and willing to give this Pudding Pantry a try at least.'

Rachel looked across at Eve. She was so grateful that their friendship had spanned the years. She felt a warm glow at her words, but was she overestimating her courage? 'Sometimes, I don't feel as strong as I come across, Eve.'

'Hey . . . that's okay too, Rach. That's when you come and find me . . . and your other friends, your family . . .'

Rachel found her vision had gone a bit fuzzy as a tear caught in her eye. 'Now look what you've made me do.' She took a delightful sip of bubbly, diverting attention from her glistening eyes. 'Mmmn, delicious. Right, let's get on with this brainstorming then.'

'Of course, yes.' Eve popped a strawberry into her mouth. 'Right, I've got some A4 paper here, some coloured pens, and we'll smash the ideas out.'

'Great. So, on the barn interior,' Rachel was eager to get started, 'I've had some ideas for general style and furniture. Can I test them out on you?'

'Go right ahead.'

'So, I'm thinking "country" and "pretty", a mix of old and new. Somewhere you'd like to hang out and relax with your friends or bring your granny for lunch, that kind of thing. Hang on, I've got some images that I've saved on my phone to give you a better idea. Now, I can picture a serving counter a bit like that one, all made in natural wood, and a glass refrigerated counter for all the puddings, cakes and other delights.'

'Of course. The puddings will be the stars of the show.'

She showed Eve a few pictures. 'The stone walls I want to keep much as they are,' Rachel continued. 'And, I'm thinking white-painted wooden furniture with a gorgeous dresser or two to display things on.'

'Ooh, yes, I love it. Yes! And what about having jam jars filled with posies on each table? And wooden spoons with the table numbers on? That'll fit so well with the baking theme.'

'Great. That'd be so pretty having flowers, and posies would be inexpensive to do . . . And, if we can afford it, look at these . . . I'd *love* two glass chandeliers, just small ones like those in the image there. See how they catch the light and make it look really special.'

'Wow, yes, it sounds unusual to have chandeliers in a barn but in fact it works really well.'

'They will be a bit expensive though, I had a quick look at prices,' Rachel admitted. 'But, if I can get the tables and chairs and a dresser second-hand and paint them all myself, then I might just be able to splash out on the chandeliers. Well, I'll have to wait and see. There'll be a lot more essential things to pay out on first.'

'Oh, I hope you can get them, they add a magical, sparkly touch.'

'*And*, there's something else I'd like to have in the tearooms. In fact, I've got a proposition for you. I've already talked it over with Mum.'

'Yes?' Eve sounded curious.

'Would you like to sell some of your wonderful crafts with us? I'm picturing a dresser filled with "Eve's Cottage Crafts".'

'Oh, my word. Are you serious?'

'Of course, I am. It'll look great with all your soft toys and folded knits on the shelves and those gorgeous stars and hearts and cards for sale. What a lovely addition to our tearoom that would be.'

Eve looked happily stunned.

'And if we agree the prices together,' Rachel continued, with her business mind on a roll, 'we'd take a small cut, and you'd get the rest.'

'I think that's an amazing idea. I'd still need to keep up with my Etsy orders, though.'

'Of course. But I know you've been making more than that. I mean, look at all the stuff you've got there piled in your dining room. It's an ideal extra outlet for you. And quality local crafts made right here in the valley will be really popular, I'm certain.'

'Eve's Cottage Crafts. I haven't named my business formally yet, but I do like that. Can I steal it?'

'Yes, course you can.'

'Brilliant, this is all so exciting. I think we deserve another glass of bubbly.'

And so, the prosecco glasses were topped up.

'Hey, who'd have thought . . . ? We're in business to-gether,' grinned Eve. 'And I'll still do all your packaging designs too, if you're happy with that.'

'Of course. And yes, it'll be great to have you on board, my lovely friend,' Rachel said with a broad smile.

This prosecco planning was rather fabulous. Who knew a 'business meeting' could be such fun! They chinked glasses, then chatted some more, talking of favourite puddings they'd need to have on the menu and headed inside for a while to print off mouth-watering images to add to the Pudding Pantry pinboard that Eve had set up – the renowned sticky toffee and chocolate puds naturally, a summer-fruits pavlova, banoffee pie, treacle sponge pudding, apple crumble, bread and butter pudding, choc-olate brownies, Rachel's white chocolate and raspberry cheesecake that Eve said was a must, and more.

'Wow, it sounds like Mum's going to be busy,' Rachel commented, as they drifted back outside to their cosy table. 'I think I'd better be donning my apron as well!'

Rachel let out a contented sigh as she popped a meringue into her mouth with the last of the sweet strawberries and sat looking out across the valley. The late spring dusk was falling; the sky settling into peace-ful pinky-peach hues. The sounds around them were calming; the odd tweet of a bird, the bleat of a lamb. The hum of a tractor working late down the valley – maybe it was Tom out and about. The thought of him nearby made Rachel's smile widen for a second. Above, a swift darted across the sky, chasing insects.

'We're so lucky to live here, aren't we?' said Rachel. 'On a night like this it's beautiful, isn't it? When you stop and really look.' With the sun going down, and a lovely feeling of warmth and friendship in the air, it was one of those rare special moments, when you take stock and simply enjoy the moment.

'Yes, we're usually running about like blue-arsed flies and don't really see it, do we,' Eve agreed. 'I love it here too. It's a little piece of heaven . . . oh . . .' Eve stopped herself, cursing her use of words.

'It's all right, I know what you mean. And you know what, despite everything. Despite the pain and hurt of these past two years, I do still love this place, the farm, this life.' Rachel looked out over the dusk-muted mauve shades and curves of the valley; taking in every field and track that she knew by heart. 'I really can't imagine being anywhere else.'

Eve placed a gentle hand on Rachel's shoulder and nodded.

Rachel sat quietly for a while with a heart full of memories, a head full of dreams and all their plans for the Pudding Pantry at Primrose Farm on a pinboard in front of them.

It was exciting and wonderful, but there was so much at stake. Boy, did this new venture have to succeed.

Chapter 19

RENOVATIONS AND ROULADE

Rachel was bristling, sat with a steaming mug of tea at the kitchen table. To her annoyance, another email had come in from Jake, asking for news on Maisy.

She'd been so cross after getting the last one, she hadn't known quite how to respond, and life had been hectic when it had landed in her inbox. Then, when Maisy made a thank-you card for her daddy with glitter and stickers and a drawing of Pete the lamb, she realised they had nowhere to post it. You can't send a handmade card to a bloody email address. It had made Rachel so angry.

But she recognised that Maisy should have some contact with her father, if that's what she wanted. Maybe she'd respond this time and attach a recent photo for him, and mention the thank-you card to try and get a postal address. Arrgh, if they hadn't had Maisy together, she'd have been happy to never see or hear from him again. Jake ready to come knocking on the door, showing renewed interest in Maisy, gave Rachel a headache that she really didn't need right now – how could he presume that he could just jump into her and Maisy's lives whenever it suited him? Bloody selfish, that was Jake all over, Rachel raged to herself.

At least she had an exciting project to distract her from the emotional tribulations with her ex. After a busy few weeks on the farm, the day had finally come for the wheels to start turning on the Pudding Pantry plans. Not to mention for the farmyard to become filled with dust and building debris. The noise of drilling, clanging and hammering filled the air, and Rachel's head, which was already in a spin after hearing from Jake, was banging too.

'Oh my God, I can't handle this noise!' Rachel broke away from her admin tasks at the laptop.

Jill quickly went to close all the windows of the kitchen, despite it being a warm day, realising that plumes of dust were already billowing in.

'Ah no, the puddings will be full of grit!' she groaned. Her latest batch of chocolate puddings for the Deli were sitting cooling on the side.

'They'll have extra crunchy toppings!' Rachel said wryly, adding, 'Well, at least it means we're on the way.' After a week's delay on their agreed start date whilst the builders were finishing off a previous project, it was great to see, if not hear, some action.

'Yes, I know, we couldn't afford to have wasted much more time. It'll be a busy, noisy month, but it also spells progress,' added Jill. 'Just think, when we get through this, we can get everything up and running and we'll be opening soon.'

'Yes, it's really happening, Mum.'

The electrician they'd hired was also coming in to get the wiring to the barn checked and improved. Rachel was quite looking forward to the electrician coming back actually. He was friendly and chatty and seemed to know his stuff when he'd called at the farm to give a quote a few weeks ago. His name was Carl, and she could picture his blond hair and grey-green eyes that had a bit of sparkle about them. It gave her a jolt of surprise to acknowledge that his face had stuck in her mind . . .

'Can I help you with anything here, Mum?' Rachel asked, bringing herself back to the here and now.

'Not just now thanks, love. I've got all these made. But I am going to experiment with some new puddings and desserts ready for the pantry's opening. We'll need an exciting selection to tempt our customers, so I'm thinking about how we can push the boat out.'

'Ooh, what are you thinking?'

'Well, we'll be right in the swing of summer when we open, won't we. So, I'll have to try a summer pudding, I haven't made one of those for ages, and I've just found this recipe for a dark chocolate and raspberry roulade.'

'Now that sounds divine!'

'Hey, come and look at this, too. I was hunting for something traditional and old-fashioned and I remembered Ruth's scrummy spotted dick recipe, so I've been looking through the old Baking Bible, and there it was.

But see this . . .' Jill was smiling broadly as she pointed to the open page.

There was a loose page tucked there with Grandma Ruth's unmistakeable neat handwriting . . . and then, beside the title of 'Spotted Dick', written in a childish scrawl, was 'Hahaha!' and a cartoonish – but unmistakeably crude – drawing! Rachel grinned – that *so* must have been Dad as a mischievous boy.

'That's hilarious! I wonder if Grandma Ruth was cross.' Rachel could almost picture the pair of them: Dad and his mum here in the kitchen baking together, or most likely Dad meant to be doing some schoolwork at the kitchen table and naughtily scribbling in her margin when she wasn't looking.

'Well, I'll have to give this a try, won't I, and some of the others to see if they work out all right. Let's see what works best and what you all like.'

'Great, so, are we going to have to be pudding guinea pigs for the next few weeks?'

'You are indeed.'

'Blimey, the things we have to put up with for the sake of the business.' Rachel gave a mock shrug. 'It's so tough, this pudding malarkey.'

Jill smiled.

'Right, well I'll get back out with Moss and start rounding up the sheep and bringing them down ready for shearing. We've got Big Bob in tomorrow,' Rachel said.

Big Bob travelled around the area at shearing time.

They had the ewes to shear, all one hundred and ninety of them, plus three tups, who were far stronger and harder to wrestle to the ground. It'd take a whole day. Shearing helped to keep the sheep cool for the warm summer months, and kept the flies from settling in the fleece and causing all sorts of bother. She and Moss would go out and herd them up today, so they were ready in The Stackyard – which was the field nearest the farm and lambing shed, soon to be the shearing shed.

Like Jill, Simon would be helping tomorrow as well – it'd be all hands on deck, with Big Bob doing the bulk of the shearing. Rachel did know how to shear, but there was an art to it and her fleeces tended to look a bit scruffy, as did the animals thereafter. It also needed a lot of physical strength for the numbers of sheep involved, so she worked better as 'shearer's assistant', rolling and stacking the fleeces. She still used the same old wool needle that her grandfather had used to sew up the wool sacks, ready for collection.

It was hard and smelly work – Rachel was already thinking about the hot bubble bath she'd no doubt be craving afterwards.

The day after the shearing – God, it had been a tough physical labour – Rachel was up sharp, despite her aches and pains. They were three days into the barn renovations and Rachel couldn't resist a look in. She swung open the barn door with a sense of expectation. Oh . . . there was dust and grime and a broken-up floor where it needed levelling out, and it all looked a bit of a mess. Her heart sank – they were at the point where you walked into a renovation project and wondered what the hell you'd embarked upon. It was early days, she reminded herself. It needed to be stripped to its shell so that they could move forward. She took a deep breath and closed her eyes, trying to call to mind the lovely interior design inspiration on her pinboard . . . it was doable, with a bit of creativity and graft.

She came back out and got on the quad ready to do her morning tour of the farm's livestock. At the top of the grassy bank, where her signal was better, Rachel took out her mobile and phoned Carl the electrician, to see if he could make it there in the coming day or two. She didn't want anything to hold things up.

'Hi, Rach.' His voice was warm and friendly down the line. 'Yes, I should be able to make it up really soon. I've a couple of jobs arranged up your way from tomorrow actually, and I've got a B&B sorted for a couple of nights near there so that ties in well. I can come in on Thursday, take a look, and maybe fit in the work Friday if that's any good?'

'Yes, that'd be great. Thanks so much for squeezing us in.'

'Okay, I'll see you around nine, Thursday.'

'Perfect.'

On Thursday morning, Carl whizzed up the farm track in his little white van that read 'CJT Electrics' on the side – *Carl John Turner*.

'Hey Rachel,' he called, stepping out of the van. He was dressed casually in jeans and a black polo-shirt. 'How's it going?'

'Hey Carl, well, it's all getting going in the barn. Looks a bit chaotic just now, but it's coming on – so the builders say, anyway,' answered Rachel.

'Ah, don't worry, that's often the way with this kind of a project,' Carl acknowledged, reassuringly.

'Right, well if you come across, I can show you where we need you. Can I get you a cup of tea, coffee? I'm sure Ian and Dan, the two builders, will be ready for a coffee now too.'

Over the past four days, the builders hadn't yet been known to say no to a cup, served strong with two sugars each – in fact, there seemed to be a constant caffeine supply wending its way across to the barn since they'd arrived, and Mum was being rather liberal with supplies of cakes and puddings too. Rachel had a feeling she was testing out her new bakes on the two workmen, and they were more than happy to oblige.

'Yeah, a coffee would be great thanks, white one sugar.' He gave a big white-toothed grin.

He was actually quite a good-looking chap, Rachel mused. 'Well, if you want to head across to the barn and introduce yourself to the other lads, Ian and Dan, I'll be across with the coffees in two ticks.'

'Great, no worries. I'll take a quick look around. Remind myself of the job.'

*

Later in the morning, Carl came knocking at the farm-house door.

'Right then, do you want the good news or the bad?' He flashed a smile, then proceeded to tell Rachel and Jill that the costs might have to be slightly higher than his original quote. He'd discovered a few dodgy bits of wiring that would need further work in the new kitchen area.

'Well, if it needs doing then we want to get it right. Can you email me the new figures to look over?' said Rachel.

'Yep, will do. It's a great place out here, isn't it,' he added, looking around him from his doorstep vantage point. 'I like to do a bit of mountain-biking sometimes, bet there's some great trails and lovely views further up the hills.'

'Oh you bet, it's a beautiful part of the world. I've never mountain-biked myself, but I know people flock to the trails from miles around.'

It was nice that he appreciated their valley.

'Hmm, might have to head back for a trip out on one of my days off. Come and say hi.' He raised his eyebrows just a touch, which took Rachel off guard. Was he just being friendly?

'Right, well that's me away till tomorrow afternoon,' said Carl. 'Need to crack on with this job over at the grain dryers in Belford, that's going to be as exciting as watching paint dry, I'm sure. I'll see you tomorrow then, yeah?' His smile was warm and friendly. 'Looking forward to it,' he added.

Rachel wasn't quite sure, but had there been a touch of flirting going on there? She was so out of practice with all that, she couldn't be certain. But she certainly did like the cheeky twinkle in his bright green eyes . . .

Chapter 20

A DISASTROUS DATE PUDDING

Friday swung around, and Carl had been working all afternoon on the barn's electrics. The builders had left at lunchtime, happy to start the weekend early and let the electrician get on with his tasks. Rachel had popped in now and again to take Carl a coffee and see how things were going, finding him singing along to the portable radio he'd brought with him. He seemed cheerful and chatty, occasionally flashing what seemed to be his trademark smile.

As early evening set in, he knocked on the farmhouse door and asked if Rachel and Jill would come across to the barn. He talked them through his handiwork, and it certainly looked like a neat job.

'That's brilliant. Thank you,' said Rachel, as she walked around, feeling a buzz of excitement that things were really starting to take shape here.

'Yes, you've been wonderful, Carl. Thank you,' added Jill.

'Right, well that's me about done then. I just need to

tidy up my tools, then I'm away. I'll send on the invoice for this by email, if that's okay, yeah?'

'Yes, that's fine,' Rachel replied.

Rachel tried not to worry too much about the money. Mum's savings pot was dwindling fast but the grants they'd applied for should hopefully come in soon – well, if they were accepted; things were still a bit tense.

'Umm, I've still got a night booked up this way in my digs.' Carl looked at Rachel with a cheeky smile. 'What would you say to coming out with me for a drink this evening?'

'Oh, I'm . . .' Was she being asked on a date, or was it just a friendly chat and a drink? She was *sooo* out of this game, she was floundering, badly.

Before she could say any more, however, Jill chipped in. 'Yes, go on love. I'm happy to look after Maisy. It's no bother, I'm at home anyhow. You go out and have some fun for a change.'

'Well, okay then.' *Why not?* It wasn't every day a good-looking guy asked you out for a drink, and he seemed friendly enough.

'Great, I'll pick you up around seven-thirty then. That'll give me a chance to get back to my digs and take a shower.'

'Great.' Rachel's voice came out slightly high-pitched, as a sudden unbidden image of Carl in a shower sprang to mind. It was certainly not appropriate thinking-matter with her mother stood beside her.

Just at that moment, to make things even more

embarrassing, Maisy skipped around the corner into the barn. She'd been playing out in the garden, enjoying the freedom of a warm June evening after school. She screwed up her nose. 'Don't like it in here, Mummy. It doesn't look very nice. It's all dug up and horrid. *And*, it smells funny.'

'Oh, it's not ready yet, Maisy,' soothed Rachel. 'There's loads of work to do here yet. Give it a few weeks and it'll all be so different.'

'Good. No-one would want to eat pudding in *here*.' She scowled with her whole face screwed up, as only a five-year-old can.

Carl finished packing up his tool box and was soon heading for the barn door. 'Right, well that's me done then, ladies. See you later, Rachel.' He ignored Maisy as he flashed a wide grin at Rachel, adding a brief, 'Bye then,' that was directed at Jill.

'Why's he seeing you later?' Maisy demanded as Carl left the barn.

'Oh, I'm going out for a chat and a drink, that's all. Grandma's looking after you.'

'Oh.' Maisy looked slightly put out, but said no more on the matter, instead running around the barn getting dust and debris all over her school shoes, much to Rachel's dismay. When she finally came back to them with a slowing skip, she crossed her arms and announced indignantly how it had looked *so* much better when it was her party, which – of course – it had.

*

What to wear? Rachel hadn't bought anything new for so long – she generally lived in jeans, T-shirts, fleeces, and often an old green boiler suit for grubby jobs around the farm. But she ought to look like she'd made a bit of an effort for this evening at least. She dug through her clothes rail in the pine wardrobe of her double bedroom, humming along to her favourite country music playing in the background, until she chanced upon a navy floral-print dress, teamed on a hanger with a short-sleeved cardigan. Would it even fit her now?

She seemed to remember the last time she'd worn it was out to a dinner for Mum's birthday. That must be about three years ago now. Maisy was still in a high chair, she remembered, and yes, Dad was there with them. Back when life was good. They still had their difficulties back then on the farm of course, but none of them had known what was to come. She sighed as she took the dress out; it was summery and pretty, but felt bittersweet.

Right, enough nostalgia, she needed to get changed and ready in fifteen minutes as Carl would soon be here. She pulled the dress on. It wasn't quite as fitted as she remembered – she must have actually lost some weight in the past couple of years, though she was still by no means thin. She'd always had curves from being a teenager and was a happy size twelve. Jake had always said they were in the right places, though he was often able to pull out the kind of lines that flattered back then. Nowadays, Rachel never really took much note of her body. It was useful, it all worked fine, and it mostly lived under layers of warm and practical clothing.

She gave a quick brush of her thick wavy dark hair – she'd wear it loose tonight, set it free from the ponytail band that usually kept it swept out of the way. It fell with a bounce to just below her shoulders. A flick of mascara, a smear of pink lipstick and a spritz of perfume, and she was ready.

When she got downstairs, Maisy came dashing over to her. 'Ooh, Mummy, you look lovely.'

'Ah, thanks, petal.'

'Yes, you do, love. I always liked you in that dress.' Jill was smiling with a soft expression on her face. Rachel wondered if the dress brought back memories for her too.

Rachel felt a little nervous, as she heard the crunch of gravel in the yard outside. Carl must have arrived. Okay, she told herself, this wasn't really a date, just a drink out. Was she okay with that? Or did she want it to be a date? She didn't have a clue.

'Right, I'm off then. Night, sweetheart. I'll see you in the morning, as you'll be all tucked up in bed when I get back.' She gave her little girl a kiss on the nose. 'Bye, Mum. Thanks again. I'll not be late.'

'It's fine, love. Me and Maisy are going to have a grand time baking some cupcakes and then we'll have a nice long story time before bed, won't we?'

Maisy was nodding happily. 'Can we do the pink icing ones?' she asked.

'Of course.'

'Okay, bye then. Have a nice evening here.'

Rachel headed out to the porch, just as Carl arrived at the door, smart in dark jeans and a blue shirt.

'Oh – hi.' She really was feeling nervous.

'Hey, you look gorgeous.' His eyes scanned up and down over her dress and curves, and he flashed a sparkling grin.

'Ah . . . thank you, you've also scrubbed up well.'

He was standing close and smelt fresh of shower gel and aftershave. His blond hair was still slightly damp from the shower, and his grey-green eyes were smiling at her. Yeah, she had to admit he looked good.

'Have a nice time,' Jill poked her head out from the front door.

Maisy stood in her pyjamas beside her. 'Bye, Mummy.'

'Bye! See you later Maisy, and be good for Grandma.' Rachel waved.

Carl also gave them a quick wave as he ducked into the van.

'Bet you can't wait to get away,' he commented, once she was sitting beside him.

'Ah . . . well . . .' Why was he speaking as though her family were a bit of a hindrance? She couldn't help but feel a bit put out, but maybe he was nervous too. Nerves were certainly getting the better of her. She started chewing a hangnail on her thumb as they sped off down the farm track, and then stopped herself, knowing that it wouldn't look particularly attractive or confident. Damn, she was so out of practice with all this stuff. Why had she said yes?

Okay, focus on the music playing on the radio, yes, that was it. They'd set off to the sounds of some kind of club-style dance music, which was probably quite trendy, but she'd never heard it before. She'd always been a bit of a country music fan herself, so she didn't even feel she could talk about that.

Luckily Carl broke the awkward silence. 'Love the dress. You look great.' They then proceeded to chat about the work he'd been doing that afternoon at the grain store. Phew. So far so bumpy . . . but at least the conversation was starting to pick up.

Rachel was quite relieved when she realised they were driving away from Kirkton, and on to a pub in Milfield, the next village along. It seemed to be just a casual drink that Carl had in mind and that suited Rachel, though she was happy that tongues wouldn't be wagging quite as much out here as they might have done in her local pub. It couldn't be helped – she'd lived at Kirkton all her life and it was the kind of place where everyone knew everyone.

The evening started okay. Rachel ordered a glass of white wine, trying to appear slightly more sophisticated than having her usual cider. They sat at a corner table and chatted about life at the farm and the plans for the Pudding Pantry, and soon the conversation switched back once more to Carl's work. He enjoyed telling her all about his latest projects and by the time he'd got on to the story of the hotel conversion he'd completed single-handedly last month, she had the feeling he might just be elaborating a touch on the truth. Were there many five-star hotel resorts on the Northumberland coast? Not to her knowledge. It was probably more like a smallish family-run hotel. But she reined in the negative thinking . . . maybe he really was the superman of the electrician world?

She bought the next round of drinks in and was quite enjoying the wine for a change. Carl had had a couple of pints of lager. She was glad they were on the English side of the border, as he'd have been way over the limit otherwise. She felt slightly uneasy about the fact that he was driving but he'd probably be fine, he'd hopefully go on to a soft drink next.

His B&B was back in Kirkton, so after chatting for another half hour, he suggested heading back that way and having a further drink back in Rachel's village. That made sense, though she knew she'd be back to the tongues-wagging-in-the-neighbourhood zone.

When they reached The Black Bull, Carl ordered a pint and another glass of wine for Rachel. The landlord, Mick, gave Carl an intense once-over before saying his hellos, and adding, 'How are you doing then, Rachel?'

'I'm fine, Mick, thanks, and you?'

'Just grand. And how's the little lass and your mum?'

'They're good, thanks. We're all getting on well just now.'

'Well, that's good to hear.' Of course the villagers all knew of the tough times that the Swinton girls had been through, and their support and goodwill was still evident.

They were soon sitting at a corner table again chatting away. Carl's arm was resting across the back of Rachel's chair in a relaxed manner that she didn't mind, when in came Tom. He spotted her and smiled at first, then his gaze shifted, taking in the man next to her. Rachel put a hand up to wave, but it lingered in the air, apparently unseen, as Tom strode swiftly on to the bar. Rachel felt slightly uneasy without really knowing why.

She and Carl chatted a while longer, talking about TV and music and his favourite films, most of which Rachel had never seen – to be fair, he seemed to be into a lot of action and war-type movies. Then Carl got up to get another round of drinks in, though Rachel was feeling she'd probably had enough by that point – the wine seemed way stronger than the cider she normally had.

'Oh, I'm not sure . . .' she started.

'Ah come on, Rach. Chill a bit. It's early yet.'

She reluctantly acquiesced and Carl headed to the bar again to order. It was obvious that Carl wouldn't be able to give her a lift home now that he'd had four pints, but Rachel was definitely feeling ready to head back soon. She'd have plenty to get up and do on the farm in the morning, and she really didn't fancy another hangover. She was about half-way through her fourth glass of wine, finding the taste a bit sour now, and was just thinking of organising a taxi for herself as the farm was a good three miles away – her 'date' hadn't seemed to have thought of that – when Carl piped up, 'So, are you fancying a nightcap back at mine? Well, at my digs at the B&B.' His smile widened as one brow arched, and she knew instantly what kind of nightcap he was thinking of.

'Oh sorry,' she blurted out. 'But I really need to be getting back for Maisy.'

Wow, she hardly knew this guy. Yes, she was aware people had one night stands all the time, but it really wasn't her thing. She knew where nights like that could end and it wasn't for her. She also had a little girl and a mother waiting at home for her.

'Ah, come on babe. The night is still young. You could still head back later.'

After a quick shag, he means. Rachel was starting to get irritated with his pushy, entitled attitude. But she didn't want to cause an argument, or a scene, and she tried to stay polite.

'Look, I've had a nice night.' *Up until now.* 'But I really don't know you that well, Carl.'

'Hey, well, I find you don't always have to know someone that well to have a good time.' His trademark smile suddenly looked way too arrogant.

So, *this* was what this evening was all about, 'having a good time', a quick shag. She hated that word, but it seemed fitting with Carl's expectations.

So, this was how it worked with Carl Turner. He bought you a few drinks and then expected a favour in return. It would pass another boring work night away. He probably had casual acquaintances all over the place. She wouldn't put it past him having a girlfriend back home too. Her guard was right up.

She noticed Tom glancing across at her from the bar just then. Was her face giving away her unease? But she was more than capable of handling this on her own.

'Well, I'm going to book myself a taxi, Carl. In fact, I can see there's one waiting at the village square.' With that she grabbed her handbag and stood up; thank heavens she still had a ten-pound note left in her purse. Carl didn't try to stop her or even to see her to the taxi. She walked tall with her head held high, out through the pub door. Phew, great, she spotted Jim, the local cabbie, there in his usual spot, and swiftly made her way to his saloon car.

'Hey there, Rachel.' You see, everyone did know everyone in Kirkton. 'Nice night, pet?'

'Not bad,' she lied.

'Heading back to the farm?'

'Yes, please.' Back to the farm. Back to normal. No more thoughts of stupid date nights. Her bloody track record with men was still abysmal. She seemed drawn to the dickheads.

That was the last she wanted to see of Carl bloody Turner. She'd obviously pay his bill for the work done on the barn, *but* . . . she'd be getting someone else in to fit the Pudding Pantry chandeliers, if she could ever afford them!

As the taxi pulled away, Rachel noticed the door to The Black Bull open. Out came Tom, looking around him with an edge of concern. He clocked the taxi, and spotted Rachel looking out from the rear window. He nodded at her then, and tentatively raised a hand, signalling goodnight. She gave him a small smile, and watched him turn around as her taxi pulled out into the night.

Chapter 21

HAY AND DELAY

A few days later, Rachel was setting out to run some errands when she saw Tom's truck coming down the country lane in the opposite direction. She felt all knotted up inside for some strange reason as he slowed to a stop, winding down his window. Rachel did the same.

'Hi, Rachel. Just to let you know I'll be cutting the rented hay fields in the next couple of days, so while I'm all set up do you want me to come in and do yours for you too? The forecast's looking good. Then we can row it up and maybe you can help me bale later in the week.'

'Well, if you're sure, that'd be great. Thanks so much. But, let me do the baling and then we'll be quits, okay?'

'Fair enough, and you can always pay me in puddings,' he grinned. 'Is it all going okay with that? It'll be full on with converting the barn, I bet. I've seen the builders' van toing and froing.'

'I wish it *was* full on,' she replied wryly. 'It's all come to a grinding halt yesterday, while we wait for missing kitchen units.'

Oh yes, Ian had caught up with her yesterday morning to enlighten them that there was at least a week's delay on the kitchen units that she and Jill had chosen, which was unfortunately going to hold up all the other works. There wasn't a lot they could do but wait and be patient.

'Ah, sorry to hear there's a hiccup.' Tom's face creased in sympathy.

'It has been pretty hectic up until now though, and yes, it's been keeping us out of mischief. Despite these last-minute hitches, we're nearly there.' Rachel was trying to stay positive.

'Great, well, I'll have to come and try it out. How long until you open, do you think?'

'Well, hopefully we'll be able to open in two or three weeks' time, in time for the school summer holidays.'

She was going to spend the next couple of weeks getting the tearoom furniture sourced. She was excited to look around the local second-hand shops or any house sales with Eve and Mum to find chairs, tables and a dresser and then get them all painted up ready. And Jill was busy with a baking production line – the big new fridge they'd invested in was bursting with puddings already.

'You will be full on then.'

'So yes, help with the hay just now will be brilliant.'

A shadow then crossed his face. 'Was everything okay the other night, by the way? You know, out in Kirkton?' There was a loaded silence, the word 'date' left hanging, unspoken, between them.

'Oh . . . at the pub, last week?' Rachel suddenly felt a bit awkward. 'Yes, that was just the electrician who'd been working for us. Seemed friendly enough, but he turned out to be a bit of a creep . . . I don't think we'll be seeing him around here again, somehow.'

'Ah, okay, well sorry to hear it wasn't the most memorable night out.' Tom sounded relieved, his shoulders visibly relaxing as he spoke. 'Right, well I'd better be getting on. See you about.'

'Cheers, Tom, see you around.'

After checking out the Kirkton antique and bric-a-brac trader for any furniture for the Pantry, which turned up a dresser but no suitable tables and chairs – she didn't think a set of Georgian furniture would quite suit the barn or the budget – and calling in at the agricultural merchant for some sheep wormer and washing powder they needed, Rachel decided to stop by at Granny Ruth's on the outskirts of the village.

Having been so busy with all the works on at the farm, and with Granny Ruth no longer able to drive herself to visit at the farm, she hadn't seen her for the past eight days, which was quite unusual.

Rachel pulled the Land Rover up on the verge in the pretty lane surrounded by country fields. Four stone cottages were lined up behind an old low stone wall, where colourful snapdragon flowers had seeded and bloomed from between the crevices. Rachel walked to the door of Granny Ruth's two-up two-down cottage, where a small-budded pale-pink rambling rose arched across in summer bloom. She knocked on the door and called a quick 'Hello Granny!' to announce her arrival, before opening the door into the cottage.

'Oh hello, pet.' Ruth was just getting up out of her armchair in her front room where she'd been crocheting. She liked to make bed throws and cushion covers which she gave to the local charity shop to sell. 'Lovely of you to stop by, I'll get the kettle on, shall I?'

'Oh, yes please. And sorry we haven't been over this week, it's just been a bit crazy with everything going on at the farm.' Rachel followed Ruth through to the kitchen.

'Don't you worry about that, pet. I'm fine. I know you and your mum have a lot on at the moment. Mind . . .' she gave her granddaughter a thorough look over, 'you are looking a bit pasty. You need to take care of yourself a bit more too.'

'Hah, I'll try. But someone's gotta do it all, Granny, the farm won't run itself.' Who on earth would get everything done if she took a back seat on it? There was no resting up for a good while yet, Rachel mused. But she knew Granny's heart was in the right place, and all she wanted was to see that Rachel was all right – even in her late seventies, Ruth's nurturing instinct was still strong.

'No, I suppose not. Now then, I made some cake yesterday, a banana loaf, would you like some, pet?'

'Oh yes, that sounds lovely. Oh . . . and before I forget I brought you some of our eggs. I'll quickly go fetch

them from the truck.' She and Jill always brought Ruth
a regular supply of their fresh farm eggs.

'Thank you. I bet you'll be needing more hens with
all the baking going on at the farm now.'

'We do, actually. I've got another dozen birds coming
this week, and I need to extend the hen house for them.'
Another job that was added to her never-ending list.
But, for now, it was nice to have a half hour of respite;
sitting with her granny, and nattering over some homemade cake and a cuppa.

Settled back in the front room shortly afterwards,
Granny asked, 'So, how's it all going with the farm developments?'

'Not bad, not bad. But we've had a bit of a hold-up
with the building work which is a bit frustrating.' She
explained about the delayed units and how the builders
had got on so far. With all the changes now happening
on the farm, Rachel felt a sense of sadness too in a way.
Ruth would understand better than most. 'I wish we
could have done something like this sooner, Granny.
That we'd thought of changing things back then . . .'

'I know, pet.' She sighed softly. 'But your dad was a
very private man. He kept things to himself and that was
how he tried to deal with it. You weren't to know then,
pet. None of us were.'

It weighed on Granny too, Rachel could see that. How
must it feel to lose a son, your child? Rachel couldn't
bear to even contemplate that . . . Maisy meant everything
to her. Rachel pulled herself back from that thought. It

didn't help to dwell on things too much. They had to look forward, not back.

'You're doing a grand job, pet. Your dad'd be proud of all that you're doing, I'm sure.'

Rachel felt a tear crowd her eye, and took a deep breath. 'Thanks, Granny.'

There was a moment of contemplation and quiet between them. Rachel looked at the photo of her dad and mum, there on the mantlepiece. It was from before she was born, and they looked so young, so happy.

'You'll have to come across soon, Granny, once the kitchen in the barn is done and see how it's all coming together,' Rachel offered.

'Oh yes, I'd like that. And if you ever need a little respite, even just a cup of tea and a chat like today, you know you're always welcome, pet.'

'Thank you.'

You never stopped being a granny or a mum or a daughter, never stopped caring about your family, whatever age you were, Rachel realised, holding onto that precious sense of love that filled this little cottage, and Ruth and Rachel's hearts.

Chapter 22

MEMORIES AND MUFFINS

Rachel was flicking through The Baking Bible trying to come up with some new inspirations ready to help out Jill once the Pantry was open, when she heard the rumble of a tractor coming up their track, two days later. She looked out of the kitchen window to see the vehicle stop at the field gate, where Tom leapt out to open it, making his way to the first of her hay fields.

'It's Tom,' she told her mum as she turned from the window.

'Ah, I guessed so. It's really good of him to help us out cutting the hay.'

'Yeah, he's been great, hasn't he?'

'A godsend. Right, well, I'm going to get on with making some more puddings.' Jill was humming along to the radio as she took out her ingredients. 'I'm thinking of trialling a selection of mini ones for our launch day actually,' she added as she began to sift some flour.

'Ooh, they sound good. So, we get to test out lots of them, a mouthful at a time. Perfect.'

She and Rachel had already discussed holding a launch party once the Pudding Pantry was ready, deciding that it was a must. A gathering of friends, family, their community and hopefully the local press – it'd be a fabulous way to publicise their opening and to thank everyone for their support.

Later that morning, Rachel decided to pop up to the hay field where Tom was working and take him some lunch as a thank you.

She made up some ham sandwiches in fresh white bread, along with a pork pie, a couple of apples, and two mini raspberry and dark chocolate muffins that Jill had baked that morning – now that she'd started up baking again, she was like a woman on a mission!

The field had already been cut and the grass was now being rowed up by the machine behind the tractor. It would dry further over the next few days ready for baling and would be ideal for keeping the sheep and cattle fed through the sparse winter months.

Rachel parked the quad at the top of the bank and waited for Tom to turn and come up the field towards her. The view from here was stunning out across the vivid green summer fields, the rolling hills, the gentle valley with its winding stream, towards an ultramarine glimpse of the North Sea on the horizon. The smell of cut grass was lush and strong. Tom spotted her, gave a quick wave from the cab of his tractor, and after completing two more rows he pulled the vehicle to a halt.

'Hey,' he called, as he climbed out. 'Everything okay?'

'Yeah fine, just thought I'd bring you some lunch; you'll need to keep your energy up.'

'That's music to my ears. My tummy's been rumbling for the last half hour. Did you hear it from the farmhouse or something?' He grinned. 'Just thought I'd keep cracking on though. Get the job done. But, now you're here . . .'

Rachel sat down on the grass verge, taking out the sandwiches from her rucksack. She'd made plenty and helped herself to one too.

Tom sat down beside her. 'Wow – this is just what I needed.' He took a hungry bite, then another. Rachel handed him a can of Pepsi too.

'Cheers, this is brilliant.'

'Just a bit of a thank you for stepping in with this job. It's given me some time to go and track down the tables and chairs we needed for the tearoom. I'm all sorted now, so that's great.'

Yes, she'd seen an ad in the local sales and wants, put in her bid for three sets that a local pub was trying to move on, and found another two in a house clearance – with a lick of paint they'd be perfect.

Tom looked up, taking in the vista before him. 'What a spot.'

'It's beautiful, isn't it.' She took a slow breath, remembering. 'I used to come up here to see Dad. Mum would bring him a picnic, when he was working up in these fields, that's what made me think of it. He used to do his own hay, back when the machinery was still in reasonable condition, when I was a little girl.' She smiled at the memory. Happier days.

Tom nodded empathetically. They were both quiet then for a few seconds.

'Thanks Tom, for doing this. I know you have all your own farm stuff to be getting on with. And, well, thanks for everything these past two years, you've been brilliant, really.' Rachel took a long, slow breath. All the emotions from that fateful day were still so heavy in her heart.

'No worries. I just want to see that you're all all right, you know, after everything . . . You, and your mum and Maisy, you've been through one hell of a time.'

Rachel felt a lump form in her throat.

'I'll pay you back properly, for all this, Tom.' They didn't have much money, but if she could ever give her time or lend a hand back, she'd do it in a heartbeat. At least she was going to do the baling for his two fields.

'I know you will.' His dark eyes were kind, his next words heartfelt: 'I saw what you went through, Rachel. No-one should have had to see what you did that day . . .'

Rachel found she couldn't speak. His words taking them back to that horrendous, life-changing moment.

'Da-ad?'

He'd been away for ages. Rachel had already driven across all their fields on the quad and still no sign of him. He'd missed supper now, and that was really unusual. She'd phoned Tom and Mr Mac next door to see if Dad had

had to go and help them out with anything, but they hadn't seen him all day.

Mum said they hadn't had a row or anything. She'd just mentioned that he'd been a bit quiet earlier, that was all, then he'd gone out, saying he was checking on what was left of their flock.

They'd had a nightmare a couple of weeks before, with heavy snows coming in early March. They'd lost forty of their pregnant ewes in the snowdrifts – the animals huddling for shelter against the hedgerows, exactly where the drifts had formed overnight. Dad had taken Simon with him that next morning and they'd tried to dig and pull them out, but many had already perished. Today, by contrast, was a fine spring day with the sun shining brightly – the weather belying its previous menace.

Mum was getting Maisy ready for bed in the farmhouse, so Rachel had offered to go out and have another look. It was seven o'clock and daylight was clinging on. Dad might just be caught up on a job that had taken longer in a further corner of the farm, or maybe he'd found one of their animals in trouble. Perhaps he'd even gone to the vets? And where was Moss, come to think of it? Oh well, she'd find them both soon enough.

She'd already checked in the lambing shed. She'd even looked in the old stone barn, and no sign of him. One place she hadn't been in yet was the old stable next to that, but no-one ever went in there nowadays. It was rarely used, only for storage, not since her childhood pony had passed away several years ago now.

But it was worth a peek in. Then, she heard Moss, and his bark had an unusual strain to it, like he was distressed. He was there in his kennel. Dad must have shut him in earlier. Strange, as they usually went everywhere together. Rachel let him out.

The dog ran to the old stable door, scratching frantically at the earth and stones beneath it, trying to get in. Her hackles rose. 'It's okay, Moss. It's okay,' she said soothingly, trying to ignore the cold feeling creeping down her spine.

The bolt was already undone. The wooden door heavy as she dragged it open.

'Da-ad?' She felt a prickle of fear.

Light shafted in through the open door, and that was when her world and everything in it came tumbling down.

'Dad. No!' she cried out. 'No . . . no . . . . no.' The shout reducing to a murmur – she didn't want Mum and Maisy to hear and come running across. There was no way they could see this.

She ran towards him. Couldn't reach him other than his feet at first. Tried and failed to prop them up. Saw the stool, discarded. Had he kicked it away in that moment of utter desperation? There might still be a chance. There had to be. If she could get on the stool. Hold him up. She felt dizzy with fear but knew she had to focus.

Fuck, fuck, fuck. This was real. She needed to act quickly. She got the stool back in place, climbed up and with all her strength lifted, then held onto him. Her father, who'd hanged himself from the rafters of the stable.

His body felt stiff, so heavy, there was no give or warmth in it. She knew she needed help desperately but there was no way Mum and Maisy could witness this. With one arm still wrapped around her father's legs she fumbled for her phone, somehow managing to call Tom.

He had come straight away. Helped her bring her father down. Stayed with her until the ambulance came.

Too late. They had all been too late.

Back in the hay field, Rachel felt herself shiver despite the glow of the summer sun. Tom put a reassuring arm around her. She leant in, finding herself resting her head against his chest, grateful for his warmth, his comfort. In that instant something shifted; this physicality between them, this sense of need, togetherness, it felt far more than simple friendship. Under his cotton T-shirt, which was soft against her face, she could hear the steady beat of his heart. The sensation reassuring and unnerving all at once.

It was because she was upset, she told herself, nothing more. There'd never been *that* kind of attraction between them. Let her girlfriends, Eve and Charlotte, have their fantasies on that front. Rachel pushed these weird feelings aside, sitting upright, telling herself they were inappropriate, misdirected, the results of her heightened emotions, their shared grief. Tom was a friend, a neighbour who'd been a great help, that was all.

But as she raised her head, he gave her a look, just for a second or two, that held so many emotions. Was he feeling something too?

Her eyes connected with his, but then confusion and fear descended. 'Ah, I'd better be getting back,' she spluttered. She was already rising to her feet. 'I'll leave you with the packed lunch. It'll keep you going for later.'

He looked somewhat surprised at her haste to get away, at the sudden change in the atmosphere. 'Okay, well . . . The lunch has been great. Thanks for bringing it across. Take care, Rachel.'

'Will do. Catch you soon.'

She was on the quad and driving away before her emotions could take any more crazy turns. She didn't know quite what was going on, but it could damn well stop before it started. Life was confusing enough as it was.

Chapter 23

A PUDDING PICNIC

The sun was warm on their backs as Rachel and Maisy knelt at the strawberry patch in the farmhouse garden. They were busy picking the now ripe, juicy sweet berries. The smell and taste of them was like candyfloss on their fingers. Maisy was eating as many as went into the punnet, Rachel noticed with a smile, taking in her little girl's red-stained lips.

As a respite from the building noise and the hot early-July weather – yes, the builders were back, just on a slightly later track, phew! – Rachel had promised Maisy a picnic after school, down by the stream that ran through their farmland. There was an amazing pool you could paddle in across into Tom's land, and he'd said in the past that he didn't mind them going there.

Back in the farm's kitchen, the picnic basket was soon loaded up with ham sandwiches, hard-boiled eggs from their hens, tomatoes from Jim's greenhouse (he'd dropped off a bag, after telling Rachel during the taxi trip home the other night that he had lots ripening up), and, of course, an assortment of cakes and puddings. Jill's latest trials were mini meringues that she thought might go well for the launch day and lemon drizzle cupcakes. Rachel, who knew she'd need to step up to the mark to assist with the Pudding Pantry supplies, had made some chocolate-honeycomb traybakes. All would go equally well with their loaded punnets of strawberries and raspberries.

They set off in the Land Rover, bumping across the fields, to park up in the low meadow, with its comforting smell of warm hay that was drying in the sun. A verge that had been left untouched was filled with deep-blue, wild cornflowers and a splash of red poppies that swayed between the pale-gold shafts of grass in a gentle breeze.

Maisy skipped down from the vehicle with Moss leaping eagerly behind her. Jill set out a tartan rug beside the stream. Moss was soon entertaining himself sniffing around the field and then playing chase-the-ball in the water, splashing them as he bounded in and out, much to Maisy's delight. With her swimming costume on and her school clothes discarded, she was soon in the water too. The stream was shallow at this time of year, with just a few slippery stones to beware of. Every now and then there was a flash of a silvery brown minnow in the waters. Rachel dipped her bare toes in and leaned back on the soft grass of the riverbank, enjoying the warmth of the sun on her face – until Moss took to shaking off icy cold droplets right next to her, that was.

'Aw, Mo-oss!'

Jill couldn't help but laugh. 'Right, picnic time,' she announced. 'Come on out of the water, Maisy. I've got a cosy towel here ready for you.'

Maisy was a little shivery as she came out the stream – the waters from the hills were cool and fresh even in summer – but she was soon wrapped up in a big fluffy beach towel.

'Look, Grandma. Look over the other side, where it's all green and shady. I think there might be a secret fairy glen there, like in my story.'

'Hmm, yes, maybe you're right.'

It did in fact look rather mystical. A small tree had uprooted on the opposite bank, and in the space between its bare and twisted roots were ferns and patches of moss, and clusters of stones that caught the light from the stream.

'You can make wishes at fairy glens,' said Maisy authoritatively.

'Oh, I see. They must be special places then,' said Rachel.

'Of course they are. You can't always see the fairies, but they're there.'

Who was to argue with the imagination of a five-year-old, spurred on by a world of magical storybooks?

Maisy sat down on the rug, her bare toes peeping out from the big towel that was wrapped around her. 'Ooh, can I have cake?' The little girl was as quick as a whip and was about to plunge her hand into the Tupperware box of lemon cupcakes.

'A sandwich first, and then you can,' said Rachel.

Maisy took the sandwich somewhat grudgingly, but was soon tucking in happily, hungry after her day at school and splash in the stream. Moss lay beside her on the rug, watching patiently, waiting for any crumbs to drop.

This was so nice, the three of them together, spending a little time out on a summer's afternoon in the sun. Time to take a pause, to breathe in the fresh Northumberland air, and enjoy the here and now. It was a rare treat with the farm always busy and their business plans in motion. The food was good, and life seemed good too just now, Rachel realised with a sense of calm relief, like the future was finally looking up for them.

Rachel batted away a wasp, and then enjoyed one of Jill's moist and zingy lemon cupcakes along with a refreshing glass of lemonade.

'Only a week to go until we open, Mum. It's crept up quickly.'

'I know, it's hard to believe it's really happening. I've got so much baking to do in the next few days. No point starting too soon though, as it needs to be nice and fresh.'

'I'll help with some of the cooking too, of course . . . for the launch party and the opening. I can do a couple of my white chocolate cheesecakes and my carrot cake is usually pretty acceptable. I could make a big one for the launch event, if you like.'

'Oh yes, thank you. I'll stick with making my traditional puds, and all the mini items for the party. Oh, and I must make a pavlova for opening day too.'

'By the way, Eve's working on a sign for us to go at the farm's front gate and also one for above the barn door. We thought a deep-grey wooden plaque with looped white writing might work well. What do you think?'

'That sounds like just the ticket.'

'She's coming around tomorrow too, to help me paint the teashop furniture white. We're hoping for a nice dry day to get it all done outside.' Eve was almost as excited as they were about the Pantry's opening, and despite being busy herself, she wanted to help out where she could.

'Mu-um,' Maisy piped up, 'Moss is back in the river, can I go play with him?'

'Have you had enough to eat?' Rachel asked.

'Yep.'

'Okay then.'

There was no stopping her whirlwind of a five-year-old. It was lovely to see her having fun. Sometimes Rachel wondered if she did enough for her little girl; it often felt that Maisy had to just muck in alongside what they had to do on the farm, and they didn't have a lot of money for expensive trips out. Life was so busy, it felt like a juggling act at the best of times.

Suddenly, there was a droning sound coming from across the fields – it sounded like a quad. Then, there was a creak of the field's wooden gate and Tom appeared. He pulled up beside their picnic area with a grin.

'Hello, there. I thought I heard some festivities going on over here.'

'Hah, Moss barking and Maisy squealing, I expect,' Rachel said. She looked up at Tom, suddenly remembering how close they'd been in the hay field just a few days ago, how his arms had felt around her. It gave her a strange feeling she couldn't quite pin down.

'Hi, Tom,' said her mum.

'Hello, Jill.'

Then Maisy, who was splashing happily away in the stream, called out, 'Tom!' and came dashing out.

'Well, this looks fun.' He took in the picnic scene, and wasn't put off by a cold, wet five-year-old appearing by his knee for a cuddle, closely followed by a very damp border collie. 'Hey, Moss. Hi, Maisy.'

His Jack Russell terrier, Mabel, then leapt off the quad to join in the fun and ran in circles around the three of them.

'Oh, I hope you don't mind us being here. We are technically trespassing,' Rachel said. The best section of stream to paddle in was here on Tom's land.

'Of course not, it's great. You're not hurting anything. Well, maybe the odd minnow, but I can live with that.'

'Would you like something to eat or drink, Tom?' Jill offered. 'If you're thirsty there's some homemade lemonade.'

'Now that does sound tempting. It's such a warm day, I'm parched.' He was in T-shirt and jeans, his forearms tanned.

Jill poured some out into a plastic cup. 'Here.'

He gulped it down quickly. Rachel noticed that there were little beads of liquid left on his top lip which he wiped off.

'There are cupcakes,' Rachel added, knowing his sweet tooth.

'Now you're talking. How can I say no?'

Jill passed him one of the lemon cakes from the Tupperware box and he took a bite.

'Delish. So, how are all the final plans going for your Pudding Pantry?'

'Good. We're nearly there, aren't we, Mum?'

'Yes, getting there now, thank heavens. We open formally to the public on Friday next week, with a launch party first on the Thursday afternoon. We have a proper invite for you at home, but it's from 2 p.m. You must come along,' said Jill.

'Oh yes, we'd love to see you there,' said Rachel with a warm smile. 'There will, of course, be pudding.'

'I'd love to, wouldn't miss it for the world. It'll be good to see what you've done with the old barn too. Well, I'd better crack on, I suppose. I was on my way to check the cattle.'

'Ah, no rest for the wicked,' said Jill.

'That's farming for you. Well, enjoy the rest of your picnic. And like I say, you can come here any time, I really don't mind. Nice to hear some laughter about the place.'

Rachel caught his eye. She suddenly thought how his home life must be so quiet, perhaps a touch lonely. A man in his thirties all on his own. Yes, she was single, but life was never really lonely what with her mum and Maisy constantly around.

She smiled at him, again remembering that recent moment of closeness. She quickly dismissed the thought.

'Well, best of luck with the barn and the Pudding Pantry. If I can help at all, just give me a shout.'

'Thanks.'

'Bye, Maisy. Have fun!' he called across.

'I am . . . but sshh!' She put her forefinger to her lips pointedly. 'I'm looking for the fairies' grotto. I think we might have frightened them away. Moss keeps splashing and barking.'

'Ah, okay. I'll drive away slowly, so the quad's not too noisy then.'

'Good.'

'Come on then, Mabel. Up.' With that the terrier bounded back on the quad behind him. 'Bye, all.'

'Bye, Tom.'

After an idyllic picnic and rare evening off, Rachel and Jill knew they had to refocus and get back to preparing for their big opening. There was still an awful lot to do. Yet, the next morning, with only a couple of days' work left, there was no sign of the builders. Their white Transit van, which had again become a fixture in the yard, was worryingly missing. All was quiet. Too quiet.

Rachel tried ringing Ian's mobile, which was the only contact number she had, to see what was happening.

They were usually there on the farm by 8:30 a.m. – neither of them had mentioned that they might be late for any reason. They had put in half the kitchen units but they still had the main area to finish off and the barn doors to replace with a window arch and a smaller entrance door to give more light.

Finally, a call came in at 9:50 a.m. 'Hi, it's Ian. Sorry pet, but we can't make it today. We're down at Alnwick. We started this job while we were waiting for your cabinets, and now the tiles they have chosen are in, they need it finished off. It'll just take a day. We've promised the customer.'

What about this bloody customer? Rachel thought with frustration. 'But won't that delay the job here? We're on a tight enough schedule as it is, and I was just about to put out a flyer and some posters around the town to advertise for the opening launch on Thursday of next week.'

'Aye, well, we'll be back with you by tomorrow lunchtime.'

'*Lunchtime?*' It got worse.

'Aye, don't fret. We'll be finished by next Thursday for you.'

'Hmm.' Rachel wasn't convinced and gave a sigh. 'Well, don't tell me that means you'll be clearing out on the Wednesday night, as we've a hell of a lot of setting up to do.'

'No worries. It'll all work out grand, pet.'

He sounded far too laid-back about it all for Rachel's

liking. Grrrr. All she could do was focus on her own tasks, and pray they kept their word.

Damn, the bloomin' lawnmower was broken now and she was so near to finishing the front gate area too. She needed to keep it tidy, ready for opening. It had chugged to a halt, there was still fuel in it, but she'd pulled the cord several times and it still wasn't restarting. Hmm, Tom might have one. She decided to quickly pop around to his farm to see. That way she might still get the job done before she finished for the evening.

It was a warm sultry afternoon; the dry spell was continuing. She jumped on the quad, drove down the lane and was soon pulling up outside Tom's house. It looked like he was about as his truck and the quad were parked outside. As she got closer to the farmhouse, she heard a 'thwack' that sounded like it was coming from around the back. She'd head there first. The chances were that Tom was working outside, given the glorious sunshine.

She went in through the little gate and followed the path in and around the side of the house. As she turned the corner, the cause of the thwacking was apparent . . . *very* apparent. In fact, it stopped her right in her tracks. There Tom was, chopping logs. His arm raised in the air, bicep bulging, with a small axe in his hand ready to swoop down. His shirt was off and his lean muscular torso bared in all its rather manly glory. There was a glisten of sweat across his chest.

'*Oh my*,' she breathed. She'd never really imagined what might lie beneath those shirts and T-shirts. Tom's chest was paler than his arms with the typical farmer T-shirt tan, which made her smile to herself. But it all looked very good, very good indeed. She gulped, quickly tearing her eyes away, aware of how badly she was ogling him.

Tom hadn't yet spotted her, being focused on his task.

Should she call his name? Interrupt him? But she had a feeling she was blushing furiously already, and she didn't want him to lose concentration and make a mistake with the axe. Mind you, she had *totally* lost concentration herself. She wasn't even sure if her voice would work properly at this point.

She decided to give herself just one more second to stay and take in the view. She'd then head back to the quad and let him finish the job. Yes, she'd just have to come back again in the morning and finish that mowing tomorrow. It wouldn't hurt really. She didn't think she could set back to work now as it was. Her legs felt oddly jelly-like.

Okay, that was it, enough girl, turn around, retreat!

She felt slightly dazed as she got back to the quad and sat down. Should she just wait a few minutes at the front of his house, then go back, do a re-take and pretend all was fine? She could shout out as she neared the house corner to give him a bit of warning, but then she'd have to try and talk normally whilst facing him, all bare-chested and tanned.

She drove back to Primrose Farm on autopilot – part of her trying not to dwell on the scene she'd just witnessed, telling herself that her reaction was just physical, that was all. God knows she'd been alone and detached for such a long time. Yet, the other half of her was *totally* wanting to re-live the moment and picture the scene in all its fine detail.

Well, she didn't see that one coming. But, she couldn't afford to lose sight of the road ahead – she desperately needed to concentrate on the new business, her mum, Maisy . . . no, this distraction – whatever it was – wouldn't do at all . . .

Chapter 24

PUDDINGS GALORE

A Sunday afternoon brainstorming session was in full flow at Primrose Farm.

Rachel, Jill, Granny Ruth, and Eve were gathered around the kitchen table, with The Baking Bible laid out open in front of them, mugs of coffee to hand and choc-dipped flapjacks on a plate within reach of all (essential brain fuel). Even Maisy and Amelia had decided to forego the garden and slide for a while to join in the important discussion that was taking place. *What should go on the Pudding Pantry menu?*

All ages were represented, and the ideas were flowing fast.

'There has to be the two stalwarts we have already at the Kirkton Deli, so sticky toffee pudding and chocolate pudding,' Jill said.

'Yes, agreed,' Rachel backed her up.

'So, what other all-time favourites do we need?' Jill asked. She was happy to try some new things as well as pitch her own ideas.

Eve added, 'I love a lemon pudding.'

'Great, I know a good one of Delia's, Canary Pudding. That'd be nice, especially in the summer months,' Jill said.

'And then other desserts?' Rachel prompted. 'Puddings don't just have to be sponge puddings as such. What about a banoffee pie or a gorgeous cheesecake or something?'

'Ooh yes, remember we chatted about that a few weeks ago, you make that gorgeous raspberry and white chocolate cheesecake, Rachel. And, what about a pavlova with strawberries and cream?' Eve was on a roll. In virtual pudding heaven in fact.

'Absolutely, pavlova was something I'd already been thinking of. I'd like to have some variety too, and the chance to keep creating new things. So maybe we could have a Pudding of the Week, like a special?' said Jill.

'Oh yes. Brilliant idea, Mum.'

'And what about a taster plate or something?' Eve asked. 'I can never decide which I want, as they are all so fab.'

'A trio of puddings, then,' Rachel suggested.

'Well, I'm already making mini puddings for the launch party. We could have a selection of those.'

'Cupcakes!' shouted Maisy. Her all-time favourites.

'With pretty flowers on,' added Amelia.

'Like sugar-paste ones, Amelia? Ones you can eat?' Jill asked.

'Yes, those ones.' The little girl was beaming, happy to have joined in.

'Great idea, girls.'

'And other cakes, of course. You can't beat a well-made Victoria sponge with jam and fresh cream,' said Granny Ruth.

'Moist yummy carrot cake,' added Eve.

'Coffee and walnut, too,' said Jill. 'Again, we can vary the cake options weekly.'

'And we need to make sure we cater for gluten free, so there'll always be an option for that,' suggested Rachel. 'I know Kirsty's little girl at school is coeliac, she always has real trouble with menus out. It'd be nice for her and others with allergies to still be able to come out for a treat.'

'That's a great idea. I can research some nice recipes, and source some gluten-free flour.'

'We need something traditional too,' Granny Ruth added. 'Proper old-fashioned puddings like jam roly-poly or a spotted dick. We used to love them back in the day. With lashings of thick creamy custard.'

Rachel and Jill burst into laughter at that point. 'Hah, we were meaning to ask you, look at this . . .' Rachel leafed through the pages of The Baking Bible to find Dad's naughty scribble on the spotted dick page.

Granny peered closer with her reading glasses poised. 'Ah yes, that was your dad all right, the little monkey. Thought it was the funniest thing ever.'

Maisy peered at the page too. 'Why?'

Oh my, who was going to tell a five-year-old what a 'dick' meant? Awkward moment alert.

215

Eve gave Rachel a cross-eyed look, trying so hard not to laugh.

'Just Grandad being a naughty boy, writing on Granny's recipe sheet, and spoiling it.' Well, it was mostly the truth.

The girls giggled innocently, with Maisy shouting out, 'Ice creams', whilst pretending to lick her lips.

'Oh yes, we can use the local Doddington's Dairy ones,' Jill replied. 'And pair the best flavours with the puddings.'

'Keeping it local is such a good idea, Mum, yes,' Rachel agreed. 'I think we need something savoury on the menu too, so people can have a lunch or brunch option. Not *too* many choices, as we obviously want the puddings to be the stars. But say some nice local ham sandwiches, and chutney with Northumberland cheeses, or we could use our own eggs from the farm for Eggs Benedict. People love the home-grown touch.'

'Or smoked salmon from the Tweed with Primrose Farm scrambled eggs on toast,' Eve added. 'That'd be delicious, and keeping it local is an excellent idea. It supports our area and it's what holiday makers want to taste.'

'We can use local bread from the Kirkton Bakery too,' said Jill.

'Absolutely. I'm loving all this already. The menu's going to be amazing,' enthused Rachel.

A little while later, when the flow of ideas was beginning to wane, and the flapjacks were being passed around for the second time, there was a knock on the farmhouse door.

Rachel went to answer it. 'Oh . . . Tom, hi.'

'Just dropping off that push mower you needed.'

'Ah, right, thanks.' Rachel found herself blushing. She had finally gathered her nerve the next day after that *Poldark* moment, and had gone back to find Tom fully clothed in a boiler suit and treating a sheep with flystrike for maggots. That scenario was far easier to handle, though she hadn't quite forgotten the image from the previous day – *still hadn't*, in fact.

'Oh . . . well, that's great. Ah . . . umm . . .'

'You okay?'

'Yes, fine.' Her words were clipped; she was aware of trying way too hard to sound normal. 'Yep, come on in for a second. We've quite a gathering here actually.'

'Hi all.' Tom poked his head into the kitchen. 'So, what's all this in aid of?'

'We're having brainstorms,' Maisy announced seriously.

'For the Pudding Pantry menu,' Jill explained further.

'But we don't have any boy ideas yet, do we Mummy? Can Tom join in?'

'I don't see why not. That's actually a great idea, Maisy. You can be the token male, Tom. As well as Moss.' Rachel added, smiling, 'Who has already advised that he'd be happy to eat the lot.'

'Mummy, don't be so silly, Moss can't talk . . .' Maisy crossed her arms, whilst shaking her head.

Rachel laughed. 'So, erm, would you like a coffee, Tom? I mean, I don't want to keep you . . . you're probably busy . . .'

'No, that would be great, I can stay a little while.' He pulled out the last chair. 'I'll get my thinking cap on. Hmm, what would I like to eat at your delicious Pudding Pantry? Obviously, that amazing sticky toffee one.'

'That was the first pud mentioned,' Jill responded.

'Ah, okay, what else have we got so far then?'

Jill read out the list.

'I'd devour all of that, no questions asked.'

'Not all in one go?' Maisy asked, astounded.

'No, maybe in two though.' Tom winked.

'He sounds like Moss then,' Eve laughed. 'It's definitely a male thing.'

'Right, there must be something else.' Tom rubbed his chin as he was thinking. 'Oh yes, what about a crumble of some kind?'

Eve caught Rachel's eye and couldn't help but snigger. Rachel felt herself blush, and gave her friend a small kick under the table.

'Of course, how did we miss that off?' Jill said. 'That's great, we could do different flavours depending on what's in season. Yes, there could be apple and blackberry, a warming winter cinnamon apple and in summertime, rhubarb or apple and raspberry.' Jill's creative flair was flowing now.

'With cream, custard or ice cream,' Rachel suggested.

'Or what about all three on top?' Tom grinned greedily.

'Sounds good to me. Delicious,' Eve agreed, with a cheeky smile.

'We're planning on having a few savoury options too.

Any ideas?' Rachel prompted, realising that it'd be good to get the male perspective. 'We're thinking more of light bites really.'

'Tell you what, after an early start on the farm, I'd love to call in for a bacon sarnie for elevenses.'

'That's it. We could use the home-cured bacon from Glendale Farm, on thick slices of Kirkton Bakery fresh bread. Wow, I think we're nearly there.' Rachel sounded animated. 'I can type all this up on a Word doc, once we've set the prices, and then print it off on some nice cream-coloured card. One for each table and another for the counter top.'

'Right then, I'd call that a success. Anyone for more flapjack?' Jill passed the plate around. 'I'd better get myself baking again soon then, I'm going to be busy.'

Rachel smiled across at her mum. She could tell Jill was excited at the prospect of opening the Pudding Pantry and it was lovely to see. There was a spring in her step and a brightness in her smile that hadn't been there for such a long while. It was brilliant that their family and friends were involved too, here around the table at the start of something special. Her wonderful support group was there rooting for her and Jill, straight from the off, and Rachel felt blessed to have them – her lovely Pudding Pantry team!

Chapter 25

PUDDING PREPARATIONS

Invites had been sent and flyers posted around Kirkton village. Friday the 12th July was officially going to be the big day for opening, with the launch for the local community the day before. It was all hands on deck getting the Pudding Pantry ready. They'd be a little pushed to have it all done in time, but they didn't want to delay any further and miss the peak summer trading weeks.

It was now Wednesday, oh yes, the day before the launch, and the builders were still in situ in the barn, much to Rachel's concern. They'd said it would only take a few hours but they had a few final tasks to tick off.

Jill was busy baking an army's worth of food in the farmhouse kitchen. 'So, I'm making brownies this afternoon and first thing tomorrow morning I've got to finish off all the mini puds and meringues. I've also got some mini cake moulds to make individual Victoria sponges for the launch party too – they'll look lovely with a swirl of fresh cream and a strawberry on the top, don't you think?'

Rachel noticed that Jill was talking at a thousand miles

an hour. She had a dab of flour on her cheek and big streaks of chocolate sauce on her apron, which looked a little skew-whiff.

'Oh yes, they'll look very summery. Are you okay, Mum? You've been running around like a whirling dervish! And I've never seen someone mix so quickly – you'll be setting a world record soon enough.'

'Oh I'm grand, don't worry, I'm well and truly in the baking zone!'

'Well, as long as you're giving yourself little breaks. Oh, and I do hope the weather holds, Mum. How many are coming now?' Rachel asked.

'It *was* going to be a small gathering but I think it's growing by the day,' Jill said, smiling as though she really didn't mind.

'Oh well, it'll be good for promotion, and you do seem to be baking enough for the whole village.'

'Hah, probably, I can't help myself. There's at least twenty or so definites that I know of, and then we put a general flyer out, didn't we, so who knows who else might decide to turn up. So, there's Brenda from the Deli with her husband, the journalist lady from the Alnwick newspaper, plus that chap from the tourist information, a few of our farming friends, Jan, oh and I've asked Tom's parents, saw them in the Co-op yesterday, then there's Eve and family, Charlotte and her Sam, the two builder chaps . . . I asked them earlier this morning, said they'd love to come.' Mum had started to tally up the numbers on her fingers, but she'd run out of digits.

'And I mentioned it to a couple of the mums from school who said they'd pop along . . . oh, plus Tom, of course,' Rachel added. 'And I imagine Granny Ruth's coming over?'

'Of course, she wouldn't want to miss out on something like this. Crikey, that's probably well over twenty already, isn't it? Hmm,' Jill confessed, 'I think I may have also mentioned it at the last Kirkton WI meeting too – a sort of open invitation.'

'Mu-um.'

'It'll be fine, the more the merrier. It'll spread the word about the Pudding Pantry and that's what we want, isn't it?'

Gosh, it was going to end up costing them quite a bit, but if it got into the local press as a feature, then that would really help publicity and hopefully increase interest in the coming weeks anyhow.

And you know what, it *was* something to celebrate! They'd put in two of the hardest and saddest years of their lives. This was a new start, a new venture and finally something to be positive about.

Despite the earlier assurances of the builders, it was five past five on the Wednesday evening when Ian and Dan put a final rub of Dutch Oil over the Pudding Pantry's new oak counter top, packed up their tools in the barn, and put their equipment away in their white Transit van. They knocked on the farmhouse door for a quick farewell chat with a slightly disgruntled Rachel and Jill, who were desperate to get into the barn and start setting things up.

'That's it all done,' said Ian.

'Nothing like taking us to the wire, chaps,' Rachel commented wryly, but with good humour.

'Come across and take a look then, before we head off. We want to be sure it's all as it should be.'

Rachel had been popping in throughout the day, but with all the tools, dustsheets and gear around them it was hard to gauge the finished job. As she walked in, along with Maisy and Jill, her mouth dropped. It was like time stood still for a few seconds as they looked about them. The Pudding Pantry was a reality, with its old stone walls all repointed and a warm-honey colour under the soft lighting, its kitchen area with the new white and grey tiles above the cooker and the glass refrigerated counter that Jill had sourced at a bargain price from an auction up in Berwick-upon-Tweed, next to the oak counter top.

Wow, look, they'd even moved the seating and furniture back in from the shed, where they'd been since she and Eve had painted them white, as well as the two dressers – one of which had been donated by Granny Ruth, who said it was just gathering dust in her cottage.

'Oh my goodness. It's just as I hoped. *No* . . . it's even better.' Rachel had tears in her eyes, as she brushed a hand over the counter top, imagining the puddings and cakes up there in all their glory.

'It's fabulous,' said Jill. 'Thank you.'

'Whoop whoop!' Maisy went dashing around, spreading her arms out like an aeroplane. 'Now, it's *better* than my party day. Can I have another party in here, Mummy?'

'Well, we've got a party for everyone here tomorrow, petal.'

'Oh, yes. Yippee!'

'Thank you so much.' Rachel went across to Ian and Dan to shake their hands warmly. 'You've made our dream a reality.'

'You're most welcome, ladies. It's been a delight working for you, though my waistline has suffered terribly,' Ian jested. 'And we wish you the best of luck with the new venture.'

'You are coming tomorrow, aren't you? To join in with the launch?' Jill asked.

'It'd be great if you can,' confirmed Rachel.

'We'll be starting another job, but it's local.' Ian looked at Dan who nodded. 'But yes, we'll call in at some point for sure. There might be room for one last brownie.' He patted his tummy as he gave a grin.

'That's great. Thank you again.' Jill was beaming.

'Well then, we'll leave you in peace, ladies.'

'Yes, there's plenty for us to be getting on with.'

There was indeed – tonight was going to be all hands on deck!

After a quick supper of bacon and eggs, Rachel and Jill set to it, cleaning and ferrying everything to the barn like their lives depended on it.

After popping Maisy to bed, Rachel came downstairs

to find Jill back in the farm's kitchen baking like a Trojan, fearing that the guest numbers might expand and they'd run out of puddings for the taster plates. (The things most likely to expand, Rachel mused, were the guests' stomachs, but better too much than too little.)

It was past eleven o'clock when Jill took the last tray of bakes out of the oven. She turned to Rachel, 'Do you think there'll be enough, love?' She looked tired and anxious, bless her.

'Mum, it's okay, you've done enough. More than enough,' and Rachel meant everything – not just the baking in these past few months – as she looked proudly across at her brave mother who'd rallied and pulled herself from the depths of her despair.

The two of them looked around the kitchen at the cakes and bakes and puddings all lined up in mouth-watering rows, and there were even more in the fridge threatening a landslide when the fridge door opened.

'Mum, if a whole army turned up tomorrow, they'd all be well fed.'

'Time for bed then, love, hey. We've a busy day ahead.'

'Yes, I think so. Sweet dreams, Mum.'

'You too.'

And they gave each other a heartfelt hug, holding on just a little longer than their usual goodnight.

'Love you, Mum.'

'You too, pet.' Jill gave an emotional sniff.

Tomorrow they'd put the final touches to the Pudding

Pantry. It would need to look its best to showcase to the world.

Lying in her bed soon after, telling her busy brain to switch off and get some much-needed sleep, Rachel's thoughts turned to her dad. She hoped he'd have given his backing for all the changes they were making here at the farm. Of course, she'd never know for sure, but she remembered how he taught her to be brave and bold, to be hard-working, and to be kind. And in her heart, she sensed he'd be cheering them on.

Chapter 26

A PROPER PUDDING PARTY

How do you launch a Pudding Pantry? With puddings of course! In fact, puddings, Pimm's and prosecco! It was summer, after all.

The most delightful selection of mini puddings were ready, laid out on blue-and-white china platters, in the barn's kitchen. There were mini sticky toffee and chocolate, there were mini pavlovas each with a blob of fresh cream and a raspberry on, the strawberry Victoria sponges, squares of moist dark chocolate brownies, some lemon drizzle cupcakes and still-warm slices of jam roly-poly pudding that Granny Ruth had made. She had also made some cheese-and-chive scones as a savoury option. Rachel had baked a large rectangular carrot cake and cut it into small squares to help out. There was probably enough to feed a sweet-toothed army – good thing considering they had at least thirty confirmed guests.

Maisy and Amelia were ready to help out as waitresses with their pinafores on – though Rachel feared somewhat for the plates and treats as Maisy could be a little accident-prone. But still, it was nice they wanted to be a part of it.

Eve was a star and had helped out all morning, setting out the wooden spoon table numbers in old-fashioned milk bottles, and her craft goodies were all ready for display on the two wooden dressers. The shelves of cute soft-toy animals, children's knits, wooden pastel-shaded hearts, stars, plaques with cute and quirky sayings and mini dried-flower bouquets looked rather wonderful. They had also scaled ladders to hang up Eve's pretty handmade bunting with its floral and polka-dot soft-green print.

On a quick coffee break earlier, she'd given Rachel and Jill a beautiful wall plaque that she'd crafted herself, as a surprise. It said, 'Welcome to the Pudding Pantry' in gorgeous white italics. It was such a thoughtful gift, and it had brought tears to Rachel's eyes as she unwrapped it from the tissue paper. In fact, it had been a bit of a teary morning all round.

With just ten minutes to go, Rachel rushed back into the barn, carrying paper napkins and plates. She stopped and looked around, taking in the transformation. There it was again, that lump in her throat. How much they had managed to achieve in such a short space of time, despite the odd hiccup along the way. The kitchen in the barn was ready for action with its pudding platters all lined up, and the newly made wooden counter looked warm and welcoming, ready for its customers. On the side, the mix-and-match selection of crockery was all set out ready for teas and coffee for their guests.

Out in the sitting area were the white-painted tables and chairs, and on every table were posies of sweet peas from their kitchen garden in pretty jam jars. The bunting was strewn along the walls with its floral and spotted flags. Rachel hadn't got her dream chandeliers yet, as funds were too tight, so there were just plain lightbulbs from the ceiling for now, but a selection of lampstands brought across from the farmhouse worked well. And with the lovely arched window built around the barn door, there was plenty of natural light anyhow.

Rachel took a deep breath. This was it, they were as ready as they could be. They had given it all they had to get the Pantry ready on time.

Jill walked in and stood behind Rachel, placing a hand on her shoulder. 'It looks wonderful, doesn't it? You've done so well, love.'

'*We've* done so well, Mum,' Rachel corrected her.

They shared a heartfelt moment – full of joy, pride, and a sense of achievement in all that they'd strived to do. And they knew they were both thinking of Dad right then. Neither voiced this, as they needed to hold it together. And then, beyond today, they knew they had to make this work as a business.

Neither Rachel nor Jill was able to speak for a few seconds, as they stood gazing at the completed barn.

The sound of a vehicle rolling up outside jerked them

back to the present. In through the barn door came Tom and, oh . . . he was carrying the most beautiful bouquet of flowers.

'Just the ladies I'm looking for,' he beamed. 'Congratulations.' He passed the bouquet to Jill. 'For you both.'

'Oh Tom, they're beautiful,' Jill said, beaming.

'Thank you so much,' added Rachel, finding that she couldn't quite meet his eye. 'And I know just the spot where they can go. Just there on the counter top, don't you think, Mum?'

'Oh yes. Pride of place. Thank you, Tom. That's so very kind.'

'Well, it's an important day. How's it all going? Ready for the off?'

'I think so,' answered Jill. 'It's all a bit nerve-wracking, but we've done all we can, haven't we pet? I'll just go pop these in a vase.'

Tom looked around at the new interior. 'Wow, you've done a great job here. So, how many have you got coming?'

'Well, we think about thirty, though Mum's been a bit free and easy with her invites so that's a ballpark figure. We'll see.'

'Can I help with anything?' Tom offered.

'Um, I think we're about there. But perhaps you could keep an eye that everyone's glasses are topped up once we're up and running. There's prosecco and Eve's making Pimm's over in the farm kitchen, so there will be a spare jug left made up in there. Just in case I get caught up chatting or something.'

'Yeah, that's fine, no worries. I'll be chief Pimm's pourer. I've had much worse jobs in my time.'

'Hah, I bet you have.' Farming was renowned for being a messy business.

Maisy came running in then. 'Tom, I'm chief waitress. I've got an apron and everything and Amelia is my helper. Can I start yet, Mummy? Can I have the cakes to carry?'

'We'll just wait a few more minutes, Maisy, until some other guests get here. If Tom doesn't mind, that is?'

'I suppose I'll just have to wait.' He pulled a face, pretending to be upset. 'No, that's fine. We'd better hang on Maisy, and do as we're told.' He winked. 'That's a very pretty dress, by the way,' he added.

'Thanks, Tom!' she said, performing a curtsy like a princess. She skipped off again with Moss and Amelia in her wake to find some other important party mission to help with.

Jill came back with the flowers in a glass vase and stood them on the oak counter top. They looked gorgeous there. The final touch.

Rachel's gut felt tight with tension as the first guests started to arrive. Eve brought out a large tray of Pimm's. She wasn't chancing the girls carrying those, even though Maisy and Amelia were clearly taking their serving role very seriously, balancing the pudding platters with expressions of deep concentration on their faces as they walked slowly between the guests.

The sun had come out, after a brief shower earlier. Some visitors were in the barn looking around the interior and praising the new developments, whilst others spilled out into the yard. With the WI ladies turning up en masse in four cars, it suddenly got a lot busier and Tom was soon on hand with the second jug of Pimm's, which raised several wide smiles and 'Yes, pleases' from the group.

Everything seemed to be going swimmingly so far, thank heavens, and the lady from the local press had even arrived, with her camera slung promisingly around her neck. The only dampener was the arrival of Vanessa Palmer-Pilkington, who was standing with a lady from the WI and sampling Rachel's very own carrot cake in the barn. The ghastly woman screwed up her pale, rather long nose exaggeratedly. 'Oh, I must say it's not as moist as it might be, is it Clara?'

'Oh, well, I think it's rather good.'

Rachel had to admit her baking wasn't quite up to her mother's super-duper standards, but still, the nerve!

'Nothing like my carrot cake,' Vanessa said loudly.

'No, *nothing* like yours,' Clara said ironically, which seemed to sail over Vanessa's head. But Rachel caught on and couldn't resist a tiny smirk as she went on her way behind the kitchen counter area to make another pot of tea.

Maisy was skipping about more confidently now with

the trays of puddings, and a tale-tale smudge of sticky toffee sauce and lemon frosting around her mouth. 'Any more? This one's chocolate brownies and roly-poly.'

Some of the guests had spotted Eve's gorgeous crafts and Rachel was proud to see that her friend had had a couple of sales already.

An hour passed by in the blink of an eye. The photographer, Amanda, had been taking lots of snaps, which she'd said she'd get into Saturday's paper with an editorial feature on the Pudding Pantry – which was brilliant.

It was time for Rachel to say a few words. As she stood up in front of the gathering, she felt a little nervous, her heart hammering in her chest.

'Hello . . . hello.' It was hard getting everyone's attention to start.

A hush began to fall across the room, except for Maisy shouting, 'Shush, we need to listen to Mummy.'

The gathering chuckled at that.

'Thanks, Maisy. I think that's done the trick!' Rachel smiled, then took a slow breath before starting her speech. This felt like such a momentous day. 'Well, here we are at the opening of the Pudding Pantry at Primrose Farm. Thank you all for coming this afternoon.'

All eyes were upon her now. She needed to get these words right. She had written something down in bed late last night, but wanted it to come from the heart, not a sheet of paper. She smiled, calming herself, as she gathered her thoughts.

'So, a lot of hard work has gone into getting this project

ready to open on time, and we've had such fabulous support from friends and the local community here, so thank you very much. A few people I especially want to thank are my mum Jill, my lovely friend Eve, wonderful Granny Ruth, Maisy and Amelia – my little helpers – and Tom our neighbour. Oh yes, and Brenda too, for supporting our puddings from the start, four months ago now, and selling them in the Deli when we weren't quite sure which direction we were going to take. Thanks to Ian and Dan our builders for the amazing job they've done here too. A total transformation.' The lads had managed to get to the launch and they nodded their appreciation, Ian giving a big thumbs up.

There was a small round of applause and a few whoops from the crowd.

'It's been a difficult few years . . . as you well know.' Rachel felt a lump form in her throat then but managed to carry on after giving a small cough. 'Me and Mum, well we wanted to make something positive happen here. A new start. A new direction for Primrose Farm.'

A loud 'Hear, hear' came from someone in the audience and Rachel was surprised to see Old Mr Mac at the back of the barn, who was nodding as he spoke, wishing them well. Damn it, the grumpy old bastard was bringing a tear to her eye now. She swallowed and managed to say, 'So thank you all. Oh, and please spread the word about the Pudding Pantry after today, that would be amazing. Please help yourself to more Pimm's – and puddings of course!'

A glass was thrust into her hand by Eve, who whispered, 'Well done,' just as Jill moved forward to add a few last words. 'A huge heartfelt thank you from me too . . . to my very special and determined daughter, Rachel, for making this happen, and for everything you've all done for our family here at Primrose Farm over the years. Cheers folks!'

'Cheers.'

'Cheers!' Tom raised his voice and his glass. 'To the Pudding Pantry.' He caught Rachel's eye, and held her gaze for a moment. 'And to Jill and Rachel.'

More 'Cheers' and chatter followed, and the party resumed with great gusto.

Rachel rubbed her sleeve under her eyes; boy had all the emotions sneaked up on her, having everyone there wishing them well. Jill gave her back a small reassuring rub, a silent comforting gesture that she'd done for Rachel since childhood. Rachel then spotted Tom smile across at her with what looked like pride in his eyes.

With Palmer-Pilkington and several of the more formal guests now away, Jill and Rachel began to feel more relaxed. The pudding platters had been enjoyed and were reassuringly depleted. Eve poured the two of them another large glass of Pimm's each – they certainly deserved it – as well as topping up their remaining guests. Most of the group were now standing outside the barn enjoying the warmth of the summer's afternoon, though the clouds had once again started to gather above.

Rachel came to stand next to Jill. 'Well, that all seemed to go off pretty well, Mum.'

'Yes love, *really* well, I'd say. Everyone seemed to enjoy it.'

'Hah – except for Vanessa moaning about my cake.'

'Ah, don't worry yourself about her. She'd not be happy if she didn't have something to moan about. Has a face like a Rottweiler on her, that woman.'

Rachel couldn't help but laugh at that.

Heavy grey clouds soon began to darken the sky, and as a few spots of rain started to fall, everyone made a dash for the barn to take shelter. It really was a typical English summer's day, filled with a mix of sunshine and showers, but it hadn't spoilt the event in any way – nothing could, in fact.

Now the remaining guests were sheltering in the barn together, Eve rapped a dessert spoon onto the wooden counter top, to get everyone's attention.

'Excuse me. Hello . . . I just have a little something to say and a presentation to make.'

Ooh, Rachel didn't know anything about this. What was Eve up to? Was it something to do with her crafts, she mused. She looked across at her mum who shrugged her shoulders. They were both evidently in the dark on this.

'Okay,' Eve started, 'so, we all know that life has been very hard for these two lovely ladies lately, and I just want to say that as well as being my absolute best friends, they are a true inspiration. What they've done here on the farm, keeping it all going, and now this, creating this gorgeous Pudding Pantry despite everything, it's . . . well, it's just amazing. You two have achieved so much in such a short space of time.'

There were lots of 'Hear hears' and a round of applause went up.

Rachel found herself welling up. She knew she should have put on the waterproof mascara this morning. She looked at her mum who was definitely a bit teary too.

'Well, several of us here have got together as we wanted to give you a little gift to help you on your way . . . So, without further ado, here you are.' Eve's husband Ben made his way through the group carrying a largish box, followed by Tom with another of the same size.

'Careful,' Eve warned. 'It's breakable.'

The lads put the boxes down on the floor in front of Jill and Rachel who knelt down and started to open a box each, both of them smiling and curious. As Rachel pulled open the cardboard lid, all was suddenly apparent. Crystal glass in teardrop shapes caught the light . . . the chandeliers. OMG. She gasped, then had a little blub, and needed a tissue passing to her.

'Oh Eve . . . everyone, oh my, they are just perfect. But . . . how did you know which ones?' She had taken one of the lights out carefully now.

Eve was smiling broadly. 'I made a mental note, then found and saved the image you'd showed me on Instagram. Just in case, you know.'

'But they were so expensive,' Rachel continued.

'Not when we shared the costs between a few of us.'

Rachel looked around at the others there, who were now grinning broadly – friends, parents from school, guests from the farming community, Brenda, Granny Ruth, Tom . . .

'Thank you. Thank you all so much. I can hardly believe it.' Rachel felt almost giddy.

'We thought it'd give the Pudding Pantry that little extra sparkle, that final touch,' added Eve. 'Not that it really needs it, mind, as it looks gorgeous already.'

'What a wonderful gift,' said Jill, clutching her own tissue. 'Thank you all so much.'

'Wow . . . well then,' Rachel announced. 'Let's carry on with the celebrations. Cheers folks.'

More puddings and pavlovas were passed around. There was still some Pimm's left. The teapot was refilled, and their friends chatted, some sat at the tables inside whilst others ventured back out again with the sun peeping through once more. Maisy and Amelia and some of the other children were happily playing in the garden, sliding bottoms on raindrops down the slide and giggling away.

With a few happy stragglers remaining, mostly close friends and family, Rachel and Jill started to clear away the debris. It was now after 6 p.m., blimey how the time had flown. As she came out of the barn bearing a stack of plates to be returned to the farmhouse kitchen, Rachel didn't hear the van pull up at the edge of the yard.

'Rachel.'

The voice stopped her in her tracks. The plates in her hands wobbled precariously. It was a voice from the past. A shock.

'Oh . . .' Rachel froze for a moment, taking in the sandy-blond hair, the frame that was shorter than she remembered, the cool blue eyes.

Just then Maisy, curious at a new arrival, skipped up to her mum's side.

'Who are you?' she asked, ready to go and fetch more cake for the newcomer at the party.

'Hi Maisy, I'm your daddy.'

From the stunned look on Maisy's face, if she had been carrying a plate it would definitely have dropped to the ground right then.

Chapter 27

BE CAREFUL WHAT YOU WISH FOR

For a little girl whose wishes had finally come true, Maisy didn't know quite what to do.

A strange man was standing in front of her telling her that he was her daddy. But he wasn't like the daddies at school or in the park playground. He wasn't full of hugs and hand-holds and pushes on the swings. He didn't even have any sweets with him.

'Hey, Maisy.' He switched on a smile, as he leaned towards her to ruffle her blonde hair. 'You okay?'

The little girl nodded shyly from the safe-zone by her mother's legs, but she didn't speak.

'She's probably just a bit overwhelmed,' Rachel explained. *Aren't we all?* She heard the tension in her own voice as she spoke – strained and mechanical. Her legs were rooted to the spot. She willed her brain into action, to act normally, for Maisy's sake. 'We've all had a long day with the opening of the barn as a tearoom today. She's been great helping out, haven't you, Maisy? So, it's been a busy day. And, *obviously* we weren't expecting you,' she added pointedly.

'Got a week off, thought I'd pop up and see my little girl.'

'Nice of you to let us know you were coming,' Rachel fired back sarcastically.

'Ah, it was just one of those last-minute things. You know.'

Rachel didn't *know*.

'Ah, Maisy, why don't you run along and find Grandma a minute? See if she needs some more help clearing up, sweetie.'

'Okay.' Maisy, in her confusion, seemed relieved to go.

The bloody cheek of him. She would *never* just turn up unannounced to meet a child she hadn't bothered to see for over two years. In fact, not seeing her own child for two years full stop was too crazy to contemplate. She was hyper-wary of this guy who'd left their lives almost immediately once Maisy was born, bar one or two casual visits. Jake had never been around when the going got tough, and now he had the cheek to turn up unannounced. Yes, she realised he'd have rights as a father, but he certainly hadn't earned them.

'Well, are you going to ask me in?'

'I suppose . . .' Rachel's tone was reluctant as she gestured towards the barn. He'd caught her completely off guard, and she was struggling to make sense of this. 'A tea, coffee . . . ?'

'You don't have a cold beer, do you? I've been driving for hours.'

'Ah, I'm not sure.' Was he expecting to be waited on? For her to slip back into an old rhythm where she'd do whatever he wanted? Well, if that's what he thought, he had another think coming. 'Umn, there's possibly one over in the farmhouse fridge. But I'm busy just now, I'll go check in a while.'

She found that she didn't want to explain exactly why they were busy – about the launch party and their new business – and didn't want him knowing about their current lives. In fact, she didn't want him to go strolling into their home fetching himself a beer, either.

'Actually, I'll go get that beer now, if you just hang on here a sec . . .' She felt distinctly uneasy and glanced about to find Jill, hoping that Maisy had located her grandma. She spotted them and noted the look of surprise and the frown that had formed across her mother's face at the sight of their unexpected guest.

'So, are you just up for the week?' Rachel wanted to clarify just how long her ex might be around.

'Yeah, something like that.' *As vague and non-committal as ever.*

'Hello, Jake.' Jill walked over to them after leaving Maisy in Eve's care. '*So*, you're back.'

Most of the guests had now left, bar Tom, Eve and her family, and Granny Ruth who was staying the night with them in the spare room. Oh, and of course Jake, who looked rather too comfortable, ensconced on the garden bench with a bottle of lager whilst watching Maisy and Amelia play.

Ben, Eve's husband, who'd known Jake briefly from their school years, had been across and had a few words with him, but he and Eve were now helping with the clearing up. Rachel stood for a few seconds as she came out of the barn, and watched. She had enough on her plate today without having to make pleasantries with this guy. She really didn't know how she felt about this new development . . . extreme unease was probably the overriding emotion just now.

It was such a shock intrusion into her and Maisy's world, and she had no idea how it might work out. Did Jake now want a part in his daughter's life? Was it going to be a regular thing? Might he even want Maisy to go and stay or see him wherever he was currently living? It was all too big and uncertain for Rachel to grasp or deal with right now . . . she was exhausted and emotionally drained after the energy she'd put into today. The Pudding Pantry launch had gone even better than they could have imagined. They were up and running and ready, and the support from their friends and the local community was wonderful. She felt positive and, yes, happy. She *would not* let Jake, of all people, put a dampener on that.

'You okay?' Tom found her where she stood by the farmhouse door.

'Ah, yes I think so. It's just been such a full-on day.'

'Yeah, you and your mum have done brilliantly here.

I'm sure it'll be a success for you, I wish you all the best.'

'I hope so.' She was still keeping a close eye on how Maisy was reacting with her dad around. She'd already 'shown him off' to Amelia once the initial shyness had faded.

Tom followed Rachel's gaze. 'I feel like I know that guy. Your ex by any chance?'

'Yes. How did you guess?' Her tone was flat.

'Just seemed to add up. He hasn't been around much for Maisy though, has he?'

'No, not so far, the bloody idiot. I have to admit I kind of liked it that way though.' The words slipped out. 'Sorry, that probably sounds really selfish. But if you knew him, how unreliable he is . . . I just don't want to see Maisy hurt, that he'll let her down again.'

'Yeah, I can understand that.'

She felt Tom's hand rest gently on her shoulder. It said, 'I'm here for you,' or that's what she imagined right then. It took her back to that moment in the hay field – that connection between them. Was it just friendship? Could it ever be more than that?

Oh, good grief, what was she even thinking? Whoa, there were so many thoughts spinning in her head, she couldn't begin to sort through them.

'Right, well I'd better be going then. You take care, Rachel. Well done on today again.' His glance strayed to Maisy and Jake. 'And you know where I am if you need anything.'

'I know. Thank you.'

If only Rachel knew what she needed herself – that might help.

Chapter 28

A CONFLAB OVER A CUPPA

As dusk descended, the sky fading into soft hues of mauve and pink, Rachel looked out of the farmhouse kitchen window, watching Jake on the garden bench and Maisy playing on her slide. Even though it was the school holidays, she was well aware it was way past Maisy's bedtime. It was time for Jake to make a move to wherever he planned on staying. (Rachel hoped he *did* have a plan and his back-up didn't include staying with them – as that was never going to happen.)

She made her way out to the garden. 'Hey, Maisy, it's time for teeth-brushing and bed,' she called out. She spotted her daughter's brown-soled bare feet. Ah, she probably ought to give her daughter a quick shower too. She hoped Jake would take the hint and make his move.

'Aw . . .' Maisy screwed up her face in protest, but Rachel could see just how tired her little girl really was.

'Five more minutes won't hurt,' Jake countered.

Hah – who the hell did he think he was waltzing in unannounced and now giving extended bedtimes?!

Rachel fumed. She bit her lip before answering. 'Actually, it's an hour past Maisy's bedtime, after what's been an incredibly busy day, so it really is time for bed. *So*, Jake, where are you staying?' she asked pointedly.

'Ah, I've got a B&B in mind.'

He sounded deliberately vague. It obviously wasn't booked.

'Can I see Maisy again tomorrow? Would you like that, Maiz?'

'Yes!' She beamed. She'd found her daddy at last and, after her initial shyness, she was clearly bursting with excitement.

'Yeah, I'd like to take her out for the day. Maybe down to the beach. Do you like the beach, Maisy?'

'Yes. Can I, Mummy?' The eagerness in her daughter's voice was almost painful to hear, but Rachel couldn't shake off her wariness. Did Jake have any experience with kids at all? Should she just let her little girl go off with him when he'd only turned up today? Was he responsible enough? Maisy was only five years old after all.

Rachel really wanted to chat this new development through with her mum, but she was faced with a dilemma with two eager faces wanting her answer now.

'Umm, look . . . Maisy, can you pop to the house and see Grandma for a minute? She was going to start the shower off for you, I think.' A little white lie to give her a chance to talk with Jake alone.

'O-kay.' Maisy lumbered off the slide. 'See you

tomorrow, Da . . .' she paused, not quite sure what to call him just yet. That moment of confusion alone broke Rachel's heart.

'Yeah, I can't wait, sweetheart.' He grinned, then as soon as she was out of earshot, his tone changed. 'So . . . ? What is it?'

'She hardly knows you, Jake. And you, really what do you know about looking after little girls?'

'It can't be that difficult. I'm only going to buy her some ice cream and take her to the beach. She's my daughter, Rach. I thought you'd be pleased that I've come up and made the effort.' He looked irked.

Rachel knew she had to tread carefully. She knew what Jake's temper looked like. 'Yeah, it's good you've come to see her,' she conceded, not wanting to get into a conflict so soon. 'It's just been so out of the blue. It's probably a bit overwhelming for her. Look, why don't you come and see her again tomorrow, but stay here? She can show you around the farm or something? You can get to know each other.' Under our supervision, Rachel was really thinking. 'Then, if all goes well, you can take her out over the weekend for that beach trip.' She felt that was a reasonable enough compromise, though she knew she'd be anxious every second her little girl was away with him.

'All right, though I don't know why you think I can't handle it.' There was a hard edge to his tone. She remembered it from years back.

'It's just about making sure it's right for Maisy, that's all, Jake.'

'Fine, well, I'll get away then. I'll be back in the morning, say ten-ish?'

'Okay.'

They finished on a frosty note with each other, but Rachel was doing her best to stay polite whilst protecting Maisy. She felt she had every right to put some boundaries in place, with Jake having been absent for so long.

Being a parent wasn't optional in her book.

Rachel headed up to the bathroom a few minutes later to find that Jill had already started the shower for Maisy.

'I'll take over now if you want, Mum.'

'All okay, love?' Jill was perched on the closed lid of the toilet seat. Her brow was creased in concern.

'Yeah, fine.' They'd chat some more once Maisy was safely tucked up in bed. 'Nearly done in there, petal?' Rachel asked.

'Ye-es,' Maisy sounded tired.

'Come on then. I've got the big fluffy towel here all ready.'

'I'll come and kiss you goodnight once you're in bed, love,' said Jill.

'Okay, Grandma,' her voice was echoey from the confines of the shower.

Rachel leaned in to turn off the water. She bundled her little girl up and dried her off, wishing she could keep her safe and warm and near like that all the time. She smelt so gorgeously of strawberry shower gel and clean fresh skin.

Pyjamas on and into bed next. Grandma Jill popped in for her goodnight kiss and cuddle as promised, followed by Granny Ruth who was staying over for the night, then Rachel perched herself on the side of her girl's bed with its unicorn duvet cover.

'Has he gone?' Maisy asked, suddenly looking vulnerable.

'Yeah, but just for this evening. It was getting late. He's coming back tomorrow.'

'Oh.'

'So how did it go . . . with your dad?' Rachel wanted to give Maisy the chance to talk if she needed.

'Okay,' Maisy sounded non-committal. She looked as though she was thinking hard, trying to untangle her emotions. After a second or two she added, 'I think he's a learner dad.'

'Hah, I think you're right.' Rachel smiled. Trust Maisy to get it spot on. 'So, are you okay with seeing him again tomorrow? Here on the farm?'

'Ye-es.' The little girl nodded seriously.

'Okay. And you know you can chat or tell me anything. It's all a bit new for you with your dad, I know.' Rachel wanted to reassure her that she was there for her if needs be, in this new territory they'd found themselves in.

Maisy nodded, then said, 'Can I have my story now?'

'Of course. The fairy glen one again?' It seemed to be her favourite lately, especially after the picnic afternoon and playing in the fern-shaded stream.

Rachel took up the book from the bedside table and

started reading, but it wasn't long before Maisy's eyes closed. In fact, Rachel's eyelids were drooping too; she would have loved to curl up and join her.

Jill and Granny Ruth were in conflab over a cup of tea as Rachel came back down to the kitchen.

'I've made you a brew,' Jill said. 'It's here on the table.'

Rachel joined them, pulling out a chair as a small sigh escaped her lips.

'So how is the little lass?' asked Granny.

'She seems okay. A bit overtired. But it's a hell of a lot for her to take in. You'd think he'd have given us some kind of a warning, so we could have prepared her a bit.'

'Typical Jake,' Jill tutted. 'What about you, love? How are you feeling?' she asked.

'Oh Mum, I'm wary. Can't help wondering what's behind all this. But I can't stop him seeing her, can I?'

'No pet, you can't, not when he's her father. But you can keep some control on it though,' Granny Ruth added.

'Yes, I've tried to do that already.'

'So, what was he saying?' Jill queried further.

Rachel repeated their earlier conversation in the garden before he left, explaining that he was just up for a few days – for now, anyway.

'I can't stop him seeing her, I know that, but I just don't trust him. Well, none of us really know him, do we? He was always so lax, so unreliable. Does he even know how to supervise a child? And then, what if he does stick around, raising her hopes, and then buggers off again like the last time? 'Scuse my language, Granny.'

Ruth merely nodded as though she realised the situation merited it.

'I know love, it's hard. I'm wary too, I have to admit,' Jill agreed. 'But I suppose we have to give him a chance.'

'And then . . . what worries me even more,' all this had been spinning around in Rachel's mind since he'd turned up, 'what if he does stay around? What will he want from her, from us? Weekends with her, a split week? What will his influence be on her? I like knowing where she is, what she's doing. She's so young, she needs routine, a steady life, especially after everything that happened with Dad.'

'Let's not jump the gun now, pet,' Granny Ruth said wisely. 'Let's see what happens over these next few days and take it from there, hey?'

'He wants to take her to the beach. I said no to tomorrow, it's too soon, and I want to see how he is with her. So, he's coming here to visit her at the farm tomorrow instead.'

'Well that sounds sensible,' Jill said. 'Don't get me wrong, I'm wary too – on high alert in fact – and I'd do anything to protect you and Maisy. But he might have changed a bit, you know, grown up.'

'I bloody well hope so.' Rachel took a slug of tea. Argh, it was all so frustrating and the timing could *certainly* have been better. 'We need to think about being prepped for tomorrow at the Pudding Pantry too, don't we?'

'Yes, we do,' Jill answered pragmatically. 'On the bright side, today went well and we're all stocked up with plenty of puddings. I'll bake a few fresh scones and a Victoria sponge first thing in the morning and we'll be ready to open as planned at ten-thirty. That'll give us plenty to think about, anyhow. Try not to worry too much about Maisy, love. It'll all work out somehow.'

'Tomorrow's another day, pet.' Granny Ruth smiled gently. All her years of experience, her life, her losses and her loves seemed to be carried in that smile, and it soothed Rachel.

'Thank you,' she responded. Her family was so precious to her.

Chapter 29

A BRAVE NEW DAY

Rachel woke up in a cold sweat with a feeling of panic racing through her veins. Had it been a bad dream or a memory? She came to, realising that she was in the warmth of her double bed, safe in the farmhouse. It was reminiscent of a long-forgotten time – when she was just Maisy's age – and she'd had a nightmare in the very same bedroom. She couldn't even remember what the dream was all about now, but the same feelings of fear and panic were rushing back.

Dad had come in back then when she was a little girl, must have heard her cry out, with his deep voice telling her to hush, followed by a bear hug and his soothing words that all was well. They had crept downstairs hand in hand, where he warmed milk on the Aga and they sat together in the comfy chair, talking about all the animals on the farm.

Rachel had been learning to tell the time and the big and little hands on the clock were both at the very top. Dad explained that meant it was midnight, and he said that Mum was fast asleep in bed. It was just the two of them up. He assured her that when she went back to bed in a minute everything would be fine until morning came . . . and it was . . . at least for the next seventeen years.

Maybe it was thinking about Maisy and Jake's shock appearance that had irked her, or the worries with all the developments on the farm . . . with their big opening day ahead. She wasn't quite sure what had set her spiralling down memory lane. But just remembering Dad and that feeling of having his arms around her was comforting. Rachel allowed herself to doze once more, until her alarm announced the new day.

Friday the 12th July, and it was now ten twenty-five on the official opening day of the Pudding Pantry at Primrose Farm. Jill was behind the counter, which was laden with freshly baked goodies, and Rachel was about to swing the barn door wide open, ready for their first customers.

They'd done it, they'd only gone and bloody well done it. The room itself seemed to glow with pride. The honey-coloured walls shone and Eve's toys and crafts were carefully placed on the two dressers. And the spread of food – just wow. Her mum had excelled herself with all the baking. Granny Ruth was keeping an eye on Maisy back at the farmhouse for them until Jake arrived. It really was a team effort. Rachel raised a big thumbs up and grinned across at her mum as she turned the handle on the new barn door.

'Ta-dah!' She opened the door with a flourish and used an old heavy iron that she'd found in the barn as a stopper. Rachel had asked Granny Ruth about it, and apparently the iron had once belonged to her mother; she'd warm it on the old range in the kitchen, ready to press their clothes and laundry. It was lovely to have another farmhouse relic, passed down through the generations.

Despite Rachel's excitement, there was no-one there waiting to come in just yet.

She sighed. 'The crowds haven't quite come flocking,' she called across to Jill cheerily, poking her head out to check the parking area in the yard. 'Shall we have a quick coffee?'

'Now that sounds like a plan. I'll get another practice in on this machine.'

They'd managed, at the last minute, to source a great second-hand coffee machine that frothed, gurgled and made the most delicious fresh coffee, though Jill was still getting to grips with the technicalities of it. (It had bamboozled Granny Ruth completely.)

'Now which bit do I fill with the ground coffee again?'

'Here,' Rachel pointed. 'And about two-thirds high for a nice strongish cup.'

'Ah yes, that's it. Got it now.'

Five minutes later, the two of them were sitting at the table nearest the door sipping their drinks. They got momentarily excited at the sound of an engine, but the little red van pulling up only announced the postman,

Trevor. Mind you, Rachel's selling skills won them their first customer with a takeaway coffee, and she told him all about their delicious bacon rolls, scones and selections of puddings to tempt his tastebuds for another day.

'Have a good day, Trevor!' they called after him as he set off, having delivered their mail. Rachel hoped the brown envelopes amongst the pile weren't bills; with all the set-up costs, money seemed to be leaching out before any was coming back in. The next few months were going to be a fine balancing act.

Jake arrived to see Maisy just before eleven – his timing as unreliable as ever. They still hadn't had an official customer yet, and Rachel couldn't help but feel a little disappointed.

'You go and take Jake across to the farmhouse,' offered Jill. 'I'll keep an eye out here ready for the big rush,' she added wryly.

'Okay, thanks.' She headed out to meet her ex. 'Hi Jake,' she said, 'I thought we'd agreed ten o'clock?' She looked at her watch pointedly.

'Ah, I was just sorting out a few things at my digs, whilst I had some internet there.'

'Okay.' She decided to let it slide, trying to keep this adult and mature. 'Well, Maisy's over in the farmhouse. I'll take you across.'

'Right you are.'

Maisy was sitting with Granny Ruth at the kitchen table, her focus intent on a half-finished jigsaw puzzle.

'Hey, Maisy.' Jake grinned across at her.

'Oh, hi-i . . .' She looked up for a second and then fitted the piece in her hand into the puzzle.

'Well done, Maisy,' praised Granny.

'Do you want a go?' Maisy asked Jake, offering him a piece from the table.

'Yeah, why not.' He stood at her shoulder frowning. It seemed to take a while before he worked it out. 'There.' He sounded relieved.

'Good.'

'So, are we going to have a look around this farm of yours? I'm sure there's lots you can show me, sweetheart.'

'Yes, o-kay.' Rachel heard the touch of hesitancy in her daughter's voice.

It was all so new, this fragile relationship. Was it going to blossom or burn? Rachel couldn't help but wonder. But she had to stand back and let them both try. It was only fair.

'Just stay near the farmyard area, Maisy, okay. You can go and see if Pete's about in the Low Field, just call him at the gate though. Pete's her pet lamb, who's all grown up now,' she explained to Jake. 'Then, there's the chickens to see. You can take Moss with you, give him a bit of a walk. I think he's bored with us being in the barn so much lately and he's not allowed in.'

'Yes, all right, Mummy.'

'Then when you're all done come back to the Pudding Pantry. You can come and have some lunch there, the two of you.'

'Ah cheers, Rach. That sounds cool, Maisy. *And*, we get to try out the food in there.'

'It's good. Tom loves the sticky toffee pudding, doesn't he, Mummy?' Maisy was just being her usual chatty self, but Jake's eyebrows rose sharply at the mention of Tom.

'Does he now?' was all he uttered in a slightly disgruntled tone.

'Yep,' Rachel said matter-of-factly. What was it to him who Tom was, or if there was anything between them? Jake had fled their lives years ago. 'Okay then, get your wellies on ready, Maisy, and have a nice time.'

Maisy got off her chair and headed for the porch. 'Come on then, Ja . . .' She stopped short, still unsure what to call him. 'I'll show you the chickens first. There's this really funny one with fluffy bits around her legs. She never stops clucking. We call her Clucky.' There was Maisy chatting away, so innocently.

Rachel and Granny shared a look as Maisy led him out by the hand. They both knew there were risks, but Maisy was still on home ground – for now at least.

At eleven minutes past eleven – Rachel knew the exact time as she had been watching the clock in the barn avidly – their first official Pudding Pantry customer arrived.

An old but well-cared-for Fiat Punto parked up in the yard and in came Frank, a pleasant old chap who Rachel recognised. He was a local, living nearby in Kirkton.

'Morning ladies,' he said, doffing his flat cap. He had

a mop of thick white hair, and a friendly sparkle about his blue eyes.

'Welcome Frank, take a seat,' said Jill with a warm smile. 'And what can we get for you? Or would you like a few moments to take a look at the menu?'

'Well, I'd love a cup of coffee to start, and I'll take a little look to see what there is to tempt me.' He picked up the cream card menu that was propped next to the jam-jar vase of sweet peas in the middle of the table.

'There's lots on display in the counter too, Frank. There might be something there that takes your fancy,' Rachel added.

'Thank you.'

'White coffee, Frank?' Jill asked, ready to get to grips with the coffee machine.

'Yes, please. With hot milk.'

'I'll make you a nice frothy one then. Here goes,' she added as an aside to Rachel, pouring milk into a small stainless-steel jug. She was getting the hang of it already.

They let Frank have a few minutes to study the menu, then Rachel walked across to see if he wanted to order some food.

'Hey, it's done out lovely in here, mind. You've done a grand job, girls. Brenda was telling me all about it down in the village. Thought I'd take a trip up and see for myself.'

Good old Brenda, spreading the word for them.

'I've had one of your chocolate puddings from there too. Lovely jubbly. Just like my Mary used to make.

And all I had to do was warm it in the oven, and I found a tin of custard I had to go with it. Delicious.'

His wife, Mary had died several years ago now. Rachel remembered them as being a sweet couple; they always went everywhere together. It must be so hard losing someone you've been with all those years, whether you had reached old age together, or were younger like Mum and Dad. Loss was all around them. But it hadn't stopped them, had it? Here they were, at the start of their brave new venture. And here was Frank out and about, taking small bold steps in his new life without Mary.

'Here's your coffee, Frank.' Mum looked so proud that she'd fathomed out the machine all by herself this time, and the cup of frothy coffee did look barista standard.

Rachel grinned and swelled with pride. 'Anything else?'

'Well then, I think I might have to try some jam roly-poly with custard. Brings back memories, that does. Takes me right back to being at home as a small boy. Sunday tea-time treat that was. My mam's special.'

'Well, I hope I can do it justice,' Jill replied.

'Aye, I'm sure you will, bonny lass.'

Just then, two ramblers arrived. They were a middle-aged couple, who told Jill they'd taken an early-morning walk in the Cheviots and were on their way back down to Kirkton and were delighted to stumble upon the Pudding Pantry.

They ordered two teas, a bacon roll and a slice of Rachel's homemade carrot cake. The couple took up their seats and Rachel overheard them saying how pretty the place looked. She felt a warm sense of achievement.

As she was making the pot of tea, Rachel couldn't help but wonder how Maisy and Jake were getting on around the farm. She hadn't seen them since just past eleven o'clock and it was now almost twelve. They weren't far away, Rachel reassured herself, and even though she was young, Maisy knew the farm and its 'rules' well. It was more her emotional wellbeing that Rachel was concerned for. This was a huge thing in Maisy's life, meeting her dad properly for the first time, and Rachel wanted it to go positively for her.

Rachel pulled herself back to the here and now, and carried over the tea, cake and bacon roll that Jill had made to the ramblers.

'What a gorgeous place you have here,' the woman said. 'We didn't know it existed. We've been here for several holidays over the years.'

'Well, today's our official opening day, actually.'

'Oh wow, lucky for us then. You've done a wonderful job. It's so quaint here. And the food looks delicious. Thank you.'

'You're welcome, you enjoy tucking in!'

Frank headed off soon after, with a wave and a smile, saying he'd be back soon and that he'd be sure to tell all his friends about them. After finishing her cake, one of the ramblers got up and started to browse Eve's crafts on the dresser. She picked up several of the farmyard-themed soft toys, settling on the sheep, and bringing it across to the counter.

'I'll take this one, thanks.'

'That's great, thank you. My friend makes them locally,' commented Rachel proudly.

'Oh really, it's such a cute toy. She's so talented, and I'm sure my granddaughter will love him.'

Rachel felt thrilled for her friend and couldn't wait to tell her.

Much to Rachel's delight, there followed a small flurry of customers who arrived around noon for some lunch – two ladies from the village, a family on holiday with a toddler and small baby in tow, and Jim the taxi driver called in for a takeaway coffee and a flapjack as he was passing.

Not long afterwards, Maisy's chatty voice announced her and Jake's arrival back at the barn, much to Rachel's relief. Maisy looked quite happy and was bossing her dad around telling him which table to sit at, which made Rachel smile.

'So guys, how was the farm?'

'Good, Mummy. Petie came to see us. I gave him some grass and a sheep nut.'

'Yeah . . . it was good.' Jake didn't sound too enthusiastic.

'So, are you hungry? What can I get for you?'

'Ooh, can I have one of Grandma's cupcakes?'

'Well, you can if you eat up something healthy first. What do you want, some soup, a sandwich?'

'Umm, a cheese sandwich. Is Jake having lunch too?' She seemed happier with that name than Daddy, and Jake didn't seem to mind.

'Yes, of course he can. What would you like?'

He scanned the menu and asked for a coffee and a bacon roll.

'That's fine. I'll get that sorted then.'

Rachel was about to head back to the kitchen area as Jake shouted across, 'Hey, it's looking good in here, Rach. Very swish. Must have cost a few quid to get all this done. You must be doing all right here.'

The cheeky git. He *must* have heard about her dad, what they'd all been through. She had to bite her tongue, what with Maisy and the other customers about. But really, if only he knew the truth.

'Yeah, reckon you must have had a little windfall,' he continued, sitting back in his chair.

Was that why he was here, because he thought they had money all of a sudden?

Rachel glared at him. How dare he imagine he knew anything at all about their lives?

'Well, it's not always as it seems, Jake. And you haven't been here to see *any of it*, have you,' she answered sharply, turning on her heels and marching across to the counter area to get their order ready.

'All okay?' Jill spotted her daughter's bristling body language immediately.

'It will be when he scuttles back to where he came from,' Rachel muttered under her breath. It was going to be a difficult week, she could tell. As long as it was only a week. She took out her frustration on the coffee machine, slamming the cup down, and wishing it was

263

more than just beans in that coffee grinder. She let Jill take the order back across to them once it was ready.

Eve popped by that afternoon with Amelia in tow.

'So, how's it going, my lovelies?' Eve asked.

'Hi, Eve. Yeah, pretty good. We've had a steady flow of customers so far and some great feedback. Oh, *and* we've sold one of your soft toys today already – Simon the sheep.' Oh yes, they all had names.

'Aw, that's brilliant, I'm so chuffed. Thanks, and well done to you, too. It looks so great in here. Oh, and before I forget, I've found someone to put those chandeliers up.' Eve knew all about the antics with the electrician, Carl, who wouldn't be invited back.

'Oh, fab.'

'Yes, Susan's husband, who sometimes does odd jobs for the school, has done a bit of electrical work in his time. He's happy to come and take a look, and rig them up for a small fee and a chocolate pudding, I believe.'

'Great. So, do you want a tea or coffee? Any of our pudding delights? Maybe a milkshake for Amelia?'

'Ooh, yes, please.' Amelia grinned. 'Mummy, can I have a chocolate one?'

'Of course. And I'll have a tea, do you have a camomile?'

'Yep, no problem.'

'Where's Maisy?' asked Amelia, looking about for her friend.

'Oh, she's just out with her dad for a while.'

They'd headed back out after their lunch.

Eve raised her eyebrows questioningly at that. Rachel just shrugged before adding, 'They're here somewhere on the farm, so you might get to see her in a minute, Amelia.'

After Rachel had got their drinks, Jill said she was happy to cover the counter to let Rachel have a few minutes to sit and talk with her friend. By the time Amelia's milkshake was slurped and the last bits of choc-olatey froth scooped up from the bottom of the glass, Maisy had come back in, delighted to see her playmate. So, the girls went running off to play on the slide in the garden. Granny Ruth, who'd been in the barn giving Jill a hand whilst Maisy was with Jake, offered to go and keep an eye on them.

Jake hung around, looking awkward, at the doorway.

'Just give me a sec, Eve.' Rachel went across to him.

'Well, that's me done for today,' he stated, as though he'd just completed an onerous task. 'I'll be back tomorrow for the beach day with her, like we agreed, yeah?'

'Okay, yes.' *Try and be positive about this*, Rachel told herself. It was just one day, and Maisy did seem to be getting on all right with him.

'I'll be over round about ten-thirty.'

'Fine.' She was being abrupt and she knew it. The word belied what her heart was telling her.

With that he set off, shouting a quick 'Bye' across to Maisy in the garden.

Rachel could see Maisy waving back. A sigh escaped her lips as she turned back around to face the pantry, well aware of the new tension knotting her shoulders.

'So, how's it going with Jake and Maisy?' Eve asked, as Rachel got back to the table.

'Ah, so, so. They seem to be getting on all right together. But he wants to take her out to the beach tomorrow for the day. I've had to say yes, but I know I'll feel nervous all day. He's just not used to kids. And they hardly know each other really. But what can I do . . . he's her dad. I can't really stop him from seeing her, can I?'

'No, I suppose not. He'll want to give her a nice day out though. I'm sure he'll try his best to look after her, and if something's not quite right, she'll put him right and tell him how it's done, knowing Maisy.'

'Hah, yes she probably will. She's already been calling him a learner dad.'

'Hah, good old Maisy.'

'It's hard though, Eve. Letting her go. She's still so young, and he can be such a prat. I'll be worried all day. Imagine if it was Amelia . . .'

'Yeah, I'd be concerned too. But it's only fair to let him try, and Maisy's been asking about him more lately, hasn't she? Maybe some good will come of it.'

'I hope so. I just don't want her upset again. I can't see him staying around for long though.'

'No, maybe not. At least if he goes again, she'll be able to remember him this time.'

'Remember what a prat he is, you mean.' Rachel

Rachel's Pudding Pantry

couldn't help herself. She was trying her best to put on a smile – for Maisy's sake more than anything – but Jake had a knack for pushing her buttons. Her little girl was the most precious thing in the word and if he even *thought* about hurting Maisy, unintentionally or otherwise, she'd have him running for the Cheviot Hills.

Chapter 30

DADDY DAYCARE

Maisy was ready, and standing looking out of the farm-house porch with her unicorn rucksack on at ten-fifteen the next morning. Rachel had made sure she had spare clothes packed, and a swimsuit – she'd make it clear to Jake for paddling up to her knees only – a towel, jelly shoes for the beach, a small juice drink and some mini raisins for a snack.

At twenty-five past ten, Jake arrived in his small, grey van – it was a minor miracle in itself that he was on time. Rachel said hello, then gave him the rundown and the rules and they agreed he'd have Maisy back by 5 p.m. in time for her tea. She also made sure he had her mobile number as well as the farm's landline in his phone, as well as checking that the number she had for him was current.

She made certain the car seat she'd moved across for Maisy was secure and was sure she could feel Jake's eyes rolling as she double-checked before letting Maisy clamber in. After strapping her little girl in and ensuring

Jake saw how the clips fastened, she kissed her goodbye, and graciously wished them both a lovely day. Then, with a small sigh, she stood back.

'We'll be fine, won't we, Maiz? We're going to have a great time at the beach,' Jake said. 'See you later then.'

'Bye.' Rachel felt her throat thicken.

'Bye, Mummy.' Maisy was waving. She managed to look both excited and slightly anxious all at once. She'd only ever been away before to Eve's house or to school. It felt weird letting her go. So many everyday things could go wrong.

Being a mum came with a million worries and a million joys, and sometimes you just had to learn to let go. It still didn't make it easy though.

'Look after her,' she whispered as she watched them set off.

She saw the van get smaller as it headed away down the farm track. As she turned, she found that Jill was stood behind her.

'All right, love?' Her mum placed an understanding hand on Rachel's shoulder.

'Yeah, I think so. I need a coffee.' Or maybe a stiff gin might just do the trick, but perhaps not at this hour. It was only ten-thirty and there was a whole day ahead. It was going to be one long one, she was sure.

'Come on then, love. Let's make a quick coffee and get ready for opening up the Pantry.' Jill diverted her, and they wandered across to the barn, where they opened up for their second day of trading.

It still felt a bit surreal unlocking the wooden barn door, turning on all the lights and putting their chalkboard sign outside. She hoped there'd be a few more customers in today. It had been steady yesterday, which gave them a chance to find their feet without a big rush, but it was already the school summer holidays and she'd hoped for a good start. They'd put lots of flyers out around the village, set up a Facebook page for the Pantry, and they'd featured in a great article by Amanda in today's local newspaper. It was hard to judge how many cakes and bakes to have in. They couldn't afford to waste too much, yet they wanted to have enough filling the counter to tempt people.

Rachel started by making them two strong coffees. It was early days and she was just being impatient, she scolded herself. Jill set out fresh scones and a marshmallow-filled rocky road traybake she'd made earlier that morning. And, if it was a steady start to their business this week, at least the traditional baked puddings had a nice long refrigerator life which would certainly help matters. Jill's first 'Pudding of the Week' was a delightful summer pudding served with local thick cream – a real summer favourite in the Primrose Farm household. She'd made lots of individual pots last night, which could be kept and turned out as required, with the rich-red fruity juices spilling into the pudding bowl – delicious. Rachel might just have to sample one later, teamed with a cup of fragrant Earl Grey tea.

Earl Grey, she had learned, had links with this very

area – oh yes, Charles Grey, the second Earl Grey's family home was Howick Hall on the Northumberland coast. He was Prime Minister back in the 1830s and loved this blend of tea flavoured with bergamot. Rachel had done some googling the other evening after thinking the name sounded vaguely familiar, and was going to add a historical note to their menu – a nice touch of culture for the customers!

She and Jill sat for a minute or two at one of the tables sipping their coffee.

'Ready for another day in pudding paradise?' Mum asked, trying to lift her spirits. She knew today wouldn't be easy for Rachel with Maisy away.

'I think so. It does look really good in here, doesn't it? And you've done so well baking all these amazing goodies.'

'Oh, I love doing the baking, I really do. It makes me feel like I'm Mary Berry every morning. And then, with the Pudding Pantry here in the barn, thinking about how far we've come, and when people come in and say such lovely things . . . Well, I just can't believe the journey we're going on, love.' Her voice trailed with a hint of a sigh.

'Yes, it's great, isn't it. Let's hope there's lots more people in today to sample your pudding delights.' Rachel was still anxious to get more trade.

'Oh yes, fingers crossed.'

'Come on then, let's get to work.' Rachel took a big sip of coffee. 'I'll pop down on the quad and put the board out by the gate.' They'd taken the large chalkboard advertising the Pudding Pantry in last night, in case of rain or dew smudging all the writing. Eve had been commissioned to complete a wooden sign for the farm entrance for them, but they'd all been so busy lately. Eve had shown her some ideas which looked fab, in a similar style to the sign she'd done for them above the barn door. She'd even drawn up some images for a Pudding Pantry logo, which was all very exciting.

Back at the farmyard, with the chalkboard now out touting for business at the end of the lane, Rachel began watering the two flower pots that stood on either side of the barn door. She'd put them out for the launch day, filling them with a mix of colourful petunias and deep blue lobelia. There were also two hanging baskets trailing a burst of pinks and mauves. They looked jolly and welcoming.

Rachel then remembered that Mum had an old, slightly rusty bicycle that she never used any more – maybe she could fill the pannier basket with compost and buy a few more brightly coloured, summer plants and leave it down by the entrance gate? That might help to catch potential customers' eyes too. They could even have one of Eve's wooden plaques on the side with an arrow saying, 'This way to The Pudding Pantry'. Hmm, she was full of good ideas today – which was at least keeping her mind off other matters. *How was Maisy getting on? Where were they now?*

The first customer of the day was the postman once

again, who stopped for another takeaway coffee and a cheese-and-chive scone. Rachel said today's snack would be on the house, and asked Trevor if he might just spread the word for them on his rounds.

Jan and Maureen, two friends of Mum's, came in for coffee and cake, and then they had a family of five call in who were on holiday and ordered a chocolate pud, a syrup sponge with custard, a caramel brownie (a new twist on Jill's traditional version), and a shortbread, along with teas and milkshakes. They were all settled happily for a while, and then the children went to check out Eve's toys. She hoped she might get another sale for her.

Just after eleven, Tom appeared. 'Morning. So, how's it going, ladies?' He gave them a gorgeous smile.

'Not too bad, I keep having to remind myself it's early days, and there have been a few more customers in the last hour,' Rachel replied.

'Well, I'm here for my bacon roll and a coffee, please. It's been a busy morning and I'm ready for a break. This saves me having to go back and make it for myself. And then, I might just have to have one of your amazing sticky toffee puddings to take away too.'

'Coming right up,' Jill smiled, taking some bacon from the fridge, ready to put on the griddle.

'Where's your little helper this morning?' he asked Rachel.

'Maisy?'

'The one and only.'

'Off with her dad for the day.'

'Ah, right.'

'First time. Can't help wondering how she's getting on.'

'Yeah, that'll be a bit tricky for you . . . and for her, I bet.' He seemed understanding of the unusual situation.

'It is a bit, but I'm sure she'll be fine.' Rachel was trying to stay positive. They were one hour down already. Only *six* to go . . . 'Much on at the farm, Tom?' She changed the subject, not wanting to dwell on Maisy's absence too much.

'Yep, got the joys of rounding up and worming the sheep today. I think we'll be starting harvesting pretty soon too, maybe early August. My wheat crop's nearly ready.' Tom had arable land as well as keeping cattle and sheep. He had a larger farm than Rachel and Jill's, and his fields went further into the flatter part of the valley, and those acres were more suited for growing crops than the land at Primrose Farm. So he had plenty on at this time of year.

'There you go, Tom.' Jill placed the completed order on the counter. 'One coffee and a bacon roll.'

'Cheers, that looks great. So, how much do I owe you?'

'Oh . . .' Jill floundered. 'Well, I don't feel we can charge you after all your help, Tom.'

'Nope, I insist. How can I keep coming back if you won't take payment? It's a business, so I'd like to start on the right footing.'

'Well, okay,' conceded Jill. 'That'll be nine pounds ninety then, please, with the sticky toffee in too.'

He settled up, took a sip of his coffee, then took a table and sat scanning the local newspaper that Rachel had left out. He looked up and added, 'And it tastes even better,' giving a thumbs up.

After a short while, Tom came across to the counter to collect the sticky toffee pud to take home.

'That's supper sorted,' he joked.

'Perfect. Who needs a main course when you can have pudding?!' said Rachel.

'Absolutely. That should be the official mantra of the Pudding Pantry! Well, that's me off to round up the sheep now. I'll see you about, yeah.' He held her gaze for a second or two, as though about to say something else, but then seemed to think better of it.

'Yeah, see you soon.' And she realised just how much she did want to see him again *soon*. He'd been in her thoughts so much more lately, and in a different way – maybe it was the effect of the *Poldark* incident, as she had named it. But taking that step further, organising a meet-up or, dare she suggest it, 'a date', seemed somehow wrong. Who knew what Tom was thinking, and she might just embarrass herself. They were far better off as they were, as they had always been: as friends and neighbours. She needed to keep her mind on the job, the farm, their fledgling Pudding Pantry business, without letting herself get caught up in fanciful, romantic ideas – which would probably just end in complete disaster.

Yes, that would definitely be for the best. But as Tom turned his back on her, she couldn't help but wish he'd turn around again, and find an excuse to stay.

*

'Trust Jake to be late,' Rachel said, simmering with frustration. She and Jill were now back at the farmhouse, having locked up the pantry for the day. 'Maisy'll be getting hungry by now.' They usually had their supper soon after five.

'I thought I'd make us some ham and fried eggs with a few sauté potatoes. There was quite a bit of ham left over today.'

'Okay, that sounds nice. Although I don't know if I can even eat, Mum, I feel like my stomach's churning.'

'Well don't worry, we'll wait a bit yet. Give Maisy a chance to get in and tell us all about her day trip. It'll have been a big day for her, I'm sure,' said Jill reassuringly.

'Yes, I wonder how she's coped with it all? I do hope Jake's been good with her.'

'Ah, I'm sure he'll have muddled through somehow. He's probably spoilt her rotten.'

'Knowing her wily ways, she'll have diverted him to a gift shop at some point.'

Ten more minutes ticked by, then fifteen, twenty. Rachel was clockwatching anxiously. Still no Maisy or Jake. She tried his mobile, no answer on that. Damn it, she couldn't help but worry. Jill tried to reassure her that they'd be back any minute, that Jake had probably just lost track of the time, but Rachel could tell her mum was getting a bit nervous too.

Finally, there was the hum of a vehicle coming up the farm track, the crunch of tyres on the gravel outside. Rachel was up and out of her seat at the kitchen table like a shot. It was the grey van, thank heavens, with Jake climbing out of it.

Rachel flew out of the porch door. 'Where the hell have you been? You said you'd be back by five o'clock! Maisy's missed her tea time and everything.' Rachel was wound up like a spring by this point.

'Hey, no need to stress, it's fine. We've had fish and chips for supper. We stopped off at Seahouses on the way back.' He sounded cool as a cucumber.

'And you didn't think to call, or that I might be worried? Jake, it's *not* fine. I had no idea where you were or if anything was wrong.' His laissez-faire attitude to life was doing her head in. It didn't work like that once you had kids.

Maisy got out of the van. She stood between them, her shoulders hunched. Rachel realised she'd better tone things down a bit. It wasn't Maisy's fault, after all. 'Well, at least you're back now.'

Maisy's hair was damp and her T-shirt even damper, as though the water from the hair on her shoulders had soaked in. Hadn't he even thought to dry it properly? Rachel clenched her fists and it took a considerable effort to stop herself from having another go.

Jake noted Rachel's stormy gaze. 'We've been swimming. Well, splashing about really. It's been fun, hasn't it, Maiz?'

Maisy nodded. Rachel could see that her hair hadn't been brushed or anything after being in the sea. It'd take ages to get the knots out now, as it was thick and wavy.

Rachel would have to wash it before bed and use loads of conditioner. She tried to keep her voice calm, however, for her little girl's sake. 'So, have you had a good time then, Maisy?'

'Yes, really good. We've had ice cream and chips and look . . .' She pulled out a new soft-toy puffin from her bag.

He was very cute. So, the gift shop ploy had obviously materialised.

'He's lovely, have you got a name for him yet?'

'Puffy.'

'Okay, good name for a puffin.'

For a brief moment, Rachel wondered whether to ask Jake in, merely out of politeness, as they were standing out on the farmhouse step, but she was still fuming that he hadn't even thought to call. Also, it was already getting late to get Maisy settled for a bath and bed. Another late night wouldn't be a good thing for her. Though she seemed okay, Rachel could spot the 'I'm tired but *really* pretending not to be' a mile off.

'Right then,' Rachel announced, as much to Jake as Maisy. 'Time to get you in ready for bath and bed.'

'Aw . . .'

'Come on, you've had a busy day and it's time to let Jake go and have a rest too.'

'Are you coming back tomorrow?' she asked, looking up at him. There was a hint of anxiety in her voice, announcing her worry that this might be it, her Daddy-time over.

'Yeah, of course, sweetheart. I'll pop in and see you. In the afternoon some time, okay?' He looked at Rachel to check, who gave a small nod. She was beginning to calm down a little now she knew that Maisy was safely home.

'Yes, that's fine,' Rachel said. It sounded more like a quick visit to the farm than a full outing this time. Maybe a whole day had worn his fathering skills down already, Rachel mused. And there must only be a few more days of his holidays left anyhow.

Jill appeared at the step. 'Hi Maisy, had fun at the beach? Hello, Jake,' she added, coolly.

'Yes, Grandma, I've been in the sea and for ice creams, and this is Puffy.' She was heading into the farmhouse now, holding out her new toy proudly.

'See ya, Maiz.' Jake smiled at her.

'By-ye.'

'What do you say, Maisy? For all your treats and your day out?' Rachel reminded her.

'Thank you.'

'Good girl.'

Maisy took Grandma Jill's hand and went on inside. The tiredness evidently creeping up on her already. Rachel knew she must be on the wave of an emotional rollercoaster, seeing her dad so out of the blue and starting to get to know him, bless her.

'She's been a good girl for me,' Jake commented.

'Good. Yes, she's generally well-behaved. They all have their moments, mind.'

'Yeah, well . . . you've done a good job with her, Rach.' Jake looked serious and appeared a little emotional. Had he finally realised what he'd been missing out on?

'Oh . . .' Well that took the steam out of her anger. She'd fully intended on launching into a more vicious rant now that Maisy was out of earshot, but – ever the charmer – Jake had managed to placate her. 'Well, thanks . . . I appreciate that. And look, if you have her again, for goodness sake ring me if you're going to be late. It's a real worry, you know.'

'Yeah, I get that. I think we must have been out of signal down on the beach, but yeah . . . okay.'

'So, you're coming back tomorrow?'

'Yep, but not till the afternoon. I'm looking at a motorbike for sale up in the Borders. Been after one for a while – looks a cracker, a Ducati, second-hand. So, it'll be afternoon by the time I'm back. Let Maisy know that it'll be later, won't you?'

'Yes, I will.' *Hah*, so he had money to buy a bloody motorbike then, but not for child support. He obviously hadn't changed that much.

'See ya, then.'

'Bye, Jake.'

Jake had come back the next afternoon as promised, and taken Maisy down to Kirkton to play in the park and have an ice cream. He was back at 5 p.m. prompt. He said he was heading back down south the next day, and swore to keep in touch more regularly, promising he'd phone Maisy once a week at least. Maisy seemed happy with that idea, and that seemed a good compromise for Rachel too.

She just hoped he'd live up to his promises, she'd heard them all before. Even if the intention was there, a sense of spontaneity and recklessness seemed to take over with Jake; he'd selfishly get caught up in whatever circumstances he'd stumbled into at the time. Maisy's face was troubled as she said her goodbyes, bless her. They watched his grey van head off – with his new motorbike in the back – and Rachel's heart felt so much for her little girl. Not having your dad around was a tough thing, whatever the circumstances.

Chapter 31

A SNAKE IN THE GRASS

A week later, the day dawned bright and sunny on Primrose Farm. It was one of those idyllic summer days in the Cheviot Hills that looked like it had been drawn from a postcard – the sky was a deep, vibrant blue, in contrast with the verdant green fields below. Rachel was struggling a little in the heat, but she needed to move the sheep down to the Low Field, where she'd set up an outdoor 'race'. She had to be ready for the next day as Simon was coming in to herd them through for worming and to check their hooves.

She set off with Moss on the quad and started in the furthest field, Hetton Ridge. The ground was rougher here with the odd gorse bush as it was nearing the moorland hills. Moss was a great worker and happily responded to her commands of 'Away' and 'Come by'. He was an old hand at this, having been well-trained by her father. He also knew the lie of the land on the farm. A couple of times he disappeared out of sight amongst the gorse and rocky outcrops, but he'd reappear again, steering some errant sheep back towards the flock. Rachel spotted another small group of ewes and lambs further up the rise and sent him up for them.

Shortly afterwards she heard an almighty yelp. Moss seemed to take a long time in coming back and, when he did, he was limping. Oh no, what had he done? Had there been something sharp in the ground up there?

'Hey Moss, what's up boy?' He reached the quad, but didn't seem right at all. Rachel knelt to investigate the damage. She checked the pads of his feet and couldn't see any sharp thorns or stones, which were often the culprits, and the leg itself didn't seem out of line or broken. He was whimpering though and seemed in real discomfort.

'Is it a sprain, lad? Did you twist it or something?' She helped him up to the quad; it was unusual that he didn't try to jump. He was heavy, but she managed to get him in the back. The sheep were beginning to drift off again, but Rachel decided to call it a day for now and take Moss back to the farmhouse. It was more important that she check his leg more thoroughly and let him rest it in his kennel. Maybe he'd trodden on a sharp stone and bruised it, or twisted it slightly. If only he could tell her what was wrong. It'd probably heal quickly with a bit of time out.

She went the quickest route by the track that adjoined her and Tom's farms, rather than opening and closing the various field gates. As she turned a bend, she spotted Tom's quad heading towards her.

'Hey,' he said, as he pulled up at the side of her.

'Hi, Tom.'

'Everything all right?'

'Actually no. I think poor Moss has hurt his paw, or leg. He seems a bit lame, reckon he's trod on something whilst herding the sheep.'

Moss was whimpering loudly in the back, as if to say 'It *really* hurts.'

'Can I take a look?'

'Yeah, of course. I've checked but can't see anything.'

'Where were you?'

'Hetton Ridge.'

'Near the moorland, yeah?'

'Yeah.'

He moved to the dog, with soothing words. 'It's okay, boy. Let's check you out.' He took the paw extremely gently and examined it closely and carefully. Moss let out a deeper whimper, as he reached a certain part of the lower leg.

'Ah . . . here. Now I see. Okay Rachel, we need to get him to a vet straight away. It's an adder bite. Here, look.'

And there on Moss's foreleg were the tell-tale two puncture wounds, which were now beginning to darken and swell.

'Right, jump on the back with him and keep him still. We need to restrict his movement to stop the venom from spreading. I'll take you down to my jeep and we'll get to the Kirkton vet, right away.'

'Oh my God, I hadn't seen.' Rachel felt awful that she'd

missed it. 'I hadn't even thought.' She couldn't let anything happen to Moss, not Dad's dog. He was such a wonderful boy, he was in his prime.

'Hey, it's all right.' Tom saw how concerned she was. 'I only know as I had a dog bitten once. It's a sunny day and the adders bask, especially up near the moorland. Don't worry, if we get him to the vets quickly, he should be fine.'

Once they'd transferred to the pick-up, keeping Moss as still as they could with Rachel still holding him, Tom made a quick call to the vets to let them know they were on the way with an adder-bitten dog, so they could get prepared. The sooner you acted the better in these cases.

Rachel was so pleased she'd met Tom on the track by chance; it might have been much later when she'd spotted the wound herself, and more damage could have been done. She tried to stay calm, soothing Moss with gentle words and stroking his soft silky head.

They soon arrived at the vets, Rachel carrying Moss in. God, he was getting heavy in her arms. The vet had an examination room ready, and they went straight in. The vet took a quick look and then administered anti-venom immediately and gave Moss some pain relief.

'How long ago was he bitten?'

'Only about fifteen minutes,' Rachel answered.

'Ah, that's good. You've acted fast and done the right things for him.'

Thanks to Tom, Rachel thought, feeling guilty that it could have been so much worse.

'Okay, so we'll keep him here just now, keep a close eye on him and see how he reacts. Give it a few hours, and I'm pretty sure he'll be able to come home either early this evening or in the morning.'

'Will he recover okay? What about his leg?' Rachel was worried there might be long-term damage.

'Most dogs recover fully in around five days, so no, no long-term damage is likely. He looks a fit and healthy dog otherwise, so that'll go in his favour.'

'Thank you.'

'You're welcome. Give us a call at, say, five o'clock and we'll let you know how he's getting on.'

'Will do.'

They headed back, Rachel feeling slightly shaken, even though the worst seemed over. She was quiet in the passenger seat of the jeep.

'He'll be okay, you know,' Tom said reassuringly.

'I just feel dreadful that I hadn't seen it.'

'It would have been easy to miss, Rachel. It's been a bit of a shock for you too, I bet. Do you want to come in for a coffee?' They were nearly back at Tom's farm, where she'd left the quad.

'Yes, that'd be good, thanks. I'll give Mum a quick ring first and explain what's been happening. She'll be wondering where on earth I've disappeared to.' And Rachel knew all too well that that in itself would bring back bad memories.

*

Sat in Tom's kitchen, with mugs of steaming coffee, they chatted for a while. She'd been in the kitchen as a girl, but it was far more modern now with light-oak units and chrome fittings. Rachel remembered being invited here for summer barbecues along with other families from the farming community, sat outside in the garden on straw bales for seats, helping herself to hotdogs and Coca-Cola, watching the teenage Tom whizz around the farmyard on his quad, and there were Christmas-time drinks right here in the cosy farmhouse kitchen served with mince pies, chocolate cake and cocoa for the children.

'Well, at least it seems like he's going to be okay,' said Rachel, starting to relax knowing that Moss was being taken care of. 'So, which dog of yours was bitten?' she continued.

'Ah, it was a while back. It was Caitlin's dog, actually. A spaniel. He ended up with a nasty lesion on his side. We hadn't seen it straight away, he just seemed a bit off. So it had taken a bit of a hold by the time we got him to the vets and realised what it was, and then the wound got infected. He pulled through okay, but it left a scar . . . It was yet another reason for her to hate the countryside.'

Caitlin was Tom's ex-wife. From what Rachel had heard in the past, it sounded as though things had become difficult between them, though Tom had never talked with Rachel directly about his relationship before.

'Country life didn't suit her,' Tom said, beginning to open up. 'She'd been brought up in Edinburgh, was a city girl at heart. We thought our love could counter that, getting married, but it wasn't enough in the long term. She grew to resent this life, me . . . farming's not a job you can just leave behind at five o'clock and weekends, is it?'

'Nope, no way.'

'And I didn't want to leave it, or my life here, though I did try early on. It's just a part of who I am . . . Anyway, I'm not sure why I'm telling you all this . . . It's all over and done with now.'

'It's all right, I don't mind you talking.' Rachel was the queen of disastrous relationships, who was she to judge? And it was nice that Tom felt he could be honest with her. She'd always had the impression that Tom was quite a closed book, a little guarded with his emotions, and he generally kept his home life private.

'Ah, don't want to bore you with it all. So, how's it all going at the Pudding Pantry?' He swiftly changed the subject.

They sat chatting for a while longer, then Rachel said she'd better go and get back to the farm and Maisy.

'Let me know, when you hear how Moss has got on.'

'Of course. Will do. Thanks again, Tom.'

They were poised on the front step. Their eyes held each other's for a few seconds, and Rachel felt some instinctive pull not to leave.

'Hey,' he pulled her into his arms and gave her a hug. It had been a bit of an emotional day with the dog, and he realised that. It was lovely to be so close, and she felt safe and warm there in his arms, and then . . . a little bit sensual. She knew all too well now what lay beneath that shirt, and it was like all her nerve endings had woken up and were on high alert.

Rachel looked up, her face tilting ever so slightly towards his. She could see the short dark stubble on his chin, was almost close enough to feel it in fact, just a shift of her lips and that would be it. A second more and she would know what it felt like to kiss Tom Watson.

What would a kiss mean? Where would it lead?

She stepped back just in time, feeling so out of kilter. 'Right, okay, I'd better go. Thanks so much again.'

To the quad, keys in, pedal down, into gear, and then go, go, go.

Chapter 32

TO KISS OR NOT TO KISS

The next day, Rachel was chatting to Eve on the mobile as she did her early evening rounds of the sheep and cattle.

'How's Moss, Rach? I saw your mum in the lane earlier and she told me all about it. Poor thing, and what a shock it must have been for you, too.'

'He's doing good now, thanks. I picked him up first thing this morning and he's just taking it steady, lying in his kennel today. Probably still a bit sore, but he's fine.'

'That's good. And it sounds like Tom did well, spotting what had happened.'

'Yes . . . .' *Tom* . . . A million crazy thoughts had been whirling around in her head all night, thinking about their near-miss kiss. Should she have gone with the moment, let it happen? Found out what it felt like to taste his lips on hers?

'Rach . . . are you still there? Are you okay?'

'We nearly kissed last night,' she blurted. It suddenly all spilled out.

'*Who?*'

'Me and Tom,' Rachel confessed.

'Wow, and you *stopped* it . . . you crazy woman. Right, well you need to come around and tell me all about it. I didn't even think you fancied him.'

'I didn't . . . I don't . . . Oh, I don't know . . . It's just kind of crept up on me.'

'Hah, you're finally seeing what we've all known for ages, how bloody gorgeous he is.'

'Oh Eve, I really need to chat about it, it's all so confusing. In confidence, of course,' Rachel said seriously. She really didn't want to get this wrong, a bit of friendly advice wouldn't go amiss.

'Of course, my love. Why don't you come around this evening for an hour or so?'

'That sounds good, I'll check if Mum can look after Maisy, but I don't think she had any plans for tonight.'

Rachel and Eve were sitting in Eve's back garden with a bottle of rosé between them under a pinky-orange sky that was deepening into dusk. It was a beautifully calm summer's evening and still warm. Ben was out for the evening and Amelia was tucked up in bed.

'So, Rachel, you dark horse you, you need to tell me all about it. How on earth have you been *nearly* kissing my all-time favourite crush?'

'Well I'd obviously been upset about Moss, and he'd helped, and I was there at his place having a coffee . . . look, I really don't know. He gave me a hug goodbye and suddenly it just felt like it should be so much more than a hug.'

'Doesn't sound like a big problem to me. If you both like each other, that is.'

'Yeah, but what if we had gone ahead and kissed, and then it ruined it all? What if he's not quite feeling the same way, or maybe it'll seem great for us both at the start but then it all falls down within a few weeks' time . . . and then it'll just be too hard to be friends any more?' It had all been racing through her mind. 'Since everything with Dad, Tom's been such a constant, Eve. He's always there if there's a problem or if there's any help needed on the farm.'

'Isn't that a good thing, Rach?'

'Yes, and that's just it, if we let it get personal and it all went wrong, we could wreck all that.'

'Why do you think he does all that for you, Rach?' Eve's voice was gentle, understanding. 'I've seen the way he looks at you lately.'

'What way?'

'Just kind of intently, and caring . . .'

'Well, we are good friends.' Rachel batted down the suggestion that he might be feeling this too and sipped her wine.

'I think it's so much more than that and you're both too frightened to admit it.' Eve looked right at her. 'So, are you going to miss out on the chance of something special just because you're afraid?'

Was that it? After her messed-up relationship with

292

Jake who just left at the first hurdle, after what had happened to her father? Too many men had left her life already. Was she afraid of losing another?

'And,' Eve continued, 'isn't that a good place to start? That Tom cares for you, supports you? Better than meeting some stranger down at the pub or something.'

Rachel let out a long slow sigh. 'Or an electrician who wouldn't even know how to screw a lightbulb!' She gave a wry smile.

'Exactly.'

'Yes, but . . .' It was hard to frame her thoughts. All she knew was that one minute she was desperate to be in Tom's arms, to make that kiss a reality, but then she was backing away, building those walls around her heart. And what was weird was that these feelings had completely crept up on her in just a few short months. Might the feeling just go again as quickly as it came? Was it just lust, seeing him with his shirt off like that? Maybe they'd get it out of their systems, only for it to fizzle out and the whole relationship would be tarnished.

'There's no real rush I suppose, Rach. Why don't you give yourselves a bit of time and see how things go?'

'Yeah.' Rachel took a long sip of her wine. 'You won't say *anything to anyone*, will you?'

'Of course not. But hey, be careful you don't miss out altogether. He might not wait around forever, you know.'

She hadn't thought about that . . . Tom with someone else. How would that make her feel? What if someone else did make a move on him? Someone else in his arms, his bed. Ooh, she felt a bit sick thinking about that.

'When did love get to be so complicated, Eve?'

'Wow, you've just mentioned the word love, Rach. Oh hun, when you're scared you know it's worth it. Because there's so much more to lose.'

Her friend's words rang true. Crikey, was she in trouble.

In bed, later that same evening, Rachel let her mind wander back to Tom. Well, it hadn't been off him for long to be fair. She allowed herself to imagine the next few seconds after that moment on his doorstep; if she'd let his lips touch hers, felt his body pressed close against her. The warmth of him, the strength of him, from the firm muscles of his torso to the delicate curve of his top lip soft against hers. But if she tasted that, could she ever bear to lose it? And risk wrecking their friendship too? It was surely best left in her imagination.

But, oh my, a sense of deep yearning was building. She realised she wanted him so much. How could she even act normally when she next saw him? She felt like she'd been zapped into some fifteen-year-old's body with all the angst that went with it. Crazy, crazy woman.

Lying in the dark, in the bed that she'd slept in on her own for years, suddenly felt so very lonely.

Chapter 33

ACHING ALL OVER

Rachel woke in the early hours of the morning feeling like she was burning up. The bedlinen was covered in sweat and she felt clammy all over.

Okay, get up . . . go and get water . . . that'll help . . . maybe take a couple of paracetamols.

But trying to move, argh no, that was no good. Oh God, her body felt like it had been kicked around The Stackyard by a donkey. What the hell? And her head . . . her eyeballs ached in their sockets. No, she wouldn't move just yet. Just stay here and lie still . . . just a while longer.

She must have gone back to sleep and woke again as the morning light pierced through the crack in the curtains. Her throat felt parched, but there was no way she could get up just yet. She curled up on her side in the foetal position. The sheep and cattle would need checking on her usual morning rounds, but not yet, not yet.

She must have dozed off once more, sleeping through her usual 7 a.m. alarm.

'Rachel? Are you all right?' Mum's voice was somewhere near.

She half-opened her bleary lids. Even that was a struggle.

'Not well,' she rasped. 'Can I have some water?'

'Oh, love.'

She felt a hand press against her brow.

'My, you're burning up. I'll go fetch you some water and paracetamol. What do you feel like?'

'Shit . . . ah, sorry Mum.' Even talking hurt. She paused, 'Aching, headache . . . like I've been ten rounds with Macduff.'

'Sounds like the flu, pet. It's been going about the village. Old Mrs Peters was terrible bad with it, ended up having to go to hospital last week. She's okay now though, thank heavens.' Jill plumped the duvet around her. 'Right, you stay here, and I'll get you some water and painkillers.'

'It's okay, I'm not going anywhere.' Rachel tried to laugh, but even her ribs ached. 'Aargh.'

'Just lie there and rest, love.'

Five minutes later, Jill came back with a large glass of water, the paracetamol pack and Maisy's head thermometer. 'Here, love.' She passed the water across, once Rachel had tried clumsily to prop herself up against the pillows. 'Maisy's asking after you, I told her to stay downstairs just now and let you rest.'

'Don't want her to catch it.'

'No.'

Mum then passed her the tablets. 'Here you go, take these straight away, they should help.'

Taking tablets was usually simple for Rachel, but her throat felt so dry that they seemed to stick. She glugged the water, until they finally shifted. As she settled back into the pillows, Jill placed the thermometer against her forehead.

'Crikey, it's up at thirty-nine degrees. We'll give it a little while and see if the tablets bring your temperature down a bit. But if it's flu there's not a great deal you can do, you just need to rest and drink plenty of fluids.'

'Yeah.'

'Don't worry. We'll be fine with everything on the farm. Simon's about, so we'll get him to do the checks on the animals and I can manage the Pudding Pantry today.' She sounded bright, breezy and efficient. Her lovely, wonderwoman Mum.

'Sorry, Mum.'

'No worries. You just get some rest, love,' Jill soothed, the tone of her voice taking Rachel back to her childhood.

Rachel nodded and took another sip of water. She was soon settling back down under the covers, and found herself dozing again. When she next looked at her watch it was almost two hours later, and she was drenched in a cool sweat. She drifted in and out of sleep once more.

Mum brought her up some scrambled eggs on toast at lunchtime but she could only manage a couple of mouthfuls before feeling queasy. But after checking, Jill was happier that her temperature had come down a little.

'Who's covering in the barn?' It suddenly dawned on her that Jill must have had to leave it. Had they had to close the Pantry?

'It's fine. Eve called in by chance, she and Amelia were happy to take charge for a few minutes.'

'Aw, that's kind of them.'

'Eve sends her love and a big get-well-soon hug for you.'

'Oh, thank her . . . Where's Maisy?'

'She's with them just now. She's desperate to see you, but I'll keep her out of the way for today. You'll probably be infectious and you need a bit of peace. Have you had enough there?' Jill eyed the hardly touched scrambled egg.

'Yeah sorry, not hungry. But thanks.' Rachel's voice was still a bit of a rasp.

'No worries, it was just in case. Right, anything else you need? A cup of tea or anything?'

'Just water's fine. Thanks, Mum.'

'Well, just shout if you need anything.' They both gave a wry grin at that. 'You can't shout, can you, sorry love. I'll come back and check on you in an hour or so.'

'Thanks.' Rachel felt terribly tired once more, and sighed as she lay back on her pillows. She hated feeling this lethargic but there was no way she could manage getting up.

'Sleep well, love.'

And Jill hushed the door to a close behind her.

However old you were, it was still the best to have your mum around when you were poorly.

The next day passed in a bit of a blur, with Rachel drifting in and out of sleep. But by early evening, she managed to sit up in bed and drink the glass of water that she found on the bedside table. She finally felt the stirrings of hunger too.

She got herself up and to the bathroom to freshen up slightly, but still felt weak, so headed back to bed. Jill must have heard the movement, the giveaway creak of the upstairs floorboards, and was soon up to see her.

'Feeling any better, love?'

'Yeah, a bit. In fact, can I have some toast? Just buttered, please.'

'Of course, you can. I'll fetch some up for you shortly.'

The toast waitress was in fact Maisy, who arrived beaming ten minutes later, with Jill close behind her.

'Mummy!'

'Hey, Maisy.'

It was the first time Rachel had been properly ill since she'd had her little girl. They'd missed each other, and the relief was evident on Maisy's face.

'I couldn't keep her away any longer,' Jill explained.

'Ah, it's good to see you, petal. So, what have you been up to?'

'Helping Grandma in the pudding place.'

'It's been all hands on deck. We've had a busy couple of days.'

'Oh yes, of course. Sorry Mum, you've had it all to cope with. Just as we were getting established too.'

'It's fine. In fact, it's been good. We've had quite a few customers through,' said Jill positively.

'And Tom helped too,' stated Maisy.

'He did?'

'Yep, he was a waitress with me.'

'*Really?* And don't you mean a waiter, Maisy?'

'Ah, yes that.'

'He'd called in for his bacon roll this morning,' Jill explained. 'And then several people came in all at once. I'd told him you were in bed with the flu, so he just got stuck in for a half hour and served.'

'He was good, wasn't he, Grandma?'

'He was indeed.'

Aw, bless him, Rachel thought. It was a bit different from handling cattle, sheep and driving the tractor, she mused.

'Here's your toast, Mummy. Grandma has the tea as it's hot. And when you've had that, I'm coming back to tell you a bedtime story.'

There was no point arguing, Maisy had her bossy tone on and had obviously set her mind to it. She was taking charge and looking after her mummy, and that was sweet. So, ten minutes later, Rachel was listening to a half-made-up version of the fairy glen book, with Maisy adding her own details when the words got a bit too tricky. There were wishes granted and magical spells. Rachel particularly liked the bit when the boy fairy became a waiter for that evening's fairy supper of sparkly cupcakes, a pure fabrication from the original story on Maisy's part, but it did make Rachel smile.

As Maisy kissed her goodnight, even though it was still early evening, and whispered 'Sweet dreams' to her, Rachel found her eyelids feeling so heavy. There must actually be something in the soothing tones of a bedtime story, as she slept like a baby after that.

Rachel was back on form and on Pudding Pantry duty a couple of days later, giving her mum a few well-earned hours off after juggling a thousand jobs. She was going to spend some time with Maisy, and pop into Kirkton with a few top-up puddings for Brenda at the Deli.

There was a steady flow of customers that morning, including a rather handsome farmer who came in for his coffee and bacon roll elevenses, which sent Rachel's heart a-fluttering.

'Good to see you back,' Tom grinned. 'Feeling better?'

'Just about. It was a rotten do though. Knocked me for six.'

'I knew you must be bad. I don't think I've ever seen you have a morning off, let alone a day or two. It's not often a farmer doesn't get out of his or her bed.'

'Ah, I was rough all right. Glad to get rid of it and be back on my feet again. Poor old Simon's been doing all the farm work and Mum's been trying to keep things going here and with Maisy. She looks knackered, bless her. Oh, and thanks for helping out the other day, by the way. Maisy tells me you made a rather lovely waitress.'

Rachel smiled cheekily, picturing Tom in a frilly baking apron.

'Hah, I did indeed. Well, it was only right to lend a hand where I could, and it meant I got my bacon roll a bit quicker that way. Actually, I know you've all had a lot on, so,' he suddenly sounded a little nervous, which wasn't like Tom, 'I was wondering if you'd like to come around to mine for supper one night . . . the three of you, I mean. Bring Maisy and your mum too.'

'Oh well, that sounds great, yes. We'd love to.' She broke into a smile. Someone else cooking their tea and, she had to admit, a chance to spend some time with Tom did sound rather good.

'Don't expect anything fancy, mind,' he warned, with a grin. 'I'm not the best cook. But I'm sure I'll be able to rustle up something. Just see what day suits and let me know, I'm busy Friday night, but any other day through the week would be fine.'

'Okay, great, I'll let you know.'

Rachel could feel the blush spreading on her cheeks. What was the matter with her? Lingering flu symptoms, that was all. It was nothing to do with Tom's unexpected invite, or the quick hammering of her heart . . .

Chapter 34

A SKY FULL OF STARS

What a gorgeous evening it had been, and it was especially lovely for Rachel to be looked after since her horrid flu. Tom had come up trumps and made a barbecue of sausages and gammon, along with a mixed salad and jacket potatoes. Rachel, Jill and Maisy were sitting on a picnic bench in his garden with dessert bowls of hot bananas that had been cooked in their skins over the glowing coals. They were soft and sweet, with a spoonful of vanilla ice cream now melting over, and a splash of dark rum for the adults. Delicious!

The sun had gone down and the sky had softened to a peachy-grey hue. Maisy was now slumped comfortably on Jill's lap, trying hard to keep her eyes open. She had a full tummy and was exhausted after an hour of play on a makeshift waterslide that Tom had set up with an old tarpaulin and lots of soapy water.

Jill finished her glass of white wine and said she'd head off soon and get Maisy to her bed. Rachel shifted from her seat, ready to help her. 'No, you stay a while if you like, love, it's early yet. We'll be fine. I'm sure Tom would appreciate some company for a bit longer.'

'Well, let me take you and Maisy back in my truck then, Jill.' Tom stood, ready to pick up the little girl in his arms. 'She'll be like a lead weight all sleepy like that. Ah . . . if you want to stay, Rachel, that'd be great. Go ahead and help yourself to another glass of wine.' He gave her an earnest look, which seemed to say that he'd *really* like her to stay. 'I won't be long.'

'Okay then, thanks,' Rachel replied, a little spark of excitement flaring in the pit of her stomach. It was one of those nights you didn't want to end too soon. A warm and balmy summer's evening with good food and pleasant conversation. Tom was so easy to talk to, they'd been chatting about farming, about Maisy's latest antics, the Pudding Pantry and all the work they'd had going on. It had been such a busy time these past few weeks, what with establishing the new business in the barn, Jake coming back and then taking off again with all the emotions around that, not to mention all the usual farm work. With having been ill too, it was so nice just to stop and relax for a few hours.

Rachel felt very mellow, caressing a glass of wine, when Tom arrived back ten minutes later. Mabel, the terrier, jumped out of his truck after him and was soon settling at Rachel's feet.

'Thanks for dropping them off.' Rachel smiled. It was typical Tom, to make sure they were back safe. He was caring, and that was a rather special trait.

'You okay?' he asked. 'Can I top your glass up there?'

'Would be rude not to,' Rachel commented wryly, the couple of glasses she'd already had loosening her tongue. They both laughed.

He poured some more of the white and then filled his own glass with red.

There was no school for Maisy tomorrow with it now being the long summer holidays. The sheep were all content out in the fields, the cattle fine too, with plenty of grass thanks to the recent wet and warm weather. As a livestock farmer, Rachel found the summer months were a little easier. Wow, she might even get a glimpse of a lie-in tomorrow. How bloody nice would that be?

Tom lit the candle in the storm lantern that he'd put out earlier, which flickered into life and then settled to a soft glow. He sat down beside her on the bench.

'It's been a lovely night, thank you,' Rachel spoke softly.

'You're so welcome.' His dark eyes were smiling and his voice golden-syrup warm. 'You lot have fed and sheltered me many a time, I think it was well overdue.'

It was he who had provided the shelter, Rachel mused, knowing he was there next door if they ever needed him. They sat side by side talking about their farms, and then he asked how Maisy had been coping since her dad's surprise appearance, shaking his head at the news of his disappearing act again. Jake had made one phone call to Maisy in the first week, but they were still waiting for the second to materialise ten days thereafter. Broken promises led to broken hearts – for Maisy, that was.

Rachel had watched her daughter with sadness as the reality began to sink in; that grown-ups didn't always do the things they said they would, even the most important things. Maisy was mentioning her dad less already, and seemed a little quieter generally, less naïve, bless her. Rachel had tried to call him herself one morning but there had been no answer – the selfish bastard.

It began to get dark; the sun melting into the horizon. Rachel said yes to a glass of the red wine next as the evening chill began to settle. Tom brought out some fleecy throws from the house to wrap around them, neither wanting to move in or indeed head home just yet.

Rachel leant against Tom with a happy sigh. It felt right and very natural, though it sent her heart rate to the moon. As she did so, she tilted her head, and caught a glimpse of the night sky above. Wow – the stars were out in full force. An inky-dark sky had crept in on dusk's tail and lit a million glinting gems. Here in rural Northumberland, with no street lights to dim them, they were just stunning!

'Look at that, Tom,' she said. 'Wow.' She was craning her neck to see. 'Hang on, I'm going to lie down on the grass and look up properly.'

Rachel got out of her seat, took a couple of paces and then lay, still wrapped in her fleecy throw, on the lawn of Tom's garden. The grass was damp with dew under her fingertips, but she didn't mind, and it felt soft as she lay on her back.

'Good view from down there?' Tom smiled as he stood up and then lay down beside her.

Rachel was transfixed by the night sky, watching the misty sweeps of galaxies.

'Oh, look, did you see that?' she whispered. 'A shooting star. You have to make a wish.'

'I'm not sure if I need to right now,' he whispered back.

His hand brushed hers by accident. Rachel felt it like an electric jolt.

She turned her head away from the stars to look at him. He was gazing at her, his dark eyes full of words not yet spoken. And the world felt like it held its breath for a second . . .

His hand reached for hers intentionally this time. The look he was giving her melted her insides. He then leaned towards her. Their lips met, tentative and tender at first, then melded in a beautiful, stunning, sexy kiss. Oh yes, it certainly lived up to her dream kiss . . . and then some.

When their lips finally parted, Tom smiled as he held her gaze. 'I've been waiting to do that for such a long time.'

Rachel felt a surge of joy. 'Me too.'

'Well then, shall we give it another try? Just to check we've got it right.' Tom's eyes were sparkling in the glow of the candlelight.

'Yes, why not.' He'd *certainly* got it right, but she wasn't going to stop him now!

So, they moved back in for another tantalising taste.

Lips warm and welcoming, bodies pressed much nearer this time, side by side on the damp grass under a canopy of stars. Tom's hands gently tugging her wavy brown hair as they kissed, hers cupping the back of his head. And it was beautiful in every way, so much so, that it almost hurt to feel that intensely. She had never kissed like that before.

After a dreamily long kiss, they sat huddled together within the fleece blankets, leaning against each other in the half-light. For a while they were silent, aware of their breathing, their warmth. It felt like words might break the spell. Bring them back to reality too soon.

'Okay?' Tom finally said.

'Yes,' was all Rachel could utter. Where was this going, what was this leading to? Her body was telling her to touch him, hold him, to make him hers in every way. But she couldn't rush this, there was too much at stake. 'Tom, I'm going to have to go.'

If she stayed much longer she wasn't sure she could stop it. And she wanted to be sure, so very sure, that this wasn't just lust or emotions getting the better of them. If there wasn't a future in this for them, then it couldn't go any further. A quick fling would just spell the end of their friendship. Oh my, they were teetering on the brink as it was. The brink of something beautiful but very scary.

Tom looked at her, disappointed, searching her eyes for a clue.

'Maisy,' she reminded him. *For the morning*, she

intended to say, hardly daring to voice the words, the implication that this might take them both to the morning, but she just couldn't risk that yet. Oh yes, she could rush things, get swept up in the moment, end up dashing up to Tom's bed as they tore each other's clothes off. *Oh goodness, why the hell not?* came a mischievous, yearning voice in her head. For all her words of leaving, she was still leaning close to him.

'Okay, I'll walk you back.' His tone was patient, even if he was disappointed.

'Thank you.'

They got up from the blankets. They'd shared that bottle of red since Jill and Maisy had left, so there was no way Tom would be using the truck now. They held hands firmly, like a small promise between them, as they made their way along the lane to Primrose Farm. It felt so very natural, like something had shifted far beyond friendship.

The night air was still and cool with the odd baa of a sheep coming from the fields around them, and only the breath of a breeze rustling the leaves in the hedgerow. It was chillier now and Rachel moved closer to Tom, feeling the reassuring warmth of his body. They walked with the sounds of their footsteps crushing the gravel of the farm track.

As they reached the farmhouse, Rachel saw that Jill had left the kitchen light on for her. The two of them stood beside the wooden front door, smiling at each other, feeling a little like teenagers. Tom looked serious as he began to trace her cheekbone gently with his finger-tips. Then he cupped her jawline, drawing her to him once more.

Three kisses! Not just the one she'd been imagining. But now she had finally tasted him, there might never be enough. This kiss lingered longer than the first two, their lips pressed firmly, tasting, teasing, tongues en-twined, causing a million nerve endings to light up within her.

As the kiss eased, coming to a natural end, they pulled somewhat reluctantly away.

'Goodnight, Rachel.'

'Night, Tom. Thanks for such a lovely evening.' Her words didn't even begin to cover how she was feeling right now.

'See you soon, yeah?'

'Yeah.' She kissed his cheek, taking in his gorgeous aftershave smell once more, then moved to go into the house, feeling a pang of reluctance to leave him.

'Bye.' She took a step, then turned to smile slowly at him.

'Bye.' His smile matched hers.

'Better go.'

'Yep.'

Rachel was surprised to find Jill was still up, reading a book at the kitchen table. It was past eleven o'clock.

'Hello, love. Nice night? Everything okay?' her mum asked, with a smile.

Rachel could still feel the linger of Tom's kiss on her mouth, his touch on her skin, and couldn't help but blush. 'Yes, great thanks. I've had a really nice evening.' She tried to keep her voice even, not wanting to give anything away. 'Maisy fine?'

'Yes, fast asleep. Went out like a light as soon as I popped her in her bed.'

'Great.'

'He's a nice chap is Tom,' Jill added leadingly.

'Yes, he is.' All Rachel really wanted to do was to steal upstairs to her room and go over this evening again in her mind, every last delicious detail, whilst it was still fresh in her thoughts. 'It's been a long day, I think I'll go on up to bed, Mum.'

'Okay, love. See you in the morning then.' Her mum's voice seemed to dip a little.

Oh, had her mum hoped for some company? Was there a touch of melancholy there in her voice?

'Mu-um, are you all right?' Rachel took a few steps towards her, ready to sit down. With all the distractions of tonight, had she missed that her mum might be silently hurting, maybe feeling lonely?

'Of course, pet. I'm fine,' Jill rallied, though she still sounded a little wistful.

Naturally, she'd have had an inkling of what was going on between them. Mums seemed to have a sixth sense for these things. Rachel was sure she'd be happy for her, but had it set Jill off thinking about her early days with Dad, she wondered? All these magical emotions that

Rachel was experiencing as a first, her mum must have once shared with Dad. Of course, every day was still a test after her dad's death. Some days were better than others, but the dreadful and painful truth was never going to go away.

'Honestly, I'm fine. Off you go to bed, sweetheart. I've been engrossed in this crime novel and I'll get back to finish the last chapters now.'

'I can stay a while. Make us a tea or something?'

'No, no. You look tired. You get yourself away to bed.'

'Okay, if you're sure.' Rachel paused for a second or two.

'Go on, off you go . . . and I'm glad you've had a good night, love.'

'Thank you.' That generous maternal spirit as Mum pushed aside her own grief brought a lump to Rachel's throat. 'Night then, Mum.' She gave Jill a kiss on the cheek, suddenly wondering if the smell of Tom's aftershave would be on her. A sure giveaway. 'Love you.'

'Love you too. Night, Rachel. Sleep well.'

'Sweet dreams.'

Love, family, life. The bliss of a kiss. The harsh finality of death. Rachel lay in her bed a short while later with it all spinning around in her mind. When you'd stared death in the face, it made you want to make the most of every second in life. But she hadn't been, had she? Even tonight, walking away – at least they'd walked away together – she knew she had been holding back on so much, playing the safe game. She had tasted something more this evening. Suddenly, she wanted to *live* life now, to dance it, taste it, touch it, kiss it.

In fact, lying there with the recent memory of those three gorgeous kisses, she knew she really, *really* wanted to make love with Tom Watson very soon indeed! Would it ever really happen?

Chapter 35

HARVEST SUPPER

The wheat was ready, and it was harvesting time at Tom's farm. Rachel knew that meant long days and late nights for him until the crop was all in. She'd left her fantasies where they were, as fantasies, and decided to concentrate on real life and the issues they needed to face at Primrose Farm.

Whilst the Pudding Pantry had started off pretty well, it wasn't exactly doing a roaring trade either. They'd nearly completed their first month and, working out all the trading figures and costs so far, they looked like they'd make a slim profit. She knew things should improve as they got more established and built a reputation, but the busier summer season would be drawing to a close in a few weeks, and they'd need to keep things going through the autumn and winter. She and Jill would need to get their thinking caps on; finding ways to promote the pudding business – there was no resting on their laurels just yet.

Whilst she was out on her morning rounds, Rachel

spotted Tom in the big yellow combine harvester, with two tractors and trailers lined up ready to lead the grain. They'd be working flat out whilst the weather was dry today. It was opportune that he did arable as well as livestock, as that meant she could always buy in a good supply of straw for the animal sheds through the winter; his farm had supplied theirs for years in that way. She gave a friendly wave across the field, not sure if he'd actually see her.

He had sent a lovely text the morning after that magical barbecue night, saying how much he'd enjoyed the evening, with two 'x' kisses at the end of the message. And they'd messaged more since, just nice and chatty. But now two days had passed and as she hadn't seen him in person, the events of that night were starting to feel a bit surreal.

It was a Sunday, and Eve had offered to have Maisy for the day, to give Jill and Rachel the chance to concentrate on the Pantry, the weekends being their busiest days.

Frank, the chirpy old gent, was back in at ten-thirty sharp just as they opened, for his morning coffee and pudding. He liked trialling the new flavours and additions to the range, giving his honest opinion to Jill on each, the clear winner for him so far being the jam roly-poly with custard, with the sticky toffee coming in a close second. There were also two elderly ladies from the village, Jean and Valerie, who loved to call in for a slice of cake with a pot of tea on a Tuesday and Thursday morning. Friday mornings generally brought in the mums and tots after playgroup for twelve-noon treats, which sometimes extended to a bite of lunch – Rachel had found and spruced up Maisy's high chair and Eve had donated the one she'd had for Amelia too, which had helped. It was fabulous to have some regular customers as well as welcoming the one-off holiday makers and day trippers, and it was even better seeing them all enjoying themselves. It was just that customer numbers needed to be higher to make the business run more profitably and to make a real difference to the farm's income.

But these things didn't happen overnight, businesses needed time to build. Rachel knew that, it was just her bank balance that was impatient.

At the end of a steady day, there were several scones left, a wedge of carrot cake, and some rashers of bacon and bread rolls that wouldn't be fresh enough to serve when they reopened tomorrow. Rachel would bet that Tom wasn't eating much fresh food just now, most likely a packet of crisps and a few chocolate bars to keep him going in the cab of the combine. Maybe she should take him and the other tractor drivers some 'bait' to keep them going this evening. It would be nice to help them out and . . . she admitted to herself, just to see him, however briefly.

Jill agreed that was a great idea and they made some fresh bacon rolls, and packed up a picnic bag of buttered scones and slices of cake. They were nearly ready to close up the Pudding Pantry with it edging close to five o'clock as it was. Jill said she was happy to finish off there.

Rachel popped some apples that they'd had in the farmhouse into the bag for good measure, and drove the quad along the lane to the field where they were working. She'd let Moss hop on the back too, as he'd been cooped up in his kennel most of the day.

Rachel pulled up on the grass verge just past the gate, knowing that Tom would see her at some point and stop when appropriate. He pulled the combine to a halt once the trailer beside him was filled with a heap of grain, and motioned to the next tractor driver that they were going to take a break.

'Hi there,' Rachel called across, as Tom came down out of the cab of the huge yellow combine harvester.

'You okay? Everything all right?' He looked a bit concerned, seeing her turn up out of the blue.

'Yes fine, sorry to stop you, but I thought you might all want some supper to keep you going. It's just some stuff we had spare at the Pantry.'

'Great, you're an angel. I'm starving.'

'Thought you might be – there're bacon rolls and more.'

'Brilliant. Couldn't have been better timing. Thank you.' He looked in the bag and grinned. 'We'll take a few minutes out, but we do need to crack on,' he explained.

'It's okay, I know that.'

He brushed his hand across her bare forearm, looking like he wanted to take her into a hug right there and then, but Jack, one of the tractor drivers, was already making his way over to them.

'Look, when can I see you?' he said hurriedly before Jack reached them. 'Can you come across to mine as we finish? It might be late, mind. I'll text.'

Now they were standing so close, that spark between them was so damned obvious.

'Yes, okay.' She'd sort something with Mum and Maisy. It sounded like it would likely be past Maisy's bedtime anyhow.

'Hey, Jack, see this. We've got a food delivery,' Tom called across with a grin.

'Ace, cheers Rachel,' Jack replied, making a thumbs up sign.

'Okay, well I'd better go and help Mum clear up back at the Pudding Pantry. Hope it all goes well with the combining this evening.'

'Cheers.' Tom didn't add anything about seeing her later in front of Jack, but the sparkle in his eyes spoke volumes.

'Come on then, Moss, we're away boy.' The pair of them leapt back on the vehicle and set off. Rachel's heart was going like the clappers all the way back as she daydreamed about what might happen later.

It was past seven o'clock when Tom's text finally came through.

Rachel had been trying and failing to concentrate on some farm documentation. She had already changed into her smarter jeans and a clean red T-shirt earlier, ready to head out. She grabbed a couple of bottles of cold lager from the fridge, said her goodbyes to Mum and Maisy, and jumped on the quad.

The sense of anticipation felt like bubbles through her veins as she sped towards Tom's farm. Although, what if it was just her imagination? It wasn't like they were going on a date or anything, she told herself. Tom would be tired, he'd had three long days harvesting – she'd heard the hum of the combine and tractors working away through the evening these past two nights, and seen the lights shifting over in the valley, well after dark.

As she turned into his farmyard, she spotted Tom at the tractor shed, where he was parking up the big yellow combine harvester, ready to secure it for the night.

'Hey,' she called out as she pulled up.

'Hi.' His smile was warm.

'Thought you might be ready for one of these . . .' She got down off the quad, pulled out a cold beer from her rucksack, and opened the lid with her penknife.

'That is just perfect, you really are my kind of woman.' He grinned. 'It's been stifling in the cab of the combine, I reckon the air con's on the blink.'

'Ah, no. Not what you need.'

Tom perched himself on a straw bale near the front of the shed, where the evening sun was streaming in. Rachel settled beside him.

He took a long slow drink. 'Ah, that's good. *So* good. You must be a mind reader.'

'Hah, I can just imagine what it's like working in one of those things all day. So, you got it all finished, then? That's great.'

'Yeah, we cracked on well this afternoon. Just in time too, mind. The weather forecast is dreadful for tomorrow. High winds and heavy rain coming in.'

'Yes, I saw that.'

You'd never guess from the balmy evening they had tonight. It was evidently the calm before the storm, the sky azure with small puffs of cloud, swifts and swallows darting around. It was an evening to make the most of.

'Well, I've been cooped up all day, so how do you fancy a walk? Stretch our legs, and take a wander up the top of Kirk Mount?' It was the nearest hill, lying behind their two farms in the foothills of the Cheviots.

'Yeah, why not. That sounds nice.' Despite being outside a lot of the time, Rachel hardly ever went out for a walk as such. It was such a lovely evening too, it'd be a shame to have to go in already.

'Great, I'll just get the padlock on the shed here and then I'm ready to roll.'

It was a gorgeous leisurely half hour, Rachel and Tom strolling with the evening sun on them, and it felt a world away from the worries and responsibilities of farming life.

They were soon at the top of Kirk Mount. A rocky rise marked the high point, and around it were patches of mauve heather and stubbly grass that had been nibbled down by the moorland sheep. The sun was setting earlier now with the August summer nights, and it had already started to dip behind the Cheviot Hills, with the sky towards the coast turning into a blush of pink, pewter and peach. It really was beautiful.

It was so special, taking a little time out, chatting away on their ascent, but there was no hand-holding like on their walk home to Primrose Farm on the night of the barbecue. In fact, Tom seemed shy of any physicality today, like he might be afraid of doing the wrong thing.

At one point on the way up, Rachel had made a move, reaching tentatively for Tom's hand, almost brushing fingertips, but then she wondered, had she got this all wrong? She felt suddenly unsure of herself.

Did Tom want to keep it as friends, after all? Was that why he'd brought her up here, to say that they ought to leave the kisses as a moment in time, and go back to how things were before? Would it be better that way? She turned her gaze from the view and found that he was looking at her. Her heart missed a beat. But what were those dark eyes really saying?

If he had doubts too, then they had to leave this right here, right now. But, could this be something so much more? She was at the edge of feelings so new, so raw, so unknown, yet powerful. Her heart seemed to ache for him.

'Rachel?' The word was clear, yet softly spoken. A question. Permission?

She turned towards him as their eyes locked meaningfully. He reached to run a hand gently through her dark wavy hair, and then moved in closer. Their eyes were still locked together as their lips met; tender, warm and loving. Oh, yes. His tongue now teasing, tempting, stirring so much longing within Rachel.

They pulled apart briefly, and smiled at each other, his caring, sexy, dark eyes intent on hers. From the stirring inside, she knew that this had gone way beyond the realm of friendship, but it didn't seem to be just about lust either. It felt like the whole damn gorgeous caboodle . . . Every nerve ending tingling, and something deeper filling up a hole in her heart.

With Jake, it had been a massive teenage crush, and yes, she'd fancied the pants off him. But she had been so young and naïve; it had been sexual and sensual but it hadn't ever reached a deeper level. She never felt that Jake really 'knew' her. *This* with Tom, it felt like coming home – a very sexy, passionate, to-the-core-of-you home.

'Tom,' was her answer. His name strong and sure on her lips.

She lost herself to his kiss once more. Then, she pulled him gently with her towards the ground, where the grass was cushion-like beneath them. Kissing, and touching, and tasting, setting free everything she'd held back on for so long. This man was beautiful and loving and caring, and she'd already glimpsed his rather gorgeous body. She shifted onto his lap, where she felt the heat and firmness through his jeans that was so sensual, so life-affirming. It was good to know how much she turned him on, it gave her confidence, fuelling her own desires.

She knew where this might be going, needed to check if this was right for them both, and if so, was Tom prepared? She hadn't had to think about contraception in such a long time.

'Tom, I . . . um, do you have something, you know, protection?'

He nodded, and couldn't hold back a daft grin. 'I was a Boy Scout once. Always prepared.'

'Okay, okay. Just checking.'

She took a slow breath, then undid the buttons of his blue cotton shirt one by one, revealing his leanly muscled torso. He was strong and healthy – a man in his beautiful prime. She traced a fingertip over his ribs, down to his abs, where the muscles tensed then quivered with a sexy shudder. She took off his shirt, tossed it aside, and made a flutter of kisses across his chest.

She paused for a second, there'd be no going back if she stayed any longer. Yet, every nerve end in her body was telling her to stay. Oh damn it, she needed to know this man, all of him. She pulled her own top off. Tom reached around to unhook her bra, which snagged for a second, making them both smile nervously, before its glorious release. Her breasts were full, and he gazed at them with a look of awe before moving in to delicately lick and suck each nipple in turn. A blissful groan escaped her lips. She kissed the top of his head, then began to lose herself to that building pleasure.

They pulled off their jeans in a fumble, just underwear between them now. Another kiss, prolonging the bliss.

Then he moved her so that she was lying on her back on the grassy hillside, and slipped her white lacy pants down over her thighs. Oh my, this was really going to happen.

He traced her breasts once more with the lightest of touches, and then trailed a fingertip down over her navel, tracing the line to her thighs, and there, yes there, he lingered rhythmically at the sweetest spot. She felt herself arch towards his touch, and he looked at her with his soulful dark eyes; it was a look that seemed to be full of love. Just the slightest of nods said the biggest of 'Yes'es. She didn't want words here now. They had gone beyond words.

And he was there ready with a sexy nudge, and then he was deep within her.

Oh God, yes, Tom.

'Rachel,' he whispered, finding himself lost to her, and then to the pulsing rhythm.

The feeling was delicious and sexy and so damned intense. The push and pull into waves of pleasure, until she felt that exquisite release as she pulsed around him.

Oh God, she hadn't known making love could be like that.

He was in no rush to pull away, just shifted his weight slightly as they smiled at each other. Then, he moved to lie down beside her, cuddling her as she nestled back against his chest. She felt totally blissed out, lying there close to him, rather like the feral cat who would occasionally get a dish of cream down at the farm and stretch out, utterly content, in a patch of sunlight. The air was starting to cool but Tom's arm was warm and protective around her.

Rachel had a sudden thought, wondering if anyone might be out rambling this evening, or if one of their farmhands was out doing their checks, and might find them there. They'd certainly get more of a view than they'd bargained for, if so. She couldn't help but giggle.

'What's up with you? Surely my performance wasn't that hilarious.' Tom tried to sound annoyed, but his voice was laced with laughter too.

'It certainly was not. Pretty damned good, actually.' She turned her head to see him give a proud beam, which made her giggle all the more. 'No, I was just picturing some hikers or one of our farmhands appearing on the quad, or something.'

'Hah, that'd give them a bit of a shock.'

'Do you think we should move, then?' But it was so cosy there, lying together in the afterglow.

'Nah, not yet.'

They stayed lying close for a while longer, chatting whilst Tom made little circles with his fingertips on her arms, then down over the rise of her naked hip to her outer thigh, but the air began to cool dramatically with the evening drawing in.

'Rachel, would you come back to mine? Can you stay the night?' Tom asked hopefully, yet aware that things might not be that easy for her with a young child to consider. Also, they were at such a fragile point in this blossoming relationship, neither really knew the rules.

She took a slow breath, thinking of all the implications, but she knew what she wanted. 'Yes, I'll send Mum a text. That's going to be a bit awkward, I have to admit. It's pretty obvious what we're up to. Hah, I'll feel like I've reverted to being seventeen or something.'

Mind you, at seventeen she had *so* fallen for the wrong guy. Was she sure now this was absolutely right? Wow, it had *felt* so right, she needed to give it a try at least. After her pep talk with Eve, she needed to be brave, live for the moment, and dive right in with a hopeful eye on the future. She couldn't lose this chance of happiness now. She couldn't lose Tom.

She gave a little shiver.

'Come on, let's get you back somewhere warm.'

'I suppose we'd better get our clothes back on then,' Rachel said wryly, Tom having stood up in his full naked glory at that point.

'For now, yes,' he replied, with a mischievous twinkle in his eye.

She'd never known it could feel like this. So bloody beautiful, giving, sensual. They were lying in Tom's bed. Making love the second time had been just as good as the first, in fact better as they were learning to know each other's bodies, to trust each other. There was something so much more than sex going on here. It was like they knew each other, *really* knew each other, and yet everything was all brand new too. She wanted to explore every centimetre, no, every millimetre, of his body.

Was this what falling in love felt like? Wonderfully, Tom seemed to be feeling it all too. Was this how Mum felt for Dad? In those early falling-for-each-other days? Oh God, poor Mum, losing that, losing him, after all those years together. She suddenly had a glimpse of a different kind of pain. The loss of a partner. She knew all too well the loss of a father. Her emotions were suddenly all over the place as she lay in the dark in Tom's bedroom. She could hear his steady sleeping breath beside her, and it was wonderful yet a bit surreal.

This evening, tonight. All these crazy, beautiful feelings. It was amazing.

And shit, did it scare her.

Chapter 36

DON'T GO BREAKING MY HEART

Rachel woke. Dark brown hair was splayed out on the pillow beside her in short bed-head tufts. The lashes were thick on his closed eyelids. The curve of his top lip defined – it was crazy to think she could kiss those lips again if she wanted.

So, it was real. Not a dream. Tom Watson was lying in bed beside her, and she felt all warm and fuzzy about that.

He stirred, cuddled her closer, then opened one eye, as if checking exactly the same thing himself.

'Morning,' he said with a smile.

'Hi . . . hello you.' Rachel grinned.

'You okay?'

'Yes, very cosy in fact.' It felt warm and safe here in Tom's bed. She had slept so well – hah, no doubt something to do with all that energetic sex. It had been so, so long since she'd woken up in someone's arms, and it was rather special.

'I'll fetch us a cup of tea then, shall I? Bring it back to bed?' Tom offered.

'In a minute . . .' There was no rush. A glance at her

watch told Rachel that it was only ten to seven. Her farm chores could wait just a little longer.

They made slow, like-there-was-no-need-to-get-out-of-bed-yet, morning love. Rachel was worried her breath might be fusty, but it didn't seem to put Tom off at all. His kisses were warm and tender.

Lying back on the pillows, Tom said, 'I can still hardly believe this . . . us.'

'Yes, I know. It's rather wonderful, isn't it.' She still felt like the farm cat, who'd now just eaten three bowls of cream.

Tom gently pushed away a strand of hair that had fallen across her face. 'I watched you grow up. We were just kids back then. Then you turned into this amazing young woman.'

'Aw . . . Hah, remember that day when you let me climb up into the tractor when you were ploughing? I begged you to let me drive.'

'Yes, you were only six or something. You were quite determined back then too.' He raised his eyebrows.

'Anyway, you let me sit on your lap just for a minute or so and steer. I loved that.'

'Yeah, and both our dads would have killed us, if they'd seen.'

'Definitely . . . oh . . .' she sighed at the mention of her dad. Their shared past entwined with so much pain as well as joy. 'Dad.'

'You've been so strong, Rachel. Keeping everything together on the farm. Being brave enough to try this new pudding venture. But you don't have to hold it all in, you know. I know the pressures, I know what you've all been through too . . .'

'Thanks.' She'd been so used to keeping it all to herself and, well, just getting on with life, it wasn't going to be shared lightly. But it was lovely that Tom wanted to give that support.

'Your dad . . .' Tom was looking up at the ceiling now as he remembered. 'He spoke with me the night before he died.'

'*He did?*' Rachel flashed her face towards him. He'd never mentioned this before. 'What did he say?'

'Oh, that it was getting to him, trying to keep the farm going, the pressures we were all under these days. That there were some problems. He didn't seem to want to elaborate, it was over in a minute. It was just a comment, you know, farmer to farmer.'

'You saw him . . . the day before? You knew something and you said *nothing*. You didn't think to warn me and Mum . . . ?'

'It was just a normal conversation, Rach. There really didn't seem anything to warn you *about*. He seemed fed up, maybe a bit down. But nothing at all that made me think that . . . God, I mean, if I'd had even an inkling . . .' the words trailed, he paused. 'Well, we were chatting in confidence, farmer to farmer, that was all.'

'Oh, my God, Tom. Maybe it was a cry for help? Did you not think to consider that?'

'Yes, of course I did, in hindsight. But at the time, no, I'd have never imagined . . .'

'Jeez Tom, if you'd only said . . . thought to warn us, it might have changed something . . . it might have changed *everything*.' Rachel was struggling to comprehend all this. The massive implications. She lay back on the pillows beside Tom, as a huge tear welled in her eye.

'I'm so sorry, Rach. I don't know what to say, I . . .'

He reached to touch her hand, which she pulled back instinctively.

She couldn't stay here now. Couldn't be near this man who'd had the chance to alter something so monumental. This man who'd witnessed her dad's fragile state of mind . . . and done nothing. Someone she'd thought they could all trust.

She was up and out of the bed, pulling on socks, underwear, her T-shirt, in a frenzy.

Tom looked shocked and sat up in the bed, trying to explain. 'Look Rachel, how could I have known? How could anyone? Like I said, he seemed a bit down, but nothing like I hadn't seen before—'

Her anger flared. 'Down, a bit *down*. He was fucking suicidal, Tom.'

Rachel bolted out of the room, down the stairs, and grabbed the keys to the quad from the kitchen side.

Go . . . get away, her bruised mind was telling her. But her heart felt so damn heavy as she closed Tom's front door. She started the quad and drove off: angry, confused, scared to look back up at his bedroom window.

*

331

Later that afternoon, back at the farmhouse, Rachel was baking as therapy. She smashed the rolling pin down onto the bag of digestive biscuits. Crush, thwack, crush.

She had kept her head down all day. Getting on with the farm work and her shift in the Pantry – although avoiding the eleven o'clock rush when a certain *someone* was likely to pop in for his bacon roll. Mum had told her that Tom had called in, looking slightly anxious and asking after her.

He had also texted several times through the day. She hadn't answered.

'Everything all right, Rachel, love?' said Jill, walking back into the kitchen after fetching washing from the line. She knew the signs of an aching heart.

'Yes, fine.' Rachel's answer sounded curt, she realised; she needed to keep her bad mood in check. She'd already decided that Mum didn't need to ever find out the truth. 'Yes, sorry. Hi, Mum,' her tone softened.

'You know you could do that easily in the mixer,' Jill prompted.

'Ah yes, but this is *far* more satisfying.' Another thwack.

'O-kay.' Jill knew when to stop delving. 'I'll just get this folded and put in a pile for ironing later, and then I'll need to crack on with something for supper.' She left her daughter to her baking, giving her a little space.

Next, Rachel began to melt the butter, popping a golden lump in a pan on the Aga's slow hob. She then took it off the heat and stirred the biscuit crumbs through it, ready to spoon and shape the mixture into the base of a flan dish, in fact, two dishes – one cheesecake would be for the Pudding Pantry and the other for them as a family, with a spare slice or two reserved for Eve. Maisy was luckily over there on a play date just now with Amelia.

Rachel had already been out and picked a bowl of plump raspberries fresh from the garden, and had her other ingredients lined up ready to mix together – white chocolate, yet to melt, along with cream cheese and double cream. Concentrating on the stirring and beating helped ease Rachel's frustrations, and she was soon lost to the task, checking the mix was at just the right consistency. After the biscuit bases had chilled in the fridge, she took them out and spooned out the deliciously sweet, cheesy mixture, layering the puddings with fresh raspberries and a little of Jill's homemade raspberry jam. She then spooned another creamy layer over the top.

'They're looking good.' Jill came back in, just as Rachel was about to pop them back into the fridge. Later, she'd add the soft, fruity-raspberry topping, drizzling it over to finish.

'Thanks, Mum.'

'*So*, do you want to talk about it, love? Was everything okay last night?' Jill prompted, concerned for her daughter.

'Yeah, fine.' Rachel's voice was way too chirpy.

'You sure? You don't seem yourself today at all, love. You can talk to me, tell me if anything's bothering you.'

'It's nothing, honestly.'

'If he hurt you, made you feel uncomfortable . . .'

'Oh no, honestly. No, it's not like that. It was nothing like that.' No physical pain, anyway. But, she was never going to tell Jill the truth. It wouldn't change anything. It would just hurt her mum to know, like it was hurting her deep inside. That sense of guilt, that they might have been able to stop it, change things, rising to the surface like a tidal wave, and wedging even deeper into her heart. 'I just don't think we're that suited, that's all. We just need to cool things, get back to being mates. It's all just too awkward otherwise.' Rachel smothered the facts.

'Well, as long as you're all right, love.'

'Yeah, I'm fine.'

'Okay, well, I'm always here if you ever need to talk . . .'

'Thanks, I know . . .' Rachel then busied herself at the washing-up bowl for a while, looking out across the fields from the farmhouse kitchen window; watching as heavy clouds – dark as bruises – moved across the sky.

Two days later, Rachel was heading into Kirkton when she saw Tom's jeep coming down the lane in the opposite direction. Her heart went into freefall. Ah no, he was slowing down . . . this was going to be so awkward.

'Hey.' He wound down his window and gave a cautious smile. 'Are you okay?'

Oh, bloody hell. She stopped too, they were still neighbours after all. But she *really* didn't know how to act, what to say, and she was still so bloody angry with him.

'I'm sorry, Rachel. If I could change anything, go back,

334

have said something more . . . You know I'd do it in a heartbeat.' His eyes were searching hers.

'Yeah, well . . . you can't turn back time, Tom.' She sounded cool, detached.

'I can understand how upset you feel, and I'm so sorry if I've hurt you. But the other night . . . well, I'd thought we had something special going on. Really special . . .'

She stayed silent. The lane was empty, there was no need to drive away, but she desperately wanted to. She couldn't cope with this right now.

'Tom, it hurts too much. I can't unknow what I now know. I don't think there's anything else to say or do now. Let's just go back to how things were. Just as neighbours.' She didn't even say friends. 'Look, I just don't think it can work out in the long run,' she blabbed.

'Oh.' His face said it all. He looked so goddamned disappointed.

If she followed this through, she might never be able to touch him again, be near him again. She held her breath. 'Sorry, Tom. I think it's better this way.'

'Okay.' He didn't look like it was okay at all, he looked totally gutted. 'Well, I guess I'll see you around, then.'

He drove off, leaving Rachel feeling sick.

'Good God, Rachel, you've been like a bear with a sore head this past week,' Jill said, openly exasperated with her daughter. 'Look, it's quiet in here now, I can manage the Pantry fine, so why don't you head back over to the farmhouse with Maisy?'

Rachel just gave her mum a look.

'Honestly, you'll be frightening away the customers at this rate,' Jill continued.

Rachel knew she had been slamming down the crockery a bit on the drainer as she was washing up, but hadn't realised quite how noisy or annoying that might be. She just felt so leaden, like a big dark cloud was crowding her mind.

She was trying so hard to put Tom out of her mind, but after that night with him, there were so many memories and moments that kept prodding at her, flashing up in her thoughts. Damn it, she missed him. But how could she even be thinking about him . . . when he'd let her dad down in the worst possible way?

It would get easier, she told herself that. But, Mum was right, she couldn't be taking it out on everyone else.

'Sorry, Mum,' she said. 'There's just quite a lot on my mind at the moment.'

Jill just nodded, as she made up a pot of tea for the next order.

'And, it is quieter in here than I'd have hoped at this stage,' admitted Rachel. 'I think we need to think of more ways to try and raise awareness of the Pudding Pantry too. People in Kirkton seem to know of us now, but do you think we're a little too off the beaten track for others to find us? We definitely need to consider more publicity and marketing – getting ourselves out there somehow.'

'Yes, I agree we could do with some more advertising,

but that can be quite costly. What about contacting the local tourist information centres again? Maybe leave some flyers with them, and look at getting a mention on their website or something?'

Rachel had already set up their own webpage for the Pantry, but maybe they could link in with the tourist board and other local attractions. It was definitely an avenue worth pursuing.

'Yeah, I'll look into it further, great idea Mum. Autumn's approaching fast, and we need to keep the momentum up. I'll get my thinking cap on. And, in the meanwhile, yes, I'll take Maisy back over to the house, she'll be getting bored spending her summer holidays sat in here so much. Just ring me if you need a hand though. You know, if a coach load of fifty turn up or something,' she jested. 'In our dreams.'

'I will. Go on, get yourselves away.'

'Come on petal, let's go then,' Rachel said to Maisy, who'd been sitting at one of the tables with her fairy glen book and some crayons and a pad. 'What do you want to do at home? We could maybe get the craft stuff out and make something?' Maisy loved drawing, painting, and creating things.

'Ooh, yes, please. Can I get my bead set out and make some bracelets?'

'Of course. That sounds a good plan.'

'Here,' said Jill. 'There's a couple of cupcakes to take back over with you, as a treat.' She passed them a plate of scrummy-looking red velvet cakes.

'Thanks, Mum.'

'Thank you, Grandma.' Maisy beamed happily.

Within the hour they'd had tea and cakes together and made two pink-and-silver beaded bracelets, one for Maisy and another to give to Amelia.

'Can I see Amelia soon, Mummy?'

'Yes, I expect so. Maybe she can come and play one day. I'll give Eve a ring.'

'Yippee!'

Rachel had been lying low for the past week as far as Eve was concerned, not wanting to tell her friend all that had happened with Tom. She had no idea that Rachel had stayed the night with him. That night and the morning after had been so momentous for Rachel that she hadn't wanted to go into details with anyone, and she knew Eve would be prying for *all* the details as far as Tom was concerned! Some things were best kept to yourself. Also, there was no point in raking over everything if it was going nowhere.

She made the call to Eve, intending to talk about the girls meeting up.

'Hi, Rach. Well, you've been quiet lately. What's up?'

'Nothing . . . well, it's just been busy on the farm and with the Pudding Pantry, but everything's fine. What about you?'

'I've got a place booked in the craft tent at the Kirkton Country Show that's coming up soon, so I've been full on trying to make lots of toys and gifts. I've got a production line going on at my place at the moment.'

'Well, why don't I help with Amelia then? Maisy's just been asking if they can get together. I could take them swimming one morning or something. Give you a break.' It was time she took Maisy out for a treat, especially whilst it was still the holidays. The Pudding Pantry had taken all their focus and energy lately.

'Oh, could you, that'd be just brilliant.'

'Yeah, I'll just check which day'll work best with Mum. I imagine one morning mid-week. I'll call you back and confirm.'

'Great stuff. And, we'll catch up for a coffee sometime too, yeah?'

'Yeah, maybe I can stop by when I drop Amelia back off that day. Just a quick one with you being so busy.' She really hoped her friend wouldn't mention Tom when she saw her next; Rachel didn't know if her face might give her away, revealing all the confusing and painful emotions that lay behind the developments this past week.

The Kirkton Country Show: Eve had set Rachel thinking. It was always on the August bank holiday Monday and it was a big event in the local area, attended by thousands of people. Rachel had often gone herself, especially when Dad was still alive. There were stalls with people selling everything from homemade pies to ales and crafts, and there were livestock parades and prizes. She remembered there was a specific food tent too. The Pudding Pantry needed publicity and more sales – this could be the answer she was looking for *and* it was virtually on their doorstep.

Maisy was now sitting happily watching a programme about puppies on the TV. Rachel seized the moment and called Eve back.

'Hi, Eve, I've just been thinking, how did you get booked on to the show? I know it's a bit late in the day, but if we could get a stall in the food tent, it'd be great for us to get our name out there, and hopefully plenty of pudding sales too.' For the first time in days she felt the stirrings of excitement.

Eve gave her the necessary contact details and wished her luck. It was a long shot, as spaces had probably been snapped up ages ago, but worth a try.

Rachel called the organiser right away, holding her breath, and, much to her delight and amazement, they were in! They'd had a late cancellation due to ill health. Rachel agreed to take the slot right away and paid a deposit over the phone. She had yet to break the news to Jill, who she hoped would be as thrilled as she was. It was just such a good opportunity. So, it'd be all hands to the pump for the next ten days – a proper pudding-making mission. They had a stall to fill at the Kirkton Show – whoop, whoop! – and it might just help take her mind off a certain Tom Watson.

Chapter 37

WISE WORDS AND LEMON MERINGUE PIE

'I'll take the eggs across to Grandma today, Mum,' offered Rachel.

So much for taking her mind off Tom. Yes, they'd been damned busy getting a zillion puddings made in time for the Kirkton Country Show, but that man was still very much lodged in her head. Seeing Granny Ruth would make for a good change of scene. And it was a chance for them to have a well-needed catch-up, one on one – Maisy wanted to stay with her Grandma Jill as they were making some brownies together, so Rachel would head across alone.

'Okay, thanks, that'll be great. Send her my love, and see if she wants to come across for supper one evening. Maybe next Tuesday, after the show's all done?'

'Will do.'

Off she set, arriving ten minutes later outside Ruth's countryside cottage. She found her granny out in the front garden with a pair of secateurs to hand, dead-heading her roses.

'Oh, hello there, our lassie. How are you?'

'I'm fine thanks, Granny, and how are you?'

'Well, the old knees have been giving me gyp – been trying to get those pesky weeds out of the borders earlier on, it was a battle to get myself back up again, but other than that I'm grand.'

'Good, that's what I like to hear.'

'Well, I think this calls for a cup of tea. I could do with a little break. Let's go out the back and have a seat, hey?'

'Oh yes.'

'Oh, and I made a lemon meringue pie yesterday, maybe we'll have a slice of that too.'

'Perfect.' Ruth's lemon meringue pies were a delight; all crispy short pastry with a layer of homemade citrus-sharp lemon curd, topped with softly baked meringue.

'I had a feeling it'd come in handy when I baked it yesterday. You never know when someone might decide to call.'

The door was always open at Granny Ruth's, so visitors were a frequent possibility. She had lots of friends in the village.

Settled on Ruth's wrought-iron bench in her small but pretty back garden, looking out over green-and-gold country fields, Granny suddenly looked serious. 'So Rachel lass, what's been troubling you this past week or so?'

Oh dear, maybe Mum had mentioned that she was acting a bit out of sorts. She really didn't want to tell Granny Ruth the truth. It was too raw; it was an emotional mess involving her son, who'd died. They were all just beginning to find a way forward.

'Oh, it's nothing Granny . . .' she batted away the question.

'Rachel pet, I know *nothing* when I see it and this is not nothing. Do you think I'm stupid? And do you think not talking about your woes will help anybody?'

This was way too close to home. 'Granny, I just don't want to upset anyone.'

'Look pet, the worst has already happened. I might be an old goat, but I want to look after the family that I have left, and if something's troubling you lass, I'd like to help. Even if it means just talking it through. Try me, I've lived a full life. There's not a lot that can shock or surprise me now.'

Rachel chewed a fingernail anxiously. Despite Ruth's assurances, she was still terrified that this revelation could hurt her lovely granny.

'Come on, lass,' Ruth tried to tease it out of her. '*Not* talking didn't help your dad now, did it?'

That was it, Rachel broke into sobs. Ruth had enveloped her in a hug within a second.

'Tell me, pet.'

'Oh Granny, that's just it, Dad did try to talk . . . to Tom,' Rachel managed to get it out. 'Tom told me he saw Dad the night before . . . the night before . . . he killed himself. Dad spoke with him. He knew he was upset.'

'Well, what did Tom say happened?' Ruth sounded calm.

'Ah, just that Dad stopped and talked to him, admitting the farm was under pressure. Tom said that he seemed a bit down but that Dad didn't want to "elaborate". Yes, that was the word. Granny, to think he might have been able to help him . . . to *stop* him.'

'Oh, Rachel lass, haven't we all been thinking that these past two years? Looking back on conversations and gestures, trying to see the signs, and how we might have changed things. But your dad was a deep soul, even as a little boy. Would Tom have known there was more to it? I don't think so. Your dad would have kept it all very close to his chest, even if he did admit things on the farm weren't so great. That dark place he was in was very private, very deep and closely guarded. It's not your fault nor Tom's, nor your mum's, nor mine. It was an illness.'

Rachel let out a long, slow sigh, words eluding her just now.

'Now then, your mum tells me there's been a bit of courting going on with you and young Tom?'

'There's no secrets around here, is there, Granny.' Rachel managed a wry smile. 'Well, we were getting friendlier, but it feels so different now, knowing this . . .'

'He's a good man, Rachel. He's kind and he cares for you, anyone can see that. Don't let this sour it all. Think about it, pet. Is it really Tom who's hurt you in all this, or is it more the feelings that have been stoked – the harsh realisation that none of us could have done anything about it?'

'I don't know, Granny. I really don't know.' Rachel

spooned some soft meringue into her mouth. She really needed comfort food right now.

'Well, if it's love, Rachel, don't you let it go to waste, lass. That's the last thing your dad would have wished for. He just wanted you to be happy.'

Chapter 38

A PUDDING STALL

The first ever Pudding Pantry stall was ready to roll in the big white food marquee of the Kirkton Country Show. Rachel had had plenty of other things to focus on in the days after seeing Granny Ruth, and she was more than happy to let the pressure of the show distract her.

Their stall was wedged in between 'The Porkie Pie Man' and 'The Chocolate Shop by the Sea' stand – the chocolates there looked divine, and that stall was so pretty. The other stallholders throughout the tent seemed really friendly, and were selling the most delicious provisions: local cheeses, ice creams, cakes, honey, jams, chutneys, sausages, and more.

Emma, the chocolate stall lady, was lovely. It was her first year there too, she'd said, coming back to the stall with steaming cups of coffee for Rachel and Jill. She also admitted to feeling a little nervous, not knowing quite what to expect.

As well as hoping to have a good day of pudding sales, Rachel and Jill really hoped to raise visibility for the

Pudding Pantry, letting both local people plus those from the wider area know where to find them. Rachel had a batch of professional-looking flyers that she'd created herself, ready to distribute around the show.

They had a Pudding Pantry sign strung up behind them – a new portable wooden plaque that Eve had made and hand-painted especially – and a mini blackboard that Rachel had carefully chalked up with a price list of all the puddings and bakes for sale. There was a table-top fridge (borrowed from the lovely Brenda at the Deli) with the chilled puddings in, set upon a green checked tablecloth, with more puddings stored in cool boxes below the table to top up from. Jill had also made a selection of traybakes – Malteser-flavour and rocky road being the most mouth-watering – along with chocolate brownies and a variety of cupcakes.

They hadn't wanted to lose custom back at the Pudding Pantry on the farm either with it being the August bank holiday weekend, so they'd decided that Rachel would head back with Maisy for the morning shift, once the stall was set up. Eve, who had her own stall in the craft tent, would cover an hour over the lunchtime for Jill and Rachel to swap over, with Ben assuring he'd give her a hand to cover her own stall.

Jill and Rachel had been baking for days now, putting in lots of early mornings and late nights. The Country Show event was very much trial and error but they were feeling positive. They still needed a big boost and were willing to try anything – the Pudding Pantry had brought in a nice steady income so far, but not quite a bank-balance altering flow.

The show officially opened to the public at 11 a.m., and before they set off back to the farm for the Pantry morning shift, Rachel had a chance to take Maisy around the various tents. The Kirkton Country Show was a fabulous end-of-summer event that had been held for over one hundred years. Traditionally, the farmers had gathered to show their finest animals, their tractor skills, sheepdog trials, with the women of the WI active with baking, flower arranging displays and more. As they weaved through the various stalls, it felt good to know that they were a small part of a bigger history – the show was a huge source of pride in the local area.

Baking was still a large part of the proceedings today. Rachel had eventually convinced Jill to enter her sticky toffee pudding into the 'Best Baked Pudding' category. She had been hesitant to put herself forward, in case her pudding didn't even get a mention in the top three, but Rachel was sure it would get a place. After all, Jill had been making the best ever puddings for years. She could see it now: 'Best in Show' and 'Prize-Winning Puddings' on the Pudding Pantry counter. But she was careful not to share her hopes with her mum, not wanting to add any further pressure.

Jill had also persuaded Rachel to enter her carrot cake in the 'Cake Made with Any Vegetable' category. Okay, so it hadn't gone down too well with the abominable

Vanessa P-P at the launch party, but then not a lot did. This prize was judged by members of the show committee, and it was Rachel's own small chance to shine. Jill ensured she gave her a tip or two when she made the cake yesterday back in the farmhouse kitchen. And, as they say, the proof of the pudding . . .

As Rachel and Maisy passed the horticultural and industrial tent where the bakes would be judged, the flap doors were closed with a small sign that read 'Tent Closed. Judging in Progress'. Rachel's heart gave a little anxious skip. How would she and Jill have done? Who would be claiming the red, heart-brimming, first prize rosettes?

Moving on past this big marquee, there were coffee cabins, fish and chip stalls, ice-cream vans, tractors and quads for sale, and all kinds of new, shiny and impressive agricultural machinery. They were headed for the craft tent, where Eve was running her stall. They eventually spotted it, over near the fair rides. Rachel promised Maisy a go on the 'Tea Cups' later on when they were back that afternoon.

It felt like they were entering an Aladdin's cave of arts and crafts in this marquee, with jewellery, woodwork, paintings, photography, and ooh, there was Eve's stall all set out beautifully – with her trademark soft toys, plaques, cards, knits and hearts and stars.

'Wow – this looks amazing, Eve. You must have spent hours and hours making this lot, for sure.'

'Yeah, there've been some late nights for me and sore

fingers with all the stitching and knitting, but I'm pleased with it all. Let's just hope it sells.'

'Well, I hope it goes really well for you today, hun.'

'And for you, too. How's it going over in the food tent?'

'Great, we've got Grandma Jill all set up, haven't we, Maisy? Just hard to know what to expect customer-wise.'

'Yes, last year I did pretty well, which is why I'm back, but you never quite know. And it costs a fair bit to get a stand, so you have to cover that much at least.'

'Well, good luck!'

'Yes, you too. Let's hope they all love puddings, soft toys and crafts. And I'm still fine to cover at lunchtime for you. I've got my mobile on me if you need anything else too. Oh and yes, once Ben's free this afternoon he said he's happy to take Amelia and Maisy around the show for a while.'

'My daddy's coming too,' Maisy piped up. She hadn't forgotten the promise that Jake had made on their last phone call.

Yes, Jake had finally called back a week ago now. He and Maisy had had a five-minute chat with Maisy telling him excitedly all about the show. He was meant to be coming up for the whole bank holiday weekend, but with Saturday and Sunday already having whizzed by, well, Rachel was doubtful to say the least. They'd heard nothing more from him since, and Rachel's texts had gone unanswered.

'Oh, well that's lovely, Maisy,' Eve said, trying to sound upbeat. She looked at Rachel questioningly though, sharing her friend's doubts.

Rachel pulled a face, silently mouthing, 'Not heard from him since,' whilst shaking her head in frustration.

'Right, well then,' she continued out loud. 'We'd better get back to Grandma at the stall, and then head home where you can be my top Pudding Pantry waitress this morning. Say goodbye to Eve.'

'By-ee,' Maisy said, with a cheerful wave.

'See you later.'

Chapter 39

BEST IN SHOW

Back at the food tent there was a building sense of expectation amongst the stallholders, with the gates due to open in half an hour. Jill was ready with her pinafore on and a broad smile in place, stood proudly behind their stand.

'Best of luck, Mum. Call if you need anything.'

'Will do, thanks, love. And, I'll nip back to the farm as soon as Eve comes to take over. Jan's all ready to give me a lift. Oh, any news from Jake, yet?' Mum lowered her voice. Maisy was over at the chocolate shop stand chatting away with Emma.

'No . . . he bloody well promised her, Mum. I'll be so damned cross with him if he doesn't turn up today.' Maisy still lived in hope, hanging onto Jake's every word like it was precious. He hadn't been back to see her since their opening week in mid-July, and it was now the end of August.

'Well, there'll be lots to entertain her today, so let's hope she's not too disappointed if he doesn't show.'

He might just turn up out of the blue, *or* he might have found something far more interesting to do this weekend than see his little girl, like going after a new woman or watching a motorbike rally. Dipping in and out of her life when it suited him was no way of being a dad, and not what Maisy needed at all. Up until the last, Rachel's own dad had always been there for her. Well, there was a slim chance that Jake might yet turn up and make Maisy's day, but Rachel wasn't holding out a lot of hope for that. A quick glance at her watch told Rachel it was nearly ten-thirty. It was time for her and Maisy to whizz back to the farm.

The rest of the morning back at the Pudding Pantry was steady but not overly busy; no doubt some of their usual customers would be at the show. Maisy kept herself occupied with a colouring book, pencils and a small pack of chocolate buttons, now and again helping to serve. Rachel let her carry a plated slice of cake across to an elderly couple whilst she took the hot drinks.

'My little helper for the school holidays,' Rachel explained.

'You're doing a grand job.' The woman smiled. 'And that cake looks amazing.'

'My grandma makes them,' Maisy answered proudly.

'Well, I wish I could bake like that,' the lady answered.

The gentleman gave Maisy a friendly wink, adding a cheeky, 'So do I,' with a chuckle.

Frank came in for his coffee soon afterwards and

ordered a cheese scone. Maisy took the scone across whilst Rachel prepared his drink.

'Thank you very much. So, little lady, how are you today?'

'Good, thank you,' she answered politely, and then proceeded to tell him all about the show, and Grandma being at their pudding stall and the fair rides and farm animals she'd seen there already. Frank slipped her a two-pound coin to spend when she went back that afternoon. Rachel said that he shouldn't – he'd only be on a small pension for sure – but he insisted. Frank was a regular at the Pantry now; he was a real gent and lovely to chat with, often telling stories of his life in the military.

There was another regular missing again this morning, Rachel realised with some relief. Tom hadn't called in for his bacon sandwich these last few days, not since their words in the lane. She couldn't blame him to be honest. It was all so difficult between them. Granny's words kept echoing in her mind. Had she judged too harshly? She knew she'd upset Tom with her doubts, her anger.

Damn, she should never have let things go so far. Getting romantically involved, as she well knew, came with big risks.

She stared out of the barn window, across the rolling fields towards his farm, and there was an ache inside. She realised she missed him and wondered what might have happened if he hadn't said anything about her dad. Bugger, it was more than an ache, it was a gaping bloody hole, but life was complicated enough. She had to let those silly romantic notions go. Better to leave well alone. Maybe in a few weeks' time things would be easier; they could claw back some kind of neighbourly friendship.

'Excuse me, can I have a refill of coffee?' It was the gentleman who Maisy had served earlier at the counter. Ooh, she'd been off in a little world of her own there for a moment.

'Ah yes, of course. No problem.' She took his cup. 'I'll bring it across for you in a moment.'

'Silly Mummy,' Maisy muttered. Rachel had to smile.

The morning passed quickly. There was still no news from Jake, no grey van turning up. Maisy hadn't asked about him again, but Rachel knew she'd still be hoping.

It was just before one o'clock when Jill arrived back at the farm to swap over.

'How's it been at the show?' Rachel asked, curious to find out.

'Great,' Jill beamed. 'It was slowish to start, but then by twelve it was crazy busy. I've sold right out of the chocolate puddings and only got two sticky toffees left. You'll need to take back some more traybakes, brownies and cake slices too. People seem to want something they can eat there and then as well as the puds.'

'Brilliant, looks like we're going to be busy then, Maisy. Right, I'll get the Land Rover loaded up. We don't want to miss out on any sales at the show.'

*

'Maisy, stay close now, darling. I can't manage to hold your hand.'

The tent was heaving. It was hard to get through the throng of people slowly drifting around the stalls. Rachel raised the boxes of baked goods higher as she pressed on, saying 'Excuse me' and 'Sorry' as she shifted through the crowd, checking Maisy was still there beside her as she went. The air was warm and it was stuffy in there, with various wafts of food hitting her as she passed different stands: sausages cooking, the ripeness of cheeses, the cocoa richness of sweet chocolate.

They finally made it across to Eve at the Pudding Pantry's stand at the far side of the marquee.

'Blimey, it's *sooo* busy in here,' Rachel said, relieved to get there and see that Maisy was still beside her.

'I know, I haven't stopped serving this past hour. It's doing brilliantly though.'

The stall did look rather depleted.

'And is that everything put out?'

'Nearly, there's about four of the marmalade puddings and a couple of ginger ones left in the cool box, that's all.'

'Amazing, that's so great. Good job I've brought some more stocks then.' She rested her cargo on the table top.

They set out the new supplies and also served a couple who were eager to check out the new produce, snapping up a sticky chocolate and two slices of coffee and walnut cake.

'Right,' Eve said, 'I'd better get back to the craft tent now and see how it's going there.'

'Yes, of course. Thanks so much for helping out here, you've been a godsend – again. How's this morning been for you?'

'Steady, I've sold a few things, but it's nothing like how busy it is in here.'

Oh, it would be such a shame if her friend didn't have a good day of sales too. Rachel knew Eve had been up until midnight finishing more of her toys.

'Your crafts are just brilliant. I'm sure it'll pick up. Hang on, have you brought any of your business cards with you?'

'Ah . . . yes, there's some spare ones in my bag.'

'Right, pass them to me and I'll pop one in with every sale we do, and I'll put some on the counter top here next to our flyers.'

'Aw, thank you. And I'll take some of your flyers and pop them on my stall too. We may as well help each other out.'

'Yep. That's what friends are for.'

'Good luck, petal,' said Rachel. 'Turn up your charmometer and go for it!'

'I'll try. Oh, and Maisy, Ben says he'll come and take you and Amelia around the show a bit later when he gets the chance, okay honey?'

'Okay.'

Maisy sounded a little subdued. Oh crikey, it suddenly dawned on Rachel – there was still no sign of Jake, no text or call – the thoughtless oaf.

'See you later, then.'

'Bye, Eve. Best of luck for this afternoon.'

With that, Eve headed off and was soon lost in the snaking surge of customers.

'Right, Maisy, let's get to work. Now, you can help me by putting the things people buy in the paper bags, like this. The right way up on the puddings, yeah, so the sticky sauce doesn't spill, okay?'

'Yes.'

'Can I have one of these, please, darling?' A blonde-haired lady leaned towards the counter. 'A sticky toffee pudding one. Oh, and I'll take a brownie too.' And with that they were up and running, mother and daughter working like a well-oiled team.

There was a constant stream of customers for the next hour or so, and the takings looked good in the cash tin. A good day here might just be the turning point for the Pudding Pantry, and knowing the puddings had been so popular gave Rachel a warm feeling of pride. Wouldn't it be wonderful if their first Kirkton Show was a sell-out?

As a quieter spell hit, Emma from the chocolate stall headed over for a natter. Rachel noted she had the most gorgeous red wavy hair.

'Wow, looks like you guys have done brilliantly, look at all those empty shelves!'

'Yeah, we've still got a reasonable selection of puddings to put out to keep us going for the afternoon, but there are only a couple of brownies left, and only one carrot cake. Maisy here has been selling like a trooper.'

'Hello again, Maisy. I can see you're doing a great job helping out.'

'Thank you, and I'm five,' she announced.

'Wow, well, you're very grown up for five.'

'Five going on fifteen.' Rachel grinned.

'A shopkeeper in the making.' Emma smiled.

'I think she might well be. Or, what is it you said you wanted to be, Maisy? An astronaut, or a farmer, or a tooth fairy?'

'Ah yes, well the world's an exciting place. Always best to keep your options open, young lady. Good thinking.'

With that, there was another flurry of customers for both stalls.

It was just after 3 p.m. when Ben appeared with Amelia, ready to take the girls around the show and the fairground rides as promised.

Rachel handed him a ten-pound note from the takings to treat them to the rides and some ice creams. 'Thanks so much for taking her, Ben.'

'That's no problem at all. It'll cheer up Amelia no end, who was getting bored at the stall.'

Again, it dawned on Rachel that there was still no word from Jake. He'd not even had the guts to call her up or send a message to apologise – the selfish git. There was Amelia holding tight to her daddy's hand, taking it for granted, and that's exactly how it should be. Rachel felt a soreness in her heart for her little girl. Being a single parent was tough sometimes, but being a single child tougher.

'Okay then, Maisy? You go and have some fun with Amelia.'

Her little girl nodded, seeming quieter than usual.

Ben knew about their situation and mouthed, 'No sign of Jake yet?' as the girls started chatting together. Rachel shook her head. He shrugged his shoulders and rolled his eyes.

Maisy then took his spare hand, so he had one girl each side and they set off together. Rachel was at least happy that she was in safe hands with Ben.

When it was time to start packing up, Rachel noticed a tall, attractive man turn up at Emma's stall. He gave Emma a warm hug and a sweet kiss, before asking how the day had gone for her.

'It's been great, Max, really worthwhile.'

Rachel tried not to be too nosey, but couldn't help watching them as they started to pack up the stall together; it was obvious they were very happy in their relationship. Aw, that was so nice to see, yet it made her own heart feel even sorer.

The food tent was definitely quietening down, but she'd wait for Ben to come back with Maisy before packing up properly. She might as well leave her last few wares out in case any stragglers were wanting some last-minute treats to take home. Just then, in the nick of time, she remembered the chocolates she wanted to buy for Mum.

'Oh, Emma, can I buy a box of chocolates from you before they're all packed up?'

'Yeah, of course. What kind would you like?'

'Oh, just a selection really, they all look delicious.'

'Yep, got just the thing. Here you go, a fiver will do fine.'

Rachel had seen earlier that the price should be more like eight pounds. 'You sure?'

'Yeah, that's fine. Oh, and before I go, here, take my card. I know you said you were just setting up, so feel free to ring me, if you have any questions about the business, or you just want a friendly ear.'

'Aw, thanks.' She seemed so genuine and warm.

'And if you are ever going Warkton way, be sure to stop by.'

'I might just do that. I could bring Maisy across one afternoon.' It would be nice to have a little trip out sometime. They didn't do that often enough. Rachel always seemed to be too busy with life and work at the farm, but it'd do them good, and make a lovely break.

Ben arrived back with Maisy and Amelia who were licking the last of their ice-cream cones.

'Hi, we've had a good time. Made sure we did the Tea Cups *before* the ice creams.' Ben grinned.

'Did you have fun, girls?'

'Yes! We had two goes on the Cups,' Amelia chimed.

Maisy's reply was a more subdued, 'Yeah.'

'She doesn't seem quite herself,' Ben whispered. 'I'm wondering if she might be a bit run down.'

'Thanks for letting me know. Her dad's still not shown.'

'Bless her, she'll be disappointed.' He shook his head in empathy.

'Yeah, I think that's what's behind it. But, thanks for the heads up.'

'No worries. Look are you all right packing up here? Need a hand at all?'

'To be honest, we've not got a lot of stock left, so I'm sure I'll be fine. There's not that much to take to the truck really.'

'Mumm-ee, I need a wee,' Maisy chanted, with a hint of desperation, already doing a little jig and crossing her legs.

'Ah, actually, can you mind the stall for a few minutes, Ben?'

'Sure, that's fine.'

'We won't be long.'

Rachel took Maisy's hand in their dash for the Portaloos. They made it just in time.

As they came out, Rachel realised they were just beside the horticultural tent. She'd never had a chance to find out how Mum's sticky toffee and her carrot cake had fared in the competition. There might just be time for a quick look before it all got packed away. She was sure Ben wouldn't mind waiting for five minutes more.

'Come on, Maisy, let's take a quick look in and see if Grandma's pudding's on show.'

'Okay.'

In they went, to be greeted by a stunning display of flowers and vegetables, which had evidently been lovingly nurtured and displayed at their prime.

'These are pretty, Mummy.' Maisy pointed at some big blooms of dahlia in bold pinks and orange. They'd won the first prize and had a red rosette.

They had a quick scoot around, oohing and ahhing as they passed all the gorgeous colours and arrangements, until they found the baking section.

Maisy skipped on ahead, scanning the labels and prize-winner rosettes.

'Mummy, Mummy, I think this is Grandma Jill's!'

There it was, Jill's sticky toffee pudding sporting the first prize red rosette. *Yes!* Rachel felt a tear form in her eye. She was so proud of her mum, of how much she'd put into the Pudding Pantry, of how far they'd come.

'Hey, that's brilliant. I can't wait to tell her.'

'Can I tell her? I saw it first.'

'Of course, let's take a picture on my phone and you can show her it when we get back.'

'Yes.'

She sounded a bit brighter, bless her.

'Where's yours, Mummy?'

'Oh yes, better find that one too.' It didn't really matter that much, thought Rachel, especially now that Jill had won the big prize.

There was a table of cakes displayed: a courgette cake, two carrot cakes, oh and look there, *her* carrot cake was standing with a very creditable blue second prize rosette beside it. Wow – not bad at all. Rachel peered closer at the other contenders. The first prize had been given to an amazing beetroot and chocolate cake, which she had to admit looked divine – no shame in coming second to that. And the third yellow rosette was sitting next to another carrot cake, by . . . Vanessa Palmer-Pilkington. Who would have thought it! Rachel couldn't help but smile to herself.

'Well done. Mummy. You've won a blue.'

'Thanks, petal.'

It was then that Rachel heard a loud, plummy and unmistakeable voice behind her. 'Well, I do think it's been *very* poorly judged this year. I've never had a third in all the years I've entered.'

Rachel gave a quick glance over her shoulder to see an indignant Vanessa P-P moaning away to the poor woman she was with. Rachel caught Vanessa's eye and gave a broad, friendly smile. No words needed to be said. The rictus smile that Vanessa gave in return was tight and forced. *Touché.*

They were just about to leave the tent when an all too familiar face appeared. Rachel froze. She hadn't seen him since their chat in the lane, and here was Tom, just metres away from her.

'Hey,' he said, tentatively.

'Hi.' Well, this was awkward. Argh. He was smiling gently and the thing was . . . he looked so bloody gorgeous.

Luckily Maisy was there to break the second or two of silence that followed. 'Tom, Mummy's got a prize for her cake.'

'Well, that's good. Well done you.' He gave Rachel a friendly nod.

'And . . .' Maisy was on a roll with the news, 'Grandma *won* the puddings!'

'Brilliant.'

'The sticky toffee one,' Maisy added.

'Oh yes. Well, I could have told you she'd get a first prize for that. That's my all-time favourite.'

He and Maisy grinned at each other. It was nice to see Maisy a bit happier now.

'I've only just got here,' Tom explained. 'Just finished the other barley field. That's the last of the arable done for now. Thought I'd nip down, see what's going on at the show. I love this tent . . . The work that must go into getting the vegetables just right, they're like works of art.' He was filling the space between them with inane chat.

'Ah, yes. There's so much expertise gone into that,' Rachel agreed. The conversation then stalled awkwardly. 'Right, well we were just nipping away, got Ben and Amelia minding the stall for us. Better get back.'

'Oh yes, of course . . . Has it gone okay today?'

'Yeah, great thanks.'

'That's good. I hope everything goes well for you.' His words seemed genuinely caring, but there was a new distance between them, a sense of detachment.

There was a heart-breaking pause. 'We'd better go.'

'It's good to see you, Rach.'

'Yeah, you too.' *Keep walking, keep going. Do not give in to silly poignant emotions, or romantic notions.*

Chapter 40

SUMMER STORMS AND SEARCHING

'Right then, I've got it all tidied up in the kitchen now.' Jill came back over to the Pudding Pantry, where Rachel was putting away the last bits of stock she'd brought back from the show. 'It was a bit chaotic getting organised this morning, what with all the last-minute baking and stuff to take,' Jill continued.

Rachel felt a sense of nervous anticipation – she was about to sit down and count up the stall's takings. 'That's good. Where's Maisy by the way?' she asked.

'Ah, I thought she was here with you.'

'Nope, I thought she was in the farmhouse with you.'

'Oh, I see . . .'

'Okay, no worries, she was with me a short while ago,' Rachel confirmed. 'She's probably just playing some-where close by. Maybe on her slide in the garden, though it looks like it's about to pour it down out there.' The sky had turned an ominous leaden grey, with late-summer storm clouds brewing. 'I'll go find her.'

Rachel headed for the garden, calling, 'Maisy, Maisy.'

There was no answer, and as Rachel peered over the hedge and into the garden there was no sign of her there either. Hmm, maybe she'd gone to check the hens for eggs, seeing as they'd been out all day. After going to the chicken coop with no luck, Rachel began to feel concerned. Maisy hadn't said anything about going to do something in particular, and she usually stuck close to her or Jill at all times.

Big plops of rain began to fall as Rachel made her way back to her mum in the barn. 'It's odd, there's no sign of her.'

With that, a crack of thunder went off like a shotgun, with a boom that shook the barn.

'Oh my,' said Jill.

'Right, we'd better get looking further.' Maisy hated storms and Rachel knew she'd be frightened, wherever she was.

'Maybe she's gone upstairs in the house, up to her room or something, and I just hadn't noticed?' Jill said.

'Yes, perhaps. We were both so busy getting things straight after the show. I just took my eyes off her for a few minutes, and I'd assumed she'd gone to you.'

'Don't worry, love. She won't be far,' Jill said reassuringly.

'Well, if you go back and check through the house, I'll try the lambing shed and the outbuildings here. We both have our phones, yeah, so the first to find her can ring the other.'

'Yes, okay, will do.'

They split up and Rachel checked the Pudding Pantry again, calling out Maisy's name, then the lambing shed, then the cattle shed and a small outbuilding next to it that they rarely used. The only other building in the farmyard was the old stable. Just the sight of it made Rachel's gut twist. But she knew she had to check it out in case Maisy had somehow found her way in. With some trepidation, she fetched the padlock key from the farm kitchen. She could hear Jill padding about upstairs, calling Maisy's name.

Rachel headed across the yard and took the padlock off the stable door. She took a deep breath before giving it a push. It was dark in there as the old wooden door creaked open. She flicked on the electric bulb, and felt her chest restrict as the place that haunted her nightmares and fears came into focus. She called Maisy's name again, somewhat shakily, and looked around all the nooks and crannies – but still no sign of her daughter.

She found Jill back out in the yard.

'Any luck?'

'No sign of her in the house.' Jill was looking concerned now.

'Nor in the outbuildings. Mum, she was really quiet and upset in the car as we came home . . . about Jake not coming back to see her. I'm worried, Mum, it's not like her to go off.'

Shit. Rachel felt sick to the pit of her stomach. What if something had happened to her?

'Okay love, let's just stay calm and think of any other places she might go.'

'Eve's, she might try and go there. To see Amelia or something. I'll ring them.'

Her heart was racing as she dialled her friend's number, hoping that that was the answer. But no, Eve said she hadn't seen her since the show. Rachel was trying not to panic now, but the fear was mounting and making her feel light-headed.

'Hang on,' Eve's voice came down the line. 'Ben says he'll come and help look for her with you. I'll stay here with Amelia in case she turns up here.'

'Thanks, okay, that's so helpful.'

Where else? Where else might she go? Rachel stood in the yard, racking her brains, with the rain and wind whipping up around her, as another crack of thunder ricocheted through her body. It wasn't like her little girl to go wandering off – she just wasn't that kind of a kid. Had she fallen and hurt herself? Perhaps she couldn't walk back to them? Was she frightened and hiding from the storm? But surely she'd call out if she'd heard their voices?

'No good?' Mum asked, already knowing the answer from the look on Rachel's face.

'No, she's not with Eve.' They were wasting time. 'I'm going to go off around the fields on the quad with Moss. He might be able to trace her scent. You stay here and look over everywhere again just in case we've missed something.'

'Okay, will do.'

As she reached the quad, Rachel thought of Tom. Could Maisy have gone there? She'd call him, it was worth a try, hopefully he'd be back from the show by now. She took her mobile out.

'Tom . . . Maisy's gone missing.' Rachel tried to stop her voice from shaking.

'From the farm?'

'Yes, we've been back around fifteen minutes from the show. She was with me at the Pantry barn, but then she just disappeared. I thought she was with Mum who was over in the house . . .'

'Okay. She hasn't called here, as far as I know. I'll get out on the quad and start looking. She can't have gone too far in that time.'

What if it was Jake – if he'd finally turned up and just taken her? Surely, he wasn't capable of that, not without telling anyone? All sorts of weird thoughts were entering her head. But then, did you ever really know a person fully – what they were capable of?

'Thanks, I've got my mobile on me. I'm going to check the whole farm area and Mum's staying near the house just in case. Oh God, Tom, I hope she's not hurt.'

'Try not to worry, Rach. We'll find her soon, I'm sure. What was she wearing?'

'Umm, a pink top and jeans. Oh, and her spotty red rain mac.' She'd put that on to get out of the Land Rover, as it had begun spitting with rain.

'Well, that's nice and bright to look out for.'

'Right, yes. Okay, well I'm going to get going.' She quelled the rising panic inside. She needed to keep a cool head to help find her little girl.

Rachel started up the quad, called Moss to her side who leapt up, and off they set, calling as they drove slowly around the farmyard first, then out to The Stackyard field. They drove on, searching the perimeters of each acre, carefully scouring the gulleys and hedgerows. The wind and the rain battering them as they went.

She then set Moss down and drove slowly, sure that he'd sniff the little girl out if he could. 'Maisy, where's Maisy, Moss? Go find her.'

She checked her phone every now and then, in case Mum or Tom or Eve had called, but still nothing. The rain streamed down over the phone screen like heaven's tears. It was teeming down, and every now and then was another boom of threatening thunder.

She'd looked in every field, every hedgerow, under every tree – where else might she be? *Think*, Rachel, *think*. She decided to head back to the farmyard; there were more places Maisy might hide in, or shelter there. A cupboard in the house, a silly game of hide-and-seek gone wrong? But, she'd been upset about her dad . . . Rachel felt that was key to this.

Mum was at the door of the farmhouse as she arrived back. She was standing there shaking her head, looking ashen, saddened to see no Maisy beside Rachel. Rachel's face must have echoed her mum's. Still no Maisy.

'I'll search the buildings again, and take Moss this

time,' she said. 'Did you check all the cupboards? Under the beds?'

Jill nodded. 'I'll do the Pantry again. That's where you last saw her, wasn't it?'

'Okay, yes.'

Rachel started the quad up again, heading for the lambing shed, muttering softly, like a prayer, 'Please God, don't let anything have happened to her. Please God.' She couldn't be sure if it was tears or rain streaming down her face.

And the search began again.

She was checking behind old straw bales in the lambing shed, when her phone pulsed in her pocket. She could hardly get her mobile out quick enough, her fingers fumbling to answer.

The caller ID told her it was Tom.

'I've found her.'

Oh God. The three best words ever.

'Oh, thank heavens. Is she all right?'

'Yes, a bit wet and shivery, but yes, she's all right.'

The relief felt like a wave engulfing her, Rachel felt weak. 'Thank God. Where?'

'Down at the stream. You know, where you'd had the picnic a few weeks ago.'

That seemed odd.

'She was saying something about the fairy glen. I don't know, didn't make much sense to me. I've wrapped her in a blanket and I'm bringing her home right now.'

'Oh, thank you. Meet you at the farmhouse then. Thank you, Tom.'

She pulled up in the yard and dashed for the door. 'Mum, Mum, Tom's found her. He's found her!'

Rachel and Jill met at the porch in a rush.

'She's all right?'

'Yes.'

'Ah, sweet Jesus.'

They clasped each other in a relieved hug. With that, the sound of a quad came buzzing up the drive. There was Maisy wrapped in a blanket, huddled in Tom's lap, his dog Mabel standing guard protectively on the rear of the vehicle.

'Oh, thank goodness,' Jill gasped, as Rachel stepped forward to pick her little girl up.

'She's okay. Just very wet and a bit overwhelmed, I think,' said Tom.

'And she was down by the stream, you say?'

'Yes.'

'Maisy, what on earth made you go there?' The frustration of the past half hour spilled out, but Rachel could see her daughter was overwrought, damp and shivery in her arms. 'Okay, okay, it's all right petal, you're home now. Let's get you inside.' They weren't going to get any answers just now, and Maisy needed warming up. 'Mum, would you mind going up to run a nice warm bath? We'll get these wet clothes off you down by the Aga, shall we, petal?' They made their way into the kitchen, shutting out the wind and rain.

'Of course,' Jill replied. 'Thank you so much, Tom,' she smiled thankfully, and patted his arm, as she turned to go on up to the bathroom.

Maisy nodded gently. She seemed a little in shock. The storm and chilling damp, no doubt, affecting her.

'Thank you, Tom, so very much.' Rachel looked at him stood there covered in mud and soaked to the skin himself.

'No worries. Just glad I was able to help and that we found her. Now, you go and get warm and dry, Maisy. I'll see you soon . . .'

'Okay.' It was the first word Maisy had uttered since getting back.

'Rachel,' Tom looked serious, his words heartfelt. 'Look, I know this isn't the time, but later, another day, can we talk?'

She nodded. 'Yeah, of course.'

They both knew she needed to get Maisy settled, and that *that* talk would have so many implications – it needed time and space.

'Bye then,' Tom added, as he turned to set off.

'Bye.'

Rachel took Maisy near the warmth of the Aga, unwrapped the damp blanket from her and peeled off her soaking wet clothes. She dried her daughter's hair with a towel, then carried her up to Grandma Jill and the bathroom. Maisy was soon soaking in a warm bubbly bath and looking much happier.

They both sat and watched her for a while, then Jill

gave her granddaughter a kiss on the forehead and said she was going to get Maisy's pyjamas ready.

'Maisy, why did you go off like that, sweetheart?' Rachel's voice was calm, soothing, but she was desperate to know what was behind it all.

'Sorry, Mummy. I went to make a wish and then the storm came and I got scared.'

'A wish?'

'Yes, at the fairy glen. My book says you can make wishes where the fairies are.'

Rachel was confused, until Maisy continued. 'I wished that my daddy would come back.'

'Oh Maisy.' It suddenly all made sense, and Rachel squinted a tear from her eye. Sodding Jake. Who the hell needed a daddy like that? But that's all Maisy wanted, to have her daddy around. Why was life so tough and unfair sometimes?

'I wanted to come back home, Mummy, but then the thunder came . . .'

'It's okay, petal. Yes, it was silly and dangerous to go off on your own like that, but I understand. Tell me next time yeah, if you're thinking about doing something like that, we can go together, or if you want to talk to me about anything. Promise?'

'Promise. Cross my heart.'

'Good girl.'

'Right, let's dry you off and get you all cosy, shall we?' Rachel helped her little girl out of the bath and had a warm fleecy towel ready. 'Then you can come down for a nice hot chocolate and a cuddle before bedtime, okay?'

''Kay.'

What a day that had been.

Rachel lay in bed in the early hours, unable to sleep, the emotions of the day's events still fizzing through her veins. A multitude of thoughts filled her mind – her dad, the farm, the Pudding Pantry, the weight of it all so heavy within her. But, losing Maisy, the fear that she might have been hurt, or worse . . . that shook her to the core. This was what mattered the most: her family, her daughter. Everything else was just the means to keep them all going, to protect them.

And today . . . she'd failed them. She hadn't taken enough care of Maisy. She hadn't noticed she'd gone; her focus had been elsewhere.

The tears that hadn't yet been shed now streamed down Rachel's face, wetting the pillows beneath her head.

It's okay, her kinder alter ego kicked in. *It all turned out okay in the end.*

She wasn't a superhero, she was just human. You can't have your eyes on your children every second of every day, she knew that. But, she'd been so busy, with the pudding stall, and the Pantry, then back home where they were still packing away, thinking about the bloody takings.

Holding it all together, trying to keep the farm going, it felt like a dangerous game of jackstraws, where one false move would send the whole pile crashing down. Today, it felt like the weight was too heavy, the load too much. Rachel didn't know where they would go from here, or if she was strong enough to build it all up again.

She felt exhausted, wiped out. Finally, she fell into a light erratic sleep.

Chapter 41

PANCAKES AND PJS

The next morning, Jill offered to go across and open up the Pudding Pantry, saying she was fine to run the tearoom by herself for a couple of hours. She could see that Rachel looked shattered, and realised that she and Maisy could probably do with some quiet time together.

As it was the Tuesday after the bank holiday, there would still be some tourists around, but generally it was likely to be a little quieter. Jill had already baked some fresh sultana scones in the farmhouse Aga, and decided to make some chocolate-mint traybakes to top up yesterday's dwindling supplies. After all the emotions of last night, and such a hectic day yesterday, it was a day to take stock and stick to routine.

Rachel had looked in to check on Maisy at 7:30 a.m. She was sleeping soundly in her bed, and looked so peaceful, so she decided to let her be – the rest would do her good. When Maisy finally came down in her pyjamas after 9 a.m., Rachel had a batter mix and all the ingredients ready to make her daughter's favourite chocolate-spread pancakes. They chatted as they ate their late breakfast, talking about all the different things at the show and the 'wonderfully-whizzy' Tea Cups ride, then they settled down to build the Lego Farm together – it had been Rachel's as a child, and was still a favourite to play with, with its mini tractor and animals. Rachel read a story with Maisy snuggled on her lap, and after that she put on one of Maisy's favourite DVDs. They spent a quiet, calm morning together, which was exactly what they both needed. (Grandmas did in fact know best!)

Just as they were nearing the end of the movie, the phone rang, and Rachel's heart started banging when she heard Tom on the other end of the line.

'Hi Rachel, just checking how Maisy is this morning?'

'Oh, she seems fine, thank you. Maybe a touch subdued, but we're making the most of a few quiet hours together. It's been really nice actually.'

'Good . . . and you, Rach?' He paused momentarily, as if nervous. 'How are you doing? It must have been a bit of a scare, her going missing like that.' His voice sounded so caring.

'Yeah, it was. It was so frightening at the time, the thought that something dreadful might have happened, but all's well that ends well. And thank you so much, again.'

'Ah, I was just glad we found her okay.'

It was good that they were talking again. Small steps back to friendship. She hated the thought that in all her own hurt and anger, she'd hurt Tom too. But she knew she had to put her focus back into her family, that was what mattered most.

At lunchtime, Maisy and Rachel went across to the Pantry to see Jill. Maisy had remembered all about the pudding competition and their photo, and couldn't wait to tell Grandma Jill about her first prize – with all the mayhem of the night before, they'd totally forgotten until now.

'Grandma Jill, Grandma Jill, you won!' She raced into the barn and it was lovely to see her back to her chirpy self. 'Mummy's got the photo.'

'It's true . . . first prize for your sticky toffee pudding,' said Rachel.

'And a red rosette,' added Maisy proudly.

'Oh, my goodness, how wonderful.' Jill was beaming.

Frank was there in the barn too, just finishing his morning coffee and cake. 'Congratulations, that's marvellous and a real achievement.' He raised his cup.

'Oh, thank you, Frank.' Jill couldn't stop smiling.

Then, Maisy and Jill had a sandwich lunch at one of the tables, with Rachel covering the counter. Maisy was chatting away happily and seemed more herself. Once they'd finished, Rachel asked if her mum would keep an eye on Maisy for a short while as she wanted to go over to the farmhouse and make a phone call. It had been brewing in her mind this past hour. There were things that needed to be said.

Jake didn't answer, not the first time or the second.

She ignored the answerphone message and dialled again, the anger rising within her.

She heard the click as it was finally picked up.

'Hey, Rach. Hi babe.'

'Don't you *babe* me.' Her tone was sharp as a blade.

'Uh?'

'Look, Maisy has been waiting for you to turn up all weekend – it was all she could think about yesterday at the show. You promised her, Jake.'

'Ah, well something turned up. It was difficult.'

'I'll tell you what's difficult – dealing with a moron like you as her father. You just can't do that to a child . . . *your* child. She was so upset that you never came. You never even bothered to ring to explain or speak to her.'

'Ah.' It was finally starting to sink in.

'You can't make promises if you're not going to follow them through. You say you'll be here, build up her hopes and then let her down, over and over. We're sick of it, Jake, *sick* of it. You can't just flit in and out of her life when it suits you. *So*, from now on, if you want to visit, you call me to make arrangements first and then you bloody well make sure you turn up, or else you can stay right away. Full stop.'

'You can't keep me away. I have rights . . .'

'Yes, and so does our little girl. I'll not let you fuck up her life any more, Jake. All I'm asking is a little consideration and cooperation.'

'I can go to the courts, you know.'

'Yeah, you go ahead Jake, and who do you think they'll listen to?'

The lioness had roared. It had needed to be said, to protect Maisy. Yes, Rachel knew she had to take some blame for yesterday, but not all of it. Here was where the main blame lay, and she was going to leave it loudly at his doorstep, like a big lion turd.

'So . . . Maisy was upset, was she?' he continued feebly.

'What do you sodding think? She's five. She believed you.'

'Ah . . . look, I'll come up soon, make it up to her.'

She'd had enough of his waffling shite. He hadn't even been man enough to apologise. 'You call me and we arrange it properly if you want to visit Maisy again. And then you come up as planned, or else don't bother coming back at all. Bye, Jake.' With that, she hung up.

She felt exhausted as she took a seat back in the kitchen, but a whole lot better having said what needed to be said. She'd been strong, assertive, proudly protecting her family – and boy did that feel good.

Chapter 42

THE BEST APPLE CRUMBLE EVER

'Rachel . . . Rach-el?!' Jill's voice rang out across the yard.

Rachel was in the lambing shed, sorting out the next batch of cattle and sheep tags, checking they were all in order. She left her task and headed out of the open shed door.

'Ye-es?' She hoped everything was okay. Thankfully, things seemed to have settled down with Maisy in the last four days since her disappearing act.

'Ah, there you are.' Mum looked relieved. 'I've just had a call from Tom. He's got a bit of a problem with the tractor. He's in his North Field, been ploughing there, wondered if you'd take a look before he calls a mechanic out.'

Rachel could be quite handy with a spanner and tools when faced with a tractor engine. God knows, they'd had to sort out their own tractor hiccups many a time. It was amazing what could be achieved with Dad's old toolkit and some YouTube videos.

'Ah, okay, no worries. I'll get across there now.'

Actually, it would be nice to do something to help Tom out for a change. And, maybe this would be a good way to break the ice too. Rachel was well aware that she still hadn't plucked up the courage to see him and have that 'talk' he'd mentioned. Much as she found she missed him, like a deep ache in her soul, she didn't know where to start. It had all gone horribly wrong since that revelation about his conversation with her dad, and she didn't know where they could go from there. Could a friendship even be salvaged?

Rachel walked back across the yard with Jill, as she'd need a vehicle to get across there.

'Oh, and if it takes a while, love, don't worry about Maisy. I'm fine with her,' Jill said, rather emphatically.

'Right, okay, good to know.' Rachel grabbed the tool box and the keys to the Land Rover, before setting off. She knew Tom would want to get the tractor fixed as soon as possible, it was already early evening, having just gone 6 p.m., and he'd want to finish ploughing that field before dusk, no doubt. It had, in fact, been a lovely day and was still warm, the sun now slipping low in its arc but still giving a honeyed glow to the softly rolling landscape.

She soon reached Tom's land and knew which fields to cross to get to the North Field. Being on the hillside, it would be one of the harder ones to plough, having steeper banks that no doubt had put stress on the tractor. She arrived at the gate to this field, and stopped to open it, concentrating on the latch, then sweeping it back ready to pass. She drove through to the other side and then came to a grinding halt, her foot coming off the accelerator as she looked at the hillside ahead of her.

Oh my, wow . . . who had done that?

Ploughed into the bank of the stubble field in huge twenty-metre-high letters was . . . 'I Love You'.

Rachel paused and pulled the handbrake on. She then stood up out of the truck. Yes, that was definitely it. 'I Love You'. It would fit the size of a full swimming pool, and was across the whole top half of the field.

Suddenly there was a toot-toot of a horn. There was Tom's pick-up at the top of the bank. And there beside it . . . Tom . . . The broken-down tractor was nowhere in sight.

Tom walked over to stand to the side of the 'I Love You' sign . . . *Was the message for her?* The penny was finally dropping.

She closed the gate on autopilot and, feeling rather stunned, she drove up the set-aside of the field, all the while admiring the view. The lettering was mind-blowing – had he ploughed that?

Could it be for her? Did he *love* her? She wasn't sure if it was excitement or incredulity buzzing through her veins. As she approached his truck and parked up beside it, she could see that Tom had set out a table and two chairs. It was like in a restaurant with a white tablecloth, candlesticks, wine glasses . . . she squinted to see more . . . little posies of wild flowers. And Tom stood there beside it all, dressed in smart dark chinos and a white shirt with a huge, if slightly nervous-looking, grin on his face.

'Hello, you,' was all he said, as she stepped out of the Land Rover.

'Hello, you,' she echoed, still wondering what the heck was going on here. 'No breakdown with the tractor?' The penny was starting to roll down and into the slot now.

'Nope.'

'Is this a set-up?' Had Jill been in on this too? Her mum's 'I'll be fine with Maisy' was suddenly sinking in.

'Now you've got me.' Tom was grinning broadly.

Oh . . . my . . . God.

Rachel looked at the table again. There was a bottle of red wine and one of white there ready by the glasses. The flowers were in jam jars and were mostly pretty hedgerow plants, including red rosehips and rowan leaves and berries, along with small pale-pink roses that were probably from Tom's garden.

'I picked them all myself,' he added proudly, watching her gaze. 'Umm, well, I said we needed to talk . . . and I'm not so good at talking . . . so I hope this says it all.'

Rachel stood there stunned and realised she wasn't so good at talking herself just now. She needed to say something back, she hadn't even thanked him yet. But it was taking a while to get her head around it all.

'Wow – this is amazing . . . and the message . . . on the hill.'

'All my own handiwork. And Rachel, I'm sorry, so sorry I couldn't have done more for your dad back then.'

'Oh, Tom.' She dashed the six paces towards him, and

flung herself into his arms that were ready and waiting – that had been for such a long time.

It suddenly felt so right, being there, being held by him. He was a kind, good man. That conversation with her father must have tortured him, and there was nothing he could have done – Rachel saw that now. And the fact that they were old family friends and neighbours, with an age gap between them, suddenly became irrelevant. Why the hell hadn't she seen it before? Or, had she and simply been running scared?

Her lips were on his; the kiss sensual, emotional, beautiful and life-affirming. It felt like very much like love.

They finally drew apart.

'I know what you've been through, Rachel, and I don't want to rush anything. I just want to be there for you, for us to be together, however that might work.'

'Oh God, yes. But Tom,' the sense of responsibility for her family weighed heavily on her still, 'it's not just about me though. There's Maisy and Mum and the farm.' She had to be realistic.

'I know all that, of course I do. You come as a team, and I'm cool with that. Like I say, we take one step at a time, and work this out together. *So . . .*' he sounded very nervous suddenly. 'Are you in?'

The smile on her face said it all, but she knew Tom needed to hear the words. It was hard for her to say them aloud even now, to let down her guard, even though every beat of her heart, every pulse in her veins was telling her it was true. She nodded. 'I'm in . . . and Tom, I love you too.'

'Woo-hooo,' he shouted out over the valley. She'd take a bet that even Mum and Maisy might have heard it. It was loud enough to startle some crows, which flapped off from a nearby tree. 'Now then, Rachel Swinton, I think it's time to celebrate. Please be seated.' He put on a mock-posh waiter voice.

She took a seat, on what she now recognised as one of his kitchen chairs.

'Red or white wine to start, madam?'

'Ah, I'll have some white, please.'

As he started to pour, she looked down at her attire, a green boiler suit fresh from the farm with smudges of muck on.

'Oh crikey, I'm not exactly dressed for dinner, am I?!' She laughed.

'No worries,' he lowered his voice. 'Did I ever tell you I find you very attractive in your boiler suit?' He gave her a sexy grin.

'Hah, no.'

'To be honest, Rach, I'd find you very attractive in just about anything right now.'

She couldn't help but smile.

'Well then, the starter is already prepared.' Tom went to the back of his pick-up, pulled out a cool box, and brought out two plates of smoked salmon, garnished with rocket and lemon slices, served with buttered bread triangles.

He placed a plate before her. 'Okay, so I hope you're not expecting *MasterChef* standard here. The barbecue is already lit. That's kind of my level.'

Rachel looked over to see a portable barbecue stood beside his vehicle. Ah, so that was the slightly smoky tang in the air. 'Sounds perfect to me, and this looks delicious.'

She sipped her white wine, which was crisp, fruity and vanilla all at once, and they started to eat.

'I can't believe you've done all this. It's crazy . . . it's lovely,' she said, between delicious forkfuls. 'And who ever said farmers can't be romantic?' she chuckled.

'No reason why not,' agreed Tom, so very glad that his plan had come together. 'Special occasions only, of course.'

'Ooh, I was hoping to get this every evening after work,' Rachel grinned. 'I could get used to this, you know.'

'Hah, we'd never get any work done!'

They sipped their Sauvignon Blanc and chatted for a while, until Tom said, 'Right, I'd better cook the main course on the barbecue. We have steak or sausages, or both.'

'Both, please.' After a day working out on the farm, she found herself ravenous.

Whilst Tom started to cook, with the barbecue coals already hot, Rachel looked out across the valley from their stunning viewpoint. The high Cheviot Hills lay behind her, and she was looking across the rolling patchwork of green, brown and golden farmland fields of North Northumberland towards the North Sea, which was a thin belt of indigo on the horizon. The sun would be setting soon and the countryside glowed in warm peach and gold tones. A blackbird hopped around near them and the last of the summer swallows and house martins dipped and swooped in the sky. It was tranquil and beautiful. Perfect.

Below her, remarkably, was *her* 'I love you' ploughed onto the hillside and she wondered if anyone had seen it as they passed through the country lanes in their cars. She hoped it had made someone else smile during their busy day. But she was so very glad that it was *her* message, and wow, looking across at Tom stood cooking at the coals, with his rather gorgeous body, warm smile and kind, kind heart, she couldn't believe this really was her man. How crazily wonderful was that!

'I didn't know you had all these hidden talents,' she called across. 'Cooking, flower arranging, waiter skills.'

'Oh, I have a whole lot more that you haven't seen yet,' he teased, and with those words he seemed to promise her a future, and new depths to their relationship, yet to discover.

'I'm glad.'

You would think that you knew someone well after all these years as neighbours, yet in a way, Rachel realised she had only scratched the surface with Tom. A rather lovely surface in fact, and that was what was so exciting and wonderful. She walked across to stand behind him, reaching her arms around his waist as he cooked, and kissed him lightly on the back of the neck. He felt warm and strong beneath her touch, and smelt of barbecue smoke and aftershave.

'Mmmn,' he sighed, adding, 'Now, don't put me off. We don't want me burning the steaks now.'

'I'll save this for later, then.' She wondered just how long Jill would be all right until, or might she need to make a quick phone call . . .

Tom served the juicy steak along with potatoes he'd roasted with rosemary and kept warm in foil packets, with a side salad (quite *MasterChef*-like after all, Rachel mused!). The candle on the table between them, which he'd lit as she arrived, was flickering gently in the light breeze, glowing now that dusk was settling.

They talked and ate, and as they finished their delicious meal, Rachel reached a hand across the table, placing it over his.

'Thank you, for all this, it's amazing. No-one's ever done anything like this for me, ever.'

He smiled warmly. 'Well, it's about time they did, then.'

She leaned across the table to kiss him. He tasted of red wine and steak, and *him*. Wow – she could carry on kissing these lips for the rest of her life. She didn't need anyone else's.

He then moved his chair to sit beside her, so they could both look out across the valley as night began to draw in. The soft bleating of their sheep provided the background noise.

'Tom, about Maisy . . .' Though this night was beautiful and promised so much, Rachel felt she had to clarify something. Maisy had to come first. It had to be right for her too.

'Yeah?'

'If we have a future together . . . she has to be a part of this.'

'I know, I understand that.'

'But how do we tell her?' Rachel was thinking out loud.

'Well, when the time's right to tell her, I'm sure you'll work that out.'

'Yes, I suppose.'

'And . . .' he added, 'knowing Maisy, I think she'll work it out by herself very soon.'

'Hah, yes, she's as sharp as a tack, I think you're right.'

And Rachel remembered the conversation with Maisy the night of her birthday party all those months ago, when her own father hadn't turned up and she'd asked if Tom could be her daddy. Rachel gave a contented smile, feeling that it would all work out fine somehow. It was early days to tell Tom that little gem yet, but in time . . .

An hour later, they were still out in the field, but it was cooling dramatically now, with night falling in a heavy, velvety blanket around them. Tom went to fetch a rug from his truck. 'This'll be better.'

He sat back down, their chairs propped close, covering them both with the rug.

'Perfect,' said Rachel, as they snuggled together. 'So, what's for pudding?' she half-joked.

'Not very demanding, are you?' he jibed.

'No, not at all. But I can live in hope.' She grinned, not really expecting him to have prepared any more food at all. The meal had been fabulous as it was.

'Well, now you mention it . . . I have made something.'

'Ooh, what is it?'

'Crumble . . . apple crumble.'

With that Rachel nearly spat out the wine she'd just sipped, and hooted with laughter.

'What's up? What's so funny?'

'Sorry . . . sorry, nothing. Oh my. It's fine. I just *lurve* apple crumble.' She was still giggling five minutes later, her sides were aching, and she knew she had to enlighten poor Tom on the antics in the pub that night.

Between fits of the giggles, she told the tale.

'Oh, that's just brilliant, I'm an apple crumble, am I?' He pretended to be put out, but was smiling broadly. 'Well, I suppose I'd better dish it out then.'

'Yes, please, hunky crumble man.'

He'd left the crumble dish he'd made covered in foil to warm at the side of the smouldering barbecue, and served out a generous portion in a single bowl to share, with a dollop of thick cream that melted down over the crunchy brown-sugar topping. It smelt delightful, all toffee-apple and cinnamon. They snuggled back down under the cosy rug together, with Tom holding the warm bowl between them.

Rachel dug in and helped herself to a delicious spoonful . . . and she knew she'd be very much looking forward to glorious seconds of *crumble* later!

She had the man of her dreams by her side, and her farm and family safe in the valley below. Her heart felt so warm and she wanted to hold onto this moment forever.

'Thank you, Tom, this has been the most amazing evening.'

He smiled warmly at her, as they sat side by side. 'This is just the start for us, Rachel. You know, there's so much more to come.'

With everything that had happened over the past couple of years, Rachel had learnt just how precarious – and precious – life could be. Amid the darkness, there was always hope, if only you had the courage to seize it. She looked up into the glittering canopy of stars above, and as they twinkled back, she felt that her lovely dad was looking down on her – telling her that everything would be all right.

And as she snuggled closer to Tom, she couldn't wait to find out what that 'so much more' would be.

A LETTER FROM CAROLINE

Thank you so much for choosing to read *Rachel's Pudding Pantry*. I hope you've enjoyed spending time with the fabulous Swinton family at Primrose Farm. Hopefully you've been curled up with this novel and a dish of your favourite pudding!

If you have enjoyed this book, please don't hesitate to get in touch or leave a review. I always love hearing my readers' reactions, and it also makes a real difference in helping new readers to discover my books for the first time. You'd make an author very happy. 😊

You are very welcome to pop along to my Facebook page, Twitter profile or blog page. Please share your news, views, recipe tips, and read all about your favourite puddings and the inspirations behind my writing. It's lovely to make new friends, so keep in touch.

Well, the next book is calling as there's a sequel coming in time for Christmas – so it's back to the writing!

Thanks again, and see you soon!

Caroline x

🐦@_caroroberts
f/CarolineRobertsAuthor
carolinerobertswriter.blogspot.co.uk

ACKNOWLEDGEMENTS

I have so enjoyed writing this book set in my local farming community – it has felt very close to home and my heart. Huge thanks to Helen and Johnny Renner and to Jane and Duncan Ord, for showing me around their farms and the animals, providing a cuppa at the farmhouse kitchen table and answering my many questions about lambing and farming life in North Northumberland. Also, thank you so much to Susan Green of The Proof of the Pudding for welcoming me to her farmhouse, allowing me to quiz her, and for giving great insight into her fabulous pudding business. I was especially grateful for the sticky toffee and ginger pudding delights she sent me home with – delicious! All in the name of research of course!

Thanks as always to my wonderful family and friends for all their ongoing support, and to the fabulous Romantic Novelists' Association, especially our Northumberland Chapter, who are always there with writerly advice and friendship.

My talented editor, Charlotte Brabbin, a massive thank you. Your skills have helped polish this book into what I hope is a little gem. And to the whole team at HarperCollins, plus my lovely agent Hannah Ferguson and the team at Hardman & Swainson – thanks so much.

Congratulations also to the two ladies who won my 'Character Naming Competition' to have a special name feature in this book: Marie Carter, whose little girl 'Maisy' features as Rachel's daughter, and Louise Adcock whose nick-name is 'Brenda' – the proud and helpful owner of The Kirkton Deli.

Last, but not least, a big hurrah for all my readers and the very supportive book blogging community! My books would be nothing without someone to read and enjoy them. I hope you've had a wonderful time getting to know Rachel, Jill, Maisy and everyone at the Pudding Pantry!

All best wishes,

Caroline x

TURN THE PAGE TO DISCOVER DELICIOUS
RECIPES TO TRY AT HOME – ONLY THE
PUDDING PANTRY FAVOURITES WILL DO!

Rachel's White Chocolate and Raspberry Cheesecake

    2 × 150g bars white chocolate
    2 × 300g tubs full-fat soft cheese
    284ml of double cream
    50g caster sugar
    200g punnet raspberries
    5 tbsp raspberry jam
    130g digestive biscuits
    50g butter

Break the chocolate into a glass bowl, put over a pan of simmering water to melt (be careful that the base of the bowl doesn't sit in the water). Take off heat and allow to cool.

Crush the digestives either in a freezer bag with a rolling pin or food processor. Melt the butter gently in a saucepan and stir the biscuits through it. Use a spoon to press into the base of a deep (ideally non-stick loose-bottom) 8-inch flan dish or cake tin. Pop in fridge to chill.

Whisk the cheese, cream and sugar together until thick (electric beaters are great for this), then stir in the almost cool melted white chocolate until fully combined.

Stir 50g raspberries with 2 tbsp jam (chopping any large raspberries in half first). Spoon half of the cheese mixture over the biscuit base, then spoon the jammy raspberries over the centre. Top with the rest of the cheese mixture, flatten with a spatula and chill again, for at least 4 hours or overnight.

Warm the remaining jam with the raspberries you have left, keeping aside about 12 raspberries. Whizz with a hand blender or in a food processor, then rub through a sieve to remove any seeds. Add a drop or two of water if it seems very thick.

To serve, top the cake with the raspberries you have reserved and drizzle the sauce over.

Ideal served with friends and a glass of something bubbly!

Jill's Sticky Toffee Pudding

For the sponge:

> 200g soft pitted dates, finely chopped
> 1 tsp bicarbonate of soda
> 200ml boiling water
> 75g butter, plus extra for greasing
> 50g dark muscovado sugar
> 2 tbsp black treacle
> 2 large free-range eggs
> 200g self-raising flour

For the toffee sauce:

> 100g butter
> 150g dark muscovado sugar
> 1 tbsp black treacle
> 150ml double cream

Preheat the oven to 180C/160 Fan/Gas 4. Lightly grease your dish (9 × 9 in/1.2l baking dish or similar).

Put the dates, boiling water and bicarbonate of soda into a bowl, stir and leave for 10 mins.

Cream the butter and sugar together in a mixer until pale and fluffy. Add the treacle and eggs, a little at a time, and blend until smooth. Add the flour and blend at a low speed until well combined.

Using a fork, stir the soaked dates, squishing them a bit, and then pour the dates and liquid into the pudding batter and beat gently to mix in.

Pour into your prepared oven dish, and bake for 35–40 mins until a cake tester comes out clean.

To make the sauce, melt all of the ingredients in a pan over a low heat, stirring occasionally until bubbling. Remove from heat.

Leave the pudding to stand for 20 mins then skewer all over and pour over half the sauce. Leave for another 15 mins then serve drizzled with more of the warmed sauce and a scoop of good quality vanilla (or honeycomb!) ice cream.

Prepare to be taken to sticky toffee heaven!

Discover more uplifting and heart-warming
romances from Caroline Roberts

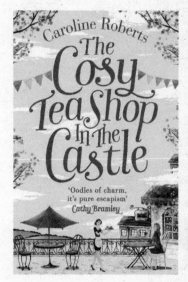 

'Oodles of charm, it's pure escapism'
Cathy Bramley

Both available to buy now!

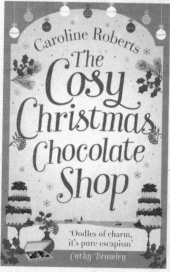

Also available to buy now!